CW01086625

THE CHEERLEADER AND THE ROOMMATE

(Style and Chord)

CHELSEA M. CAMERON

About Style

Kyle Blake likes plans. So far, they're pretty simple: Finish her senior year of high school, head off to a good college, find a cute boyfriend, graduate, get a good job, get married, the whole heterosexual shebang. Nothing is going to stand in the way of that plan. Not even Stella Lewis.

Stella Lewis also has a plan: Finish her senior year as cheer captain, go to college, finally let herself flirt with (and maybe even date) a girl for the first time and go from there.

Fate has other plans for Kyle and Stella when they're paired up in their AP English class and something between them ignites. It's confusing and overwhelming and neither of them know what to do about it. One thing they do know is that their connection can't be ignored. The timing just isn't right.

But is there ever a good time for falling in love?

For all the girls who like girls. This one's for you.

Chapter One

KYLE

"She's like . . . Satan in a blonde package," Grace said as Stella Lewis walked by. Grace had it right. I slammed my locker and leaned my back against it as Stella went around the corner, her skirt flipping, but not showing *too* much. Just enough. Her ash-blonde hair was curled perfectly, as if she had a team of stylists in her home to get her ready every day.

"Well, I don't think she's *that* evil. Just . . . driven? Assertive?" Grace just rolled her eyes.

"Those are just other words for 'bitch', Kyle." I shrugged as we walked beside each other to class. A few people stared as we went by, but I ignored them. Grace had the misfortune of being one of the only black girls at a small high school in Maine; and then there was me. They looked because I walked with a visible limp, mostly due to the fact that one of my legs was longer than the other, and even with multiple surgeries to lengthen it, there was still a discrepancy. Not to mention the scars. It was so much better than it had been, but in high school any physical anomaly was reason to stare, especially in a homogenous community.

I took my messy bun down and then put it back up again. It was a habit I had when I was annoyed by something. Or nervous. Or stressed. Or tired. Grace took the seat next to me in AP Chemistry and sighed.

"What?" I asked, hauling out the enormous textbook and dropping it with a thud on my desk.

"Nothing. Just thinking." She pushed her dark curls out of her face and glared up at them.

"Be careful. That could be dangerous," I said, pushing my black-rimmed glasses up my nose. Yeah, yeah, I was the stereotype. Girl who loved academics and wore glasses. I'd heard all the jokes before, so save it.

Something was bothering her, and as usual, she was going to hold it in until she couldn't stand it anymore and then it would burst out of her at a totally inopportune time. Like when we were in the middle of dinner with my parents. Or at the movies. Or in the library. Or in the middle of a test.

"Whatever," she said, pulling out her Chapstick and slicking it on her lips. Mrs. Collins started class and I knew I was going to have to wait.

We were working on diagramming chemical bonds, so I let my brain be taken over by that and pushed Grace's potential problem to the side. Science wasn't my best subject, but I did well enough to make it to AP Chemistry my senior year, so that had to count for something. Grace and I split up, her to head to Art and me to AP Geometry and then we met up again outside the cafeteria. Like always.

We got in line and filled our trays with pizza, and I decided to grab a salad because pizza and salad cancelled each other out. By the time we got back to the table, Molly, her boyfriend Tommy, Paige, Monica, and Chris were already eating.

"Whoa, what's with Grace?" Molly whispered in my ear as Grace glowered at her food like it had offended her in some way.

"No idea," I said back as Tommy and Chris debated something politics-related that would probably end in them agreeing to disagree. Again.

"Hey, is anyone going to the game on Friday?" Monica asked. She, Chris, and Molly were in the band playing flute, bass drum, and clarinet respectively.

"Yeah, sure," I said. I tried to make most of the games to support them, and we all showed up for Grace and Monica when the drama club put on productions. My friends were pretty spectacular and I didn't know what I would have done without them.

"Everyone else in?" Monica asked, and we all agreed. I couldn't have cared less about the actual sport (football), so I usually brought a book and only looked up or paid attention when the band was doing something.

Don't get me wrong, sports are fine, but they're not really my forte, considering running isn't my thing and most of them require it. I would much rather spend my time reading or . . . doing anything else.

"What the hell?" Grace said, finally looking up and turning toward a commotion on the other side of the cafeteria.

"Oh God, what are they doing now?" I said. It was one of the tables for the football players and they were always up to something. Brad Harding was standing on top of one of the tables and chugging . . . something from a glass bottle.

"What is that?" I said, squinting.

"I think it's hot sauce," Molly said, shaking her head.

Yup, definitely hot sauce. Brad's face got red, he started gagging and then hurled all over the table before one of the lunch monitors hauled him off the table and down the hall to the principal's office. A surly custodian came over to clean up as groups of students clapped in support.

I was about to turn and say something to Grace when my gaze snagged on Stella. She stood with her arms crossed as she rolled her eyes. Tossing her hair over one shoulder, she just happened to look in my direction and catch me staring. I looked away fast, so she didn't think I was . . . well, anyway.

"I can't believe people think that's funny. I mean, how old are they?" Grace said, her brows furrowed. If she didn't tell me what was up by the end of the day, I was going to confront her. Because this was downright ridiculous.

"Well, he's going to get suspended, again," I said. Brad got suspended a lot, but it never stuck because his dad was a lawyer *and* a former politician *and* crazy rich. So Brad was basically the worst because he could get away with it.

The topic changed from Brad's idiocy to Homecoming weekend and I checked out. It wasn't that I didn't care . . .

Okay, that *was* it. I just couldn't get so whooped up about something that didn't really mean anything. These weren't the best days of our lives. I was always looking forward to college. If I could just get to college, I knew my life would start.

I'd finally get a boyfriend and my obsession with academia would be appreciated and I'd be out on my own. Not that I didn't adore my parents, but I was an only child and living with their expectations hanging over my head had been intense, to say the least. Good thing I was smart, or else I would have had to work my ass off at something else to meet their expectations of being an extraordinary child.

College was going to be it. I just had to get to graduation and then I would be free.

INSTEAD OF HEADING home after school, I always took my laptop downtown to the library and got most of my homework done. It was a hell of a lot easier to work on everything when I didn't have one (or both) of my parents leaning over my shoulder asking what I was doing and if I was sure I wanted to use that exact word, or if that number was right. They put the *hel* in helicopter parenting.

After I finished everything I needed to get done homework wise, I let myself do some work. Last summer I'd gotten a job at a small IT support company in town and my boss, Jason, had taught me a little bit of coding and graphic design, so I'd started doing a few freelance jobs here and there. Just basic stuff like Photoshop editing and basic web design, but you could make pretty decent money at it. I wasn't sure if it was what I wanted to do when I got to college, but if I could make a few bucks and enjoy what I was doing, then why not?

My current project was a blog redesign for a new book blogger. I hadn't even known book blogging was a thing until I posted some of my ads in online forums. She was also a senior in high school and didn't have a whole lot of money, so she couldn't hire a real professional. We'd exchanged emails back and forth and I'd liked her and knew I could give her a great design. She'd already done part of the work; finding me stock images and colors and fonts that she wanted to use.

I'd just gotten started, but she was happy with the progress. I put on my coding playlist (which included everything from Adele to the Hamilton soundtrack to Muse) and before I knew it, the head librarian was tapping me on the shoulder and kicking me out.

Time to go home.

∾

"HOW WAS YOUR DAY, HONEY?" my mom said the second I shut the door. She gave me a hug and a kiss on the cheek and then Dad was there too.

"Fine," I said, knowing that wasn't an acceptable answer. She gave me the Mom Look and I sighed internally.

"It was good. Got a 98 on my AP Chem quiz and Mr.

Hurley assigned us *Jane Eyre* for our next book." I would be asked to give many more specifics, but that would happen at the dinner table.

To be fair to my parents, they did only want the best for me. Neither of them had gone to college, but had been almost entirely self-taught and didn't want me to struggle like they had. Granted, the economy was a hell of a lot different now than it was when they were growing up, but I didn't want to burst that bubble. In the end, we both wanted the same thing. Me, at a good college and getting at least a master's degree. In . . . something.

Still figuring that out.

"I'm going to take a shower," I announced and escaped to my bathroom for a reprieve.

My room was kind of a disaster, as usual. I nearly tripped over a pair of sweatpants on my way to the bathroom. Might be time to do some laundry. I picked them up and tossed them on top of the overflowing hamper.

I turned the water on nearly all the way and stepped under, yelping a little. No doubt when I got out there would be no hot water. I was a fan of long showers, especially when my parents wanted to ask me to describe every moment of my day.

I closed my eyes and leaned my head back, letting the water soak my hair. Sighing, I slid my hand down my stomach and between my legs. I was paranoid that my parents would hear me somehow, so the shower was ideal for "relieving stress." It probably wasted water, but whatever.

I kept my eyes closed and ran my fingers up and down the inside of my thighs. As always, I tried to picture my ideal man. I needed some sort of visual stimulation to get off. I created him in painstaking detail, but it just wasn't working. He was . . . blurry. I stroked myself and tried harder. He would have blonde hair and wasn't too muscular, just enough so that you knew he probably ran or did some sort of activity. He had a sexy voice and didn't call me "baby" because that was patronizing. He had just a few tattoos on his chest.

I growled in frustration. It wasn't working. There was just too much on my mind to get myself there. That had been happening more and more lately. Stupid stress. Stupid senior year messing with my masturbation. I opened my eyes and gave up. Maybe I'd try again later when I was in bed.

My mind drifted to other things as I washed my hair. I replayed the day and for some reason, I kept seeing Stella walking by me this morning. Like my brain was stuck and just kept replaying it.

What the hell? I shook my head and shoved it aside, but the moment I did, there was a twisting in the pit of my stomach. My heart started to race, as if I was running from something, and I quickly finished my shower and got out.

After I scrubbed myself with the towel so hard that my skin was red and raw I yanked a brush through my hair. It snagged more than a few times and I ripped out a few hairs. I told myself to calm the fuck down and get my shit together. It was nothing.

It was totally nothing.

～

STELLA

"Pull up, pull up, you've almost got it," I said to Joy as she attempted to hit her scorpion. She was so close to having her back arched perfectly with her foot pulled behind her head. Almost. Just a bit more stretching and she'd have it.

She made a face at me and then let her foot snap back to the floor.

"I feel like I'm bending myself in two," she said, getting down on the floor to work on her splits.

"Well, you kind of are," I said, getting down on the mat

and joining her. As a senior captain of the cheer squad, one of my jobs was to take some of the JV girls under my wing and help them out. Sort of like a big sister/little sister situation. It could be kind of a pain in the ass, but at least Joy wasn't obnoxious and really seemed like she wanted to listen to what I had to say.

After we stretched, we hit the locker room. Our big/little time was supposed to happen outside of practice, so we had to work it around both our schedules. If I didn't hurry, I was going to be very late for work, so I took a quick "baby wipe shower," changed my clothes, and said goodbye to Joy before rushing to my car. I knew I was sweaty and my hair was a mess, but that couldn't be helped.

I pulled into the vet's office and I was two minutes late. Shit. I dashed in the back door and nearly crashed into Maggie, who was dealing with a very grumpy golden retriever who didn't want to be doing whatever she was trying to get it to do.

"Sorry!" I said as I nearly tripped over the leash and we got tangled together. I regained my balance and we untangled ourselves as the dog moaned and groaned.

"What are you doing to this poor boy?" I asked.

"Giving him shots. I'm a terrible person, aren't I, Gunnar?" We both looked down at the dog as he howled like we were murdering him. I just laughed and moved past her to the back room where I could stash my bag. My scrubs today had little hearts on them. I'd gotten them around Valentine's Day, but I figured hearts could be worn year round. I hustled to the front desk where the receptionist, Margie, gave me a look.

"Sorry, sorry," I said, sitting down and booting up my computer. It was one of those terrible ancient desktops that was roughly the equivalent of a computer dinosaur, but the clinic didn't have a lot of extra funds for new computers.

I signed in and got to work. Since I wasn't even a vet tech, I didn't get to interact much with the animals outside of checking them, and their owners, in. Most of my job involved boring clerical work, but if I wanted to get into vet school, this was one of the first steps.

I worked on schedules, checked people out, filed, organized, and did a bunch of other little tasks, and soon it was time to clock out. That was one of the reasons I loved it. Never a dull moment. I ended up breaking up a potential fight between a dog and a very old, very mean cat whose owner refused to use a cat carrier, and then ended up consoling a girl whose hamster was put to sleep.

"Busy day," Margie said as I organized my desk again. I wanted it to look the same every day when I came back. I was weird that way.

"Same as always," I said, giving her a little wave. "See you tomorrow." She covered a yawn with her hand and I made my way into the back to grab my stuff. A few of the dogs who were there for overnight observation barked as I went by, begging me to release them.

"Not today, guys," I said, but they didn't listen and kept barking. My stomach yelled at me as I got in my car and turned it on. Shit. I was almost out of gas.

"Perfect," I sighed. Just one more thing I had to do today.

"I'M HOME," I called an hour later when I came through the door with a few bags of groceries.

"Hey, Star," Dad said as I dropped the bags in the kitchen and gave him a quick hug, then he started helping me put everything away.

"How was work?" he asked, putting the cereal box on the wrong shelf. He didn't appreciate my organizational skills, but that was fine. I'd arrange them correctly later.

I filled him in on my day and asked how his had been.

"Good, good. I assigned *Hamlet* today so we'll see how that goes." He rolled his eyes and I laughed. He was an English professor at the local community college and needless to say, a lot of the students in his classes weren't exactly fans of literature. They were forced to take English and liked to punish my dad when he tried to teach them something.

"*Sweets to the sweet*," I quoted, handing him a bag of apples. I'd grown up with him testing me on literature by quoting passages and asking me what book they were from. Sometimes he'd reward me with Hershey's Kisses.

"*To thine own self be true*," he said, pointing at me. I rolled my eyes.

"I'll get right on that."

After we put the groceries away, dad started making dinner and I went to do my homework in the den. This was one of those times when I was happy that it was just the two of us. My mom had left us when I was a toddler, and my older brother Gabe was off at Columbia studying journalism. I missed him like crazy, but we talked at least a few times a week and he texted Dad nearly every day.

I worked steadily, hitting my least favorite subjects first and leaving my English reading for last. Dad was still pissed that I hadn't signed up for AP English, and I didn't think he was going to let it go anytime soon.

"Are you coming to the game?" I asked as I twirled spaghetti on my fork.

"I'm going to try. I have exams to grade, but I'll do my best." He always did. Sometimes he made it to see me cheer and sometimes he didn't, but he tried. He always tried and that was what mattered.

"Have you thought any more about signing up for AP English?" he said and I sighed. I knew it.

"No. I just think that it's not worth it. They don't weigh AP classes, so I can get a perfect grade in regular English. Or I can take AP and have my GPA potentially take a dip. I don't want to do that." Now he was the one to sigh and I was treated to another lecture on the fact that I could gain college credit for taking and doing well on the AP test and blah, blah, blah.

He put down his fork and gave me a long look. Fortunately, I'd gotten most of my looks from him including hair color, eye color and shape, and our mouths did the same thing when we were trying not to smile.

"What if I told you I would give you some money so you could trade in your car and get a nicer one." Shit. He'd picked the *one thing* that I would go for. My car wasn't exactly a piece of crap, but it wasn't really nice either.

I glared at him and he narrowed his eyes and glared back.

"Fine," I said through gritted teeth. "I'll sign up for AP English."

~

WE WATCHED TV TOGETHER; we always liked the same shows, and then I headed to my room. I worked through my nightly stretches and then got in bed.

The lights were off, but I closed my eyes. This was the only time I let myself think about it. About how when I thought about kissing, it wasn't a boy I imagined. It was a girl. All sweet curves and soft lips. Sometimes her hair was long, and got in my way, sometimes it was short, the blunt ends tickling my fingers. We'd twist around each other until it was impossible to tell us apart.

The desire rushed through me and I welcomed it. I hadn't, at first. It had always been followed by shame. By guilt. Why was I thinking about girls that way? I'd been twelve and most of my friends were swooning over the boys, but I couldn't seem to feel that way. I tried. I tried so hard. I put posters of boy bands in my room and danced with them and tried to flirt with them, but it was just . . . wrong. I didn't like it.

I dated boys here and there, but never went further than that. They would try and I would slam a door in their face. Eventually they lost interest and moved on. I'd given up on that charade a while ago. I was who I was and no boy was going to change that.

I couldn't imagine telling my father and my brother, at least not yet. I would have to someday, obviously, when I got into a relationship. They weren't homophobic, or at least they had never said anything overt, but I didn't want to test them either. Things were fine right now and soon I'd be off to college and I could go all in with whomever I wanted. I'd set that goal for myself and I was going to stick to it.

The last thought I had before I fell asleep was of kissing a set of sweet pink lips.

Chapter Two

KYLE

I was distracted the next day and I wanted to pretend I didn't know why I was distracted but I totally did.

"What is wrong with you today?" Grace asked when I nearly knocked her can of soda off the table at lunch.

"Sorry. Just . . . thinking about stuff." I didn't sound convincing at all. Even to myself.

"Okayyyyy," Grace said, drawing the word out. "You've been weird all day. What's up?" I gave her a look.

"Really? Whenever you have an off day and I ask you what's wrong, you lie to me and now you expect me to talk to you?" She scowled.

"Ugh, whatever. Just be all weird and grumpy. See if I care." She turned away from me to talk to Molly about something.

I tapped her on the shoulder a few minutes later.

"What?" she snapped. You couldn't be sensitive and also be friends with Grace. She could be prickly, but she still had my back and if I needed to hide a body, she would be the one I would call.

"Sorry, I just have a lot on my mind. I had this . . . crazy dream last night and it's been throwing me off all day." So that wasn't a huge lie. I had had a dream last night. The kind of dream that left me waking up gasping and turned on. I could feel my face getting red as I told her. Thankfully, Grace couldn't read minds.

I looked away from her and it was like my eyes were drawn to Stella's table. She was there, sitting and laughing with her friends. Her hair was down in curls and she tossed them over her shoulder. Like she was in a fucking shampoo commercial. I felt my face get redder and told myself to stop looking at her. Not only was she a total bitch, she was also a *girl*.

I shouldn't be getting turned on by a girl. I was straight. I'd had crushes on boys plenty of times. Had even dated a few, but decided that there was no point until I got to college. It was a waste of time that I could better use for studying. Besides, my parents had been super strict about it, so it wasn't worth it.

I didn't like girls. I was just . . . whatever.

Grace snapped her fingers in front of my face.

"Are you there?"

"Yeah, sorry. Just thinking." I kept saying the same thing over and over again and Grace was definitely suspicious.

"Uh huh," she said and I knew she wasn't going to drop it, but the bell rang and we had to go. I kept my head down when I walked by Stella's table and was so focused on not looking at her that I smashed right into someone.

"Oh, I'm sorry!" I said, looking up into a set of crystal blue eyes. They narrowed before she rolled them back in her head and flounced off as I gaped after her.

"Who peed in her Cheerios?" Grace said as Stella flounced away. I felt like I couldn't breathe.

"Don't know," I said, shaking my head and starting to walk again, paying more attention to where I was going.

"She's such a bitch," Grace said, winding her arm with mine.

"Yeah," I said.

~

THE REST of the week was similarly weird. It was like Stella kept getting tossed in my path. Or maybe I just had never noticed her as much. Hell, I was noticing her now. I hated how much I was noticing.

How thick and long her eyelashes were. How her hair fell over her shoulder. How delicate and small her hands were. How her voice had a husky, smoky undertone that was . . .

No. I wasn't noticing things about Stella Davis.

Finally, it was Friday and time for the weekend. I could hang out with Grace and the rest of my friends and not notice Stella Davis for two whole days.

I had not counted on the fact that, of course, Stella would be at the football game. She was captain of the cheerleading squad for fuck's sake. She'd be front and center the whole time. It was going to be even more of a chore not to look at her. I was totally up to the challenge, though. I'd spent the last three years ignoring her (for the most part). How hard could it be?

~

"WHAT ARE YOU STARING AT?" Grace said, nudging my shoulder.

"Hm?" I said, turning to face her. I had *not* been staring at Stella's ponytail. At all.

"Um, I'm watching the game?" I said, wrapping my arms around myself. It was cold tonight and my ass was already numb on the hard metal bleachers. Grace lifted one edge of her blanket and I scooted closer and we snuggled together.

"You know, we should get one of those family-sized Snuggies," she said as we huddled closer to the rest of our friends.

"That isn't a terrible idea," Paige said. Tommy made a grunting noise on the other side of her. He was too busy watching the game to chat.

"Unpopular opinion time," I said, but only loud enough for Grace to hear. The ref blew a whistle on the field and all the players jogged back to their benches for a time out.

"Yeah?" Grace said, watching the huddle.

"I'm not a fan of football," I said. "Shhh, don't tell anyone." I put my finger to my lips and she rolled her eyes.

"Tell me something I don't know." I went to say something else, but she shushed me. Grace did like football, which was one of the other reasons I came to these things. She got all riled up and it was really funny. More often than not, I watched her instead of the game.

Tonight was different. Tonight I was extremely distracted by a certain cheerleader with blonde hair. It was so cold that instead of wearing the skirts they usually wore during basketball season, they had pants on, but those didn't leave much to the imagination either.

God, what the fuck was wrong with me? I looked around to make sure no one had seen me staring and felt my face get hot. Of course no one was paying attention to me, which was a good thing.

How was it possible that you could be in school with someone for nearly four years and then BAM, you can't stop thinking about them or staring at them or wondering about them . . .

It couldn't be due to Stella's awesome personality. She was generally acknowledged to be not very nice. Not that she did anything overtly mean, but she just gave off that "I'm better than you" vibe and walked around like she owned the world.

I shook my head at myself. I wasn't going to think about

Stella's personality. It was irrelevant. I forced my eyes back on the players on the field. I had no idea how anyone could tell them apart with all that gear on Sure, they had their names and numbers on their backs, but still.

Of course, the minute I decided to actually pay attention to the game, it was halftime. The band played first, walking in unison over the field, making a few different formations. We all cheered for our friends and then it was time for the cheerleaders to perform.

Great.

"Wanna get some popcorn?" I said in a strangled voice, grabbing Grace's arm.

"Yeah, sure. You okay?" I nodded jerkily.

"Yeah, just hungry and cold." I didn't let myself watch as they started their cheer and got the crowd to yell back at them. Nope. I kept my back turned and stood in line at the concession stand with Grace.

I was so focused on not paying attention to what was happening on the field that after we got our snacks loaded up in our arms, I nearly ran right into Stella.

"Sorry," I said and she just gave me another look. Like I'd done it on purpose.

"What is your problem?" Grace said. She'd been next to me and had seen the whole thing. Fortunately, only a few kernels of popcorn spilled and I had managed to keep my balance. I wasn't normally this bad at bumping into people. It felt like someone was playing a joke on me.

Stella glared at us both for a second. Her makeup was perfectly in place, despite the fact that she'd been cheering for half of the game. But that was normal. She always looked perfect. Even when she was glaring.

"Nothing. I just don't like people getting in my way," she said and then crossed her arms. I kept my eyes on her face, but I could feel my face getting red.

"Well maybe you should watch where you're going and then it won't happen," Grace snapped, shifting the food so she could take my arm to lead me back in the direction of the bleachers. I couldn't make my mouth work and say words. Why couldn't I say words?

Stella Davis had me tongue-tied and I wanted to scream.

Her blue eyes locked on mine and it was one of those moments when everything goes quiet and it's like you're the only two people in the world. And then she blinked and rolled her eyes.

"Come on," Grace said, tugging at my arm. I stumbled a step before I could regain my footing. Grace was always nice about not walking too fast for me and she held onto my arm all the way back to the bleachers and we sat back down in front.

We handed out the snacks and then Grace turned to me.

"Okay, what the hell was that? You looked like you were . . ." she trailed off.

"I looked like I was what?" A cold drip of fear slid down and pooled into my stomach. I didn't want her to say it at the same time I almost did.

Grace studied my face and then pressed her lips together.

"Never mind," she said, brushing a hand over her hair. It sprung back immediately.

I let it drop. I had been friends with Grace for a long time and I knew her face probably better than my own. I knew what she was going to say without her having to say it.

And it scared the ever-loving shit out of me.

STELLA

Was it karma that kept dropping Kyle Blake in my path? That was the second time I'd nearly knocked her over in one week. I felt bad about it, mostly because she had a difficult time walking, but I couldn't bring myself to not be a bitch about everything. If people saw me get soft, things would go back to the way they'd been in middle school and I would die before I let that happen.

So I let her think I was an asshole. I let everyone think that. Hell, I encouraged it. People didn't mess with a bitch. They steered clear of her. They didn't spend their time trying to knock her down and make her suffer. My exterior was steel, topped with razor wire. Come at me and you are going to get cut.

Anyway, I stepped away from her, but not before I got a weird vibe. Like, she was staring at me in a way that she hadn't before. If I didn't know better.

Yeah, no. She was definitely into guys. I'd heard her talk with her friend Grace (another person who didn't take shit from anyone, which I actually admired) about the hot football players and so forth and I was pretty sure she'd had a few boyfriends.

She was kinda cute though. Had that nerdy thing going on with the glasses, and she could do a messy bun that I envied. Ugh, it didn't matter. I wasn't going to go after anyone here. College. Just wait until college.

WE WON the game and afterwards the cheer team went out for pizza. There was a party at Maria's house and since I didn't have anything better to do and the whole squad was going, I went.

It was pretty typical. A bunch of us in the huge basement of her parent's house, some smuggled alcohol, and crappy music. I tried to let go and have a good time, but I couldn't seem to do it.

"What the hell is up with you?" Midori asked me as I

sipped a weak wine cooler. I never got plastered at these things because I didn't see the point. Not that I hadn't been wasted before, but the experience had not been enjoyable and I didn't want to repeat it.

I didn't answer as I watched Destiny Cook tangle her tongue with Brett Forrester's. Gross. I made a face and looked back at Midori. Her brown eyes were studying me in a way I didn't like.

"Nothing," I said, shrugging one shoulder and sitting next to her on the leather couch that had seen better days.

"Yeah, somehow I don't buy that," she said, leaning back. I was saved from having to answer her by a totally bombed Brian Sharpe trying to hit on her and Midori shooting him down. And cursing at him in Japanese until he went away.

She turned her attention back to me and I tried not to squirm under her scrutiny. She'd never said anything about me, never asked, but that didn't mean that she didn't know. I had the sneaking suspicion she did. But she was too much of a good friend to put me on the spot like that.

"So?" she said.

"Just not feeling it tonight. Got a lot on my mind. Dad made me sign up for AP English. I have to start on Monday." I made a face. I had a ton of homework this weekend to catch up on everything I'd missed in the first few weeks of school. It was going to take me several days to get it all done and I wasn't looking forward to it. But I'd suck it up because next weekend Dad was taking me car shopping and I couldn't wait. My car was making a weird grinding noise and I was hoping it would hold out until then.

"That blows." I nodded and she didn't push further. We left early, before things got really out of hand.

"Call me if you need a break or anything," she said when I dropped her off.

"Will do," I said and then headed home. Dad was already in bed, but I went to say goodnight to him.

"Did you witness massive amounts of debauchery?" he asked with a raised eyebrow.

"The usual. It was pretty boring, actually. I'm tired." He kissed my cheek and I went to take a shower before crawling between fresh sheets.

I closed my eyes and sighed. It had been a long day and it was going to be a long weekend. I let my mind wander away from the stress and toward something much more pleasant. Smiles and soft skin and laughter. The stress of the day evaporated and I felt my shoulders relax.

Freedom.

I MADE sure I had my resting bitchface fully activated before I stepped into the AP English classroom on Monday. Still, a few people looked up and whispered to each other.

"Oh, hello, Stella," Mr. Hurley said. I'd had him my freshman year for English, so at least I didn't have to worry about dealing with a new teacher. I handed him all the makeup work and he gave me a smile. He reminded me a lot of my dad, only he was a few years younger and a little less put together. His glasses were always a little askew and his sweaters usually had at least one hole by the cuffs or the hem.

"Well, you were busy," he said, licking his thumb and then flipping through the pages of essays and handouts I'd nearly killed myself to get done this weekend.

I didn't answer him.

"And you got all the books for this semester?" he asked. I nodded and pulled my copy of *Jane Eyre* out of my bag. It was a worn copy that Dad had given me. I'd read it a few times already. Having an English teacher as a father was a literature class in itself. I'd already devoured most of the required reading list in my younger years and had copies of all of the books at my disposal.

"Great, why don't you take a seat and we'll get started." I turned and looked around. I wasn't friendly with any of the people in this room and as fate would have it, there was only one open seat near the door. Right next to Kyle Blake.

She was doing her best not to look at me, keeping her eyes on the surface of her desk, tracing a pattern with one finger over and over. I heaved a sigh and sat down next to her. She didn't acknowledge me and Mr. Hurley got class started a second later.

"Okay, so we start *Jane Eyre* this week," he said, clapping his hands and rubbing them together as if he'd announced we were going to Disney World. God, he was like my dad. I smiled a little to myself and looked to my left. Kyle had been looking at me. She quickly fixed her eyes back on the front of the class and her cheeks went red.

Weird. I looked back at Mr. Hurley just as he announced that we'd be pairing up to discuss the first three chapters of *Jane Eyre* and filling out a worksheet with our partner. And he pointed to me and Kyle to pair up.

I almost sighed again, but restrained myself. I slowly turned to face her, and she didn't look happy about it either. Mr. Hurley handed out the worksheets and I grabbed it first. Never rely on someone else to do the work in a group project.

"Okay, did you do the reading?" I asked, scanning the questions. They weren't too hard. Just basic information. I could answer all of them by myself, which was good.

"Um, yeah," she said, flipping through her book. The spine was worn and there was some clear tape holding it together. Huh. It was probably one of the school's crappy copies and not a personal copy.

"What are you doing in this class?" she asked as she

chewed on her bottom lip and pushed her glasses further up her nose. Had she always had green eyes? I didn't think I'd ever noticed them before. The glasses somehow hid them.

"I transferred," I snapped, starting to work on the first question.

"Hey, what are you writing?" She reached for the paper, but I jerked it away.

"I'm answering the questions. My father is an English teacher. I could do this in my sleep." She gave me a skeptical look and I glared back. This was going so well.

"Well, we're supposed to be doing it together." She waved her hand to indicate the other pairs who had pushed their desks together and were talking.

"Fine," I said, getting up and dragging my desk closer to hers. "Happy?"

For a second I thought she was going to laugh, but she just grabbed the paper out of my hand and put it on her desk, sliding it over so we could both see it.

"There. Okay, so what do you think for the first one?" She bent her head over the paper and I swallowed and leaned closer. I'd never been this close to her and I could just barely smell her perfume. It was like a mix of coconut and vanilla. Like dessert. I tried not to think about it.

She started talking, but I wasn't really listening. I blinked a few times.

"Wait, what?" She gave me a confused look and repeated herself. She pushed her glasses up again and I wondered if it was a nervous habit. They were black plastic frames, but they totally worked for her.

I forced my eyes back on the paper and slowly but surely, we got through the worksheet. I was so relieved when Mr. Hurley asked for us to pass them in and I could move my desk back to where it was supposed to be. But then he made us have a group discussion, which meant moving the desks again into a lopsided circle.

Kyle was having a bit of difficulty getting her desk flipped around so I just grabbed it and did it for her. Instead of getting a "thank you," she looked pissed before slumping into her seat, jaw clenched.

What the hell did I do?

"You're welcome," I said.

"I didn't ask for your help," she said through clenched teeth. I couldn't figure out why she was mad, but I had to admit, she was kinda hot when she was pissed. She had an amazing jawline.

Mr. Hurley cleared his throat and I had to shove my head back into the discussion so I didn't sound like an idiot.

KYLE DIDN'T LOOK in my direction for the rest of class and when it was time to move our desks back, I just went ahead and let her do it, putting my stuff in my bag and leaving without another word.

This class was going to be so much fun.

Chapter Three

KYLE

Seriously. Stella was a straight up bitch. I had only ever had one class with her freshman year; since then we hadn't had much contact, except for last week when we'd kept colliding. Grace was right, though. She was an asshole.

I was still mad about her "helping" me without asking when I met up with Grace for lunch.

"Whoa, you look like you're super pissed. What happened?"

"Stella Lewis is now in my English class. For some reason. No idea how that happened, but she said her dad was an English professor so maybe he pulled some strings for her or something. Basically it means that she's going to be glaring at me and giving me the cold shoulder for the rest of the year," I said, barely taking a breath. I'd been holding onto that rant since I left class.

"Tell me how you really feel, Ky," Grace said, slinging her arm around my shoulder.

"She's just so irritating," I said as we dropped our backpacks at our table and went to get in line for food.

"Uh huh," Grace said, prodding me in the back.

"No I didn't," I said, looking over my shoulder at her. She just smirked and I had no idea what the hell that meant.

"What is happening right now?" I asked as I handed her a tray.

"Oh, nothing, nothing," she said, fiddling around for the silverware. I tried to prod her about it as we got food and then again when we sat down, but she just pretended to zip her lips and refused to talk to me.

I chatted with Molly instead, but I couldn't help but look over at Stella's table. She was sitting with her back to me, her hair draped perfectly over her shoulder. She really was pretty. That kind of easy but polished pretty. And she didn't have to wear a massive amount of makeup to achieve it. The raw materials were all there. I bet she looked amazing with no makeup on.

Yeah, I needed to put a stop to those thoughts like yesterday. I made myself stop looking at her by reminding myself how annoyed I'd been earlier. I just needed to distract myself with something, so I started going through the steps to create different effects in Photoshop. It worked well enough that by the time lunch was over, I had only looked at Stella a few times.

"SO, ANYTHING NEW HAPPEN TODAY?" my mom asked at dinner and I nearly choked on my asparagus.

"Not really," I said after I sipped some water to clear my throat. I hadn't told them about Stella joining my class because it didn't seem important or relevant.

"You okay?" Dad said, rubbing my back.

"Yup. Just went down the wrong pipe." I changed the subject and then my mom changed it back to my college applications. She'd been into the guidance office at least three times already, begging for applications. They weren't due for months, but she wanted me to "get a jump" on them. Mostly this required me writing tedious essays about my high school experiences and the volunteer work I'd done since I was eleven. It had been mandatory, but I'd enjoyed it. Soup kitchens, building houses, walking shelter dogs, that kind of thing. They wanted me to do it for college, and I just thought it was a nice thing to do. My parents had one-track minds.

I escaped to my room as quick as I could and went back to working on the web design for the blogger. I was so close to being done, I was just doing tweaks and testing to make sure that everything was going to work out and that there weren't any bugs.

I had my headphones on and was blasting Halsey so I didn't hear it when my mom knocked, and I nearly bit m tongue in half when she tapped me on the shoulder.

"Oh my God, Mom, don't do that!" I put my hand on my chest and tried to get my heart to beat at a normal level. She handed me a cup of tea.

"I thought you could use some tea. How's it going?" Um, what? We'd already talked at dinner not that long ago.

"Fineeeee," I said, drawing the word out.

She smiled, but it was one of those placating smiles that parents used right before they dropped bad news.

"Good, good," she said, sitting on my bed. Uh oh. That was the second bad sign.

"Mom, is everything okay?" I asked, knowing I was probably going to regret the answer.

"Oh, fine, fine. Just making sure everything's going to okay. You seemed a bit off at dinner." Shit. My parents were too observant for their own good.

"No, I'm fine. Just busy. Start of the year, you know?" I laughed a little and cringed at how fake it sounded.

Mom patted my arm and I sipped my tea so I wouldn't have to look at her.

"Well, you know that you can talk to your father and me about *anything*." Okay, this was getting weird. They couldn't possibly know anything about . . .

"Yeah, I know, Mom," I said in a voice that was a little too loud. "I have to get back to work, okay?" I said, pointing at my laptop.

"Sure, honey. Sure." She gave me another smile and put a kiss on the top of my head before leaving and shutting the door quietly behind her.

Um, weird.

STELLA

Practice that night was brutal. Everyone was off, even me. I kept having difficulty with my heel stretch, which was nuts because I'd been doing them fine since I was eleven.

Coach ended everything early so there weren't any permanent injuries.

"I don't know what is wrong with all of you, but I hope it's fixed by next practice. None of those stunts should have been falling. You've been doing them for years. Go stretch out and then go home." She walked away, muttering to herself.

I shared a look with Midori.

"Ouch. It's like there's something in the water," she said, stretching her neck out. I got down and started working on my hips and then sunk down into my spits, right, left and middle.

"You okay?" Midori asked as we gathered our stuff and headed out to the parking lot.

"Yeah, just feel off. Maybe it's PMS," I said, even though I knew it wasn't that. She gave me a weird look as we got in the car.

"Are you sure there's nothing you want to talk to me about?" I shook my head.

"Okay, okay. Then will you give *me* some advice?"

"Of course, you don't even have to ask." She took a breath and proceeded to tell me that she had a huge crush on Nate Klein. I had suspected as much, since I'd caught her staring at him during lunch at least ten times in the past two weeks.

"But I don't know if I should go for it. I mean, what's the point? We're just going to end up dating and then breaking up when we go to separate schools. And I'm not in the mood for just a fling." I knew what she meant. Not that I had my eye on anyone. I wasn't dating boys anymore. It sucked and I hated it and I always felt like a liar when I did it. When I first realized that I was attracted to girls, I thought maybe I liked them in addition to boys. And then I'd dated a few boys and realized there was just nothing there for me. But girls? Oh, yeah.

"Well, I guess you have to decide if it's worth the risk. Maybe you won't break up at the end of the year. Maybe you'll stick it out for the long haul. And maybe not." She laughed a little.

"You're so practical sometimes." I guess I was. I never really thought about it much. Sure, romance was fun and wonderful, but it was also work and didn't just happen by magic. Or at least I didn't think it did. To be honest, I didn't think I'd ever really been in love. I'd had feelings for the guys I went out with, but they were only ever friendly. I was just waiting for that one girl to knock me off my feet and then I'd be all in. Just had to get through this last year of high school and then I could go to college and start looking for her.

KYLE WAS pissy again when I sat next to her on Wednesday.

"This is the only seat in the room, so it's not like I can sit anywhere else," I said, low enough for her to hear, but no one else.

She just made a grumpy sound and I risked a look at her. Cute. She was dangerously cute. I watched as she took down her hair, combed through it with her fingers and then put it up again, exactly the same way. She caught me looking, so I quickly turned and pretended to pay attention to Mr. Hurley, who was going on and on about the paranormal aspects of *Jane Eyre* but I wasn't paying attention. My focus narrowed to one particular point. And she was sitting right next to me, taking notes with her left hand. Had I noticed she was left-handed before? Probably not.

There were a lot of things I discovered about her in that period. Like the fact that she had large, looping handwriting. That she pushed her glasses back up on her nose. A lot. That she had just a few freckles on her nose. There were also several holes in her ears, but only the bottom hole on her lobe had a silver stud in it.

At the end of class, I'd barely taken any notes on the material, but I'd made a hell of a lot of notes about Kyle. This was going to be a continuing problem.

I packed up slowly so we could leave nearly at the same time. I wanted to say something to her, but she just ignored me and kept walking. That made me realize that I couldn't say something to her. I couldn't be friendly toward her. That was *definitely* out of the question. I had to put Kyle Blake out of my mind. Nothing was ever going to happen, so it was crazy to even try.

YEAH, the not-thinking about Kyle lasted until Friday, when I walked into English and realized just how cute she was. How in the hell hadn't I noticed her before this year? She was a neon sign in front of my face and not looking at her was nearly impossible. Somehow she'd flipped a switch and it didn't matter what she did, I was aware of it. I swore I could smell her even after I'd left the room. And at night . . . I thought about taking down her hair and running my fingers through it. It looked soft and smooth. Just the image of wrapping it around my hands was just . . . yeah. I was terrified that she was going to somehow find out that I was thinking about her like that. So my only option was to be ice cold to her. Well, colder than I already was.

That became a problem when Mr. Hurley kept pairing us up to do things in class. Kyle treated me with open disdain, which made being attracted to her even harder than it already was. I had come to the realization that glasses made any girl about five thousand times hotter than she already was. And Kyle had all the raw material. She barely wore any makeup, but I liked that. Sloppy sexy.

"What is your problem?" she hissed at me when she caught me staring.

"Nothing," I said, keeping my tone cool. "Just wondering if you actually read these chapters, or just skimmed Cliff's Notes online." It usually gave me no qualms being like this with most people because the alternative was getting hurt again. I would do whatever it took to not go back there. But I did have a twinge of guilt for being snappy toward Kyle. Didn't stop me from doing it, but it did make me hesitate a little.

"Yes, I did read the chapters," she fired back and grabbed the paper from me. "God, why are you like this?"

I shrugged one shoulder.

"Because."

Her jaw got all clenchy and pretty and I wanted to run my finger along her cheek.

"I get it, I get it. You think you're better than everyone." She rolled her eyes.

"I don't," I blurted out before I could stop myself. Shit. I tried to slam my bitchface back on, but she'd caught me. Her eyebrows flew up and she narrowed her eyes as she looked at me.

"You don't?"

I cleared my throat and grabbed the paper back from her, trying to think how to change the subject.

"Hey," she said, her voice so soft that I couldn't ignore it. I shut my eyes so I couldn't see the way she was looking at me. If I did, I didn't think I'd be able to deal with it. What was wrong with me? I'd barely spent any time with her at all. She was an easy target for a crush, that was all. She was new(ish) and she was here. It was opportunity. And she was cute. Nothing more. Hell, I didn't know anything about her, other than what I could observe. I didn't know what she ate for breakfast or if she was a morning person, or what she wanted to do when she graduated. That was what made a crush. This was . . . nothing. It was nothing.

I opened my eyes and narrowed them.

"Let's just get this done," I said. Instead of reeling back, she gave me what was almost a smirk. As if she knew she'd gotten under the surface that I glossed on for everyone else. I was going to have to work twice as hard now to undo that. Great. Just fantastic.

KYLE

Interesting. Very interesting. Not that I really cared about Stella, but I could have sworn she had a moment of humanity. I didn't know it was possible. That meant one of two things. Either it was a fluke, or it was a moment of weakness. I'd never considered the fact that she might not be a total asshole. The only question was, if asshole wasn't her default setting, then why did she do it?

I guess I could understand a little. I mean, she was captain of the cheerleading team and she hung out with the so-called popular crowd and seemingly had everything. I wouldn't be surprised if she was in the running for prom queen. If it was fake, it was obvious that it had worked for her.

I shook my head at myself. I was thinking way too much about this. She was definitely just a horrible person and would continue to be so. Such a shame because she was definitely pretty. So, so pretty.

"UNGH," Grace moaned on Saturday. We were hanging out at her house, stuffing our faces with pizza and garlic knots and marathoning *Faking It*. I didn't want to watch it, but Grace did, so I'd caved. The thing that made me not want to watch it was the fact that the two main characters were pretending to be a lesbian couple to get popular at their liberal high school. I had to look away every time they kissed. I hated the way it made me feel. Not bad. Good. *Really* good.

What the crap was happening to me? It was like I'd flipped some sort of switch and now all I could do was notice girls in a way I had never thought to notice them before.

"Hey, I forgot to ask, how's class going with Stella?" Grace said. I hadn't been thinking of Stella up until that moment, but the instant Grace said her name, I couldn't get her out of my head.

I laughed nervously. Great.

"She's still the worst," I said, and Grace was preoccupied by the show and didn't see how weird I was being.

"I think she's one of those girls who will always be terrible, but good things will continue to happen for her. Like, she's blessed or something," Grace said. She was blessed all right.

UGH. I needed to stop having those thoughts. But how did you stop your brain from thinking? Other than doing permanent damage.

"Yeah," I said, and got up to stretch.

Grace looked up at me from her position on the floor.

"You sure you're okay?" she asked.

"Yup. Just going to get another soda," I said. "You want anything?" She shook her head and I headed to the kitchen. Her house was quiet since her mom was at the hospital where she worked as an ER doctor and her dad barely left his law practice. Another reason we hung out at Grace's a lot was that her house was five thousand times nicer than mine. It was also about three times the size.

I pulled a Coke out of the fridge and leaned on the marble countertop of the kitchen island for a minute. When I was little, I used to be terrified to make a mess in such a pristine house, but now I was more comfortable. It still didn't feel like a home, more like a movie set, but Grace's room was cozy and comfortably messy.

What was going on with me? I mean, I thought I knew, but that was impossible. I mean, I was straight. Always had been. I'd had plenty of crushes on boys and wanted to get married and all that stuff. I mean, not right now, but in the future. He'd be nerdy and sweet. We'd watch a lot of Doctor Who and maybe cosplay and he'd work for a lab or something.

I had it all planned out. That was what was going to happen. It was what had to happen.

This whole thing with Stella was just a distraction. I was just . . . I don't know.

I peeled myself off the counter and went back to Grace's room. She was laughing her ass off when I got there and pulled me back down to the floor to fill me in on what I'd missed in the show. But my mind was still reeling and my stomach churned as I sipped my soda. The churning had nothing to do with the carbonation.

∽

I WAS a big fan of research. If I didn't absolutely know everything about a subject, I was determined to learn. So when I got home on Sunday after crashing at Grace's, I locked myself in my room, pulled out my laptop and opened a search engine. I had to figure this out.

My fingers shook at little as they hovered over the keys.

I typed in a few letters, erased them, typed again, erased them. That went on for at least ten minutes until I finally typed in *how do I know if I like girls?* and hit Enter.

And then clicked out of the window before I got any results.

∽

STELLA HAD her bitchface back on Monday. I should have been relieved, but it didn't stop the little fluttery feeling from starting in my chest. She really was a beautiful girl. I wished I could get my eyebrows to look like that.

But her personality was horrible, which was fair. No one should be both gorgeous and have a stunning personality. I was just praying that we didn't get assigned to work together. Fortunately, Mr. Hurley had us read passages aloud, starting with me and going down the rows and back up. I hated reading out loud, but I suffered my way through it. I snickered to myself when a few of the other kids in the class stumbled over some of the more difficult words.

And then it got to Stella and I riveted my eyes on my desk, so I wouldn't look at her. She started to read and for some reason, her voice got all low and melodic and holy *shit*. She didn't stumble on any of the words and didn't read it in the same robotic voice as everyone else. She read as if she was on stage, doing a dramatic recitation and I looked up to see if anyone else was being affected by it like I was.

A cursory glance around the room said no. I felt my face going red and I looked back at my desk. She finally finished and sat down. I breathed a sigh of relief.

Out of the corner of my eye, I saw her look over at me. I wasn't going to turn my head because then we'd make eye contact and I just couldn't.

English class had never been fraught with so much tension ever in my life and I just wanted it to be over.

There were several feet of space between me and Stella, but I wished there were miles. I just couldn't NOT be aware of her. Every time she touched her hair, or moved her legs, or breathed, I was aware of it. She had skinny jeans on that hugged and accentuated everything, a filmy top that I could never pull off, and cute little ballet flats. As always, her hair was perfect.

I wanted to run away, but class was almost over. I made a frustrated sound that was louder than I thought it was. Finally, I turned and saw Stella giving me a puzzled look. I just wanted to grab her snotty, stuck up face and . . .

I raised my hand and asked to go to the bathroom. Mr. Hurley let me go and I nearly knocked my desk over in my haste to leave the room. I nearly fell when I got through the door because my brain was moving faster than my feet, but I caught myself on the wall and headed toward the bathroom. I didn't care how it looked; I was camping out in there until English was over.

It was only ten minutes. I could do it.

~

I HAD ABOUT two minutes left before the bell rang when someone came through the door. I had sequestered myself in the last stall, hoping that no one would notice that I was standing.

I waited for them to pick one of the other stalls, do their thing and leave, but the footsteps just kept advancing until the person was right near my stall. I wondered if I should flush or something, but then whoever it was spoke.

"Kyle?"

Chapter Four

STELLA

I don't know what made me do it. But she looked so freaked out and she'd hurried so fast to get out of class that I couldn't just sit there. What if she was sick and needed help?

Okay, that was a flimsy excuse, but it didn't stop me from asking Mr. Hurley if I could run to the office for something. If someone else had asked, he probably would have said no, but he liked me too much and went ahead and let me go.

I figured she'd gone for the bathroom, so I headed that way and saw her black Chucks under the door of the last stall. I didn't hear anything but her breathing, so I decided to risk it.

"Kyle?" Silence. "Are you okay?" She coughed and the toilet flushed before she pushed through the door. Her face was totally red and I wondered what the hell I was doing. Why had I followed her in here like a total stalker?

I needed to turn around and run away. There was no easy way to salvage this situation.

"I'm fine," she said, and it sounded like those two words should end with a question mark. "Why are you in here?"

I opened my mouth to answer and then the bell rang. Two seconds later, the door opened and we weren't alone. She pushed past me and headed out the door.

I stood there for a second before a girl gave me a nasty look. I gave her one back and left, heading to my locker.

MY DAD HAD KEPT his word about the car, so on Saturday he'd taken me shopping and I was now the owner of a new-to-me vehicle.

"Not bad," Midori said when she got in after practice. It had a lot of upgrades over my old wheels, namely the leather interior and Bluetooth capability. I'd already synched all my music, which was awesome.

"Not at all," I said.

"So," she said, taking down her ponytail and combing her fingers through her hair. "Everything okay? You were a little out of it today." I knew she'd noticed. After the weirdness with Kyle, I was off the rest of the day. I forgot to be so much of an asshole and got some strange looks from my friends when I wasn't at my normal level of icy composure.

I was able to throw myself into practice because we were working on heel stretch double downs and I had to focus or else I would seriously hurt someone.

"Yeah, fine. Why?" I switched the songs to have something to do.

"Don't know. You just seemed . . . off." I flipped through songs until Midori put her hand on mine to make me stop.

"Stel." I looked at her and then back at the road.

"I'm fine. I just don't want to talk, okay? I just . . ." I gripped the steering wheel. I knew Midori wouldn't care about me liking girls. I knew it wouldn't change anything. But actually saying the words out loud and telling her was something I just couldn't do. Not yet. College. I would be who I wanted to be in college. It just wasn't the right time. I wasn't ready.

"It's fine, it's fine. Don't worry about it." She pulled back and I was so grateful. The pressure to tell her weighed on me, but it was a weight I could deal with. I'd been handling it for years.

So why did it suddenly feel like it was crushing me?

"HOW'S THE CAR?" Dad asked when I got home. He had dinner ready, but I wasn't that hungry.

"Great. The heated seats are going to be a bonus in the winter." He smiled at me and we chatted about this and that for a few minutes, but then my phone rang and it was my brother. I answered at the table.

"Hey, Gabe," I said.

"Hey, Star. How's life?" My brother was the most upbeat member of my family. And I was a cheerleader.

"Good, how's school? You failing yet?" He laughed.

"Hell no. Dean's list, Sis." I rolled my eyes. Stupid smart family full of overachievers.

"You would. Are you having any fun?"

"Here and there. Not the kind of fun you're thinking of. I don't think passing out on the sidewalk naked and being found by campus security is my idea of a good time." I agreed and we talked more about his classes and campus life. He was so lucky to be in New York and surrounded by so much culture and life and diversity. I couldn't wait to get the hell out of Maine.

Dad motioned for the phone and I handed it over so he and Gabe could chat about his assignments and his recent articles he'd had published. I knew that was going to take a while, so I took our plates and rinsed them in the sink.

After Dad was done, I took the phone and headed into my room so I could talk to Gabe without Dad overhearing.

"Okay, so tell me what you're really up to now that I'm not sitting next to Dad," I said, flopping on my bed.

"Nothing. I told you, I've been a good boy. I honestly don't have time to get shitfaced with all the work I'm doing in class and on the paper and freelancing. You'll understand when you get to college next year. It's so much more work than people say it is." I could believe that, but I could also believe that Gabe was taking on too much. He always did. If he wasn't careful, he was going to run himself into the ground before he turned thirty.

"Have you even been on a date?" I asked. I would much rather grill my brother about his love life than talk about mine. Or lack thereof.

"Not really. I've been doing the casual sex thing."

"Ugh, TMI, Gabe. TMI!" I wished I could throw a pillow or something at him. He just laughed again.

"I'm kidding. Sort of. Sometimes this girl from one of my study groups comes over, but usually we're so tired that we just pass out before we can even get to the sex. I figure I'll get to have sex when I graduate." I rolled my eyes at him, but he couldn't see.

"How's your love life? Any developments there? Still sticking to the 'no dating until college' rule?"

"Yes, I am." I didn't sound sure. Oh, hell.

"Is that some hesitation I hear in your voice? Did you meet someone?" He didn't specify a gender. We hadn't for a long time. But I still hadn't told him that I wanted to date girls.

"No. Definitely not." I didn't sound sure about that either. But just as I thought he was going to start interrogating me, I heard someone call his name.

"Shit, listen. I have to go, but we need to have a longer talk soon. Oh, and when are you coming to visit?" I always flew down to see him at least a few times a year on our school breaks. He took me around the city and we went shopping and he let me see what it was going to be like to be a college student. I couldn't wait to get back.

"I can't remember the exact day our break starts on, but I'll text you." We said goodbye and hung up. I was actually relieved that I didn't have to talk to him anymore.

Gabe was perceptive as hell and I was ninety percent sure he already knew. Once again, saying the words just seemed impossible. For the millionth time in my life, I wished I just liked boys. I'd tried. Sometimes I still tried. I'd look at a popular male actor or model and ask myself if I found him attractive.

Nope. Nothing. Absolutely nothing. It was like looking at marble sculpture. Pleasing to the eye, but I didn't want to buy it.

Kyle still floated in the back of my head. She'd been lurking there all day in all her adorable glory. She really was cute as hell. I was an idiot for ignoring it so long. Now I couldn't see anything else.

She had definitely looked freaked out in the bathroom today, but that was probably because she hadn't expected me to come and find her. I groaned and rolled over onto my stomach. I was such an idiot. Why had I done that? Things were going to be so awkward on Wednesday when I saw her again.

I turned back over and put my hands behind my bed as I stared up at the ceiling.

I was just going to go back to avoiding her. It would be easy. Totally easy. Impossibly easy.

∾

I DIDN'T LOOK up when I walked into class and took my seat, but she was there, fiddling with her hair. She let it down long enough for me to see that it hit the middle of her back before she swiped it up again.

I'd considered saying something, or apologizing about the bathroom weirdness, but my instinct told me to just let it go and pretend it hadn't happened.

And then, in his infinite wisdom, Mr. Hurley said the words that every student dreaded, "Okay, pair up." I searched around the room, but in the seconds after he'd spoken, the pairs had already formed, as if they'd just been waiting for this moment. There was the sound of desks sliding and people moving seats and then it was just me and Kyle.

I looked at her and she looked at me and it was inevitable.

"Guess I have no choice," I said, trying to sound bored while my heart was beating roughly three thousand miles a minute.

"Yup," she said, sounding irritated. Mr. Hurley handed out our assignments. Great. We had to pick from a list of topics, write a three page paper together and do a presentation for the rest of the class. We were going to have to work together for the next two weeks.

Oh, hell.

~

KYLE

I was really beginning to hate Mr. Hurley. Did he understand how horrible it was to make you work with someone you didn't want to work with? Hadn't he been in school once? Maybe it was too long ago. He was old and had gray hair.

Whatever the reason, I had to look forward to working very closely with Stella for the next two weeks. No way around it.

She and I would have to work in-class and outside to get everything done. Great. Just great.

"So . . ." she said, grabbing the topic list before I could reach for it. "I think we should do the one about feminism. Because *Jane Eyre*'s clearly a feminist text." I hadn't even seen the choices and I wanted to smack her because that did sound awesome.

"Do I get a say, or are you just going to do the entire thing yourself?" I said, my tone dry. She raised one absolutely perfect eyebrow and handed me the paper. I scanned the topics and I could feel her studying me. I pushed my glasses back up my nose and looked at her. I hadn't really absorbed what the paper said and I couldn't tell her that.

"Fine, we can do the feminism thing. But I want to write the paper. I type really fast." She gave me another eyebrow raise and I tried to do it too, but failed. My eyebrows weren't that coordinated.

Something passed over her face and she slid her eyes back down to the paper.

"Fine. But I get to do the presentation."

"Fine." I was absolutely fine with that. She was much more of a performer than I was, with the cheerleading and all. I'd probably end up stumbling over my words and messing it up. Stella probably knew that too.

There was a moment where neither of us knew what to say. The quiet hum of talk seemed distant. It almost felt like the two of us were completely alone. And then Mr. Hurley walked over and cleared his throat.

"Better get started, ladies." He gave us a Stern Look and I glanced at Stella. For a brief second, I could have sworn she was holding in a smile. But she smoothed her expression like a wrinkle out of fabric and it was gone.

"Guess we should start," I said to her.

"Guess we should."

～

THE REST of the class we spent in terse conversation. I was in charge of pulling quotes from the book we could use in our paper and Stella was busy looking up other sources on one of the classroom tablets.

For the most part, we could work quietly, but when we did have to exchange a few words, it was short and to the point.

Still, I couldn't take my eyes off her. As if it was planned that way, a shaft of sunlight broke through one of the windows and lit her hair on fire. If I didn't know better, I would have said she looked like an angel. And then she turned and gave me a look and I edited my assessment. Fallen angel. Fallen angel that was kinda bitter about the whole thing.

It was just then that I realized I'd been staring. Dammit.

I shoved my face in my book and tried to get back to work. A moment later I looked up because she'd cleared her throat.

"What do you think about this?" Her voice was softer than I'd ever heard it and I nearly fell out of my seat when she leaned over with the tablet to show me whatever was on the screen. I looked down at it, but it could have been written in emojis for all I noticed. She was too close. Way too close and I was freaking out about it. My heart was pounding so much that I was sure she could hear it and my hands suddenly went cold and then hot.

"Well?" she said, her voice totally breathy and low. I turned my head just a fraction and whoa.

Her eyes were crazy gorgeous up close. They weren't just blue. They had little flecks of green, right around the center. Like emeralds in a pool of water. She blinked the longest lashes I'd ever seen on a real person and suddenly breathing became a chore.

A rush of heat started from the top of my head and poured down my body into my toes. I had never felt this way before and it didn't seem to be going away. Stella stared at me, lips slightly parted and then jerked back, as if I'd punched her.

"Stop staring at me," she snapped, putting her icy face back on. I blinked a few times and it was like coming up for air after being underwater. I was gasping and disoriented.

I coughed once and then sat back. I'd leaned way far over without realizing it. Stella didn't appear affected at all.

Except.

Except for the slightest tremor in her hand as she held the tablet.

Huh.

"SO I THINK we should get a head start on everyone else," she said briskly, just before class ended. We'd made good headway on our project, but I had the feeling Stella wasn't going to be satisfied unless it was absolutely and totally perfect.

"What do you mean?" I asked, knowing the answer wasn't going to be good.

"I think we should get the paper done by the end of this week so we can perfect the presentation. As much as I hate to say it, I think we should get together outside of class and work." She made a face like the idea disgusted her, but I wasn't buying it. I'd seen a few cracks in her shiny surface and I was just waiting to see more. People were right when they said Stella was like ice. An iceberg was a little more accurate. There was something below the surface that no one had seen before. I didn't know what made me want to figure her out, but I did. I wanted it a lot.

"Okay," I said, a little too quickly. I shouldn't have been so eager.

"We'll have to do it later because I have practice. And at

one of our houses because the library will be closed." Great. Just what I needed.

"Not my house," I said, my voice too loud. "My parents are insane and will drive both of us crazy." She gave me a look and then said, "Fine. My house."

"I mean, really. They're like the textbook definition of helicopter parents." Why was I still rambling? She just sighed and looked toward the door as if she wanted to escape.

"It's fine. Seriously. Look, I have to go." Her eyes snapped back to me and then she lunged out and grabbed my phone from where it rested on the corner of my desk. Before I could protest, she handed it back.

"There. I'll text you when practice is over and give you directions. You'd better be there on time and ready to work." With that, she got to her feet, threw her hair over her shoulder and was out the door.

Ice storm Stella strikes again.

∼

I DID *NOT* SPEND the rest of the day freaking out about going over to Stella's.

Okay, that's a lie. I did.

"I bet her house is all white and you can't sit on the furniture," Grace said, which was a little funny, considering the house she lived in. But she was trying to be supportive.

"I have no idea. It's going to be beyond awkward. My plan is to get in and get out as fast as possible." With hopefully my dignity and sanity intact. It was definitely going to be harder to stop staring at her and being weird if it was just the two of us. If she suggested we do this in her room, I was going to veto that. I didn't want to be anywhere in her personal space. For some reason.

"Well, you can always text me and I'll come rescue you

with some sort of emergency." Grace was that kind of best friend who would fake a life-threatening emergency to get you out of an awkward situation. She'd done it many times before with great success.

"Thanks, I might take you up on that," I said as we headed to our cars.

Chapter Five

STELLA

I wasn't nervous. Not at all. I wasn't fidgeting and re-arranging the shakers on the dining table and then going to the fridge to make sure we had enough soda and then checking the couch to make sure there were no dust bunnies underneath.

Nope. I wasn't doing any of those things.

I'd booked it out of practice so I could get home and get a shower in (and redo my hair) before she came over. I sent the text with shaking fingers. I almost wished that Dad was home to distract me, but he was working late tonight so it was going to be just me and Kyle.

Bad idea.

Such a bad idea.

I'd regretted the words almost the instant they were out of my mouth, but there was no way to pull them back so here I was, fiddling with my hair and waiting for her to show up. I drew the line at waiting by the door.

Finally, what seemed like hours later, a car pulled into the driveway. God help me.

I WAS able to pretend that I totally didn't care that she was here, in my house with me, alone. She'd changed into low-slung grey sweatpants that left just a hint of belly showing under her t-shirt. Just that little whisper of skin was enough to make my mouth go dry and I had to remind myself to look up at her face, but that was somehow worse.

The lighting in my house must have been designed to make her look as cute as possible or else I was just imagining things. I narrowed my eyes and led her to the dining room table where I had my laptop set up and my book out already, with passages I'd highlighted. I'd needed something to do while I was waiting for her.

"Do you want anything?" I said, trying to sound bored as I went to the kitchen.

"Um, Coke? If you have it." Her eyes kept darting around, as if looking for a neon sign to point her toward the emergency exit. I was feeling a little that way myself.

I grabbed two cans and two glasses and nearly dropped everything when she got up to help me.

"I've got it," I snapped and she put her hands up and backed away.

"Sorry, sorry. Just trying to be nice, no need to bite my head off." I'd like to bite her, but not in the way she was thinking.

I could feel my face starting to flush, so I got busy pouring out the sodas and then asking her if she wanted a snack. She declined, but I was still starving from practice, so I grabbed a few bags of chips and some berries from the fridge.

Kyle gave me a look when I set them down between us.

"The chips and the berries cancel each other out. It's basic food science," I said and I swore she almost smiled. Almost.

"I'm pretty sure that's not how calories work, Stella." Wow. I really liked the way my name sounded in her mouth.

Stop thinking about her mouth.

Hard to do when she scooped up a handful of berries and started popping them in said mouth.

I was going to die. This girl was going to kill me.

I cleared my throat and put my laptop screen in front of me so it blocked the view.

"So, I pulled a few passages already, if you want to look at them and then copy them down for the paper. I could also have my dad go over it before we hand it in," I said. He'd already been doing that for every paper I'd ever written. It was a habit that I didn't intend on breaking.

She raised her eyebrows and there was a smudge of berry juice in the corner of her mouth. I stomped on a mental image of leaning forward to lick it off.

"Yeah? You're going to give it to your dad and he's going to rip it apart and then you're going to have him fix it and hand it in anyway," she said, crossing her arms.

"No, he's going to tell us where it's weak and where it's good and make sure that the grammar is correct," I said, keeping my eyes on my laptop. I was pretending to type, but really, I was just pressing random keys.

"Or, stay with me here, you're going to re-write the entire paper, slap our names on it and then hand it in. I get it, you're a control freak." My mouth almost dropped open and I risked a look up to stare at her.

"What the hell are you talking about?" I'd been called worse before, but for some reason this really got under my skin.

"Uh, is this new information? Like, are you really surprised?" Her voice was totally dry and I wished I was less attracted to her because that would make things so much easier.

"I'm not a control freak, I just like things a certain way."

She let out the cutest little snort-laugh and it did funny things to my stomach. Was there anything she did that didn't make me want her more?

"That's a diplomatic way of putting it, babe," she said and then we both realized she'd called me "babe."

Oh. Hell.

We just sort of stared at each other and then she cleared her throat and looked down at her book.

"So we should probably get to work," she said in a low voice.

"Yeah."

NEARLY AN HOUR LATER, we'd demolished the berries, one bag of chips, three sodas between us and we hadn't gotten much done. It wasn't for lack of trying. We just didn't see eye-to-eye on the paper.

"This was such a bad idea," she said as she typed in the Google Doc that I was also working on at the same time. "You just keep deleting everything!"

I hadn't been. Just editing here and there. Picking a better word or making a sentence stronger or adding a comma. Nothing major. But she saw it as an assault against her writing skills, which were actually better than I thought they would be.

Not that I doubted her ability to write, but I just thought that numbers were more her speed, but she had some excellent points and used a lot of words that I didn't know she knew.

She was smart. Really smart.

If only she'd been pretty and dumb, I might have been able to resist her. But the smart/sexy combo? I was a goner.

"I like to think of it more as polishing what's already there and making it shine," I said.

"You always have the most diplomatic way of putting

things. Makes me wonder where all those rumors come from." She tried to make it a throwaway comment, but it definitely wasn't.

"What rumors?" I asked, as if I had no idea. Hell, I started a lot of them myself. Had to keep reminding people not to mess with me.

"I'm sure you're familiar with them, Stella."

"Why would I be?" I asked, trying to sound oblivious.

She just rolled her eyes at me. Cute. So cute.

"You also don't seem like an idiot, so let's cut the crap, okay? You know exactly what people say about you. I wouldn't be shocked if you were the one who encouraged it."

No. This was bad. This was why I didn't let people get too close. Midori was one of my exceptions. When people got close they could see me clearly and I didn't like it. If they really saw me, they wouldn't like me.

I just narrowed my eyes at her and didn't answer. Most people looked away from me after a few seconds, but Kyle held my gaze and then one side of her mouth turned up in a smirk. The smirkiest of smirks.

"You get quiet when you don't know what to say. Means I'm right."

There wasn't much I could say without digging myself an even bigger hole, so I just turned my attention back to my laptop and thought about highlighting the entire paper and deleting it like a bitch, but then I'd have to spend even more time with her and that wouldn't be good for anyone.

"I think that's enough," I said after a few minutes of silence. I had to get her out of here. She was all I could see and all I could hear and all I could smell and it was a real problem. I had to get her out of here before I did something stupid.

She took off her glasses and rubbed her eyes before putting them back on. I still had a bunch of other homework to do and I was sore from practice.

She looked at me and then down at her laptop.

"Yeah, I guess." Was she reluctant to leave? After all the stimulating conversation?

"What, you want to stay and hang out with me?" I injected just the right amount of acid into each word.

"It's better than being at home," she muttered, as if she didn't want to admit it.

"Are you parents really that bad?" I asked before I could stop myself.

"Not really. I mean, it's that they *care* too much. How can you be pissed that your parents care too much about you and want you to succeed? What kind of asshole am I?" I wasn't going to answer that right away.

"I'm sure there are plenty of people who wish they had two parents who aggressively cared about them," I said. I hadn't been speaking specifically about me, but I guess I did fit the bill. My mom had cared about me long enough to give birth to my brother and then me, but had decided that being a mom just wasn't for her. You know, she couldn't have figured that out until after she'd gotten married and had us.

"That's right, make me sound like an ungrateful bitch. Perfect. Way to go, Stella," she said, grabbing her stuff and heading toward the door. I wanted to go after her and tell her that she was the opposite of a bitch, but then that might have led to all sorts of other things, so I let her go, calling "bye," after her.

∾

KYLE

Seriously. What a fucking bitch. Her personality was just that terrible. I'd been wrong. Maybe the glimpses of nice I'd seen were an act. Who the hell knew?

I was fuming when I got home and that made my parents

go into a panic and have another one of their little "interventions" with me. Any time I showed any sort of excessive negative emotions, they sat me down and had a "chat."

I wanted to tell them that I was fine, just annoyed. That I wasn't secretly depressed, or cutting my wrists, or hiding an eating disorder. In addition to being human helicopters, they were also hyper-hypochondriacs. Everything had the potential to be life-threatening, from a cold to a slammed door. When I was younger I used to wish at every birthday and every Christmas that I would get a sibling that they could focus on. Never happened and I was pretty sure that ship had sailed a long time ago.

Once I got them off my back and assured them that I was not going to hurt myself or anyone else, I barricaded myself in my room to fume.

I didn't know why she drove me so crazy. Just . . . everything she said and did just . . .

Fuck.

I could pretend the little fluttery feeling in my chest wasn't there, but that wouldn't make it go away. I . . . liked her. Or something.

I didn't know why. I didn't know when it had started, but there it was. I liked her in a way that made me wonder how soft her lips would feel and if her hair was silky to the touch. It made me think of lots of other things too. Things that made me want to get in the shower and spend some time alone.

Dangerous. Those were very dangerous thoughts that I should not be having, but there really wasn't any way to stop them. They were happening and I had to just get through it. I was stuck with Stella for the foreseeable future, unless I dropped out of AP English, but that wasn't an option.

I'd just have to keep a lid on it. Keep it to myself. It was just a little crush (I hated even calling it that) and I could handle it.

I was a nearly grown-ass woman and I could deal with a tiny crush on a terrible girl.

I could deal.

~

IT DIDN'T HURT that she was so cold. If she'd been nice to me, I might have liked her more. Or maybe not. Verbally sparring with her was kind of sexy.

Fuck, fuck, fuck.

Somehow the two of us got through the week without killing one another and I managed to not do anything that would have let her know how I felt. She pulled back a lot, but wasn't as critical. She'd press her lips together and I knew she was trying not to say something she wanted to say.

Friday night was another home game and I was there on the bleachers in the front row with Grace. And there was Stella, her hair up high and a smile on her face. It was a little funny that she was so frigid most of the time, but chose a sport like cheerleading to excel in.

And holy shit, did she excel. Flips and stunts and all kinds of stuff that made me think about all kinds of things. My face was probably beet red the entire game, but I couldn't take my eyes off her.

Fortunately, she seemed oblivious of me. Except for one moment when she was front and center, leading a cheer where the crowd had to respond. Her blue eyes seared into me for one moment and then slid back to scan the rest of the crowd.

Fuck with a side of fuck.

Grace didn't say much during the game, and I realized she was upset about something. Her eyebrows were drawn together in a constant frown and I decided that I had to get my head out of my own ass and be a best friend.

"You okay?" I asked, touching her arm when we went to get sodas at halftime.

"Yeah, sure," she said, totally unconvincing.

"I'm sorry I've been distracted. What's up with you?" I turned her to face me and she wouldn't look at me. Yup, something was definitely bothering her.

"It's my parents. They're being stupid about college. They want me to get a 'sensible' degree." She used her fingers to put air quotes around sensible.

"And what does that mean?" She sighed and rubbed her hand through her hair.

"I don't know, business or something? Pre-law? Pre-med? Anything with the word 'pre' in it? Not art or music or anything like that. And don't even get them started on journalism or graphic design." Now this, I could relate to.

"You've met my parents, right? They're going to flip their shit if I don't get a PhD in something fancy and have a six-figure starting salary." Not because they wanted me to be rich, but because they wanted me to be *secure*. Their word, not mine. I had no idea what the hell I wanted to do, and that was a serious problem for them.

"Yeah, I know. It just sucks when I think they're going to let me do what I want, but then lay down the hammer. They're saying that they'll only pay for school if I major in something they approve." Well. That sucked. My parents didn't have a whole lot of money to send me to college, so I was going to have to rely on a lot of scholarships, which was one of the reasons I took so many AP classes and had taken the SATs four times to get a good enough score to qualify for more than a few. I was going to be spending a hell of a lot of time writing essays and so forth after I applied. Just my idea of a good time.

"Hey, you still have a lot of time. And do you honestly believe that they won't support you financially if you become an artist? Please. You're going to be amazing at whatever you do, Grace." I slung my arm around her shoulder and she leaned her head against mine.

"You always make things sound easier than they are, but I totally appreciate it," she said.

I heard a throat clear behind us and I turned to find Stella there, with one exquisite eyebrow raised.

"Can I help you in some way?" I said, trying to sound as icy as she did.

"No, you're just holding up the line," she fired back. I had no idea what she was talking about and then I realized Grace and I had been kinda holding up the line.

"Sorry not sorry," I fired at Stella and then moved to the counter to order.

Stella definitely muttered something under her breath, but I didn't quite catch it.

"So I guess she hasn't sweetened any," Grace said as we walked back to the bleachers. Everyone else was deep in conversation about the upcoming Fall Formal, so I let myself be drawn into that conversation.

"Are you going to ask someone?" Grace said, a weird look on her face.

"No, why would I? I haven't had a date to any of the other dances, why start now?" Our group always went together and I didn't see a reason to mess with tradition.

"No reason. But if there was someone you wanted to take, you could, you know."

"I know," I said, slowly.

"Okay," she said, giving me one last look before turning to Paige and asking if she'd gotten her dress yet and if we should plan a shopping trip for the next weekend. I agreed, even though I had a perfectly cute dress already in my closet that I'd bought last summer. I needed a weekend that didn't involve football, Stella, or my parents.

∽

I WAS twitchy on Saturday and Sunday, constantly checking my phone. I told myself it wasn't because of Stella, but that was a huge lie. I didn't know why I wanted her to text me, because it would probably be something mean anyway. There was no way I was going to text her anything. Not even if my house was on fire.

Still, I typed out a few terrible messages and then deleted them. I cringed at myself and went back to watching re-runs of Buffy.

∽

"SO, did you finish the edits I suggested?" Stella said to me on Monday. We'd nearly finished, but she still wasn't satisfied. I was beginning to think that nothing ever satisfied Stella Lewis, but that wasn't my problem.

"I did, but I really don't think that comma belongs there," I said. We'd had a comma battle last week that had almost ended in bloodshed. I'd even gone so far as to look it up online and print out a few articles that proved I was right. I had them in my bag, ready to show her.

But then she did something that had me so shocked I almost fell off my chair.

"You're right."

I sputtered for a second.

"I'm sorry, could you repeat that for the people in the back?" I said, cupping my hand to my ear.

She rolled her eyes and then narrowed them.

"You heard me. I'm not going to say it again, so drop it." I couldn't contain the laugh that bubbled out of my mouth.

"You don't like being wrong, do you?" She looked back down at her notebook and turned a page of her notes.

"It doesn't happen very often. I'm nearly always right."

"Wow, you should really work on your self-esteem issues, Stella," I said and she gave a little start when I used her name. I couldn't seem to stop using it whenever I could. It was a pretty name for a pretty girl.

"I can't help it if I'm right. It just happens," she said and I almost caught a smile.

"What a hardship for you," I said, but I realized that we were teasing each other. Holy shit, I was flirting with her.

I was flirting with Stella and she was kinda flirting back.

What the fuck was even happening?

The moment died when she brushed her hair back and turned toward me.

"Now. About the presentation." We were back to business.

TWO DAYS later I was at Stella's house again and she was giving our presentation for an audience of one. Me.

I was trying to keep my mind on what she was saying, but it was hard to focus on that because of the way her mouth moved when she talked. The tone of her voice. The way she stood. It was all . . . sexy. So sexy.

Just a crush. A weird, out of the blue crush on a girl. Everyone had had one of those in their life, right? It didn't mean I was . . . I mean, I still liked guys. I totally liked guys. I totally . . .

Was staring at her boobs.

I was just jealous of them. Mine weren't shaped that nice. That was it. And her shirt was cute. I was not staring at her boobs, imagining what they would look like without the shirt.

Nope. Not even a little bit.

I dragged my eyes back up to her face and found her staring at me expectantly.

"Well? How was it? And keep the editorial comments to a minimum." Oh. She'd finished the presentation and I hadn't even noticed. Because I'd been staring at her boobs.

This was starting to be a serious problem. Thank God our presentation was on Monday and then we wouldn't have time alone together anymore. I couldn't handle it.

"Uhhh, good. Really good," I said, stumbling to come up with something, anything, to say. She sighed and threw up her hands, notecards scattering to the floor.

"You weren't even listening. I can't believe this. You may not care about this class, but I do." Now that made me mad.

"I do care about this class, seeing as how I've been in it since the beginning of the year. Where the hell were you?" I got to my feet and then we were standing about a foot apart, both equally pissed.

"That's irrelevant. I'm in this class now and I don't want to get a shitty grade because I'm stuck working with you."

I took a step forward and we were almost chest-to-chest.

"Oh, I'm so sorry that it's been so *awful* to work with me, you should have just gone to Mr. Hurley asked him to do the whole thing yourself. Oh wait, you pretty much did that anyway!"

Our eyes are locked and I could feel that this was one of those intense moments where the world just stops.

We're both breathing a little too hard for what happened and then Stella did something that shocked me more than if she would have pulled out a gun and shot me.

She kissed me.

Chapter Six

STELLA

I had no idea what made me do it. Maybe I was hormonal, or hadn't kissed anyone in a long time, or maybe I had been poisoned during lunch and this was some side effect, but one minute she was standing in front of me yelling and the next I had pressed my mouth to hers.

The contact lasted all of a half a second, because she pulled away so fast. I teetered on my toes and nearly lost my balance. I'd been leaning so far into her that I had to grab the back of a chair so I didn't crash to the floor.

"What the fuck, Stella?!" she said, putting her hands up and backing away. "Seriously, what the *fuck*?"

"I'm sorry," I said automatically. "I'm sorry." I had no idea why I was apologizing. I mean, yeah, it probably wasn't the best idea to kiss her, but I'd thought . . .

No, that was impossible.

"I'm sorry," I said again, my voice sounding robotic. She spun around in a circle while ripping the elastic viciously out of her hair. The brown semi-waves tumbled down to her shoulders and she was so cute. So, so cute.

Cute and pissed, but that was a good look for her.

"You just . . . You just kissed me," she said, spinning around. "You just fucking kissed me. What the fuck?" She certainly liked to swear a lot when she was taken off-guard. But I thought her reaction was a little extreme for the situation. I mean, was me kissing her the worst thing that had ever happened to her?

"I don't know," I said. That was the truth. I didn't know. Well, I did. I knew that I thought she was adorable as hell and that I had wanted to kiss her for a while and that it had finally become too much and my body had sort of taken over, but other than that, I had no idea why I specifically liked *her*.

Sure, there was the cute factor and she was smart and sexy and she could be funny when she wanted to, but she wasn't . . . I mean she wasn't, say, Natalie Dormer, who was hot as fuck. She was just Kyle.

I licked my lips and tried to tell myself that I couldn't taste her.

"I have to go. I seriously have to go," she said, grabbing her things and stumbling, dropping her copy of *Jane Eyre* in her haste to get out. Her limp slowed her down a little and I grabbed her arm, reaching down to get the book.

"You don't have to go. I'm sorry. I shouldn't have done it. I don't know what happened." Oh, what a lie.

"This is just . . . so, so fucked up. You're seriously fucked up, Stella." My insides clenched when she said my name. She wrenched her arm away from me.

"Stay away from me." I let her go because what else was I going to do? I couldn't force her to stay and I wasn't going to explain everything and I was still so messed up from the fact that I'd even done it that I just let her walk out the door.

~

"HOW DID STUDYING GO?" Dad asked an hour later when he came home. He'd been working a lot of extra hours at the college lately, but it made him happy, so I didn't mind. Plus, it had been a blessing in disguise tonight. I didn't know what I would have done if he'd walked in on me kissing Kyle.

I choked on a piece of popcorn and had to chug some water before I could breathe again.

"Fine. We, ah, practiced our presentation so I think we're ready for Friday." I knew my presentation was solid, but now I had this fear that I was going to mess it up due to what happened earlier.

I wanted to groan and bury my head in the couch cushions. I'd definitely messed up and the embarrassment was now taking the place of shock from earlier.

Oh. Hell.

What if she told someone? Fear prickled my skin and my chest started feeling tight. What if she told someone? What if that someone told someone and then tomorrow everyone would know that Stella Lewis, Queen Bitch, was a dyke?

I pulled out my phone and texted Kyle with shaking fingers.

Please don't tell anyone about it. Please.

I knew it sounded desperate, but I was pretty desperate. This could undo everything I'd worked for in high school. I swore I would never be the girl that everyone mocked and teased and made fun of. Just thinking about it made my stomach heave and I had to run to the bathroom. All the popcorn came back up and I gasped, resting my forehead on my arm.

Dad knocked softly.

"You okay, Star?" He had enough courtesy not to bust through the door and ask if he could hold my hair or something.

"Yeah," I said, getting to my feet and flushing the toilet. I grabbed my toothbrush and started scrubbing my teeth hard.

"Let me know if you need anything," he said before I heard him walk away from the door.

My phone buzzed and I nearly swallowed my toothbrush.

Don't worry. I won't say anything.

I slumped against the sink and spit out the toothpaste before rinsing my mouth out.

Thank you.

I left it at that. I should probably just pretend that it didn't happen. Yes. That was the best way to deal with this. Kyle wasn't going to say anything and I was sure she wanted to forget about it.

There was only one problem.

I couldn't forget about it.

LATE THAT NIGHT, in the throes of sleep, my brain took hold of the kiss and let it go further. One kiss became two and then there were tongues and hands and clothes on the floor and before I knew it I was awake and panting with my hand between my legs and the sweet burn of desire flooding my veins.

I moaned and there was no way I could get back to sleep, so I slid my hand under the waistband of my panties and got to work. I was so close that it was only a few moments later that I came, shuddering and biting my hand so I didn't moan too loudly.

Dad's room was down the hall, but I didn't want to take any chances that he'd hear me. Sometimes he stayed up late reading or doing work for his classes.

The shudders slowly stopped and I had to lay there for a second before I could even think about moving. I hadn't come that hard in a long time. And I wasn't done. The ache started up again a few seconds later and I was back at it, with the dream-kiss scenario fueling me.

Three orgasms later, I was finally done and ready to sleep. I went to the bathroom to wash my hand on semi-shaky legs.

That was when the guilt and the shame set in, but I refused to feel bad about it. I wouldn't let myself go there. I'd had plenty of fantasies about girls before, they'd just never been very specific. So I'd used Kyle to get myself off a few times, so what? It didn't mean anything. She was just there and she was cute and I'd kissed her.

Didn't.

Mean.

Anything.

～

KYLE

I sat in my car for a few minutes after I'd rushed out of Stella's house. Because what the fuck.

She . . . she definitely kissed me. There was no way around that. I mean, it wasn't like she'd leaned in to pluck an eyelash off my cheek, or was checking me for cavities or something. Nope. That was definitely meant to be a kiss.

It . . . kind of was, before I realized what was happening and flipped out. Because why wouldn't I flip out? Stella was . . . the last person I thought would ever kiss me. I mean, the fact that we had been yelling at each other and the next second she thought "hey, I should kiss this girl right now" was fucking crazy.

Fucking crazy.

My hands shook on the steering wheel as I gripped it. I needed something to ground me or else I was going to float away in a haze of confusion.

I should probably go. Like, right now. Definitely before her dad came home and caught me loitering in the driveway. I wouldn't even know how to explain that.

Telling myself to get my shit together, I rolled my shoulders and turned my car on. I wasn't going home right away, I couldn't. My parents would know that something had happened and then I'd have to come up with some sort of story that they'd buy. I mean, I was still going to have to do that because my parents were my parents, but at least if I had some time, I could hopefully calm myself down and come up with something good.

～

NEARLY AN HOUR of driving later and I didn't feel any more calm. Stella had texted me and begged me not to say anything. That hadn't even occurred to me. What kind of person did she think I was? The desperation seethed through the texts. I could almost smell it. Belatedly, it hit me that if I wanted to destroy Stella, I had the perfect ammunition.

Lucky for Stella, this wasn't a stupid, vapid teen television show where one rumor would destroy a reputation forever and a day. I didn't hate Stella. Well, maybe a little, but only because of the way she made me feel. Sure, her personality sucked sometimes, but she had her moments. They were few and far between, but they were there. We'd sort of flirted and traded barbs back and forth and I saw what she might be if she let her guard down. Also made me curious why she kept a guard up. If she wasn't a bitch, then why did she want people to think that?

Stella Lewis was a fucking mystery and I just kept sinking deeper and deeper.

～

I COULDN'T SLEEP that night. I was still thinking about the sort-of kiss. Trying to remember what it had felt like, but it had been too short to really judge. I'd never kissed a girl before. I mean, I'd never wanted to.

Did I want to kiss Stella?

Well, if I asked my body, then it was a resounding YES. If I asked my brain . . . it was NO followed by a very quiet yes. Followed by a no. And then another yes.

Yeah, okay, I was confused. Even more confused than before the not-kiss.

I kept trying to get comfortable and couldn't. Every position I tried I'd get uncomfortable after about five minutes. I tried everything. I pillow under my knees, my feet by the headboard, on my back, on both sides, nothing.

My mind was too busy thinking about too many things to let my body slow down long enough to get into sleep mode. I finally gave up and grabbed my phone. At least if I couldn't sleep, I had something to distract me.

I hit Tumblr and then Snapchat and, for some reason, I clicked on my Messages. The last one I'd sent or received was Stella's. Before I could tell myself that it was a bad idea, I sent her a text.

I'm not going to tell anyone. I promise. Just wanted you to know. Again.

It was totally stupid and I didn't know what she was going to think, but I went ahead and sent it anyway. Her phone was probably off, or on silent, so I didn't expect a response.

And then the little typing bubble popped up that told me she was responding. It went away and then popped up again. And went away. Popped up. Went away.

Just hit send. I can see you trying to figure out what to say.

What the hell was I doing? Ugh. I needed to stop this ASAP.

Don't tell me what to do.

I snorted, because I totally read the text in her voice.

Then don't be indecisive. Why are you even awake right now?

Her responses came quicker.

Why are you?

Texting with her is just like talking to her. Only easier because I don't get distracted by her face and her voice.

No reason.

I could just picture her face. Perfect eyebrow arched.

Uh huh. I believe you.

The sarcasm was thick with this one.

Well, I could call you a pot or a kettle so . . .

I had a stupid grin on my face and I kinda hated it, but couldn't stop it.

Oh, you're so funny. I never could have come up with that one.

I heard a sound and realized I was laughing.

You know you laughed.

Did not.

Are we arguing again? Because earlier when we did that, you decided to kiss me.

She typed for a long time after I said that.

It wasn't a kiss. Not really.

I snorted again.

Then what would you call it? Mouth-to-mouth? Because I definitely wasn't drowning.

I could hear her sighing from here.

Shut up Kyle.

You're the one answering me.

She answered with a middle finger emoji.

Cute.

There was another long pause.

I'm turning my phone off now.

I laughed to myself.

Ok. Go ahead.

I am.

Fine.

Fine.

She stopped answering after that. But I kept checking my phone into the wee hours of the morning. Just in case.

~

I GOT to English early the next day and was waiting and waiting for Stella to show up. She rushed in, at the last minute and for the first time, probably in her life, she looked flustered. Her hair was messy; not in its characteristic spirals. Her face was free of makeup and she had jeans and a simple t-shirt on. She sat down without looking at me, but I couldn't stop looking at her.

Okay, so I'd pulled back when she tried to kiss me last night, but if she did it now? Looking like that?

I definitely wouldn't have pulled away. Oh no. I would have twisted my fingers in that shirt and pulled her closer so I could feel her body against mine and OH MY GOD I NEED TO STOP LOOKING AT HER RIGHT NOW.

With a herculean effort, I tore my eyes away from Stella, who hadn't moved her eyes from her notebook or acknowledged my presence.

Class. I was in class. We were learning . . . things. Our teacher was saying words.

But the blood that was supposed to be running my brain was going to other places and I kept crossing and uncrossing my legs. I had never been this fucking turned on during school hours. Was this how guys felt? Like, things were almost getting painful.

I was actually considering running out to my car to get some relief, but then something poked me in the arm. It came from my right, and there was only one person sitting on my right.

"You look like you're in pain," she hissed. It was hard for us to talk to each other without getting caught since we were in the front row, but Mr. Hurley was standing by the window on the other side of the room, waxing on about literary theory or some such bullshit. He was all caught up in it and a quick glance around the room confirmed that just about everyone else had also checked out of this particular lesson.

"I'm. Fine," I said through clenched teeth. I so wasn't fine.

"Don't look fine," she said with a bit of a sing-song.

"I. Am," I said. She really was asking for it. I turned to glare at her, but was arrested by the sight of her makeup-free face. Freckles.

She had freckles. Just a few on her cheeks, under her eyes that looked so, so beautiful. How was it that she looked better with a totally clean face? It didn't make sense.

I realized my mouth was open a little so I closed it. The only indication that she wasn't totally fine too was her appearance and the tiniest hint of pink in her cheeks.

Guess I wasn't the only one knocked off their game today.

"I think we need to talk," I said in a low voice that only she could hear.

"Right now?" she said, a hint of irritation in her tone.

"Well maybe not right now," I tried to say, but then she raised her hand and said that she had to go to the bathroom. She tossed a meaningful look over her shoulder and I got the hint. But I couldn't say that I also had to go, because that would be way too obvious. So it was time to embarrass myself in the name of talking with Stella.

"Ow! Oh my god!" I yelled out, clutching my bad leg and effectively putting a stop to the lecture.

Mr. Hurley rushed over and knelt down. Every now and then I had nerve pain, so this had happened before. But never this dramatic. I was laying it on thick.

"Is it your leg? Do you need to be excused?" he said as

everyone else stared and whispered and made suggestions and some muttered words that weren't very nice. Fuck them. I didn't care.

"Yes, I think so," I said, biting my lip and hoping he believed me. It was kind of awful to take advantage like this, but I needed to get out of this class and have things out with Stella. We hadn't gotten anything out last night via our text messages. Now she couldn't run away from me and we could figure this shit out.

"You're excused. I'll email you tonight with everything you've missed. Go see the nurse." And with that, I gathered up my things and limped (harder than normal) out of the room and then resumed my regular walk. I was headed toward the bathroom when a hand reached out and yanked me into a corner shielded by a wall of lockers. We'd be pretty safe here until the bell rang in a few minutes.

"Hey, watch it," I said, yanking my arm back. She put both palms up in surrender.

"You were the one who wanted to talk. So. Talk." She crossed her arms and I tried not to stare at her chest. Somehow it was even more on view in the tight t-shirt. I could just see the line of her bra through the fabric.

Definitely not the point. I pulled my gaze up to her face. Those freckles. *Those freckles.*

"We need to talk about it. Whatever it was. I promised not to tell anyone, but I'm going to need an explanation. Because . . . what the fuck, Stella?" That was the only thing I could come up with. "I mean, did I give you some sort of signal that I wanted to kiss you or . . ." I trailed off. Oh. God. She knew. She must know. I'd been too obvious.

I opened my mouth, but nothing came out.

"No! No," Stella said the second no more quietly. Her arms uncrossed and she twisted her fingers together and looked at the floor. I'd never seen her look so . . . vulnerable.

"I don't know why it happened. I don't know what's wrong with me." She sounded small. And scared. I knew the feeling. My stomach was flipping all over the place and I almost had the urge to hug her. Just gather her in my arms and let her rest her head on my shoulder. I wanted to do that. I really wanted to do that.

"Do you? I mean, are you . . ." I couldn't finish.

"Did I try to kiss you because I like you and I'm a big fat dyke?" I flinched at her words. "Don't flatter yourself."

"Uh, okay, then what was it?" Because generally, you only kiss people because you want to kiss them. Because you want your mouth and their mouth to touch as a sign of affection. I mean, I didn't have a lot of kiss experience, and none with another girl, but I was pretty sure that was how things worked.

She tossed her hands in the air and a few wisps of hair floated around her face.

"I don't know! God."

"Jesus, I'm not interrogating you. I just want to know what was going through your head," I said, trying to use a calm tone. She looked on the verge of flipping out.

"I . . . It was just . . ." She clamped her teeth down on her bottom lip and shook her head.

"You wouldn't understand."

"What would I understand?" I asked gently. She shifted her feet; ready to bolt.

"You just wouldn't, okay?" she snapped.

"Try me." I was both curious and freaked out to hear what she had to say. Because I was pretty sure I understood exactly what she was talking about and what she'd been thinking because I had been thinking the same thing about her. There was no denying it now.

I liked Stella. I really, really liked her and if she kissed me again, I'd kiss her back. I would so kiss her back.

Chapter Seven

STELLA

I shouldn't have left the classroom, but I had to get out. She was looking at me in a way that made me want to drag her out to my car and throw her in the backseat. She was still sort of doing it, actually.

I mean, I was a total hot mess, but I guess that worked for her?

I kept telling her that she wouldn't understand why I tried to kiss her, but I wasn't getting that vibe now. I was getting a completely different vibe that made my cheeks flush and my skin too tight.

I'd already told her that I didn't want to kiss her because I was into her, which was the biggest lie ever.

I liked her a lot, but I had no idea if I could trust her. She could just as easily turn on me and I couldn't handle that. I stood there, weighing the risks as she waited. She tilted her head to the side just a little and it was so unbearably cute.

"Come on," she said, lifting her chin.

"Come on what?" I said.

"Come on," she said, backing up and heading toward the

door. All of my stuff was still in English, except for my purse, which was in my locker.

"Okay," I said. This was either the best decision I was ever going to make, or the worst.

Time would tell.

I FOLLOWED Kyle out of the building, after a brief stop at my locker. We didn't say much until we were in the parking lot, presumably headed toward her car.

She stopped and unlocked the door with the press of a button on her keychain.

"Get in," she said, but it wasn't a command. It was more a question.

I looked over my shoulder toward the school. The minute I got in this car, things were going to change. They already had. They had the second I'd signed up for AP English. That first day that I looked at her and felt something new and hot swirling inside me.

I got in.

KYLE DIDN'T TURN the radio on and the car was terribly quiet.

"Where are we going?" I finally asked.

"You'll see," she said. That was it.

"If you're going to take me out to the woods and strangle me, I'd like to inform you that I've taken several self-defense classes and I think I could take you." For a moment, she took her eyes off the road and gaped at me.

Then she laughed. Such a surprised and delighted sound that it made little things in my chest start fluttering.

"You're adorable," she said when she was done, a smile lingering on her face.

"Am I?" I asked.

She sighed.

"Yes. You are. It's driving me crazy." I froze. I stopped breathing and thinking and I was pretty sure my heart stopped for a moment.

"I drive you crazy?" I asked in a small voice.

She pressed her lips together and her face flamed up. I didn't think she was going to answer.

"Just a little," she said with a wry twist of her lips. "Just a little bit, Stella." I wasn't sure what to say to that, so I didn't say anything.

Kyle kept driving and I kept stealing glances at her. Maybe more than glances. I wanted to lay in a flower-filled field and stare at her skin as shadows and sunlight played across it.

Ugh, I wanted to punch myself in the face for that thought. I was making myself sick.

I shouldn't have gotten into this car, but here I was and we were headed somewhere and . . . I had no idea what was going to happen.

I didn't like Kyle being in control. I didn't like anyone being in control of my life but me, ever.

"I don't trust you," I said.

"Oh, I'm sure you don't trust anyone. Even yourself." Ouch. She'd hit too close to home on that one.

"Shut up," I said. Brilliant response. She laughed a little.

"You don't like it when other people figure things out about you either."

"Just stop talking." I was getting more and more irritated and annoyed.

"I never should have gotten in this stupid car with you. I have no idea why I did," I said, crossing my arms.

"But you did, Stella. You did get in the car and now here we are."

Here we were.

"And also, here we are," she said, stopping the car.

We'd arrived at the lighthouse. I'd been here before on class trips and so forth, but not in the fall. In the summer the parking lot was be jammed with tourists, but now there were just a few cars here and there.

And us.

"Come on," she said again. And again, I did what she said. We both got out and I wrapped my arms around myself because it was always chillier on the coast than inland.

"Here," Kyle said, handing me a sweatshirt. I gave her a look, but she just shoved it at me. Reluctantly, I put it on. And almost passed out because it smelled like her. The sleeves were a bit too long, so I rolled them up. Kyle coughed and I turned to find her staring at me, her face red.

"It . . . it looks good on you," she said, looking at the gravel parking lot.

"Thanks," I said. "So should we . . . ?" She nodded and we walked, not toward the lighthouse, which stood like a tall white sentry protecting boats from the ravages of the rocks below, but toward those rocks.

A portion of them jutted out into the ocean, like granite fingers. Kyle and I picked our way down and headed toward the water, but not too close. One nasty fall could send you tumbling into the water, and you probably wouldn't make it out alive. The water rushed and smashed against the rocks, as if it had a vendetta against them.

I could understand that anger.

Kyle and I sat on a rock that was far enough away from the water that we wouldn't get sprayed, but close enough that we were surrounded by the rushing sound and it felt a little bit dangerous. As if we were on the edge of something dark and all-consuming that didn't care about us and our problems.

"Why did you bring me here?" I asked, pushing my hair back. It kept blowing in my face. Kyle reached into her pocket and pulled out a hair tie, handing it to me without a word. I tried to pull my hair back like hers, but I could feel that it didn't look half as good.

"Not sure. I just always come here when I need to think about something. I know it's cliché, but I don't care. Hashtag deep-thoughts." I laughed a little and she looked at me.

"This is kind of crazy, isn't it?" she asked.

"Yeah, you could say that." She scooted a little bit closer to me. Our legs were almost touching.

"Do you? I mean, you kissed me because you wanted to. And I freaked out. And I'm assuming you think it was because I didn't want you to kiss me," she said, tracing a black vein in the rock we sat on.

I couldn't move. If a wave came right then, it would sweep me away and I wouldn't move to get out of its way. The ocean churned and I waited for her to continue.

She didn't.

"Did you want me to kiss you?" My words were so soft, they were almost lost to the noise surrounding us.

Her response was even quieter, but I would have heard it in a room with a thousand other voices.

"Yes."

We stared at one another and something crackled between us. And then I was leaning forward and she was leaning forward and our mouths were meeting. We both initiated it this time and the brush of Kyle's lips over mine didn't stop. Didn't end.

It was delicate, hesitant. She shook just a little. A whisper against my mouth, but we both waited. Held onto that moment.

It was unlike any other kiss I'd ever had and I melted into her. One of my hands slipped up to cup her cheek and the other wound around the back of her neck. Her hands were on me too, but not to push me away.

To pull me closer.

Her mouth opened and her tongue darted out to tease the seam of my lips. It was sweet and a little aggressive at the same time and I moaned in the back of my throat because hell, she tasted so good. Completely different than kissing anyone else.

Our tongues touched so carefully and then something ignited and we were devouring one another. Her nails dug into my skin and the little jolt of pain made it even better. She stole my breath and my lungs ached, but I couldn't stop.

Kyle could. She pulled away and I opened my eyes to see hers. Behind her glasses, her eyes were green. So green.

Beautiful.

"Wow," she breathed over my lips and I almost reached out to capture her mouth again.

I couldn't talk.

"So that's what it's like to kiss a girl," she said, moving her face away and studying me. Her lips were a little red and her cheeks were flushed.

I could stare at her forever.

"Stella, can you say something? I really need to know what you're thinking right now." I opened my mouth and then licked my lips. They tasted like her. I shuddered and gathered myself.

"I don't know what I'm thinking, Kyle. I have no idea. All I can think about is that I want to kiss you again."

"Really?" Her face broke into the sweetest smile ever.

"Yes. Really." She let out a breath, as if she was relieved.

"Fuck, I was scared there for a minute, thinking I was the only one. Because holy fuck, Stella." I wanted to roll my eyes at the excessive cursing, but I couldn't.

"I know. I know." That was all I could say.

"So we should probably do it again. Like right now, yes?"

"Yes."

～

KYLE

Who knew that Stella Lewis was an amazing kisser? I mean, seriously. Like a stop your heart, make you feel like you're going to die, never want it to end kind of kiss. The kiss to end all kisses.

Kiss wasn't even the right word. That was so much more than just a kiss. We should invent a new word for that. Maybe after we stopped kissing each other we could. I mean, if we stopped. I didn't want to and the way she was moaning and making these cute little noises, I could get the idea that she didn't either.

My ass was completely numb on the rock, but I couldn't have cared less. All I wanted was to keep my lips attached to hers as long as possible.

I tried to take my glasses off because they were getting in the way, but she told me to leave them on.

Unfortunately, we had to stop, but only because her phone buzzed with a text.

She jumped away from me and fumbled for her phone. I sat there and waited as she frowned and typed out a response to the message. As I freaked the fuck out. I'd just made out with a girl. I'D JUST MADE OUT WITH A GIRL.

"Just Midori. Asking where I was."

"Oh, right," I said, still dazed by the kissing. I could feel the echo of her hands on the back of my neck.

"So . . ." I said, dragging the word out. "That happened."

"Yeah, it did," she said, as she took a strand of her hair and wound it around her fingers.

"And it was good. Really good."

"Yes."

"And now we have to figure out what the fuck to do from here."

She nodded slowly and stared out at the waves. Deep blue, topped with whitecaps here and there.

"I don't know what this means. I don't know if this means that I like you, which is crazy to begin with because you're kind of awful, or if I like . . . girls, or if I like boys and girls, and I'm really, really confused." The words tumbled out of my mouth, tripping over one another.

Stella listened and twirled her hair.

"You think I'm an awful person?" she asked.

"I didn't mean it that way, but kind of?" How was it that I could want her so much, but also know that she wasn't the nicest of people? How could I be so attracted to her and completely ignore that?

"No, you're right. I am an awful person. I like it that way." She turned back toward me, her mouth a thin line.

"Why?" I just didn't get it.

Her eyes narrowed.

"Because. You wouldn't understand." It was like she'd slammed a wall between us and I felt the chill of the ocean air at last. I wrapped my arms around myself.

"You're going to shut me out. Just like that?" She raised her chin.

"Just like that."

Unbelievable.

"Okay, fine, fuck you, too." I slid away from her on the rock and contemplated stomping back to the car like a petulant child.

"Look, don't act like just because you had your tongue down my throat that you know me now. You don't."

"Yeah, well, I know that you don't have to be a bitch all the fucking time. Not to me." My stupid voice cracked on the last word.

"You're pretty presumptuous, you know that? What do you think's going to happen? That we're going to kiss some more and then hold hands in the hallway and go to prom and get crowned queen and queen? This is the real world and stuff like that doesn't just happen." Her words were sharp and sliced across my skin.

"Well obviously I know that's not going to happen, Stella, I'm not a fucking idiot. But there's something here and I think we need to at least . . . I don't know, give it a chance." I tossed my hands in the air. I didn't even know what I was saying.

She pushed herself off from the rock and started picking her way back to the car. Joke was on her, since I had the keys.

"You can't just walk away from this," I called after her.

"Watch me," she yelled back.

Oh, I was. She was in excellent shape from cheerleading. Amazing legs.

I had no control over the fact that I was definitely into her. In that I wanted her naked with my hands all over her.

Two hours ago, that thought would have freaked me the fuck out, but now it was just . . . there. It was there and it didn't feel wrong. I didn't get this twisting in the pit of my stomach telling me to stop thinking things like that. No.

It felt right. Easy. So. Damn. Easy. How had I not figured this out by now? I didn't need Google. I only needed the way she kissed and the way she felt and the way I wanted her.

Fuck, did I want her.

I GAVE her a head start and then followed her over the precarious rocks and back to the car. But I found her staring up at the lighthouse. It had been built in eighteen-hundred-something and was still in use.

"Whatcha looking at?" I asked and she startled a little at the sound of my voice. There was only one other car in the parking lot now, way down the end of the lot.

"Nothing," she muttered. She'd tucked her hands inside the sleeves of my sweatshirt and her anger seemed to have cooled off again.

"Do you want to go back on the rocks and make out?" I asked, only half-joking.

"No."

"Okayyyyy. Wanna make out in my car?" She fixed me with a withering look.

"No. I don't want to make out with you." I snorted out a laugh.

"Yeah, okay. Sure."

Stella turned her back on me and then . . . her shoulders started shaking. Either she was laughing or crying. Pretty sure it was the latter.

"Hey," I said, putting my hand on her shoulder. She tried to throw me off, but didn't resist when I turned her back around.

Yup. Crying.

"Hey, what's the matter?" I mean, I could probably guess, but I wanted to hear it from her.

She just shook her head and then just kind of fell into my arms. At first I didn't know what to do but after a second of being stunned, I wrapped my arms around her and she buried her head on my shoulder as she kept crying.

"It's okay. It's gonna be okay," I said, because what else was I supposed to say? I wasn't really good at this kind of thing. Grace was much better. She always had the right words at the right time.

My hands ran up and down her back in what I hoped was

a soothing way. No idea if I was helping or not, but she was just sniffling now.

Stella raised her head and wiped her eyes. She looked ridiculously good for someone who had been crying. Using the sleeve of my sweatshirt, she swiped her nose and eyes. I didn't mind at all.

I kept my hands on her shoulders.

"Stella. Talk to me. Please talk to me. I know you think that I don't know you, but I know a few things." She huffed and rolled her eyes, as if this was one giant inconvenience when she'd been the one crying two seconds ago.

"It's nothing. I just . . . I had a plan, you know? I was going to get through high school and then when I got to college, I'd go full gay and meet a girl and I'd finally be able to be myself. But then you had to come and . . ." she trailed off and put one of her hands on my chest, just below my throat.

"Everything was working fine until I signed up for AP English and sat next to you and started to feel things that I didn't want to feel. I was going to ignore it but then we got paired up and I couldn't anymore." She sniffed again.

"Yeah, I know the feeling. Except I was totally going to date guys when I got to college. So this is a little weird for me." That was an understatement.

"You didn't know? That you liked girls?" I shook my head. It was hard to think with her hand there, her fingers just barely sneaking under the collar of my shirt to caress my skin.

"Oh. I figured you did. That was probably why you freaked out so much when I kissed you, huh?" She laughed once.

"Yeah, maybe that was it," I said, my tone dripping with sarcasm. But then I looked at her face and realized I was being harsh. "Fuck, Stella. I had no idea."

"Yeah, well. No one does. Until you." Until me. Stella Lewis liked girls. And had for a while. Thoughts and questions were popping in my brain and I was getting close to overload.

"I think I need to like, sit down for a minute," I said, and this time she took my hand and led me to the car.

~

"SO HAVE you ever been attracted to guys?" I asked after I'd sat with everything for a few minutes.

"I don't think so. I mean, I've dated and kissed them, but it's not what I would choose. So no, I'm not bisexual. If that was what you were asking," she said. Clearly, she was a lot more comfortable with . . . everything than I was.

"Oh, wow, there are so many things going through my head right now," I said, resting my head on the steering wheel.

"So I'm guessing this is all new for you?" she asked softly.

I nodded against the wheel and then raised my head.

"I mean, yeah. I just . . . I have no idea when it started, but it turned into a thing and now I don't even know what to do or what to think. I tried Googling it, but couldn't follow through." There was a cute little snort next to me.

"You Googled it?" She gave me a look as if she thought that was precious.

"Yeah. What did you do?" Why was that outrageous? Google had never failed me before.

She pulled her hair out of the elastic and it tumbled over her shoulders. The fact that I was just this year learning I was attracted to her seemed ridiculous. How could I not be attracted to her?

"I don't know. I was like, thirteen? I think I just assumed everyone looked at girls that way. Because girls are beautiful and pretty and why wouldn't you want them? Took me a little while to realize that wasn't the case and I had to hide it. But I never denied it to myself. I know who I am, Kyle."

"Wow," I said. "I had no idea." She gave me a wry smile.

"It's not something I want anyone to know. At least not

now. I was going to head to college and be a completely different person in a different place." She looked out the window at the ocean.

"I know what you mean," I murmured. I'd thought the same thing. "I mean, I was going to wait until college to date guys. But now I'm not sure if I want to. Date guys." My head started spinning again and my stomach growled. This had been one of the longest days ever and I was starving.

"Do you want to get something to eat?" I blurted out.

"Sure," she said.

BECAUSE WE LIVED in a small ass town and there would have been questions if we went somewhere alone, and discussed the things we were going to discuss, we went back to my house. My parents were at work, so I didn't have to worry.

It was a fine plan until I remembered that it wasn't that clean and it was smaller than and not as nice as hers.

"Um, yeah. So . . . this is it," I said, waving my arm around and cringing inwardly. I waited as Stella's eyes swept the room and then she headed toward the kitchen. As if she'd lived here for years. I followed in her wake as she popped open the fridge and stuck her head in.

"What are you in the mood for?" I gaped at her back as she bent down and pawed through the crisper drawers.

"Um, my own food because this is my house?" I said and she straightened.

"Well, I'm in the mood for something smothered in cheese." She slammed the fridge shut and opened the freezer.

"Aha!" she said, pulling something out. "This will do."

It was a box of frozen spinach and artichoke dip.

"Do you have some chips or something . . ." she trailed off

as she searched the counters and then grabbed a bag of tortilla chips.

I watched as she read the instructions on the box, set the oven to preheat, found a bowl to put the chips in and then handed me a soda.

"Um, thanks."

"Sure," she said with a little smile. I'd never seen her so . . . relaxed? No, that wasn't the right word. Un-frozen? Warm. I'd never seen her this warm.

Even the way she moved was different. More like when she was cheering.

She hopped up on the counter and munched on a chip as the dip cooked in the oven.

"Make yourself at home," I said and she pushed the bowl of chips toward me. I nudged over the little step I used in the kitchen to help me climb up onto the counter.

"So, am I the first girl you've ever had a crush on?" she asked and a chip crumb went down my windpipe and caused me to cough.

"Uh, I guess so? I'm not really sure."

"You're not. My first, I mean." She sighed, as if at a good memory. "Shannon O'Shea. I was eleven and she was fourteen. God, she was so beautiful. I used to imagine just running up and kissing her on the cheek, and spent hours fantasizing about holding her hand. Then she got a boyfriend and went to high school. You never forget your first, though."

I gaped at her.

"Are you drunk right now?" There was no way, but holy shit, she was telling me all kinds of things without me even prodding her.

"Haha, no. I'm just . . . I haven't had anyone to talk to about this so it's all kind of coming out at once. Sorry." She shrugged one shoulder and grabbed another chip, smiling as she bit into it.

"Yeah, me neither. But I didn't think I was ready? I don't know. I'm still . . ." I trailed off.

"Hey," she said, brushing a hand down my shoulder. It made me shiver inside. Just being near her was driving me crazy. I wanted to dramatically swipe the bowl of chips off the counter and tackle her and do a lot of other things that involved tongues and fingers and secret places.

The timer dinged and I nearly fell off the counter, but I needed to put some space between me and Stella.

I nearly reached for the little tub of hot dip without an oven mitt, but at the last second I remembered.

"It's probably still too hot, so," I said, fumbling as I set the dip on top of another oven mitt. "Um, do you want to maybe sit in the living room?"

I really had no idea how to handle this situation. I was flying without a safety net and I was freaking out. Stella seemed so comfortable and I wished I could be like her.

"Sure," she said, pushing herself off the counter and grabbing the bowl of chips. "Lead the way."

Chapter Eight

STELLA

It was adorable how nervous she was. It was almost like a movie, how our hands collided as we both reached for a chip at the same time. Kyle blushed and yanked her hand back. So far, we'd been sitting in her living room eating steadily through the chips and dip and not talking.

I was fine with silence, but she was fidgeting and it was super distracting. Seeing Kyle flustered was fun.

"Do your parents know?" I asked and she froze. Her face went white. Okay, guess that hadn't been the right question to ask. I wasn't one to talk. I hadn't told Dad or Gabe and had no intention of it for a long time.

"Uh, no. *I* didn't even know. I still don't really know. I think I need to figure things out before I tell them anything." We were down to just chip crumbs in the bowl and I kept picking the smaller ones, leaving the bigger ones for her.

"That's probably smart. You might wake up tomorrow and totally be straight." I grinned at her and she gaped at me in surprise before smacking me on the shoulder.

"Brat."

I shrugged.

"I'm just saying. I know this one time I hit my head a little too hard at practice and that night I dreamed about dicks. So many dicks. I was just surrounded by them. Mmmmm . . ." That really shocked her. But that was my goal.

She burst out laughing and it was totally worth it. Her face lit up and it was a whole other level of cute for her.

I was in serious trouble.

WE LOUNGED on the couch and flipped through the channels.

"There are never enough shows with lesbians," I said.

"Aren't there any? I never really noticed." Oh, sweet gayby. I kept forgetting that she was so new to this. But maybe I could educate her. That would be fun. Potentially in a lot of ways.

"You're different," she said after a few minutes of silence. She wasn't looking at me and had taken off her glasses to polish them on the hem of her t-shirt.

"What do you mean?" I asked, but I knew exactly what she meant. I wasn't being a heinous bitch was what she meant.

"Well, you're not . . . um . . ." She pushed her glasses up on her nose and waved her hands as if she was looking for the right word.

"A bitch?" I finished. Her face went a little red.

"I wouldn't necessarily put it that way." I rolled my eyes.

"Yeah, you would. You and everyone else. I know what people say about me, Kyle. It doesn't bother me." Not even a little. It was so much better than the alternative.

"It doesn't?" I shook my head. I expected that to be the end of the questioning, but it wasn't.

"Why not?"

"Because I don't care what they think." This was a lie, but

she didn't need to know. I wasn't sure what this thing was between us, but it definitely wasn't going anywhere. We weren't going to hold hands and ride off into the gay sunset.

"Really?" She raised one eyebrow, calling my bluff. I gave her the same look.

"Really."

She went to say something else, but then all the blood drained from her face.

"What time is it?"

"Um, four thirty," I said, checking my phone that I'd set on the coffee table.

"Crap, my mom is going to be home any minute. I hate to do this to you, but you've got to go. My parents are insane and if you want to not be interrogated about every single detail of your life, I would leave now." I knew her parents were a little obsessive and I definitely didn't want to have a conversation with a mom about who I was and what I was doing here.

"Point taken," I said, getting off the couch, grabbing the empty chip bowl and the disposable dip bowl and heading back to the kitchen.

"You didn't have to do that," Kyle said, trailing after me. I just shrugged again and turned to face her.

"Well. I guess I'll see you in class." It was an anticlimactic end to what had been a strange day.

"Yeah, see you in class." I almost leaned in to kiss her, but she just stared at me in that cute-but-stunned way and I couldn't do it.

"Okay then." I pivoted on my heels and headed out the front door.

That was when I realized she'd been the one to drive us here.

I STOOD OUTSIDE FOR A MINUTE, wondering what to do, but there was no option but to go back inside, which was what I was preparing to do when the front door opened and she walked out.

"Oh, yeah. I forgot that you didn't have your car here. I can drive you back." I nodded and got in the passenger seat.

"I had fun today," I said and then cringed. I sounded like an idiot.

"Me too," Kyle said, turning the car on.

She drove in silence for a few minutes, her hands clamped on the steering wheel.

"So, what happens now?" Kyle said.

"What do you mean?" Once again, I knew exactly what she meant.

"I mean, with you and me. Not that there is a you and me. I don't even know what the hell happened today other than we made out and I would really, really like to do it again." Fuck, that made me want to tell her to pull over so I could yank her into the backseat.

"Are you saying that you want to come out, and then be my girlfriend?" I asked, not looking at her.

"Oh, no. We can't do that." No, we couldn't.

"So there are two options. One, pretend this never happened and go back to hating each other, or two, we make out when no one else is around." I hoped she would go for the second option, because it involved more kissing. I was in favor of any plan where I could kiss Kyle some more. That girl knew what she was doing and would have been totally wasted on boys.

"So, be like secret girlfriends?" I wanted to roll my eyes at that. It sounded stupid. Like a plot of a bad movie.

"No. We'd just be two girls who sometimes hang out and kiss. And potentially do other things. No pressure. But I don't think we should like, be best friends or something." I already had one of those and I didn't need another one. Besides, I didn't want to be Kyle's friend. I wanted to kiss her until she couldn't breathe. That wasn't usually a friendship activity. Unless you were friends with benefits, but that wasn't for me either.

"Okay, but what would we call it?" I sighed.

"Why do we have to call it anything?" I asked, turning to her. We were almost to the school.

"I guess we don't have to." No, we didn't. We didn't owe anyone anything.

"So how will this work?" She asked so many damn questions. I was going to have to kiss her more so she'd stop.

"No idea. We'll figure it out. Just text or call or whatever. And don't act any different at school. Promise." That was very important. I didn't want anyone catching on that things had changed between me and Kyle.

"Uh huh." She still looked a little dazed. I had the feeling she was going to be up late tonight. So would I, but for different reasons. I was going to spend a lot of time thinking about kissing her and what that tongue of hers could do if it were applied to places other than my mouth.

She pulled into the parking lot and I realized that if I didn't hurry, I was going to be late for cheer practice.

"I have to go. So I'll see you around," I said, my hand on the door.

"Yeah, okay," she said, giving me a little jerky nod. I got out and closed the door, thanking the stars that there was no one around to see me get out of Kyle's car.

~

KYLE

What a bizarre day. I couldn't stop thinking about how things had changed in only a few hours. Just last night Stella

93

had kissed me and today I was making out with her and now I was gay.

I mean, I'd sort of known? But kissing Stella and wanting her kind of cemented it. My parents were mad at dinner when I wasn't as open about my day as I could have been so I escaped to my room and shut the door.

I just wanted some time to THINK. There was so much noise in my head and I couldn't sort out any of it.

Yes, I liked Stella. But was it just her or other girls?

I knew the answer to that. Yes, it was other girls. No one specific (until now), just . . . girls. Their hair and the way they walked and not to mention the way their bodies were. Just perfectly shaped. It was everything about them. How had I been so blind to it?

That was what got me. How could I live eighteen years and not know? If I hadn't known this about myself, what else didn't I know? That was the scariest part.

And my parents. What would they say? What would they think? They'd struggled and pushed me to be the absolute best and to have a better life than they'd had. How would me being gay change that? Sure, marriage was legal all over the United States, but that wasn't everything. There was so much more.

They weren't anti-gay, but I didn't know how they would feel about having a gay daughter. If I was gay. I guess technically I was a lesbian? How did I decide what I wanted to be called?

There were just so many questions that I didn't have answers to. So I asked someone who might.

Do I have to call myself a lesbian now?

I knew she would be up.

No. You can be gay or queer or whatever you want. You don't owe anyone a label.

She sounded so different now. It just blew my mind how I had known her for so many years and not know what she was really like. It was obvious to me now that she put on a bitchy front, but I didn't know why. Her real personality was great. She was snarky and funny and thoughtful. At least she'd been that way today. Why would she hide that? I didn't get it.

Are you still going to be a raging bitch to me in English?

I felt like I could hear her laughing.

Absolutely. What you saw today was an anomaly.

But WHY?

I knew I wasn't going to get a straight answer from her so I changed the topic.

Do you know anyone else who's gay?

I could think of a few kids off the top of my head and I knew there was some sort of rainbow organization. I'd never really paid attention to it because I didn't think it was for me. Guess I was wrong.

Yeah, there's a group of them.

Was I now required to be friends with them? I had so many questions about this. There really should be a rulebook.

You don't have to do anything you don't want to, Kyle. Seriously.

I knew that, but I almost wished there was someone standing next to me and telling me what the rules were, what the steps were. I had so much uncertainty. Part of me even wondered if I'd just made a huge mistake or had a brain tumor or something.

I know. I guess I just have to get used to it.

She took a long while to respond and I saw her typing and then deleting a few messages before she sent one.

I'm here if you need me.

The words hit me like a punch. How had this Stella existed and I had no idea?

Thanks. We should probably go to bed. School night and everything.

This time her response was lightning fast.

We could always pass the time by sexting. What are you wearing?

For a half-second I thought she was serious and I realized

just how much I would enjoy that. And then she sent a little winky face and I wanted to kick myself for thinking that. Of course she was joking. We had literally just kissed today. I mean, last night too, but it had been only about 24 hours from the first lip contact. Sexting was getting a little ahead of things.

Wouldn't you like to know . . .

I hoped she was laughing.

Yeah. I would.

Wait, was she serious? This had been the most confusing day ever. Thank God tomorrow was Thursday and I wouldn't see her in class.

But that meant that I'd see her on Friday and then at the game. Stella was definitely going to be there and I had no idea how I was going to handle that situation. Some of my other friends might not notice, but Grace definitely would know something was up with me. That was what best friends were for.

I realized I hadn't responded to Stella in a while.

I sleep naked I typed and hit Send before I could second-guess myself.

So do I.

Well, shit. This was definitely not helping. I was turned on as fuck and I only had myself to blame. I shouldn't have texted her.

Goodnight, babe.

I groaned into my pillow. What was she *doing* to me?

Chapter Nine

STELLA

I was still thinking about the text messages and the kisses and everything about Kyle when I woke up the next morning. My blood still felt like it was on fire and didn't want to cool anytime soon.

Kyle Blake was going to be the death of me. Fortunately I only caught a glance or two of her in the hallways on Thursday. If I saw her every day I didn't know how I'd handle that. It was too much already.

Thursday I had a shift at the vet clinic and I was totally out of it. I messed up several times and my boss actually asked me if I was okay and suggested that maybe I should go home early. I wanted to kick myself for getting so distracted by the hot nerd.

She didn't text or reach out to me at all that day, so our first contact was on Friday in class. She got there first and I slid into my seat beside her. At least she didn't flinch.

"Hey," I said and she looked at me as if I'd done something completely insane.

"What?" I said, looking around, but no one was paying attention to us. They were all on their phones or talking to each other.

Kyle leaned closer and I told myself not to inhale too deeply and remember how her mouth tasted.

Tried and failed on both counts.

"I thought we were going back to the status quo. You never said 'hey' to me before," she said in a low voice, eyes darting around as if we were going to get busted for just talking to one another.

I rolled my eyes.

"We can at least be cordial without raising too much suspicion," I said. At the beginning, I hadn't wanted to set off any potential red flags, but the more I tried to avoid Kyle, the more obvious it was that I was trying to avoid her. So maybe if I allowed myself a little contact, things would be okay.

A cynical voice in the back of my mind told me that it was a stupid plan and that someone was going to catch on, but I told the voice to shut the fuck up. That same voice would be telling me to go for it if it had had the chance to make out with Kyle.

"Oh, we can?" she asked, raising one eyebrow. I wanted to grab her face and kiss the shit out of her, but that would definitely not be a good idea at this moment.

"Yes, we can," I breathed, leaning a little closer and smiling in satisfaction as she swallowed hard.

Mr. Hurley started class then and our heads snapped forward at the same time. Not suspicious at all.

"My dad looked over our paper on Thursday night," I said when Mr. Hurley told us to keep working together in groups as he wandered around the room and "kept us on task." There were only a few groups that needed him to hover to make sure they were doing work and not screwing off. Kyle and I were not one of them, so he generally left us to our own devices.

"And?" Kyle said, looking at the printout I'd given her with my dad's correction marks on it. There weren't many.

"And he said it was good. So I think we're pretty much set." She flipped through the pages, her eyes scanning before she set it back on her desk and turned to me.

"So, what now? We're basically done and we have a whole week to work on this." I wasn't sure, so I raised my hand and Mr. Hurley came over. I told him the situation and he just gave me a smile.

"I had the feeling you were going to be an overachiever in this class, Stella. Are you sure you're absolutely finished with everything?" We nodded in unison. He sighed.

"You have two options. You can either use the next few classes as time to work on an extra credit project, or I can send you to the library to work on something else." I glanced at Kyle. I knew what option I wanted.

"Library, I think," Kyle said and I nodded. Good. That had been my choice. The library was full of all kinds of corners and nooks and there were rarely people up there during the school day, so we would potentially have privacy.

Mr. Hurley wrote us both notes and we hurried as fast as we could out the door.

"I can't believe he let us do that," Kyle said as I slowed my pace to match hers.

"He knows my dad so I think he lets me get away with a lot," I said with a smirk. Kyle rolled her eyes as we headed out of the English building and toward the library. It was at the top floor, so we got to take the special elevator.

"Look at you with your fancy key," I said when Kyle pulled it out of her back pocket and put it in the hole above the buttons to unlock it.

"If I had to take the stairs, I would get there about the time class was over." Ninety percent of the time I didn't even think about her limp, but then we'd be confronted by something like stairs and I'd remember that it wasn't as easy for her to get around as it was for me.

"No way," Kyle said as we strolled into the library and looked around. There was no one in sight. Not even the librarian. But then she bustled around the corner with a stack of books in her arms and glared at us as if we'd walked into her house without permission.

"We have notes," I said, extending my hand out. She snatched them and looked at them as if they were fake IDs or something. After deciding on their authenticity, she told us to find a corner and be quiet and that if we caused any shenanigans, we would be booted out.

"No problem," I said, jerking my head in the direction of one of the corners. Kyle nodded and followed me. It was in a little alcove and had two beanbag chairs crammed in between the stacks. The only way you could see us if you walked between those exact rows of shelves and looked around part of the wall. It was perfect and almost private.

I set my stuff down and held out my hand to Kyle. She blushed but then accepted it as I helped her flop onto one of the beanbags as I crashed on the other.

"This is perfect," she said in a whisper.

"I think we can talk at almost normal volume, but I've never tested that theory," I said, a little louder than a whisper.

"Do you come here a lot?" she asked as she pulled a bag of gummy bears out of her backpack and offered me some. I took a handful as she did the same. Food was forbidden in the library, but we'd only get caught if the librarian happened to check on us and we'd have advance warning from her footsteps. So we were good.

"Not a lot, but I love libraries. Wherever I go, I always have to visit the library." I didn't know why I was telling her that. It was something only Gabe and Dad knew about. My desire to visit hundreds of libraries in hundreds of countries someday.

Kyle snorted and I pelted her with a gummy bear.

"Hey, don't waste those." She picked it up off the floor and made a face at it, but then put it in her mouth.

"Ew! Do you know what kind of germs there could be on that?" She just grinned and kept chewing.

"You just don't seem like a library kind of girl. I mean, no offense." I narrowed my eyes.

"Why? Because I'm a cheerleader? We're all supposed to be bitchy airheads, right?" She crumpled the empty bag and shoved it in her backpack.

"You know that's not what I mean. It doesn't matter that you are a cheerleader. You just seem more the social butterfly type than the library type."

"Why can't I be both?" She opened her mouth to respond, but then nodded.

"I guess you're right." I twirled a curl around my finger.

"People aren't just one thing, Kyle." She nodded.

"You mean like people aren't just lesbians?" I hadn't been talking about that, but sure. That was a good example.

"Exactly." She nodded again.

"And you're not just a hot nerd," I said, bumping my shoulder with hers.

I was rewarded by a blush that made me want to grab her face and lick her cheeks. I really had self-control issues around this girl.

"You think I'm hot?" she asked, looking down at her feet as she set her chin on her pulled-up knees.

"Kyle. Have you *seen* you?" She gaped at me.

"Um, yeah, I see myself in the mirror and it's nothing to lose your shit over, I'm pretty sure. And no one's going to put me on a magazine anytime soon."

"That's just because people are fucking idiots. You're gorgeous. Like, it's really hard for me to *not* look at you." She started to laugh.

"Are you serious?" I nodded.

"Yeah, it's a real problem. You've got that sexy nerd thing and I'm pretty sure it's designed to drive me crazy." She bit her lip to hide a smile.

"No one's ever called me sexy before." A year ago, I probably wouldn't have. But now it was so obvious to me that I couldn't ignore it even if I wanted to. She took her hair down and started to put it up again.

"Wait," I said.

She froze, her hands pulling her hair back from her face to pile it on top of her head again.

"What?"

"Let your hair down," I said, hating how breathless my voice sounded. But I'd pictured Kyle with her hair tumbling over her shoulders so many times and I just wanted to see it for real.

She gave me a look but let her hair drop, settling on her shoulders like a mahogany cape.

"It's gorgeous," I said, reaching out and running a few strands through my fingers. She didn't flinch, or tell me to stop.

"I always think I want to cut it because it drives me crazy, but I don't know if I could rock short hair." She could rock anything and look gorgeous.

I let go of her hair.

"But then your hair always looks perfect, Stella." I scoffed. My hair definitely didn't always look perfect and I spent a fair amount of time on it every day anyway.

"*You* always look perfect," Kyle said in a lower voice and now I was the one blushing.

"Thanks," I said, biting my lip. We both laughed a little.

"This is a little awkward, isn't it?" Kyle said and I nodded. Neither of us really knew how to do this. If Kyle was a boy, it would be different. So different.

Girls were complicated. Me being one didn't make Kyle any easier to figure out.

"Do you want to do something this weekend?" I blurted out. I knew that I couldn't go the whole weekend without seeing her, that was for sure.

"Um, sure. What did you have in mind?" Making out with you and maybe convincing you to take off your clothes? But I didn't say that.

"There's not a whole lot to do. Maybe we could go shopping or drive around or something." I didn't care as long as it involved her mouth and my mouth.

"Well, uh, my parents are going to this thing on Saturday to learn about financial aid for college and won't be home until late." Perfect. "You could come over. If you want." Yes. I did want.

"Sounds good. Do you want me to bring a pizza or something?" My heart fluttered at the idea of an entire day with Kyle when we didn't have to worry about being caught.

"Yeah, that'd be great." Silence descended on us again.

"Are you going to come to the game tonight?" I'd gotten used to seeing her in the first row of bleachers. Most of the time I cheered directly to her, as if the other fans didn't even exist. I didn't mean to do it; it just happened. I had Kyle blinders.

"Yeah, do you not want me to? Would it be weird?" I put my hand on her arm.

"No. No, it wouldn't be weird. I want you there. I like it when you watch me." It sounded more intimate than I meant it and Kyle blushed again and ducked to hide a smile.

"It doesn't hurt that you look hot as fuck in your uniform." I raised one eyebrow.

"Is that so?" She sighed and tilted her head back, looking at me out of the corner of her eyes.

"You *know* you do, babe." It was hot as fuck when she called me "babe." I'd always found guys giving their girlfriends cutesy nicknames to be patronizing, but I think I was finally understanding it. It made my insides feel like warm mush and my skin all prickly. In a good way. A very good way.

"Oh, well. Sorry?" She shoved my shoulder and I tipped back so she fell against me.

"Sorry!" she said, trying to scramble off me, but I clamped my hands on her arms.

"Don't be." I couldn't take it anymore and I pushed myself up so I could kiss her. Just a little one. Just because it had been so long. Like, more than twenty-four hours, which was basically an eternity.

Kyle let out a tiny little moan and I had to stop myself from pulling her on top of me so I could feel her body pressing against mine.

But she pulled away, looking over her shoulder, as if she was going to find the librarian standing above us and glaring down in disapproval.

Of course no one was there.

"We shouldn't," she said, sitting up again. I sighed. She was probably right. I didn't know how the administration would deal with finding two girls making out in the library. Probably not as well as they would if one of us was a boy. Fucked up, but true.

And this was exactly why I'd wanted to wait until college for all this. And then Kyle Blake came and smashed all my plans.

"It's okay," I said, reaching out to stroke one finger down her cheek so she knew I wasn't mad. "We should be careful. You're right. I guess you're the one with the most common sense out of the both of us." I laughed a little under my breath and then the bell rang, making is both jump.

"We should go," I said as I stood up and held a hand out to Kyle. She took it and didn't let go right away. I had a brief flash of what it could be like, if she didn't let go and we walked out of here together, still holding hands. What would happen? Would people stare and scream at us for being dykes? Or would they not even notice? Or would they spit on us? There was just no way to know for sure. And then we'd have to tell our parents and hell to the no.

Kyle gave me a sad little smile, as if she was sorry before she dropped her hand.

"We should probably leave separately," she said and I nodded.

"I'll go first, I guess." She shrugged one shoulder. I started to walk away. Another anti-climactic ending for us. We seemed to have a lot of them.

"I'll text you later," she said with a wink and I couldn't keep the smile off my face.

"Later," I said, giving her a little wave as I walked away with a bounce in my step.

~

KYLE

I couldn't believe I'd asked her to come over. Again. But I wanted to see her and that was the best option. I didn't want to take the chance that if we went out that we'd see someone from school or someone's parent or someone else from this damn small town. Gossip spread quicker than a wildfire in a field of dry grass. Everyone knew everyone's business, no matter how small or insignificant.

Fortunately, Stella got it, which made things a lot easier. If I could use that word in this situation, which wasn't very easy at all.

I was still coming to terms with the fact that I liked her and wanted her. Why now? Why *her*?

"Your face is all red, are you okay?" Grace asked as we headed down to the field for the football game. Of course most of the town was here, because what else was there to do on a Friday night in Maine? Other than drive out to someone's gravel pit and get drunk and shoot shit with a pellet gun, which was probably what the people who weren't here were currently doing.

"Yeah, fine, why?" I'd been blowing Grace off a bit, claiming that I was stressed with schoolwork, but that wasn't going to fly. Not with Grace.

Her fingers dug into my arm and she made me stop walking.

"I swear to God, if you don't tell me what is going on right now, I am yelling out that you're not wearing any underwear for everyone to hear." I gaped at her, but knew she was dead serious.

Shit.

I bit my lip and looked toward the field where the cheer-leaders were warming up. Of course, Stella chose that moment to laugh at something Midori had said, her face lighting up. So gorgeous.

I opened my mouth.

"Not here. I can't do it here." So Grace and I went back to my car. The doors shut and I was having trouble breathing.

Grace reached out and took one of my hands.

"Before you say anything, I want you to know that you can tell me literally anything and I will still love you. Even if you killed someone. No conditions, okay?" I squeezed her hand and forced the words to come out.

"I think I'm gay. No, I know I am." My entire body shook and I felt like I was going to die. Grace just started laughing.

"Yeah, and I'm black. What else is new?"

Did I hear her right?

"What?" I said and she stopped laughing.

"Oh, Kyle. I know you. How long have we been best friends? I've known for a long time. Maybe forever. I was just waiting for you to tell me." Words deserted me. I just kept opening and closing my mouth. Grace leaned forward and pulled me into a hug.

"It's not a surprise and it doesn't make me think any differently of you. How could it? You're you and I love you." Before I knew it, I was crying onto her shoulder and she was holding onto my shaking body.

"Oh, Kyle, I'm sorry this is so scary for you. I can't imagine, but I'm here for you. Whatever you need." Apparently I'd chosen well in my best friend. She rubbed my back and let me cry it out. I didn't even know why I was crying that much, but I finally got a hold of myself and pulled back. I'd gotten Grace's shirt all wet, so I popped open the glovebox and pulled out some napkins. I handed a few to her and used a few to blow my nose and wipe my face.

"So that happened," I said, laughing a little.

"Yup. It did. How does it feel?" I wasn't sure. My heart was still pounding, but I didn't feel any different. A little better, maybe. Because now someone other than Stella knew.

Stella.

We were very late for the game, but I knew that I needed to fix things with Grace first.

"You can ask," I said because I knew she would. Anyone would.

"Ask what?" she said and I rolled my eyes at her as I crumpled the napkins up and threw them in the backseat.

"How I figured it out, am I in love with you, that sort of thing." She snorted.

"You've already told me a ton, so I don't need to know anything else unless you want to tell me and I know you're not in love with me. Not that way." Lottery. I'd won the Best Friend Lottery.

"Oh. Okay," I said. She wasn't going to push, which was kind of a first for her. And totally at odds with the fact that she'd dragged me up here in the first place. Weirdness.

"Do I look like a hot mess?" I asked and she used some of the napkins to wipe the rest of the tears from my face and told me when my face wasn't red anymore.

"Your eyes are little puffy, but there's not a whole lot you can do about it. It'll go down. Just say that you had an allergy attack if anyone asks." Yeah, that wasn't going to work. I wish I had ice or some cold spoons or something, but it couldn't be helped.

"Come on," Grace said, getting out of the car. I took a breath and opened the door. She strung her arm through mine and we walked together back toward the football field.

"Where have you been?" Paige asked as we took our seats again.

"Robbing a bank," Grace said, putting the hood on her jacket up. It was a chilly night and I was wishing I'd brought gloves. The cheerleaders had their pants on tonight, but Stella still looked great. She looked good in anything. And probably nothing.

Grace nudged my arm and I looked over at her.

"What?"

Her eyes flicked to me and then where I'd been staring. At the cheerleaders. I looked away as fast as I could, but the damage was already done. Now Grace knew I was into a cheerleader. I just didn't want her to find out which one.

But she didn't drag me back to the car to grill me about it. She just turned back to the game and started clapping as our team scored a touchdown.

And my eyes slid back to Stella.

~

GRACE DIDN'T SAY anything else after the game, but gave me a huge hug and told me that if I wanted to talk, she was always there. And that she loved me. I almost cried again, but made it home without losing it.

I feigned a headache and went to my room, but I spent my time lurking around the gayer parts of Tumblr. I discovered there were a lot of people in similar situations and I stayed up late reading through stories. For the first time since everything had started, I felt like I could take a deep breath because there were people who had been through the same thing. I could feel myself nodding as I read the posts. And I'd told Grace and the world hadn't ended. She didn't hate me, or think I was a freak, or not want to be friends with me anymore.

I wasn't crazy and I wasn't alone. I clicked out of Tumblr and texted Stella. She'd caught my eye a few times at the game, but we hadn't said a word to each other. But she'd texted me about an hour after and we'd been talking off and on the whole night. Nothing earth-shattering, just stupid little things and memes and jokes. Still, every time my phone dinged with a new message, my heart tried to smash its way out of my ribcage.

I hadn't told her about Grace. Mostly because I didn't know how she would react. If she'd think that I had outed her, or something. That would kill me if she thought that.

You can bring some movies, if you want. Or we can see what's on Netflix.

I cringed at how stupid it sounded, but I didn't want us to spend the whole day being awkward in my living room. I still had some fear that our chemistry would suddenly die and there would be nothing left for us to talk about.

Movies with girls making out?

Whoa.

Maybe? Do you have a lot of those?

I could almost hear her laughing.

Maybe . . .

I wasn't sure if that was a good idea or a bad idea. Or both.

Chapter Ten

STELLA

I didn't get much sleep that night, and when I finally woke up the next morning, I couldn't resist bouncing out of bed. I hadn't been this giddy in a while. It was like being ten again and going to my first concert.

I did my hair extra carefully, hoping that by the time I came home, it would be messed up from having someone's hands running through it. I also wore my favorite jeans that made my butt look great and a simple tunic with a t-shirt underneath. Casual, but cute. Or at least I hoped so.

I had a moment of panic just before I pulled into Kyle's driveway.

Was this a date? Were we dating? Was that what this was? We hadn't talked or used any definitions. Fuck.

What were we doing?

I was still flipping out as I walked to the front door with a pizza, a bag of chips, and sodas and rang the doorbell. She opened it with a grin on her face.

"Hey," she said, a little out of breath.

"Is this a date?" I blurted out and her smile fell.

"Um . . . Do you want it to be?" she asked. I opened my mouth.

"I have no idea." She laughed and pulled me into the house.

"Let's not worry about that now, I'm starving." That broke the ice a little as she led me into the kitchen to get out plates and so forth.

"How's your day been so far?" I asked, cringing at the terrible small talk.

"A little manic. I've cleaned the house within an inch of its life." I looked around and it was definitely cleaner than it was last time, not that it had been dirty or messy. Just lived-in.

"You didn't have to do that," I said, touching her arm as she popped open the pizza box.

She turned and her mouth was so close that I couldn't resist giving her a kiss. We were almost exactly the same height, so no one had to bend in half.

Kyle smiled as I kissed her and then stroked my face.

"I was trying to impress you. You're intimidating. You also look, really, really good today," she said and I couldn't help but grin. There was nothing like a compliment from Kyle to make me feel like I could conquer the world. Or at least a few countries.

"Thanks," I said, running a few strands of her hair through my fingers. She'd worn it down and I hoped it was for me. She'd also dressed up, or at least as "dressed up" as Kyle got with a nice pair of jeans and a short-sleeve button up that was white with pale green stripes.

She looked amazing.

"Is this a date?" I asked again.

"I don't know yet," she said, kissing my cheek and then turning her attention back to the pizza.

We both filled our plates, grabbed sodas, and put the chips in a bowl.

"Look how healthy we are," Kyle said as we both sat on the couch, putting our plates on the coffee table. Sitting at the dining room table would have been weird and too formal.

"The pizza has sauce on it, which is made from tomatoes, which are fruit. And potatoes are vegetables," I said, pointing to the chips. She laughed.

"Good point."

WE STARTED out sitting with several feet of space between us, but when we were done eating, we'd somehow slid until we were sitting right next to each other.

"Hey," she said, bumping my shoulder.

"Hey back," I said, turning to face her. "What are we doing?"

She took a breath and shrugged.

"I don't know. I mean . . . do you want to talk definitions? It seems a little early for that. And weren't you the one who, two days ago, didn't want to label anything? Just wanted us to be two people hanging out and having fun in secret?" I opened my mouth to argue, but she was right.

"Well, I guess I changed my mind," I snapped and she laughed.

"There's the bitch queen," she said, but it didn't sound like an insult. It sounded more like an endearment.

"Shut up," I said, fighting a smile. "I don't know. I just . . . it's not enough. I feel like I want to have some sort of claim on you, which is totally ridiculous, but I can't help it." I hated admitting that to her. How much I wanted her.

"Wow," she said, blushing.

"What? Does that scare you?" She bit her lip and shook her head slowly.

"No. Because I kind of feel the same way about you. And it's crazy. This is crazy, Stella. We kissed for the first time less than a week ago. I thought you didn't even have a heart less than a week ago. It's not supposed to happen like this." How was it supposed to happen? It also wasn't every day that a girl fell for another girl. Maybe that was it. Maybe girls were just different. I didn't know, I'd never felt like this before. Not even about Shannon.

"It doesn't matter if it's supposed to be this way or not. It is what it is. And I like it. Like you." She snorted.

"Somehow I like you too. In spite of seeing you act like an asshole for years." I mean, I hadn't been mean to anyone. Just cold. Just closed off. Protecting myself.

"I don't get why you want people to hate you when, if they knew you like this, they wouldn't." I pressed my lips together. I had strong feelings for Kyle, but I definitely wasn't going to talk about that. Not this soon. Maybe not ever.

"I get that you don't want to tell me, but it still has me puzzled. Anyway," she said, waving that off and grabbing the remote.

"What do you want to watch?" she said, turning on the TV. I wanted to talk some more, but she'd clearly shut the door on that conversation for now. I guess she was probably still a little new to all of this anyway. I'd had years to deal with these feelings and she'd just started.

So I looked at the TV as she scrolled through Netflix. I thought about asking her if she wanted to watch *Blue is the Warmest Color*, but that movie had a ridiculously long and graphic sex scene between the two girls, so probably not the best idea at the moment. It was also kind of a pain because of the subtitles.

"I'm fine with whatever." I realized I didn't know a lot about Kyle. What movies she liked, music, what she did when she was home alone in her room.

"Okay, then you don't get to complain about what I choose.

That's how this works," she said, scrolling through until she found what she wanted.

"Are you serious?" I asked.

"Yup," she said as she selected *Tangled*. I'd never seen it.

"You're such a dork," I said as she turned up the volume and sat back happily.

"Yeah, but you like me so what does that say about you?" Good point.

"Is there singing in this one?" I asked and Kyle gaped at me.

"You've never seen this? What is wrong with you?"

"Um, I'm not six years old?" Kyle rolled her eyes.

"You don't have to be a kid to appreciate Disney. Besides, the animation they had to do for her hair is worth watching alone." I knew it was a Rapunzel retelling, but not much beyond that.

"Okay, okay, if you say so," I said.

"You're going to like it," she said taking my hand and kissing the back of it."Promise."

She didn't let go of my hand for the entire movie.

"SO?" she asked as the credits rolled.

"So, what?" She used the hand not holding mine to pinch my shoulder. "Ow!"

"You liked it. I know you did because you smiled and laughed." There was the cutest smug smile on her face. Made me want to kiss her.

"Fine. I liked it. Happy?"

"Ecstatic," she said, letting go of my hand and getting up to clear away the pizza stuff. I helped her bring everything into the kitchen and couldn't help myself from standing directly behind her and putting my arms around her waist as she rinsed off the plates.

She gasped a little and one of the plates clattered as she dropped it.

I pressed up against her so there was nowhere for her to go. So slowly, she turned in the circle of my arms until she was facing me. She swallowed and I couldn't stop staring at her mouth.

My fingers clutched her shirt and I leaned in the few inches between us to kiss her. Her hands, wet and soapy, gripped my head as I kissed her harder. She returned the force and I thought my knees were going to give out. Good thing I was holding onto her.

I pulled back just a little and was pleasantly surprised when she shoved her tongue into my mouth and dug her nails into my scalp. Sometimes I thought that the desire was one-sided, or at least that I wanted her more than she wanted me, but she was showing me that she definitely wanted me back.

My blood pounded in my ears and I couldn't breathe and my heart was going to explode. It was terrible and wonderful at the same time.

She finally pulled back, shaking a little. Kyle pressed her forehead against mine and licked her lips.

"I keep thinking that it's going to stop. That I'm going to kiss you and it's going to suddenly feel wrong and that I've made a mistake. But then I touch you and all the doubts are gone. Fuck, Stella." Her voice shook when she said my name and I brushed her hair back from her face.

"I feel the same way," I said and she dropped her hands from my head and neck to my shoulders.

"Sorry about the wet hands," she said, and I felt the wet spots on my shirt.

"Doesn't matter. I'd rather make out with you than have

dry clothing." She laughed and I reached up to stroke her hair again. Kyle really had great hair.

She giggled.

"That sounded dirty." That started me laughing and I leaned forward to rest my head on her shoulder.

"This is really nice," Kyle said, moving her hands up and down my back. "I didn't know it could be this nice with someone. I thought maybe I was broken, or that I just hadn't met someone I was attracted to yet. A late bloomer." I nodded and kissed her neck. She shivered and I couldn't resist using my tongue a little.

"Stop it," she said, but her tone told me she didn't want me to do that. I laughed.

"You know you like it," I said and she made a little sound in the back of her throat that turned me on so much that it was painful.

"I do, that's the problem. I like it way too much. Your tongue makes me stupid." I barely understood what she was saying as I moved up and softly drew her earlobe between my teeth.

"Fuck, Stella." I wanted to make her say that again. And again. And again.

Her fingers dug into my shoulders and then she was suddenly gone.

~

KYLE

It was just . . . too much. Too much of a good thing. Not a good thing. The best thing. So good it hurt. I couldn't handle all of that at once. It was like I'd been asleep my entire life and had been blasted awake by a tornado of color and sound and feeling.

I didn't know it was even possible to feel like that in every cell of my body. I needed some air. I couldn't take it.

Stella looked at me and I realized she'd thought I didn't want her.

"I just needed a break. When you do that, it makes me want to do a lot of things that I'm pretty sure neither of us are ready for at this particular moment." I ran shaking hands through my hair and she nodded.

"I understand. We shouldn't get carried away until both of us are ready for . . ." she didn't finish. A few weeks ago the thought of having sex with a girl would have been something I would have scoffed at and said I was not interested in at all. Now it was at the forefront of my mind and I couldn't see straight for thinking about it.

"Uh huh," I said, still finding it hard to breathe.

"We should —" she started to say, but her phone went off. She went back into the living room to get it.

"What's up?" I asked, following her.

She shook her head and set the phone down.

"Nothing. Just Midori wanting to know if I had plans tonight." She sat back down on the couch and I sat as well, but kept plenty of space between us. Neither of us could keep our hands to ourselves otherwise.

"Oh," I said. "You can go, if you want." She shook her head again.

"No, it's fine. I want to hang out with you." My heart got all warm and gooey when she said that.

"Where does she think you are?"

"Home, probably. Not sure. I don't tell her where I am every hour of every day. Where does Grace think you are?" I opened my mouth and then shut it.

"Hanging out by myself, I guess." And there was the problem. No matter how much chemistry we had, we couldn't ignore the fact that we were lying to everyone. Not even lying.

Hiding. As if we were ashamed. I wasn't, that definitely wasn't it. I just had no idea what would happen if my parents walked in right now and found me holding hands with Stella on the couch. And I wasn't ready to find out.

"It's okay, you know. Keeping things like this. I don't want to force you to do anything. Especially since I'm not willing to tell anyone either," she said with a sigh, combing her fingers through her hair.

"This is going to get more complicated," I said, which was one of the reasons I hadn't wanted to talk about it earlier. But it was inevitable.

"I'm not a fan of hiding things, but . . ." she trailed off. There was no easy answer.

"We could just start making out again. We're really good at that," I said, and a smile lit up her face. I loved those smiles because I was pretty sure not a whole lot of people got to see them on a regular basis.

So beautiful.

"Mmmm, if we do that, then I might not be able to control myself," she said, slinking across the couch toward me.

"What if I don't want you to?" I whispered as she straddled my lap. Her fingers pushed back my hair and she smiled.

"Then I won't."

"You should. One of us should be able to say no." I clearly wasn't very good at it.

She laughed low and sweet. Fuck.

My hands rested lightly on her hips. If she shifted just a little, we would be in quite a position.

"Where's the fun in that?" she asked, and then did rolled her hips against me in a way that made me nearly black out. A moan escaped my mouth and she was very pleased with herself.

"Not fair," I said, digging my fingers into her hips. She bit her bottom lip.

"Never said I was going to be," she whispered, lowering her face to kiss me.

And then my parent's car pulled into the driveway.

I NEARLY THREW her off my lap in my haste to put as much distance between the two of us as possible.

"I thought you said they weren't going to be here until later!" Stella hissed as she got up and tried to fix her clothes and hair. There wasn't a whole lot she could do.

"They weren't supposed to!" I hissed back and then grabbed her arm. My plan was to hide her in my room, but there was a huge hole in that plan because her car was in the driveway.

"Calm down," I said, putting my hands on her shoulders. "They won't think we're doing anything if we don't make them think that we're doing anything. We're just two girls hanging out. I should have told you to bring homework to make it more authentic." Stella swallowed and sat back down on the couch way over on one side and I sat on the other, turning the TV on. I took a few deep breaths and tried to calm my pounding heart.

"I'm sorry," I said before my parents came through the door.

Chapter Eleven

STELLA

Well, I hadn't planned on meeting Kyle's parents. Ever, really. I mean, I knew who they were because everyone here knew everyone else's parents, but this was a completely different situation. I swore they could hear my pounding heart when they called out to Kyle and she said she was in the living room.

They both came around the corner at the same and weren't surprised to see someone else in the living room with her.

"Oh, hello," her mom said. Her parents were young and Kyle definitely resembled her dad more than her mom, who was willowy and blonde. Kyle's dad had her hair and was a little shorter than his wife.

"Mom, Dad, this is Stella. She's my partner for that English project and we were just finalizing our oral presentation," Kyle said and I almost choked on air when she said the world "oral." There wasn't anything she could say that would not make me think of sex.

"Oh, how nice," her mom said, beaming and coming over

to shake my hand. I shook her father's as well. Guess he was the quiet one.

"Yeah, well, I should probably go. My dad wants me home for dinner." It wouldn't hurt to start laying groundwork to show them that I was a good influence.

"Of course, of course," Kyle's mom said before Kyle walked me to the door. I wanted to kiss her more than I wanted to take another breath, but that definitely wasn't going to happen.

"Oh, hey, do you have that book for me?" Kyle said, her hand on the doorknob. Her parents hovered a discreet distance away. Kyle gave me a look that they couldn't see.

"Yeah, it's in my car," I said, understanding what she was saying.

"Cool, I'll just come get it," she said, loudly and we both headed out the door.

"I wasn't going to let you leave without kissing you," Kyle said as we walked toward my car.

"My parents are totally watching right now, but . . ." she said, trailing off and jerking her chin at a particularly thick and high bush that happened to be right next to my car and blocked us from view of the house.

"Come here," I said, grabbing the hem of her shirt and pulling her to me. She stumbled and nearly fell.

"I got you," I said and she smiled before our mouths touched.

"Thanks, babe," she said and I got that little thrill.

"Anytime," I said as she left little short kisses on my lips, like she couldn't stop.

"I'll see you on Monday. Text me," she said, stepping away from me, still holding my hand. I tugged to make her stop.

"Wait! If you go back in there without a book, they're going to be suspicious." Her eyes went wide.

"Shit, you're right."

"Give me a second." One of the upsides of having a father who was obsessed with literature was that you never wanted for reading material. I always had a few paperbacks in my car, just in case I got stuck somewhere.

I looked through my backseat and found a copy of *War and Peace*. I smiled and handed it to Kyle. She raised her eyebrow at it.

"What?" I asked.

"Really? Have you actually read this?" What was she talking about?

"Of course. Several times. I had a summer of Tolstoy a few years ago." Kyle snorted.

"Summer of Tolstoy," she said, looking at the back cover with a little smile.

"Yeah," I said, wondering what she was thinking. But then she took a breath and looked up.

"Talk to you later." She brushed one finger along my cheek and then turned to walk back into the house.

If this were a movie, it would start raining and I'd run after her and pull her into a passionate kiss that somehow didn't leave both of us drowning or with hair in our mouths.

I sighed and got in my car and shut the door.

This wasn't a movie.

I'D TOLD Midori I didn't want to go out, but that was because I'd thought I was going to be with Kyle until late, so now I was stuck. Unless I just wanted to sit in my room, read, and text Kyle. That didn't sound too bad, but when I got home Gabe called.

"Aren't you supposed to be out getting wasted and not talking to your little sister?" I asked.

"I'm going to a wine and cheese party later. I'm classy as

shit." I snorted and sat down on my bed. Dad was in his office grading papers. As usual.

"I'm pretty sure classy people don't use the word 'shit', Gabe."

"Anyway, what's new with you?" I opened my mouth to tell him everything about Kyle, but then I slammed it shut. Hard enough to hurt my teeth.

"Nothing, really," I said, trying to make it sound as casual as I could.

There was a pause.

"Now, if I was an idiot, I'd believe that. But sadly for you, I'm not an idiot, so why don't you tell me what's really going on." For a second, I thought about hanging up on him and then just never answering his calls again, but that wouldn't really work when he came home for Christmas.

"Just school. They're up our asses about college applications already." That was a terrible excuse and I knew he wasn't going to buy it.

"Try again," he said. He was patient and would wait all night if he wanted to. I'd been down that road with him before. He was much better at it than I was.

"It's nothing, Gabe. Let it go." I didn't want to talk to him about Kyle. I didn't want to talk to anyone about Kyle. Part of me liked keeping her as a little sexy secret, even if it wasn't going to work, or was unhealthy for both of us. Sooner or later, someone was going to notice and hiding would only be sexy for so long before it got old.

"Star. You know you can talk to me about anything. You know if you told me you killed someone, I'd be in my car and heading to help you hide the body. Always." I knew it. I knew he loved me. I knew that love came without conditions, but telling him was just . . .

"I can't," I said, my voice breaking. "I just can't."

He sighed.

"Oh, Star. I wish I could be there for you right now. I can tell you're going through something and I wish I could be your big brother in person and help you slay those dragons." I laughed. When we were little, Gabe used to pretend to read to me, but all the stories he told me were ones he'd made up, with me as the main character. It was no wonder he was in college for writing, but I always thought he would become a novelist instead of a journalist. Maybe someday he would.

"Yeah, I know. But I can deal with this. I'm a big girl." I'd be heading off to college in less than a year. And I'd never been someone who needed to be coddled. Not having a mom growing up might have something to do with it, or maybe it was just me.

"Even big girls need help sometimes." I hated that he was right.

"Who do you go to when you need help?" I asked.

"Dad," he said. "Or you. You're really good at giving advice. For a girl." I snorted. He didn't mean it.

"Yeah, I know."

"Why don't you talk to one of the girls on the squad? Midori?" I wish. But this was definitely something I wouldn't talk to them about unless it was a last resort. Gabe would be most likely, and I still couldn't do it.

"This isn't the kind of thing she can help me with."

"Hmmm . . . Then I don't know what to tell you. Can't give me even a tiny hint?" A tiny hint would give it all away. There was no subtle way to say "I like girls and one in particular."

"No," I said. "Look, can we talk about something else? How's school?" I thought he would protest, but he started talking about his classes and the articles he was doing research for. Gabe's passion was feature articles, where he could get in-depth with one subject. He always sent me his articles and they were brilliant. He was going to win a Pulitzer someday, I swear.

I got off the phone with Gabe and headed to the kitchen to get something to eat. The pizza had been a long time ago. Just as I was rummaging through the freezer for something easy, my phone dinged with a text.

I'm sorry about my parents. Again.

Kyle.

It's NBD. You didn't know they were coming home. It's fine.

It was cute how bad she felt. At least she heard the car before we'd started making out again. Having her parents catch us in the act would have been . . . Well, I didn't even want to think about that.

I miss you. Is that weird? Sorry if that's weird.

So adorable.

If you're weird, then I'm weird because I miss you too. I'm just having dinner now.

I found a bag of pasta with chicken and shoved it in the microwave.

What are you having?

I told her and then asked what she was eating. That led to a somewhat heated discussion about olives, (terrible or delicious) guacamole, (terrible or delicious) and beets (we both agreed they were terrible).

I liked learning those little things about her. The things that not everyone knew. I wanted to know them all. I wanted to know what song she had stuck in her head. I wanted to know her most embarrassing moment. I wanted to know what side of the bed she liked to sleep on.

I wanted to know it all.

MIDORI TEXTED me again to ask if I was sure I didn't want to go out and I said no again. I was too busy texting with Kyle. It was so much easier than actually taking face-to-face or on the phone.

She started sending me silly selfies and I sent a few back and we had a whole section of the conversation that were just emojis.

I really, really liked her.

She was funny and sweet and I couldn't believe I hadn't seen it sooner. How could this amazing girl have been there all along? Was I that self-absorbed?

Probably.

The last message she sent me had a kissy emoji and two words.

Goodnight, babe.

KYLE

On Sunday I was forced to do all the homework I'd ignored on Friday night and Saturday, along with listening to my parents go through all they'd learned about financial aid at the seminar.

Riveting stuff.

I could feel my eyes glazing over and the words were going in one ear and out the other. Basically, I had to apply for any and every scholarship I could, stay in state and maybe sell an organ or two.

My parents had been scrimping and saving my entire life, but it still wasn't going to be enough. I hated it for them and I planned on getting at least two jobs this summer and stashing away as much money as possible to pick up the slack. They shouldn't have to pay for *my* education. At least not all of it.

Stella was probably going to have no problem. Seeing as how her dad taught and I knew they had more money than my family. Whatever. It didn't matter. She had her situation and I had mine.

Thinking about college just reminded me that it was happening in less than a year. Things with Stella were . . . complicated already. Neither of us knew what we were doing, or if anything was going to come of it. How could anything come of it? We'd not only have to both come out and hope everyone accepted us, but then deal with going to different colleges. There was just no way it was going to work out.

I guess I should just stop worrying about the future and just think about now. About how I wish we were making out instead of me sitting here and listening to my mom explain the FAFSA form.

I was about to head to my room when something my mom said made me stop in my tracks.

"So, who is that girl, Stella? She doesn't seem like your kind of friend." Ouch. But I knew what she meant. Stella looked like a princess and I looked like the stable-hand or something.

"Oh, we're just working together in AP English. That's it." I shrugged and tried to slip away to my room, but my mom was giving me a look. Uh oh.

"It's just that you don't invite a lot of people over. We hardly even see Grace." That was true. I didn't like subjecting my friends to the nuttiness of my parents.

"Well, we had to work on the project, so . . ." I trailed off. Dad was still staring at the forms, but Mom was giving me one of those looks where you knew she knew you weren't telling the whole story.

Shit.

"Okay, well, I'm going to do my homework." I gave her what I hoped was a normal smile and headed off to my room.

I sat on my bed and wondered if I should text Stella. I was really terrible about keeping this secret and it had only been a couple of days. I'd make a horrible secret agent.

I'd told Grace and now my mom knew something was up. How long would it take everyone else?

The thought made my stomach churn.

I picked up my phone and texted her.

I think my mom knows. She was asking about you and I am pretty sure I'm a terrible liar.

Her response took a few minutes.

I mean, it was bound to happen, right? Guess it was just sooner. What did you tell her?

This was different than Grace knowing because now Stella was involved. Revealing my secret meant revealing hers and that made me feel sicker than anything.

Just that we were working on a project. I tried. I'm so sorry.

Kyle, it's fine. I know you didn't do it on purpose. We just have to be more careful. Or tell people. Those are the only options.

Two options; I didn't know if I could handle either of them.

～

ON MONDAY it was so hard not to kiss Stella when I walked by her in the hallway. She glanced at me, but didn't give me a smile. I tried to keep my face neutral, but I couldn't help but be happy to see her.

Grace was talking in my ear, but all I could see in the crowd was Stella. She passed me and it was so close that she just barely brushed my hand with hers. I shivered.

"Are you even listening?" Grace said, grabbing my other arm and stopping me.

"Yeah, sorry. I was just off in the clouds," I said, refusing to look over my shoulder to see if Stella was still there.

"Uh huh," Grace said and pulled me into the bathroom. We were going to be late, but something told me she didn't care.

"Is this about what we talked about on Friday? I wanted to give you some space this weekend, but maybe I shouldn't have?" I had been sort of surprised that she hadn't texted me, but I'd been so wrapped up in Stella I didn't really notice. It made me feel like a shitty friend.

"No," I said too quickly. Grace crossed her arms and leaned against the wall as if she was going to stand there all day and wait for me.

"It's not about that. Not exactly. Things are just . . . a little weird. Because I always thought I was straight," I said the last part in a whisper, even though we were the only two in here at the moment.

"Yeah? I bet. Are you having second-thoughts?" About my sexuality? Oh, hell no. Definitely 100 percent gay. Gay, gay, gay. Lesbian. Whatever.

"Nope. I know that it's right and that it's true." Grace opened her mouth as if she was going to ask me how, but then shook her head.

"You want to know how I know. I know you do. If the situation were reversed, I'd want to know. But I can't tell you that. Just that I do." Her eyebrows drew together and we stood there in silence for a while.

"I'm sorry, Grace. I don't like keeping secrets from you. I don't like keeping them from anyone, but I need you to trust me on this one. Please?" She bit her bottom lip and sighed, putting her arms around me.

"I know. I'm sorry. I just hate that you feel like there are things you can't tell me. But of course I trust you." I rested my chin on her shoulder for a second and thought about how different hugging Grace was than hugging Stella.

Two different galaxies.

"I promise that if/when I tell someone, you'll be the first. Okay?" She let me go and nodded.

"Okay. And if you need a friend to go to the Pride Parade,

I'm your girl. I mean, your heterosexual girl," she said, giving me two thumbs up. I laughed and we headed off to class.

～

STELLA and I headed to the library again during English class.

"This worked out in our favor, didn't it?" she asked as we sat next to each other. I was starting to think of this corner as our place. Or one of our places.

"Totally," I said, kissing her cheek. She wrinkled her nose in the cutest way and then kissed me on the lips.

"No tongue," I said into her mouth. She pulled back and pouted, which made me laugh.

"I love your tongue, but it makes me forget everything and that's probably a bad idea to do in a place where someone could catch us," I said and she moved away from me.

"Yeah, you're right. So tell me more about how it went with your parents." I told her and that made me want to tell her about Grace.

"I'm worried you're gonna hate me," I said as I handed off the bag of gummy bears. I'd made sure I had some when I left for school today.

"Why would I hate you?" Stella said, running her fingers up and down my arm, causing goosebumps.

"Because I told Grace I was gay." The fingers stopped and I couldn't look at her face.

"How did that happen?" Her voice was level, so maybe she wasn't going to be pissed?

"Basically I was ignoring her at the game and she made me go back to my car and tell her what was wrong. She's not really good at letting things go." I looked up at her and she had a neutral expression on.

"So I basically broke down and told her. I didn't say anything about you, I swear, but today she talked to me about it again and I think she's on high alert for any lesbian behaviors. Like me not being able to stop staring at you." She gave me a half-smile.

"Well, you're not the only one who's guilty of that. I would stare at you all day if I could." I loved it when she said things like that.

"Anyway, I just . . . I'm really bad at this secret thing and I just wanted to let you know that I might do something that is going to out us." Both of us.

She sighed and looked down at her nails. They were polished in a soft grey today.

"It's not your fault that you suck at lying, I guess. And our friends and family would be pretty stupid if they didn't notice at least some change." She took a breath. "I think my brother knows. Or at least suspects."

She'd talked to me about her older brother, Gabe, who she absolutely idolized. It was so sweet and I was a little jealous, being an only child.

"Yeah?" She nodded.

"He's really perceptive, but he hasn't pushed me or anything. If I told anyone, I'd tell him. Or at least I'd tell him first." I nodded.

"I hate that we feel like we have to lie. I mean, we *shouldn't* feel this way," I said. Stella gave me a sad smile.

"It's just the way things are right now. They've changed a lot. At least we're probably not going to get stabbed or spit on, but who knows? There are still plenty of homophobes in the world." I bet there were. It wasn't something I'd given a lot of thought to. Until now, of course. Now it was something I had to consider.

My mind was starting to spin again.

"Hey," Stella said, squeezing my shoulder. "I'm not going to lose you again, am I?"

"No. I just . . . I was thinking about homophobes and that

got me thinking about a whole lot of other shit. There's a lot to this liking girls thing, isn't there?" Stella scooted over and put her head on my shoulder.

"But there's a lot of good things too." I rested my head on hers. That was true. It wouldn't be worth doing if there weren't more pros than cons.

"Should we make a list?" I said, almost as a joke.

"Let's do it."

She laughed a little and I decided her laugh was number one.

"Girls are prettier," Stella said.

"Girls smell better."

"Girls are better listeners."

"Girls have better boobs."

That one made us both laugh.

"Boobs are pretty fantastic. How did I not notice?" I said, looking down at my own chest.

"Yours are really nice. In case you were wondering," Stella said. "But don't get a big head about it."

"Why, Stella, that's the nicest thing anyone's ever said to me." She smacked my shoulder.

"Shut up."

"Girls have better nails," I said, taking her hand and stretching her fingers out.

Stella was just about to reply when the bell rang, shattering our little bubble. We both got up and it was almost painful to walk away from her.

We would text later, but it wasn't the same. I just wanted to be with her. As much as I could. Basically all the time. Being with her was like breathing fresh air for the first time and it was so hard to let go. I hoped it wasn't going to keep getting harder.

Chapter Twelve

I was totally off again at practice on Monday night and coach was not pleased. I kept messing up simple choreography I could do in my damn sleep. It was so bad that she pulled me aside.

"Is everything okay? Everything at home or in class?" Everyone else had headed to the locker room to change or had left, so it was just the two of us in the gym.

"No, I'm just tired," I said. I figured it was a good enough excuse. "Or maybe I'm coming down with something." Mysterious illness was another good one. Maybe I should have said I had PMS.

Coach put her hand on my shoulder and did that thing that adults do when they sort of lean down and look deeply into your eyes as if they're going to decipher all your secrets with one look.

"I'm fine, Coach. Promise." I gave her a smile and she pulled me into a hug.

"You let me know if you need absolutely anything. You got it?" I hugged her back and thanked her. I was all gross and I just wanted to go home and take a shower. I grabbed my stuff and headed out the door, taking my hair down and running my fingers through it. I was thinking about other things so I didn't notice that someone was standing beside my car. It was almost dark, but not so dark that I didn't recognize who it was.

"What are you doing here?" I said, nearly dropping my bag in shock.

"Um, waiting for you and feeling like a creepy stalker?" Kyle said, crossing her arms in the cold. I was still overheated from practice so I didn't have my coat on.

"Do not tell me you've been standing out here for hours, because that might veer into stalker territory." I unlocked my car and threw my duffel in the back and shut the door, walking over to where she was leaning against the driver's side.

"Yeah, no. I definitely didn't do that. I went home and did homework and thought about you and figured I would come and bring you a little pick me up." She held out a bottle of green juice and a paper bakery bag.

"What's in there?" I asked. She smiled.

"Open it and find out." I moved so I was under the streetlight and opened the bag. A chocolate croissant.

"Because the green juice and the croissant cancel each other out. Calorie-wise," she said, pushing her glasses up on her nose.

"You know that's not how it works, right? I thought you were supposed to be the smart one." She snorted.

"See if I do anything nice for you again." I reached out and took her hand.

"I love it. Thank you. And I'm really happy to see you. Even if I'm all gross." Kyle laughed and pushed some of my hair over my shoulder. We looked more alike now, with me in sweats and with my hair all messy.

"You are so beyond gross right now," she said, and demonstrating by pulling my face forward for a kiss. It was quick, because we didn't want anyone to see us.

"Thank you for the croissant. And the juice." I kissed her cheek and squeezed her hand again.

"You're welcome, babe." She let go of my hand and headed back to her car across the lot.

"Girls are more thoughtful," I yelled after her and she gave me a thumbs up.

"Definitely!"

I ATE the croissant first and had the juice second, but I was still starving when I got home, so I made myself some dinner.

"How was practice?" Dad asked.

"Good," I said, which was what I always said.

"And how's your presentation?" I froze in the act of putting together my salad.

"Good," I said again.

"Are you going to give me any more details than that? I thought we'd passed this phase a few years ago." He leaned against the counter.

"It's good. We're basically done and we made the changes you suggested. We're ahead of everyone else, so we've been using our class time for studying." Studying, cuddling.

"Good, good. And how's it working out with your partner?" I'd told him the bare minimum about Kyle. And now I was starting to get suspicious.

Were the two of us wearing neon signs on our foreheads advertising that we were hanging out together? Or did we just have very perceptive people around us?

Or was I just paranoid?

"Fine," I said, for some variety. "She's actually really cool." I could talk about Kyle as a friend without raising too many red flags. Because his assumption wouldn't be that Kyle and I were into each other.

"That's nice. It's good to make new friends. I mean, friends that are more into academics." I gave him a look.

"You're saying Midori isn't into academics?" I asked. "She's a National Merit Scholar." He sighed and looked at the ceiling. He was more than used to debating with me.

"That's not what I meant and you know it. I like seeing you branch out and meet new people. Why don't you have her over sometime?" Um, I'd already done that and it had ended in me kissing Kyle. But my house was a better place for the two of us to hang out, if only because my dad was gone so much.

"Yeah, maybe I will. She'd probably like to get out of her house. Her parents are a little obsessive and hovery," I said and cut it off there because I was saying too much.

"Is she an only child?" He crossed his arms and smirked.

"Yes, as a matter of fact she is." We both laughed.

"I can understand that. You only want what's best for your kids and sometimes it's easy to go a little overboard." I finished making my salad and started pouring on the olive oil dressing.

Dad came over and stole a cherry tomato before I could swat his hand away.

"I'm glad you didn't hover. I mean, not like that. They're constantly checking in with her, making sure she's happy and healthy and everything." I started eating while standing up because I was still so hungry.

"She'll be grateful for it one day, I'm sure." I had no idea if she would or not. Would I even know Kyle down the road? I didn't like thinking about the future that far ahead. I was so focused on college that I couldn't really see beyond that. Everything else was blurry.

"Uh huh," I said as Dad drifted back to his office to burn the midnight oil.

~

"YOU'RE ALL GLOWY TODAY," Marcey, one of the vet techs said on Tuesday when I was at the vet clinic.

"I am?" I asked, putting one hand to my cheek.

"Yeah, you look really happy lately. Could it be because of a boy?" There it was. The assumption that all girls were into all boys. My face froze and I shook my head.

"Nope. Guess I'm just getting a lot of sleep or something." She got distracted from replying by the entrance of one of our problem clients, Rufus, with his owner Geoff. Rufus was already howling and whining and practically dragging Geoff out the door. It took three of us to get Rufus into the exam room so Dr. Cope could give him his vaccinations for the year.

You know what I hate? The assumption that all girls like boys.

I texted Kyle when I got home, after I'd showered and was toweling my hair off.

Same. It's the default and it's stupid. I mean, MOST girls like boys, but not all.

Not us.

I liked talking about her and me as one unit. Neither of us was close to being ready to call us something like girlfriends, but I did like thinking of us as . . . something.

Gal pals.

Yeah, no way. That was stupid. Maybe we needed to make up a new term.

Nope. Not us. That's another one for the Pro list. We're unique.

You mean "not normal"

I wasn't sure if she was being sarcastic or not.

Do you really think that? That we're not normal?

I waited and waited for an answer, but then she just ended up calling me.

"No, I don't think we're not normal. That wasn't what I meant," she said without any preamble.

"What did you mean?"

She sighed.

"I don't know, Stel. I don't know. I didn't mean it. I'm sorry. That came out completely wrong. I was more talking that other people would think that. Not me." I moved my hair over one shoulder.

"I know. I know you don't think that. It just caught me off guard, I guess. I'm sorry I got a little defensive." She sighed.

"No, I'm sorry that I said it. Typed it. Whatever. Ugh, why is this all so complicated?" It sounded like she'd slumped on her bed.

"We don't have to make it complicated. We could always end it. Go back to our regular lives. Try and be straight again." I was joking about the last part and she laughed a little.

"Yeah, I think I'll pass. Also, I like making out with you too much to give that up."

"Same."

There was a beat of silence and I sat back on my pillows.

"What are you doing right now?"

"Just sitting in my room and praying that my parents won't barge in and give me more practice essays for scholarships. I already had to do one today." Sounded awful. And she didn't need practice. She was smart already.

"I'm sorry. You could always sneak out of your house and come over to mine." I wasn't serious, but I almost wished she would do it. Just show up and stay with me.

"Yeah, my parents would definitely notice if I was gone. They have a security system. But I would if I could. Would it earn me extra points in the romance department?" I smiled.

"Maybe. You earned some today when you showed up after practice." She laughed.

"Good to know. I'm trying to out-romance you."

"Oh, so it's a competition is it?"

"Yup, and so far, I'm totally winning." I scoffed.

"Yeah, so far. But I'm pretty sure I can beat you."

"Oh yeah?"

"Yeah."

She heaved a little sigh.

"I miss you. Even though you're on the other end of the phone. I wish you were like, sitting next to me. Could you sneak out? That would earn you some romance points." I chewed my lip. I mean, hypothetically I could. Dad was knee-deep in work and left me to my own devices.

"But how would I sneak in if your parents have an alarm system?"

I could hear the smile in her voice.

"I go to bed after they do. I'm the one who sets it."

I sat up.

"Are you serious right now?"

"Why not?"

I opened my mouth to argue.

"I don't know," I said and got up. "Give me twenty minutes."

KYLE

I didn't think she'd actually do it. I totally expected a text saying *nevermind*, but then my parents went to bed and I didn't set the alarm and went to my room to wait. Fortunately, my house was a ranch style, so my bedroom was on the first floor. Although, if I'd been on the second floor, it might have been interesting to see her try to get up there. I imagined a trellis would somehow be involved.

But then, almost exactly twenty minutes later, there was a soft tap at my window.

I skipped over and pushed it up, finding a smiling Stella on the other side.

"I can't believe I'm doing this," she whispered as I helped her scramble through the window and into my room.

"I can't believe it either," I said, not letting go of her. She stepped forward.

"So do I get romance points?" she asked, a smirk on her face.

"Definitely," I said, giving her a kiss. She laughed and we tumbled onto my bed together, tangling our limbs. Her hair was still a little damp from her shower earlier.

"This was such a good idea," I said as she kissed me with desperation. I kissed her back just as hard, both hands fumbling with her clothes. She just had a sweatshirt on with a pair of yoga pants and they were both driving me crazy.

"Such a good idea," she said, just before she drove her tongue into my mouth. I moaned and she somehow flipped us so she was on top and I was flat on my back. Her fingers tangled in mine, raising them over my head.

"Fuck, Stella." She pulled back only to bite my bottom lip and laugh.

"I love it when you say that. It turns me on so much I feel like I'm going to die."

"You saying that turns me on so much I feel like I'm going to die," I said as she looked down at me, her hair falling. I wanted to push it out of her eyes, but my hands were already occupied.

"I should have put my hair up," she said, sitting up and letting go of my hands so she could pull a hair tie off her wrist and put her hair back in a ponytail.

"I'll remember that for next time," she said before she attacked my mouth again. She stole my breath and made my bones turn to warm caramel and I'd never felt anything so good. I tried to pull her closer, but I couldn't get her close enough. My glasses were smashed to my face but I didn't want to take them off because then she'd be all blurry.

"More. I want more," I said into her mouth and she laughed.

"Are you sure?" she said, looking down at me with swollen lips.

"Yes," I said, the word more breath than substance. Stella cupped my face with both hands and kissed my forehead. Instead of ramping up, she slowed us down, laying kisses across my entire face until I was trembling under her, my fingers digging into her sides. She didn't seem to mind. Or notice.

Her lips skipped over my jaw. I made a sound of frustration and she smiled against my skin and just barely kissed my chin.

"You said you wanted more. I'm giving you more, babe." I took a deep breath as she moved further down. To my neck where the skin was sensitive and her kisses made me see stars.

My blood pounded in my ears as she reached the neck of my t-shirt and pulled it down just enough so she could kiss the top of my collarbone. A breath hissed through my lips.

I wanted her to take my shirt off. I wanted her to take everything off and I wanted to take her clothes off and do everything, but a very quiet voice in the back of my head said that wouldn't be a good idea.

Not yet.

Not tonight.

So I shifted under her so she'd look up.

"My turn," I said, crossing my legs around hers and rolling us over again. She squealed a little, but the change in position was definitely nice.

"Oh, I like this," I said, looking down at her, laid out on my bed.

"God, you're beautiful." The only light in my room was moonlight that spilled in through the window and it lit up her hair and made her eyes look mysterious.

"Thank you. You're beautiful too, Kyle." I sighed.

"We can argue about who's prettier, or you can let me kiss you."

"Fair point." I laughed as I kissed her forehead and gave her the same treatment she gave me. She held onto my arms as if holding on for dear life and she unconsciously thrust her hips into mine.

I was going to lose my mind.

We were both completely clothed, but I was so fucking close to coming that I didn't know what to do.

I tried to focus on kissing Stella. Doing whatever I could to get her to make those little whimpering sounds in her throat. I was gentle, because neither of us needed a hickey because then there would be questions. We didn't need questions.

I tasted the underside of her jaw and the pulse on her neck and the hollow of her throat. It was good. It was all good.

So much different than any of the times I'd kissed a boy. I didn't even know what those had been, but this was something else entirely. I was never, ever, going to kiss a boy again. Like ever.

I stopped kissing her, just so I could watch her.

"What are you doing?" she asked, looking up at me.

"Watching you. I don't get to do it that often when I won't get caught. Or when it's okay." I ran one finger from her forehead, down her nose and to her chin, down her neck and stopped just at the top of her sweatshirt.

I could tell she wasn't wearing a bra and I wanted so much to shove my hands under her shirt and feel them. Feel her nipples against my palms.

"Kyle?" she asked. I had been very obviously staring at her chest.

"I was just thinking about touching you. Here." I skipped my hands over her boobs and she arched up into me.

"I want you to," she said, her words uneven.

"I think . . . I think we should slow down." The words

sliced me to say, but I knew that we were very close to stepping over the edge.

"I know you're right, but I seriously hate you right now. I'm not getting to sleep anytime soon." Me neither.

I climbed off her and sat on one side of my bed, with her on the other. We were both still breathing hard.

"How did you get here?" I asked. Probably a little belated.

"Drove my car without the headlights until I got far enough from the house. And I parked a few houses down so your parents wouldn't get suspicious. I think we're fine," she said, taking down her ponytail that had gotten a little messed up, and combing through her hair with her fingers.

"I was thinking what we'd say if we got caught. And then I decided we just shouldn't get caught," I said.

"Solid plan." The air between us cooled a little, which was probably a good thing. I still could barely think of anything other than her, but at least now I was keeping my hands to myself.

"So this is your room," she said, looking around. It was small, but cozy. I'd done what I could with the space and fixed up furniture from yard sales and discount stores.

"This is where the magic happens. And by magic, I mean me and my hand. Sometimes both hands." She snorted and rolled her eyes.

"Perv." I gave her a look.

"You can't tell me you don't."

She fiddled with her hair.

"No, I do. Doesn't everyone?" Pretty sure. Unless they were too uptight or something.

"We probably shouldn't talk about that right now anyway," I said and she nodded.

"You okay?"

She sucked on her bottom lip.

"I've just been thinking about . . . about next year and

144

college and how all of my plans basically went out the window. Thanks a lot, asshole." She found a shoe on my floor and chucked it at me. I caught it and tossed it back on the floor.

"Why is it my fault? What did I do? She rolled her eyes.

"You're irresistible." I tried to hide a smile.

"I'm sorry?"

"You should be. Asshole." She got up and came to sit next to me again. I put my arm around her shoulders and she leaned into me.

"I don't like that I can't see you whenever I want. That we can't just do this without hiding," she said. I rubbed her shoulder because I didn't have a good answer.

"Well, Grace took things really well. Maybe you could try Midori? Or your brother?" She stiffened.

"I'm scared," she whispered. "I'm scared they won't love me the same way."

"Oh, babe. You know that's not going to happen."

"But it could. It could." Never let it be said that Stella Lewis wasn't stubborn.

"You're right. It could. But that would mean they didn't love you enough in the first place. Because if this is the thing that makes them love you differently, then that love wasn't that strong anyway. Okay?" She sniffled and I moved her so we were facing each other.

"I wish it wasn't like this," she said as I brushed her tears away with my thumbs.

"Shhhh, it's okay. It's okay, baby." I kissed her and she melted into me, letting me hold her. It was a different kind of kiss than earlier. A softer kiss. Something more like comfort than desire.

"Do you want me to come with you?" She shook her head.

"No, that would definitely not help. Because then they'd look at you and assume we were together." Right.

"Or, you could tell your brother on the phone and I could

be here and hold your hand. I wouldn't say a word," I said, pretending to zip my lips shut.

She thought about that.

"Not right now. But maybe this weekend. Maybe. I don't know." She took both of my hands.

"I should probably go. I really don't want to risk getting caught and the longer I stay, the better the chances are that we will." She kissed both of my hands and then my lips.

"Goodnight, babe. Drive safe," I said as I walked her to the window.

"Thanks." With one last kiss, she was out the window again and I went to set the alarm.

Chapter Thirteen

STELLA

Kyle had planted the seed of the idea of telling Gabe in my head and it was starting to grow. I imagined all the potential scenarios and went over them with Kyle on Wednesday when we were in the library together.

"Okay, what is your absolute worst case scenario?" Kyle asked as she tossed gummy bears into her mouth.

"Um, him telling me that I'm going to burn in hell, that he's never talking to me again, and that he's telling Dad. That's pretty much the worst." Kyle raised one eyebrow.

So. Fucking. Cute.

"Don't do that, it makes me want to kiss you." She started wiggling her eyebrows up and down and I couldn't stop laughing.

Of course the librarian chose that exact moment to come around the corner in search of who was destroying the peace of her library.

Kyle and I froze. Fortunately, we hadn't been in a compromising position.

"If you two are just going to come in here and goof off, I'm

going to send you back to class. Don't make me tell you again."
Since we were sitting, she was a lot more imposing. Especially
when she wagged her finger at us.

"Of course. Sorry," I said, trying my best to look contrite.

"We won't do it again," Kyle said, moving her leg so it hid
the bag of gummy bears.

"It better not." With one last glare, she turned on her heel
and marched off to do whatever she did all day.

"Whoa, that was close," Kyle said, picking up her gummy
bears again. "No more laughing. Or smiling." She made her
face devoid of emotion and it was so ridiculous that I started
giggling and slammed a hand over my mouth to muffle the
sound.

"You're not supposed to be doing that," she said, shaking
her finger at me.

"Shut up. You have to stop or else I'm going to laugh
again."

She heaved a sigh.

"Fine."

"HEY, I feel like I haven't seen you in forever," Midori said on
Wednesday afternoon as we headed to the locker room to
change for practice.

"I know, I've just been really busy," I said, my mouth going
dry. It was a bad excuse. I'd been using most of the time I
usually spent on Midori with Kyle and sooner or later, something was going to have to give.

"Yeah, I can tell. Busy with what?" She set her bag down
and whipped her shirt over her head. She already had her
sports bra on underneath. I turned my back and fiddled with
my bag, grabbing my clothes.

"Just . . . school. I've been stressing about college. And I've been working more hours." I pulled off my shirt, unsnapped my bra and traded it for my sports bra and a tank top. I didn't turn back around until I was covered again.

Midori was standing with her arms crossed and her eyes narrowed.

"Uh huh."

I groaned and sat down on the bench where I'd put my bag.

"What do you want from me? Do I have to tell you every single fucking detail of my life?" A few other girls passed by and gave me weird looks, but went to change.

"Whoa, no one said that." She sat down next to me and I could see the concern on her face.

"What's going on with you? Are you okay? You've just seemed different lately." Guess Kyle and I were perfect for each other because neither of us could hide anything.

"It's just . . ." For a second, I almost blurted it out. But I couldn't tell her before I told Gabe. That was the new plan and I was going to stick to it.

"Can you come over on Sunday? Or maybe we could do something on Saturday night?" That would cut into my time with Kyle, but both of us had been neglecting our best friends and there had to be a way to balance the different parts of our lives and still see each other.

"Yeah, sure. You want to maybe grab some pizza? Just the two of us?" We hadn't done that in so long.

"Absolutely." I gave her a smile and she patted my shoulder before grabbing her cheer shoes and slipping them on.

Guess I was telling two people this weekend.

It was like being on a train that wasn't slowing down.

Kyle. I had to remember I was doing this for Kyle. And for me. Hiding this part of myself hadn't been fun. Each time someone talked to me about having a boyfriend or a husband or anything like that, I felt like a liar. It made me feel awful and honestly, even before Kyle I'd been sick of it. But I told myself I could hold on until college.

Not anymore. I'd had enough, and it wasn't just about her. I was tired of not being able to be myself. To be scared of myself. I didn't want to do it anymore.

I had a weirdly good day at practice, nailing my tick-tock heel stretch three times in a row. I was feeling good when I walked out to my car and there she was again.

"I figured we could make this a thing," she said, handing me a juice (mango, this time) and a glazed donut.

"It should definitely be a thing, thank you," I said, giving her a quick kiss and looking around. There were a few cars still in the lot from other cheerleaders and teachers working late.

"I decided I'm going to tell Midori," I said as we sat in my car and I split the donut in half, offering it to her.

"Oh, yeah? How are you feeling about that?" She took a bite and I licked the glaze off my fingers.

"Good? I guess? I wanted to tell her today because she sort of cornered me, but I want to tell Gabe first. And that probably means I should tell my dad soon. I don't want to make Gabe keep that secret from him." She nodded and we munched on our donut halves.

"Grace is still watching me. I think she knows that I have a thing with someone, or at least a crush and she's taken it upon herself to find out who. Oh, and she's also started pointing out cute girls. She's really taking this ally thing seriously." I laughed. I couldn't picture Midori taking things that far.

"I think you'd like Grace. And she would like you. Once she found you weren't actually a raging bitch." She grinned at me and I wiped some glaze from the corner of her mouth and licked my finger off.

"But I've been so careful to make her believe that. Wouldn't want to ruin things now." Her eyebrows drew together.

"I still don't get it. Why you're so different with me and

like that with everyone else. I'm guessing you're not like that with Midori." No. Not completely. She got to see bits and pieces of my real self, but Kyle was the only one, outside of family, who saw me. Just me. Unvarnished and real.

"You wouldn't get it," I muttered and shoved the last bite of donut into my mouth.

"Oh, that's nice, Stella. You're literally the only person I can talk to about liking girls, but I 'wouldn't get' what you're going though. Yeah, okay." Her words hurt, but not enough to make me tell her the reason why.

"Look, it's my thing. Can you just drop it?" I knew exactly what was going to happen when I said those words, but it didn't stop me from saying them.

I expected Kyle to tell me to go fuck myself and slam the door, but she didn't. She just sat there and waited.

"I know what you're trying to do. You're trying to be a bitch to make me leave, but too bad, because I don't believe you. So I'm just going to sit here." She crossed her arms, as if she really meant business.

Damn. I'd underestimated her. And her bullshit tolerance when it came to what I could give her.

"Fine, do what you want to do." The words didn't come out as forceful as I wanted. I gripped the steering wheel to have something to hold onto and smeared leftover donut glaze on it. Great.

"Stel," Kyle said, touching my shoulder, but I jerked away from her.

"You don't even know me. Just because you've had your tongue in my mouth and we've talked a few times, doesn't mean you know me." I couldn't stop the words from coming. I was just so used to curling in on myself and going on the defensive before someone could hurt me.

I had to hurt them first.

"Good effort. I'd give it an eight out of ten," she said, giving me a smirk.

"What the fuck is wrong with you?" She shrugged one shoulder.

"I like you. And I'm not all that sensitive, I guess." I opened my mouth to say something else, but short of screaming at her, or throwing her out of my car, she didn't seem to be budging.

"You are weird." She grinned.

"Never claimed to be otherwise."

I fought a smile and lost.

"Ha," she said, a little sound of triumph. "I win."

"Brat," I said, smacking her in the shoulder.

Somehow she'd defused the situation and got me to smile. No one else had done that before and I didn't know what to do with it.

"But I'm your brat. You know you like it." I did. Too much.

"Anyway, I'm going home. But I'll text you later." She smacked a kiss on my cheek and was out the door, heading to her car.

I shook my head and started my car.

KYLE

I was definitely going to have bruises when this phone call was over. It was Saturday and I was next to Stella in her bedroom, holding her hand as she prepared to call her brother.

"He's probably busy," she said, staring at her phone. "He probably won't even pick up."

We'd been going through this same thing for a while now, but I wasn't going to force her before she was ready. Grace had sort of put a gun to my head and I didn't want that for her.

"We don't have to do it today," I said. She shook her head.

"No, it has to be now. Because I'm going out with Midori

152

later and I promised myself I'd tell Gabe first." With a nod of her head she hit send for his number and raised her phone to her ear.

I was sitting so close that I could hear it ringing.

He picked up on the third ring.

"Hey, Gabe," she said, her voice a little shaky. I couldn't hear what he said in return.

"No, I'm fine. I just . . . There's something I need to tell you. Do you have a minute to talk?" She waited and then took a deep breath. We'd practiced what she was going to say all week.

"Dad's fine. No, I didn't get kicked out of school. Can you just shut up for a second?" She took another breath and somehow squeezed my hand harder. I wouldn't be surprised if she snapped one of my fingers. Damn cheerleading muscles.

"Gabe, I'm gay." Her entire body shook with the words and her hand trembled in mine.

You got this, I mouthed at her, but she was too busy with Gabe.

"No, I'm sure. Yes, I'm serious. No, I haven't told Dad. You're the first." Second. Technically.

She opened her mouth to say something else, but Gabe must have been talking.

"Shut the fuck up, you did not know," she said, letting go of my hand.

"No you didn't . . . No . . . No, Gabe . . . Stop it . . ." Okay, was it going bad or . . . ?

I was dying to know what he was saying. I wished she'd put him on speaker.

"I'm not going to say that because you did not know before me. You're just saying that because you want to be right." She rolled her eyes, so that was a good sign.

"Look, I'm not fighting with you about who knew I was gay first. The bottom line is that I am and I like girls and Dad doesn't know yet, so don't say anything. I'm going to tell him. Probably tomorrow." Wow. Her brother, Midori, and dad all in one weekend. She was better than me.

"Oh my God, Gabe. Yes, I did kiss Shannon. No, I do not have a girlfriend." She gave me an exaggerated wink and I had to muffle a laugh.

"Okay, I'll tell you when I get a girlfriend so you can do your brotherly thing and interrogate her to figure out what her intentions are. Okay. I'll talk to you later, jerk. Okay, bye." She set the phone down on her bed and I pulled her into a hug.

"I'm still shaking," she said and I could feel it.

"I'm guessing it went well? From what I could hear." She snorted into my shirt.

"Yeah, you could say that. He basically said that he's known for years and doesn't give a shit and just wants me to be happy." She sat back and pulled her knees up.

"I mean, I *knew* that was what he was going to say. I know my brother. But I still was scared out of my mind. My heart is pounding." She put her hand on her chest and let out a little breathless laugh.

"I think I need a drink now."

SINCE WE COULDN'T HAVE an alcoholic beverage, we had seltzer water with maraschino cherries in it.

"Too bad I don't have any cherry stuff or we could have made Shirley Temples," she said as we sat in the living room.

"How do you feel now?" She set her drink down on a coaster and shrugged.

"The same? I guess I thought I would feel different or something. But I'm still me. Still gay." I laughed.

"Lucky for me."

She gave me a half-smile that made my heart do flips.

"I'm really proud of you. For doing that."

"Thanks," she said, looking down at her hands. Stella painted her nails every week without fail. They were painted a cute mint green.

"Hey, would you do my nails?" I asked. She looked up.

"Yeah, sure. I can do your toes too."

"Cool." She skipped off and came back with one of those clear plastic containers and it was filled to the brim with polish. There had to be at least fifty or more bottles.

"Polish much?" I asked when she set it down on the coffee table with a clunk.

"It's fun. Something to do." She shrugged and set out the supplies and I scooted closer, flattening my hand on her thigh.

"That's not going to be distracting at all," she said, lining up the bottles of polish for me to choose one.

"I have no idea what you're talking about," I said, pointing to the same color polish she was wearing.

"This one?"

"Yeah, I want us to match." She beamed. How cute.

"Okay," she said, unscrewing the top of the polish and starting on my pointer finger.

"Can I run a hypothetical situation past you?" I asked as her head was bent over my hand to make sure everything was perfect.

"Sure."

I took a breath.

"What if I told my parents and you tell your dad and your brother already knows and our best friends will know so . . . what would you think about us maybe telling more people? Or, if not that, just . . . hanging out? In public?" More and more, I was learning that I was willing to risk/give up a hell of a lot of things to get more time with Stella. I'd do just about anything for more time with Stella.

She looked up as she finished my first nail.

"Hypothetically?" she asked, raising one perfect blonde eyebrow.

"Hypothetically."

She put the brush back into the jar of polish.

"I think . . . I think that I'd be okay with that." I exhaled shakily.

"Really?" She took my polish-free hand.

"Really." Stella lifted my hand to her lips and kissed the back of my hand like she was from an old movie or something.

"So you'd be willing to hold my hand in public and go on dates outside of either of our houses? Hypothetically." I felt like I had to keep adding that.

"I'd be willing to pretty much go anywhere with you, Kyle. In case you didn't know that," she said, twisting her fingers with mine.

I loved the idea of being out with her, our hands entwined, walking together.

"It wouldn't bother you to be out with me?" She shook her head.

"No, why?"

"Because I am easily defeated by stairs. And if we were chased by a murderer, I'd probably end up dead." She stared at me for a second and then it hit her. My limp.

"Oh! Oh, no. I guess I don't see it as something that's bad or wrong, or whatever. It's just you. And I like you. All of you." That was something I'd definitely considered when it came to dating, but I'd figured I would just find a guy in college, since colleges were generally liberal places. But it had still been in the back of my mind.

"I won't always be able to keep up with you." I started to say something else, but she shook her head.

"I like *you*. Whatever form you come in. The packaging isn't important. And I happen to think your packaging is perfect." I bit my lip and looked down at my nails again.

"Thanks."

"You wouldn't feel weird about being out with me?" she asked, going back to painting my nails.

"No. When I really think about it, no. It feels right. Sometimes I look at you and I wonder how I ever could have thought I was straight." She giggled.

"Yeah, I feel the same way sometimes. But I haven't been 'straight' for a long time."

I rolled my eyes.

"Okay, okay, you win. You knew before me." She looked up.

"It's not a competition. You got there in the end. And there are some people who go almost their entire lives without figuring it out."

"I guess you have a point."

"I do." Stella concentrated on my nails and I watched her work. It wasn't an uncomfortable silence. Just the two of us being together. She finished my first hand and I blew on my nails as she worked on my second hand.

"We'll have to do another coat," she said after she'd finished the first. I waved my hands in the air to dry them.

"Want me to do your toes while you wait for those to dry?" she asked. I slipped my socks off.

"As long as you don't think my feet are ugly," I said before I put them in her lap.

"Aw, your feet are cute. Cuter than mine. My second toes are longer than my first and I hate it." I bet it wasn't that bad. Maybe I'd ask if I could do her toes. Not that I was great at nail polish. I just didn't use it that much because it chipped after two seconds.

I was glad she couldn't see my leg, because I wasn't ready for her to see all the surgery scars. Most of the time I didn't think about them, but I definitely didn't want to when I was with Stella.

"So, you're going to tell your parents?" she asked as she finished my second toe.

"I think so? I mean, it went well with Grace and you told your brother and I think it'll be okay. I hope it'll be okay. I just hate feeling like I'm hiding something from them. As much as they drive me crazy, everything they do is because they want the best for me. And they've sacrificed their entire lives to see that I didn't grow up like they did." Both of my parents had had rough childhoods. They hadn't given me a lot of details, but I knew enough. And I could read between the lines.

"That's sweet."

"Yeah. Bottom line is that I know they love me. And if they love me, they have to love all of me, right?" She nodded.

"Exactly."

Chapter Fourteen

STELLA

I was second-guessing my choice of venue for my talk with Midori that night. It meant that anyone walking by or eavesdropping would hear what we were talking about. Fortunately, there was a booth tucked into a corner near the kitchen that the waitress seated us at and if I spoke low enough, no one would hear.

"I wonder if she thinks we're on a date," Midori said after she'd taken our drink orders.

"What?" I said, nearly choking on my water. I felt all the blood drain from my face.

"I just said what if she thought we were on a date. It was a joke. I wasn't serious." That didn't stop me from shaking. But this was Midori. My best friend. The girl who had had my back. Literally, in some instances at cheer practice.

"Oh, yeah, right," I said, pretending to laugh, but probably sounding deranged.

We talked about what to order and homework and the new stunt our coach wanted us to try.

I was trying to figure out how best to tell her when I just blurted it out.

"I'm gay," I said as she picked up the first slice of pizza. The waitress had just left us, so we were alone.

Midori froze.

"I'm sorry, what?"

"I'm gay. That's what I didn't want to tell you." She set the slice of pizza down on her plate and opened and closed her mouth a few times.

"Okay." She picked up her napkin and set it on her lap and started to eat.

"That's it?" I asked. She wrapped a string of melting cheese around one finger and then put it in her mouth.

"Is there more?"

"I guess I just expected you to have more of a reaction." She smiled and took another bite of pizza.

"I mean, I think I sort of knew, but it doesn't change who you are. I don't see you any differently. And you're my best friend. So that's it." Oh. Okay?

I opened and closed my mouth a few more times and Midori laughed.

"Stella, it's not a big deal to me. I know that there are some assholes out there, but I'm not one of them. If girls are what you want and they make you happy, then that's what I care about." Well.

"Wow," I said and she shrugged one shoulder.

"Do you want to talk about it? Or not talk about it?" she asked. I finally picked up a slice and bit into it.

"If we didn't have to talk about it that would be great. I feel like it's all I've thought and talked about for weeks and I'm a little bored to be honest." We both laughed.

"Okay then. So, what do you think about fundraising online for the new uniforms? Because car washes are so overdone and I really don't want to wash a car in a bikini so some gross old guy can ogle me." I made a face.

"Totally agree." So we talked about fundraising for cheer and how we couldn't wait for this year to be over and the ridiculousness of college application essays.

It was amazing.

Before she left, I gave her a huge hug.

"Thank you for being my best friend," I said.

"Anytime," she said, hugging me back.

Two down, a bazillion to go.

I WAS on such a roll that when I got back on Saturday night from hanging with Midori, I sat Dad down in the living room and told him.

He just sort of blinked at me and told me he'd known since I was five or something.

"You're my daughter. It's my job to know you." He smiled and gave me a hug. I started to cry a little and he held me and told me that he loved me.

"I thought this was going to be horrible," I said, wiping my eyes. He kissed the top of my head.

"Why? Why would you think that this would change the way I see you?" I didn't know for sure.

"I'm really proud of you for trusting me with this, Star. And I know that you'll be happier when you can live openly as yourself." My stupid heart kept swelling due to these amazing people I had in my life.

"So you're not going to disown me or take me to 'pray away the gay' camp?" I asked, totally joking. He shook his head.

"You know, it always fascinates me that when people are

having a child, they say 'we don't care what we have, as long as it's healthy' but if that child turns out to be gay, or transgender, suddenly that's not good enough." I nodded and we sat down and did what we always did and had a lively discussion of gender and heteronormativity and he even gave me a list of books that he'd read. My dad had read a little bit about almost everything, so he always had a ready book recommendation. If you needed a book on pangolins, he'd have a title ready and waiting in his brain to give you. Sometimes he made me feel stupid. But he'd had more years of reading under his belt than I had.

So that was Gabe, my dad and Midori down. The three most important people (other than Kyle) in my life. Everyone else? I kind of wished I didn't need to tell them. Why was the pressure on me?

I texted Kyle because I needed to talk to her.

So Midori and Dad were fine. NBD.

Wow! That's awesome. I'm telling parents tomorrow. Might call you sobbing and ask if I can come live with you if things go badly.

Aw, I wished I could go and hold her hand. Or even do it for her. I was getting pretty good at it by now.

You don't have to, Ky. It can wait.

I know, I know. But I just want to get it over with, you know?

I did. I absolutely did. Now that my family knew, I almost felt . . . light? Like something that I'd been carrying for a long time inside me had lifted. It was nice.

I wanted that for Kyle too and I hoped beyond hope that she'd get it.

I'm here for you. No matter what. Okay?

Okay. I'll let you know how it goes. Goodnight, babe.

I sighed and set my phone to charge as I climbed into bed.

Everything and nothing had changed in just a few days. I guess I expected to feel more of a change in myself, but I felt the same, but better. The best word to describe it would be "quiet."

Maybe it was supposed to be this way. I didn't really believe in fate or that shit, but this felt right. The timing felt right. *Kyle* felt right.

KYLE

My mom looked like she was going to die from a heart attack when I sat her and Dad down in the living room on Sunday afternoon. I had a whole speech prepared, with answers to any potential questions and I wasn't going to cry this time. I mean, I was going to try not to cry this time. No promises.

"Kyle, you're scaring us," Mom said, clutching Dad's hand. "Are you pregnant?" she said in a whisper.

And I burst out laughing. Oops.

"This is not funny at all, Kyle," Dad said, putting his arm around Mom.

"I'm sorry," I said, trying to stifle the giggles. "I'm really sorry. It's not funny. I mean, it is in the context." I bent over, my stomach aching.

"Kyle!" I straightened up and swallowed the rest of my laughter.

"I'm sorry. It's funny because I'm gay. As far as I know, two girls can't make a baby, so that's not something you have to worry about. Yay." I raised my hands and wiggled my fingers like jazz hands.

They both stared at me.

"You're gay?" Mom said. "You're not pregnant, you're gay?"

Uh oh.

"Yes?"

She let out a huge sigh and fell back against the couch.

"Oh, thank God. I thought it was something bad. I need a

163

minute to get my heart back to normal." She put her hand on her chest and I looked at Dad.

"Well, thank you for telling us, but you didn't need to make a huge production out of it. We were both preparing ourselves for the worst."

"I'm sorry?" I said. What was going on here?

"It's okay, kid," he said, getting up to give me a hug. Mom joined him a second later and we had a family hug. I couldn't remember the last time I did that.

"We love you, Kyle. You're *our* daughter and we are beyond lucky that we got you." That made me cry. Guess I couldn't come out without crying. That was going to be really embarrassing.

"I love both of you," I said. "I know I don't seem like it sometimes, but I do. And I appreciate all of the sacrifices you've made for me and all that you do." Mom pulled back from the hug and held my face between her hands.

"If you think about it, we're even luckier because not everyone gets a gay child. You're rare. Like a diamond." She kissed my forehead and I cried some more.

After that, they sat me down and I told them that I'd recently come to realize these feelings and I could tell Mom wanted to say something.

"That Stella you had over is really pretty," she said, totally obvious. I felt my face go red.

"Are you two . . . ?" she trailed off.

"Um, kind of? It's very, very new. We've just been hanging out and stuff. She hadn't told her family either, so we had to do that before we could really, you know, move forward." Why was this so awkward to talk about? If Stella was a boy, it wouldn't be a big deal.

"Well, I think you should have her over for dinner so we can officially meet her. She must be pretty special," Dad said with a wink.

"Yeah, she is," I said, biting my lip. "She really is."

"You look happy, baby," Mom said, tears glistening in her eyes. "Really happy."

"I am. I think," I said. We talked more about life and whether or not I'd want to propose, or get proposed to, and how a wedding with two brides works, and it was the best conversation I'd had with my parents in ages.

It made me feel guilty about how often I brushed them off or shut them down or closed my door in their face. I vowed that I was going to stop doing that so much. Shutting them out of my life.

We had another group hug and then Dad said we should celebrate and go out to dinner, which we almost never did, so I went to put on one of my nicer button up shirts, black pants that didn't have rips in the knees, and my black Chucks. I even made some effort with my hair, got out the curling iron I'd bought on a whim years ago, curled the ends of my hair and left the rest down. I even did eyeliner and put some colored gloss on my lips.

"You look so pretty!" Mom said.

"Thanks." She gave me another hug and we headed out to the nicest restaurant in town. "Nicest" meant they had white tablecloths and tall candles on the table and had a huge wine menu.

I didn't get to text Stella until after we'd gotten home from dinner, and I bet she was climbing the walls to know how it had gone.

So Mom asked if I was pregnant. And then I laughed. And then I told them and she said "oh thank God. I thought it was something bad."

OMG! I can't believe it. So they were fine?

Uh, yeah. They were more than fine. Mom said that since being gay is rare I'm like a diamond or something.

WOW. That's . . . wow.

I know. So that happened.

What do we do now?

I wasn't sure. I was still reeling from the fact that my parents were all aboard the rainbow train.

Can we give it another week? Please? We had our presentation on Monday, which meant that after that, there would be no more private "study" sessions in the library and we'd go back to being on display all the time. It sucked, but I just wasn't ready to face everything else yet.

Sure. Whatever you need. BTW, I'm really proud of you.

I couldn't help but smile. Hearing that she was proud of me made my heart want to smash out of my chest.

Thanks. That means a lot. And I'm proud of you too. We both did a lot this weekend, didn't we?

That we did.

WHILE STELLA GAVE our presentation about feminism in *Jane Eyre* I couldn't take my eyes off her. If I hadn't liked her before, I probably would have when she started to talk. She was incredible. Smart, articulate, and beautiful. She absolutely nailed it and I could tell Mr. Hurley was pleased when I handed in our paper.

"Well done, ladies," he said.

I looked at Stella and held my hand up for a high five. She looked quickly around before she connected her hand with mine, ever so briefly. It took all my control not to grab her hand and hold onto it for the rest of the class. We had to sit through the rest of the presentations, which were mostly a snore-fest.

"Finally," Stella said when the bell rang and we were dismissed. I got up and expected her to go back to not wanting to be seen with me, but she packed up her bag and waited for me.

"Oh, are you going to walk with me?" I asked.

"Maybe," she said, her voice all flirty. Most everyone had already left, so we were pretty much safe, as long as we talked in a low volume.

"You gonna carry my books too?" I asked and she rolled her eyes.

"No, because this isn't a television show from the 1950s. Come on." I left the room first and she followed after me, keeping pace. I realized I didn't even know what class she had next.

"Where are you headed?"

"Calc. You?"

"Health." I made a face. It was the worst class ever. The gym teacher just stood up and told us not to have sex and talked about the different muscle groups. I pretty much slept through most of it, but it was a requirement for graduation and there was no way out.

"Well, I'll walk you as far as the health room," she said with a smile before looking around to see if anyone was watching us. As far as I could tell, no one was.

"Thanks," I said and she turned to look at me again. "You look really cute today, by the way. I wanted to tell you earlier." She ducked her head as we walked and blushed a little.

"Thank you. I hate that compliments from you turn me into absolute mush." I laughed.

"Well, that makes two of us." People passed by us and didn't even look twice. They were all dealing with their own shit and insecurities and thoughts. One good thing about teenagers; we were so absorbed with our own issues that we didn't notice other people's.

"So, what are you doing tonight?" I asked and she stopped walking.

"Are you asking me out?" Her voice was loud and I stepped closer to shush her.

"No, I meant that we should hang out. At your house or something. By the way, my parents want to meet you. Like, officially. Even though we haven't decided what the hell we're doing. They want you to come over for dinner." I cringed as I said it, but she laughed.

"Wow, meeting the parents. That's a big step, Ky. Is your dad going to bring his shotgun to the table and start cleaning it?" We were both definitely going to be late, but I didn't care. I slowed my pace even more and she did too. Like we didn't want to leave each other.

"Uh, I don't think so. Seeing as how he doesn't have one? And you can't get me pregnant, so there's that." She snorted.

"Yup. That's one thing we don't have to worry about. Should we add it to the list?"

"Definitely." We finally reached the health classroom and Mr. Varney was already trying to get everyone in order, which usually took at least five or ten minutes of threatening everyone with detention. He never actually gave them out because he wanted everyone to like him. Adults were weird sometimes.

"Um yeah, you can come over. My dad might be home, but he'll be working and he's pretty shy so he'll leave us alone. Unless that's not okay with you?" Mr. Varney was yelling at someone and I hoped I could slip in while he was distracted.

"Yeah, that's fine, I guess. I'll meet him eventually, right? You want me to just meet you there at like five?" I knew when her practices got out now because she'd texted me her schedule.

"Perfect. I'll see you later. Babe." She whispered the last word and gave me a wink before strutting off to Calculus. I definitely watched her walk away.

I slid into my seat in the back of the room just as Mr. Varney was threatening Esther Wilson with detention for being on her phone already.

Phew.

~

I WAS FLIPPING out a little as I drove to Stella's house. I'd brought green juice and Boston cream donuts for each of us this time. I wasn't scared of her dad, exactly, but knowing that he knew that Stella liked girls and her suddenly having me over looked a little suspicious. Or maybe I was thinking too much. Probably.

I took a breath and got out of my car with the bakery bag and the juices. I walked slowly so I didn't trip and drop anything. I made it to the front door and knocked, feeling like a weirdo.

"Hey," Stella said as she opened the door. "Come on in." I did, reluctantly, and she shut the door behind me. I pretended that I wasn't looking for her dad, but I totally was.

"Relax," she said in my ear. "He's already in his office." I shivered as she ran her hand down my back and then plucked one of the juices out of my hands.

"Thanks, babe." I followed her into the living room and she sat down. Her hair was still wet from her post-practice shower and she had a tank top and shorts on. I was pretty sure she was not wearing a bra under the tank top, which was a little distracting.

A lot distracting.

"How was practice?" I said, forcing myself to look at the juice as I unscrewed the cap.

"Good," she said, lifting her hair off her shoulder and draping it over the back of the couch. "I'm sore. Coach made me do a million scorpions and my back is mad." I had no idea what she meant. She must have seen the question on my face. She sighed and then got up. I had no idea what she was going to do until she took her foot in one hand and swung it behind her head.

Holy. Shit.

She popped her foot up until she was almost bent in half and then leg go, acting like people did that every day.

My mouth was dry as she sat back down.

"Who says cheerleading isn't a sport?"

"Not me," I managed to say. "Doesn't that hurt like hell? Your body isn't really supposed to bend like that. Unless you don't have a spine."

"You dork. I've been cheering since I was a kid. If you get flexible when you're young, it's easier. I barely feel it anymore, as long as I make sure I stretch every day." I just stared at her.

"What?"

"That was some contortionist shit right there," I said. She waved me off.

"Eh, everyone can do that." I shook my head.

"You're crazy." She grinned.

"Shut up and hand me whatever you have in there." I passed the bakery bag over to her and she pulled out the donut.

"Oh, helloooooo." She gazed lovingly at it.

"Should I leave you two alone?" I said, pretending to get up. She bit into the donut and rolled her eyes at me.

"I love carbs," she said through a mouthful of donut. I shook my head at her and pulled a napkin out of the bag and started wiping her face.

"Stop it," she said, pulling away. I was just about to tackle her against the arm of the couch when someone cleared their throat. I whipped around to find a man with graying blonde hair, glasses, and Stella's eyes looking down at us.

"Oh, hello Mr. Lewis," I said, putting distance between me and Stella and hoping that my face wasn't too red.

"It's nice to finally meet you, Kyle," he said. Right. Stella had already told him about me. I glanced at her and she was still staring down at her donut as if it was going to start talking for her.

He stepped over and put his hand out. I shook hands with him, feeling more awkward than I ever had in my entire life.

"I heard your presentation went well," he said and I could feel him trying to make conversation, but it was just making the whole thing worse.

"Yeah, Stella was amazing," I said and then wanted to kick myself.

"Whatever," she said, fighting a smile.

"What? You were. You were the only one who knew what they were talking about." I needed to stop right now, so I shut my mouth.

"Do you girls need anything?" he asked, shifting from foot to foot. He was nervous, which almost made me feel better about the whole situation.

"No, we're good, Dad. Thanks," Stella said, finally looking up. She was more than a little red and I had the feeling she and her dad were going to have a chat about me when I left. I didn't want to know.

"Okay, well, if you do, just let me know." He shuffled to the kitchen and made himself some instant coffee and then headed back to his office.

"So that was your dad," I said when I was sure that the door was closed and he couldn't hear us.

"Yup. That was my dad. And I'm pretty sure that I'm due for a lecture after you leave." I bit my lip.

"Sorry about that. I guess I got a little carried away. That seems to happen a lot around you." She couldn't hide her smile.

"I guess that's okay, because I feel the same way about you. But I definitely think that in the future when my dad is here, we should have at least two feet of space. Just . . . so we don't get carried away. It happens so fast." She was right, as much as I hated it.

I sighed and moved a little further away.

171

"Should we measure? Should we draw a line?" She crumpled up the napkin and threw it at me, but missed.

"I'm only protecting us from the horror of my dad walking in while we're in a compromising position. I would rather die than have that happen." Yeah, me too.

"I know, I know. All these rules," I said, taking my hair down. It was pulling at my scalp and I could feel a headache coming on.

"If you were a boy, he'd still have the same rules. Probably more." True. There was that.

"At least he didn't ask me if we were seeing each other," I said, shuddering. That would have been the worst. The "so what are your intentions with my daughter" speech. Ugh. I hoped I would never have to hear one of those.

"Yeah, but he will after you leave. What do you want me to tell him?" Since my parents knew about her, I figured it was only fair.

"You can tell him. I mean, he's going to find out anyway at this point, so lying would just be silly." And I knew he wasn't an idiot. Stella had gotten her smarts from somewhere.

"Yup. You're right."

There was silence as she finished the donut and I sipped my green juice.

"So, what do you want me to tell him? That we're seeing each other? That we're dating?" I tried to answer, but the truth was that I didn't know.

"I guess? I mean, for lack of a better, more accurate, term." She nodded.

"Do you think that at some day, you might want to call what we're doing dating? Or be up for calling yourself my girlfriend?" My heart fluttered when she said the word "girlfriend." I wanted that. I wanted to talk about Stella as my girlfriend. I wanted to introduce her as that.

Definitely.

But was I ready for that?

Was I ready for a girlfriend and all that came with it?

I didn't know. Not yet.

"I'll be totally honest with you: Yes. I want that, but I don't know if I can handle it yet. I hate being the one who's not ready because I feel like I'm holding you back, but I don't want to say yes, and then let you down. That would be worse." So much worse.

She reached out and took my hand. The one that still had the polish on it that matched hers.

"I don't want to push you or rush you into anything. I totally get it. This is all new and scary for me too. We'll get there. Because I like you and you like me and we're excellent at making out." I laughed as she squeezed my hand. I never knew hand-holding could be so awesome. I mean, seriously.

Awesome.

"Cool," I said, kissing the back of her hand.

"Want to watch a movie and hold hands?" she said and I nodded.

"Yeah."

So we did. I scooted a little closer to her, but still with enough room that if her dad came out again, we could play it off.

I let Stella choose the movie because I didn't really care. I just liked being with her.

She chose the newest movie with Rebel Wilson, which I was fine with because she was funny as hell. Plus, it let me watch Stella laugh a lot and that was pretty damn great too.

We held hands the whole time, even though they started getting sweaty. Stella's dad didn't come out, which was great. I wondered if he was hiding in there, wary of walking into something.

"Stop being so paranoid," she whispered in my ear as my eyes flicked down the hall to look at his office door.

"I can't help it," I hissed back.

"Stop it," she said and then her tongue was licking my earlobe and I stopped thinking about just about everything.

"Fuck, Stella, you have to stop. What if he comes out?" My eyes fluttered shut as she kissed down my neck. This girl was trying to kill me. In the best way possible. I'd happily die at Stella's hands.

"But that's the fun. The almost getting caught," she whispered against my skin as her hand crept under the hem of my shirt. Just the barest brush of her fingertips on my stomach nearly had me losing my mind.

"Seriously, Stella." My protests were getting weaker and weaker.

She laughed against my skin and her fingers kept working. I was dying. I was actually dying.

And then I nearly did when my phone vibrated.

"Shit," I said, reaching for it. My parents were calling, wondering where I was. I looked at the clock and it was five after nine. They were super strict about school nights. I mean, not that they really had to be. Until now, I guess. I'd always had a curfew, but they'd never had to enforce it.

"I should go," I said after I got off the phone with my mom. I'd told her that I was with Grace. I hated lying, but I didn't know if she'd approve of me hanging out with Stella now.

"Okay," she said, walking me to the door. I put my coat on and told her to say goodbye to her dad for me.

"I hate to say it, but you should probably meet him in some sort of official capacity." She cringed as she said it.

"You're probably right." Meeting the parents. Big step. For any relationship.

"I'll see you tomorrow after practice?" she asked. As if I needed a reminder.

"I hope so. Have a good night, babe." I wasn't sure if I

could kiss her or not and then she grabbed my coat and pulled me in, capturing my lips with hers. We both kept our tongues to ourselves and the kiss was over far too soon.

"I wasn't letting you leave without my goodnight kiss," she said, tapping my nose.

"Bye, baby," she said as I opened the door.

Chapter Fifteen

STELLA

I did see Kyle the next day before she met me by my car. We just happened to be walking into the cafeteria at the exact same time. Totally unplanned. I was with Midori and a few of the girls from the squad and she was talking with Grace and Molly.

I had a brief moment of terror, but then she beamed at me and my heart did back handsprings.

"Hey," she said, as if we did this every day. My mouth was dry so I had to swallow before I could respond.

"Hey." Wow, amazing response. I was so good at this.

Grace and Midori were both watching us and the other girls had puzzled looks on their faces.

"Do you want to sit with us?" Midori said and I whipped around to stare at her. She just shrugged one shoulder.

"Um, thanks. We're good," Grace said, hiding a little smile. Kyle and I didn't hang out with the same people. It wasn't as if there was an impossible divide between us, but meshing our two groups didn't seem like something that was going to happen. At least not without a reason.

"Okay," I said, and started walking.

"Okay," I heard Kyle say behind me.

"That was a little awkward," Midori said in my ear. "Are you into her?" I gave her a look.

"Ohhhhhh," she said as it dawned on her. "Don't worry, I'll keep my mouth shut." We grabbed trays and got in line.

"What was that?" Courtney asked.

"What was what?" I said, trying to play it off.

"You talking to Kyle. Did anyone else get a weird vibe there, or was it just me?" Nope, wasn't just you, Courtney. Pretty sure everyone felt it.

"We got paired up in English for a project so we've been talking. She's nice," I said, hoping that would satisfy them.

"Huh," Courtney said and got distracted by a cute boy. As usual. Midori poked me in the back and winked. She was definitely going to want details later. Well, as many details as I could give her. There weren't a whole lot. I bet Grace was going to do the same thing with Kyle.

What had we gotten ourselves into?

"SO?" Midori said as we changed for practice. I looked around; I really didn't want to discuss this in the locker room. Especially not while I was getting naked.

"So, what?" I said. "I don't think this is the right venue for this discussion." I looked around and popped my shirt over my head and switched out my bra.

Midori huffed.

"Fine. But after practice, you're going to tell me. Because I definitely saw something going on there," she said in a sing-song voice.

"Shut up," I said.

"Hey, I'm not criticizing. She's cute. In a nerdy kind of way.

Is that your type?" We were not having this conversation right now.

"I will talk to you later," I said through gritted teeth.

"Fine, fine. But we will talk." Guess I wasn't getting out of that one.

She winked at me and then skipped out of the locker room while I tried to get my shit together.

PRACTICE GOT CUT short because one of our freshman flyers had a bad fall and needed to go to the hospital with a potentially broken wrist. Coach was beside herself and it was chaos until the ambulance came, and then she left with Macey, so the rest of us rolled up the mats and headed home.

I took my time in the locker room and so did Midori until we were the only two left.

"Okay, it's just us," she said after she'd walked around and made sure we were alone. I sat down on the bench and she sat facing me.

"Is she your girlfriend?" was the first question.

"Um, yes and no. We aren't official, but I think we will be soonish. It's still weird and new and scary so we're taking things slow." I was absolutely fine with that. I knew Kyle thought she was dragging her feet, but I was happy with how things were going with us. I didn't want to rush and then fuck this up. I didn't want my first relationship to end in complete disaster. I didn't want to end it at all, really. But I couldn't think that far ahead. Not yet.

"Oh my God, that is so cute! I can't even deal with this." I gave her a look.

"You seem more excited about this than I am." She laughed.

"I'm just excited *for* you. Because I can see how much you

like her. You look at her like you're falling in love with her. If you haven't already." I froze.

What?

I tried to make words come out of my mouth, but I couldn't. I was out of them.

"I wish you could see your face right now," Midori said. She looked like she was highly enjoying this. And I was ready to slide off the bench and onto the floor.

Falling in love.

Falling.

In.

Love.

What?

I wasn't in love with Kyle. I barely knew her. We weren't even dating, for fuck's sake. We'd only kissed a little. Okay, a lot. But we hadn't even gotten close to being naked. Or anything else.

Shit.

My mind started reeling and I could tell that I was starting to hyperventilate.

"Whoa, Stella, breathe." Midori clamped onto my hand and helped me calm down.

"I don't know what that was," I said, feeling cold sweat run down my back.

"I think that was you freaking out about Kyle. I'm sorry, I think I said too much." I shook my head and swallowed a few times.

"No big. I think you just blew my mind a little. And I need to sit here alone and think for a minute. If that's okay with you?" She got up and squeezed my shoulder, but left me alone.

One of the sinks had a leaky faucet and the dripping was driving me crazy. I got up and went to turn it all the way off and stared at myself in the mirror. My face was all shiny from sweating during practice and my hair was a mess. I pulled it out of my ponytail and then put it in a bun on the top of my head.

Like Kyle's.

I couldn't stop thinking about her. My fingers dug into the porcelain of the sink.

I wasn't going to think about what Midori had said. I wasn't going to think about the feeling I'd had when she said it. Nope. I wasn't.

Once I'd finally gotten a grip on myself, I threw everything in my bag and headed out to my car. And froze when I remembered that Kyle was meeting me.

"Hey, what took so long? I was going to come in and make sure you hadn't drowned in the shower or something." She saw my face.

"What's wrong? Did something happen?" I took a breath and tried to act normally.

"Uh, yeah. One of the girls had to go to the hospital and she might have broken her wrist. So things were a little crazy." I took the green juice with a shaking hand that I hoped she didn't see. It was freezing, so we got in my car and I cranked the heat for her.

"Oh, I'm sorry. But you looked really freaked out." I was. Still. Sitting next to her wasn't helping. I realized I hadn't kissed her, so I leaned over and gave her a peck.

Shouldn't have done that.

"Okay, something is definitely wrong." I shook my head. She didn't let me get away with anything.

"I just had a talk with Midori. About us." She groaned.

"I had one with Grace too. She wanted to know a lot of details and got . . . really personal about things. She knows way too much about what lesbians do in bed, by the way and I really don't want to know how she knows all that." She shuddered and I wished I could laugh.

"Yeah, Midori didn't do that. She just . . . said some

things." I knew I was digging myself into a hole, but I didn't know what else to do. Short of pushing her out of the car and driving away.

"Okay, babe, you're being really vague and it's freaking me out a little." She turned to face me and I scrambled to figure out what to say to her.

"It's nothing. It's nothing." I turned away from her, but she grabbed my face and made me look at her.

"Nope, I'm going to sit here and stare at you until you're uncomfortable enough to tell me. So there." I tried to get away, but she just held on.

"This is ridiculous," I said, but she just smiled.

"It's only ridiculous if it doesn't work."

"Kyle, please. I don't want to talk about it. Please." Her fingers stroked my cheeks.

"Oh, babe, what's got you so rattled? I want to help. Talk to me." Her voice pleaded and I wanted to tell her. But I couldn't. I just couldn't.

I closed my eyes and tried to pull away again, but she wouldn't let me.

"*Please.*" Her eyebrows drew together in concern, but she nodded.

"Okay," she said, but I could tell she was hurt.

"I'm sorry," I said, my voice cracking. Her thumbs brushed my skin.

"It's okay, babe. It's okay." She brought my face forward and kissed me. Even though I was being an asshole. Even though I was hiding something from her. She kissed me anyway.

～

Kyle

Something major was up with Stella. I'd never seen her so

freaked out. Completely freaked. She almost looked like she was going to be sick.

I wanted to know what it was, because I wanted to help her, but she closed right up and wouldn't tell. Just like she wouldn't tell me why she was such a bitch in front of everyone else, but not with me.

Stella had her secrets and I guess part of being with her was living with them. I could do it, because I wanted to be with her no matter what. It was a small price to pay for getting to kiss her and laugh with her and hold her hand.

She seemed like she wanted to be alone, so I left her and went home, feeling on edge. My parents asked what was wrong at dinner and I caved and told them. Not everything, but that Stella was being weird and I didn't know what to do about it.

"Do you think someone maybe said something mean to her?" Mom asked. That had been my first thought too. And my second thought was that someone had maybe threatened her. Who knows? But I was pretty sure she'd tell me about something like that. No, this was something different. And I was pretty sure Stella would have no problem telling someone that they could shove their homophobia right up their own ass.

"She just won't talk to me about certain things and it drives me crazy," I said, putting my head in my hands. I sighed and looked up to find my parents giving each other one of those looks that parents did when they didn't say anything out loud, but you could tell they were thinking the same thing. It was weird.

"Well, maybe you should give her some space? Some time? She might find that she'll want to come and talk to you, if you give her a little room." I'd thought about that and I didn't like it. I didn't like anything that put more space between us than there already was.

"I just don't want this to end before it's even started."

"Aw, honey, I'm sure it'll work out," Mom said. I loved that she was acting like this was just another relationship because, to her, it was.

"Girls are tough," Dad said and I burst out laughing.

"Doesn't make them any easier to understand being one, let me tell you," I said. In some ways I thought it was harder.

I TEXTED Stella once that night, telling her I was thinking of her and if she wanted to talk, I was there. She sent a goodnight message back and thanked me, but that was it. I knew I was going to see her in English the next day and I had no idea what she was going to say or what I was going to say or what the hell to do.

I made the mistake of looking online and succeeded in confusing myself and making myself more anxious about the whole thing. I stopped before I worked myself into a frenzy and tried to sleep, but it didn't work.

My alarm rang after only a few fitful hours of sleep and I wanted to tell my mom that I was sick and stay in bed and have her skip work and fuss over me like I was a little girl again. But what if Stella decided she did want to talk and then I wasn't there? I couldn't risk it.

So I dragged my ass out of bed and got dressed and threw some concealer on under my eyes, grateful that my glasses distracted people from how bad my dark circles were.

I wanted to chew on my nails, but they were both still polished, which only made me think of Stella even more. To be fair, just about everything made me think of her.

She beat me to English and her head snapped up when I walked in. She looked gorgeous, as always, but I could tell she hadn't slept well either.

"Hey," I said, sliding into my seat next to her.

"Hey," she said, her voice rough.

"Are you okay? I was worried about you," I said under my breath. "I almost called you so many times." She looked straight ahead.

"I'm sorry."

I didn't want her to apologize. I wanted her to talk to me.

"It's okay," I said, feeling a horrible sinking feeling in the pit of my stomach. "I just wish you would trust me." That made her look at me.

"I do trust you," she said, as if I'd uttered something ridiculous.

"Then why won't you talk to me?" I hissed. Shit, girls were difficult. Worth it, but difficult.

She looked like she was going to respond, but then didn't.

"I'm sorry," she said again, and I could tell she meant it. There was something holding her back. Someone must have broken her trust. Really broken it. There was so much more to Stella than met the eye and I was determined to find out. I wasn't going down without a hell of a fight. If she wanted one, she had one on her hands. I was stubborn as hell.

SHE HAD to work at the vet clinic on Wednesday night, so I drove there and waited for her to come out. I didn't think this would qualify as stalking. If she told me to leave, I'd get in my car, but I was going to give this a shot. I had to.

She didn't look surprised to see me when she came out, dressed in scrubs with her hair up. I'd never seen her in her work clothes and what looked like crap on most people on her, of course, were painfully cute.

"Just tell me to go, and I'll go," I said, holding my hands up to stop her from having the first word. She pulled her keys out of her purse, and when she exhaled her breath clouded in the air.

"I don't want you to," she said, and I knew she was really struggling.

"You don't have to talk to me. I don't want to put you in crisis. I don't want to tear you apart. I just want you to be happy." She started to cry and I pulled her into my arms, letting her rest her head on my shoulder. We were both freezing and she started to shake, but I wasn't moving. I would freeze to death out here. I would let all my fingers and toes turn black and fall off from frostbite. I would stay here and hold my girl.

I had come to the realization that I liked Stella. A lot. A lot, a lot. I wasn't going to call it "serious" yet, but it was getting there. This girl was probably going to wreck me and I was going to stand there and let her.

She finally lifted her head and sniffed. She had snot coming from her nose, but it was a testament to her beauty that she still took my breath away. I pulled her toward my car and made her get in, fishing a tissue out from the center console and handing it to her. She dabbed at her nose and her eyes and then stared out the windshield.

"You only know me now. You know me as the ice-cold bitch. I wasn't always like that and I think you know that. But I never told you why." I waited, nearly holding my breath.

"I wasn't popular in school. At all. I was more into books and my mom ran off and I don't really know why people didn't want to be friends with me. I tried. I tried so hard and in third grade, a group of girls that I wanted to be friends with started asking me to hang out with them. I was so excited that they invited me to their parties and sleepovers, but they only invited me to torment me. And it wasn't just stuff they said, there were other things they did." She shuddered.

"Anyway, I was so desperate to be friends with them, that I took it. I let them treat me worse than garbage. For years. There wasn't a day that went by that they didn't do something awful. As we got older, they got better at hiding what they were doing, so teachers didn't notice. I never told anyone. I had myself convinced that if I only put up with it long enough, they would let me in. They would like me." She inhaled and closed her eyes for a minute. I reached out tentatively and took her hand. She let me.

"I don't want to talk about the details, because honestly? I think I blocked a lot of it out. I didn't tell my dad. I wanted to handle it myself. Gabe knew, but there wasn't much he could do to protect me. So when I finally got to high school, I decided that I wasn't going to let that happen again. I wasn't going to be a victim. I was going to be a stone-cold bitch and not let them see that they could hurt me." Everything completely clicked into place. I knew she had a good reason and that was definitely it.

"That makes sense," I said and she looked back at me.

"Really? It doesn't make me a terrible person?" I frowned.

"Why would it make you a terrible person to protect yourself from people who hurt you for years?" She looked down at our hands.

"I don't know. I've never told anyone this. Midori already knew because she moved here in seventh grade. But other than that, no one else knows." I was honored. And totally pissed off. I wanted to throttle those stupid girls. WTF was wrong with them?

"I want to throat punch them all," I said and she laughed, just a little.

"I would like to see that," she said. "Anyway, things are different now and I guess I just got so used to it that I don't really know how to stop. And I was scared that if I let people see who I really was, that they wouldn't like it." Now that was ridiculous. Her personality was awesome. She was funny and sweet and so, so smart.

"Everyone would love you." There was a voice that whispered in the back of my mind *you already do.*

"I think that's an overstatement and you're a little biased, but thanks. That's really nice, Ky." I put my arms out and she let me hug her.

"Thank you so much for trusting me. I know this is a big deal for you. I just want to live up to it." She kissed my cheek.

"I do trust you. I don't know if I've ever trusted someone like I trust you. I mean, my family yes, but this is different. And then there are ways I don't trust you." The bottom dropped out of my stomach.

"What do you mean?"

She stared into my eyes, unblinking.

"I'm afraid that you're going to break my heart."

I couldn't breathe for several seconds.

"Well, that makes two of us," I said and we just gazed at one another.

"So, this is happening," she said and I nodded.

"This is happening."

Neither of us could say it. Not yet.

"Will you be my girlfriend?" I blurted out to stop myself from saying something else.

"Yeah. Yeah, I will." It felt like a proposal. I almost wished I had a ring. A visual reminder that we were together.

"This is a very intense moment," I said, stating the obvious. Stella just closed her eyes and brought her face to mine.

"Shut up."

"Shut up, *girlfriend*," I said into her mouth.

"Shut up, girlfriend."

Chapter Sixteen

STELLA

I couldn't believe that I told her, but just one day of essentially ignoring her was too much. I had been so miserable at work that even a basket of kittens couldn't cheer me up. It wasn't that I couldn't live without her, it was that I didn't like the way I'd treated her. I didn't like the words I'd said and I couldn't let it end like that. I would hate myself forever.

Even before she showed up, I vowed that I was going to call her and ask her to meet me somewhere so we could talk. But, of course, she beat me to it.

And then we'd talked and I'd told her and it was okay. Better than okay. I told her that I more than liked her and she felt the same and now I had a girlfriend.

My very first girlfriend.

We both had tons of homework that couldn't be ignored, so we couldn't hang out for long, so making out in the backseat of her car had to be cut tragically short.

I'd managed to get my hand most of the way up her shirt, brushing the underside of her bra. So. Close.

"We should stop," she gasped, breaking our kiss. I nodded, and ran a shaky hand through my hair.

"Uh huh," I said, pushing myself up with my arms. We'd gotten horizontal and if we'd had more time, we probably would have gotten a lot more naked.

My brain was scrambled and I was so turned on that I was in pain. I needed a shower. Stat.

We both scrambled out of her car and we were a little shaky, trying to get ourselves together to actually drive.

Kyle kissed me goodbye and whispered in my ear.

"I'm going to think about you all night." I shivered and she gave me a sly smile and wave before she yelled "Bye, girl-friend!" and drove away.

"Well, shit," I said, leaning against my car and telling my heart to calm down.

"YOU STAYED LATE TONIGHT," Dad said when I walked through the door and into the living room. I bet my face was still a little red, even though I'd driven past the house twice to try and get myself looking normal so I could face him. I sat on the couch nearest his leather wing chair where he read for pleasure.

"Um, sort of? I stayed late, but not to work. I, ah, had a talk with Kyle. You remember meeting her, right?" He put down his book.

"How could I forget?" A hint of a smile started to emerge.

"Stop it," I said, blushing.

"She's very cute. And smart, I'm guessing, if she's in AP English." I nodded.

"She is. She's number four in our class."

"Very nice. Is there something you want to tell me about

her?" Not really, but if I wanted to have her over, I was going to have to do this.

"Kyle and I are kind of . . . together. Together, together." He laughed.

"I get the point, Star. She's your girlfriend. Is that the term teens still use?" I raised one eyebrow. What else would you call it?

"Um, yes? A new term hasn't been invented yet, so we're going with girlfriend for now." Saying the word out loud made me want to do a bunch of standing back tucks.

"That's a big step. But she seems like a very nice girl. I'd like to meet her, talk to her more, if you want to have her over." My dad had never been one of those overbearing types that would threaten anyone that Gabe or I dated.

"Yeah, she's forcing me to meet her parents, so it's only fair, I guess." He chuckled.

"Seems so." We lapsed into silence and then I couldn't deal with it.

"I really like her. A lot." He gave me a gentle smile.

"You seem giddy. I haven't seen you like that." Because I never had been. I'd never felt so many overwhelming and fluttery and confusing and wonderful things all at once.

"The timing sucks. Because it's going to end. We're both going to head to different colleges and maybe try and stick it out for a while, but then we'll stop calling and it will just end." Dad leaned back in his chair. He always did that when he was going to give me some advice. He was very good at it.

"Or maybe it won't. Usually going into something thinking that you're going to lose is an excellent way to ensure that you do." I knew that, but could it really work? How many people actually stayed with their high school sweethearts? I'd heard the statistics and they were low. I bet they didn't even have any on LGBT couples in those kinds of surveys. Because we didn't really exist, probably.

"I don't know. I hate thinking about it. I just want to think about now and then deal with that later."

"That's probably a good idea. But give it a chance before you write it off completely. Love doesn't work out for everyone, I should know, but it can for some people. You might just get to be one of them." It was a little pessimistic, but Dad was like that. He didn't sugarcoat reality. Never had.

"Yeah, I guess. Anyway." I got up and gave him a kiss on the forehead. He wrapped his arm around my waist.

"I'm so proud of the woman you're becoming, my Star. So proud to call you my daughter." I had tears in my eyes that I wiped away before I hugged him back and went to the kitchen to make some dinner.

"YOU'RE TOTALLY MY GIRLFRIEND," Kyle said later that night as we sat in our separate beds in our separate rooms, pretending that we were together.

"Yup. You talked me into it. I was powerless against you," I said, being dramatic.

"Oh, shut up. I'm not the hot one." I snorted.

"I beg to differ, but we're never going to agree on that one."

"Probably not."

I leaned back and twirled some hair around my finger.

"Are we going to be out now? At school and everything?" I asked.

"Can we wait until next week?" she said.

"Absolutely. And I think we should prepare ourselves for people being . . . less than welcoming. Our families and besties are one thing, but who knows. That's another reason I didn't want to come out until I was in college. I figured it would just give everyone ammunition to shoot at me again. But now it doesn't seem so bad. I mean, I haven't dealt with it yet, so I might totally regret this." I laughed.

"Yeah, I've thought about that a lot. I mean, I don't care what people think, but having someone say something horrible about you in front of me is something that would make me so angry, I can feel my blood boiling just thinking about it. Ugh, I don't even want to talk about it." I could hear the anger in her voice and I felt the same way. I had protected myself, but I would slay some fucking dragons for Kyle.

"We aren't the first couple at school, though. There's Jane and Lexi and then Polly and Tris. I know there are more. They all hang out in a group together." It was a small school, but I'd always consciously avoided even making eye contact with any of them. Afraid that they would know. Afraid that they could see me. With their gaydar.

"That's true. Do you think we should make friends with them? It might be nice to talk to someone else who's been through this. Other than us." I'd thought about that too. As much as I loved the girls on the cheer team and Midori, this was something I couldn't share with them. They could sympathize, but they didn't know what it was like to care about another girl like this.

"But how do we go about it? Just walk up to them and ask to join their group?" That sounded painfully awkward. Definitely didn't want to do that.

"I don't know. Let's get through this week and tackle that next week. I feel like we have to go about this in steps. We'll get there eventually. I honestly can't wait for the day when I can just walk down the hallway with you and not worry." Yeah, me too.

"And when we can go on real dates not in one of our living rooms. I want to show you off, you sexy nerd." That made her laugh.

"I wanna show you off too, you beautiful thing. People are

probably going to think I've lost my mind for going out with you. After they get over the initial shock that Kyle Blake and Stella Lewis are gay as fuck." I burst out laughing and couldn't stop.

"I'm kind of looking forward to the looks on people's faces," she said. I hadn't thought of it that way. I'd always thought about it in a negative way. But maybe it would be good. It had been so far.

"You have a bad case of the giggles tonight, baby," she said because I couldn't stop laughing. "I think it's time to go to bed."

I stopped laughing and took a deep breath.

"Okay, I guess. I'll see you tomorrow. Bye, Ky."

I SENT her a text the minute I woke up with a picture of me doing a kissy face.

Good morning, my girlfriend.

She sent one back of her blowing me a kiss.

Hey, girlfriend, hey.

I skipped to the bathroom and I couldn't stop smiling. I also couldn't wait to get to school, which was pretty unusual. I didn't hate school, but if I had a choice, I wouldn't go there every day. I'd much rather hang out in a huge library somewhere, reading whatever I wanted, day after day. Someday I'd get to do that. Maybe.

I just happened to see Kyle getting out of her car when I parked in the student lot and I honked at her. She turned around to glare at the asshole who'd honked and then her face lit up when she saw me.

That look. That look was everything. I wanted to see that look on that face every day. Forever.

I told myself to chill out, but it was hard when I got out of the car and Kyle came over to say hello. The lot was busy and people were calling out greetings to one another and talking, so we had an audience so we couldn't kiss or anything.

"I couldn't wait to see you, is that crazy?" she asked as we stood with several feet of space between us, both leaning on my car.

I looked up at the grey sky. They were calling for snow, which was bizarre since it wasn't even November yet. It would definitely mess with the football schedule.

"No, because I couldn't wait to see you," I said, turning back toward her.

"I want to kiss you so bad right now, baby," she said, reaching out to touch my face, but then pulling back.

"Soon. Soon you can do that all you want. It's Wednesday. Just a few more days and the week is over. And next week . . ." I trailed off.

Next week.

"We'll have to make a plan." She agreed.

"Definitely. I think that means we should spend the entire weekend together making said plan. We really have to think through all the possible scenarios." She was saying one thing, but meaning something entirely different, something that made my skin tingle.

"I think that can be arranged," I said, my fingers aching to touch her.

"Good. It's a date." She winked and then pushed off my car to walk to homeroom. I gave her a head start and then walked behind her. Mostly to check out her ass. She'd started wearing tighter jeans lately for some reason and I was very much enjoying the view.

I had to go to a different building and by the time I sat down in homeroom, I had a text on my phone.

Stop ogling my ass.

I snorted and then sent her back a winky face.

KYLE

"So? What's the update?" Grace said to me as we were supposed to be doing an experiment in chem.

"With what?" I asked, adjusting the height of the flame so it didn't hit the ceiling and burn a hole through it.

"With you-know-who?" I stood up.

"Voldemort?" Grace gave me a look like I was being dense.

"Oh, oh, *that*. Things are good? Really good." I bit my lip and Grace bumped her hip with mine.

"Sounds like it. So are you guys going public?" I did a quick sweep of the room, but everyone else was immersed in what they were doing.

"Soon," I said and then we both pretended to be working very diligently as our teacher walked by.

"I've got your back. And hers, by extension. And I think I should get to hang out with both of you. I've never seen you in a relationship like this before." That was because there hadn't been one. There was nothing like this. I didn't know if it was because we were both girls. I'd never find out. But I did know that what I felt for Stella was something big.

Something beautiful and new and amazing.

"You get all smiley when you're thinking about her."

"Stop it," I said, smacking her arm.

"I FEEL like we haven't seen you in forever," Paige said at lunch. I had no idea what she was talking about. I'd eaten with them yesterday.

"Okay?" I said, unsure of whether or not I was supposed to apologize.

"You've just seemed kinda distant," Molly chimed in. I

looked around and every single one of them was wearing an uncomfortable look.

"Is this some sort of intervention?" I said, looking around and landing on Grace. She had her arms crossed and looked like she didn't approve of whatever they were doing.

"No, that's stupid. We just miss you, that's all." Molly's face went red and I had half a mind to get up from the damn table and leave all of them.

"I'm literally sitting right here. Talking to you. I'm not off slitting my wrists, or hanging out and smoking pot under the overpass. So I really have no idea what the fuck is going on." I didn't mean to get so pissed, but I felt like I was being attacked or something.

"Just leave her alone, guys. All of you," Grace said, sending a glare around that made some of them cower. The guys had been avoiding eye contact with me the whole time.

"So, did anyone hear what Chad Hoskins got arrested with?" Grace said and that got everyone talking again. Thanks, Chad.

But I still had an uneasy feeling in my stomach when I tossed my tray.

"I told them not to," Grace said in my ear. "I really did. I told them to leave you alone and that you were fine, but then Molly started going on and on about her cousin who's on crack or something and it got blown out of proportion. If you decide to, ah, *tell people*, next week, I think they'll lay off. Not that that's a reason to do it. But it would give them an explanation. You know?"

I understood what she was saying, but I still felt like they were backing me into a corner.

Fuck it. If they were going to be assholes about me being happy, then they weren't my real friends anyway. And since when did happy = being on drugs?

Fucked up. I sent Stella a text about it.

OMG, your friends are weird. But maybe they'll leave you alone next week?

Hopefully. We didn't have anyone else gay in our group that I knew of. No one really said anything outright that was homophobic, but you never knew. It was like rolling dice, but instead of winning money, you got the freedom to live and not be harassed.

~

"SO I TALKED to one of the other gays today," Stella said that afternoon as we hung out at her house. Her dad was teaching late tonight, so we had several hours of uninterrupted time. I wanted to spend most of it making out and doing other things, but she seemed to want to talk.

"Which one?" I asked.

"Tris. It just kind of happened. She was in the bathroom and we were using the sinks at the same time. I said hello and she gave me a look like I was going to punch her in the face. So then I tried a smile and she sort of gave me one back and then scurried away." I couldn't stop laughing. My girl was intimidating.

"You probably scared the shit out of her. I bet she thinks you're going to target her or something. It's going to be funny to see what she says when she knows the truth." She laughed with me and then moved so her head was in my lap. I ran my fingers through her hair and she closed her eyes.

"That feels really good. I can't remember the last time someone else played with my hair." She curled up almost like a cat. I wouldn't have been surprised if she started purring.

"Don't fall asleep, baby." We had some stupid reality show on that neither of us was paying attention to. I was too busy focusing all my attention on her.

"I won't. What if they hate us?"

"Who?" She turned her head and looked up at me.

"The other gays." Was she serious?

"Why would they? And don't they kind of have to accept us? Based on the fact that there's safety in numbers." I had no experience with this, but it made sense. And we had a lot in common with them, so why wouldn't we get along?

I had definitely realized, early on in knowing her, that Stella had issues when it came to trusting other people. Especially trusting that they weren't going to hate her right off the bat. It was shitty, but the only way she'd realize that not everyone was an asshole was to introduce her to more people who were going to adore her just the way she was. Not the bitch queen. The beautiful girl who spent an entire summer with Tolstoy. The girl who loved animals and laughed in the library and was passionate about cheerleading. If anyone didn't like that girl, they had some serious issues.

"I guess you're right. I just don't like meeting new people." I stroked her temple.

"I know, baby. But I think this will be good. For both of us. As much as I like living in our bubble, I think it's time for us to get out. I don't want to turn into people that never leave their houses or go out in the sunlight." She giggled.

"I think we're going to be fine." I leaned down and kissed her head.

"Yeah, we are. We're gonna be fine."

THE WEATHER WARMED UP AGAIN (if you don't like the weather in Maine, wait five minutes) so the game was on for Friday. I was a little nervous about going, but excited about seeing Stella cheer. She was just so good at it.

My friends had backed off after that little "talk" they'd had with me during lunch on Wednesday, but I could tell they were still watching me.

"Don't let them force you into anything," Grace said, leaning over as we froze our asses off on the bleachers.

"I'm not. Stella and I are tired of hiding. We want to be like everyone else. And it's not like we're ashamed, you know? I'm proud of her." My eyes flicked over to her as she made a funny face at Midori.

"Good. And if you need anyone to kick someone's ass for you, I volunteer." I didn't want her to do that, but her heart was in the right place.

"Thanks."

"What are best friends for?" She put her arm around me and we snuggled closer together.

"I wish someone looked at me like that," she said and I tore my eyes away from Stella. Again.

"Huh?"

Grace nodded in Stella's direction.

"I wish someone looked at me the way you look at her." I gaped at her and she just grinned.

"It's really sweet. I'm not jealous, I swear." Last year, Grace had broken up with her boyfriend she'd had since junior high when he went to a private school an hour away. I knew she still cried about it every now and then. I almost felt like I was rubbing my happiness in her face.

"Grace—" I started to say, but she put her hand up.

"It's not your fault. I'm really, really happy for you. Just makes me miss when I felt like that." I put my arm around her.

"You will again."

"Promise?"

"Promise."

The game finally started, but I paid even less attention to what was happening on the field than I usually did. Too busy looking at my girl.

She kept flashing looks back at me and once she even winked. She'd asked me if I wanted to come hang out with her and her friends after the game and I'd turned her down, but now I was rethinking it.

"Do you want to go to the barn party with me?" There was a guy, Raylan Ford, whose parents had a farm with an old barn on their property and didn't really care what he and his friends did to it since they were just going to demolish it anyway.

Grace made a face.

"I'd rather not subject myself to the rednecks tonight." I had a feeling she'd say that, and I didn't blame her. As liberal as our little town was, it was still incredibly white and people didn't get called out on their shit as much as they should sometimes.

"Yeah, okay," I said, looking back at Stella.

"But for you, I'll do it. Unless someone says something. Then I'm out." I stared at her.

"Seriously?" That was a best friend right there.

"Yeah, who knows? It could be fun." I wasn't sure about that. I'd never gone to one of the barn parties because it had never appealed to me, but Stella appealed to me and anywhere she was, that was where I wanted to be. So we were going to a barn party.

I WAITED on the bleachers for Stella to pack up her stuff and for most of the crowd from the game to disperse. Grace said she had to "get something from her car" so she'd left me by myself a few minutes ago.

"Hey, baby," Stella said, coming over. "I bet I could give you a hug right now and no one would think anything." I got up and put my arms out and she walked into them.

"Hi," I said, hugging her and not even caring that she was sweaty.

"Hi back. I saw you staring at me."

"Am I not allowed to stare at my girlfriend?" She pulled back and I reached up to adjust the bow she had on top of her head, adorning her high ponytail.

"Oh, that's right. You totally are." She gave me a sweet smile.

"So, I think Grace and I are going to the barn party." Her face lit up.

"Really? That would be so great. Then we can all hang out together. My theory is if we bring our groups together enough, they'll just mesh and make one big group." She was so cute.

"We'll see." I gave her another hug and said I would meet her at the party with Grace.

I headed to my car and found Grace leaning on it, messing with her phone.

"I can drive so we only have to take one car. You just say the word and I'll bring you back."

She gave me a thumbs up and we got in the car.

Chapter Seventeen

STELLA

I was both apprehensive and exited that Kyle was coming to the party. Both feelings churned in my stomach as I drove myself and Midori way out to the boonies where the barn was.

"So she's coming?" I'd told Midori that Kyle and Grace were going to meet us there.

"Yup. We're not going to be official, but this is the first time we've hung out in public together, so . . ." I turned off onto a dirt road and slowed down so my car wouldn't bottom out on the potholes.

"It's a shame you can't just be together like everyone else." I swerved to avoid a huge branch and winced as we bumped over the uneven road. We'd had to take the back way to the farm because the cops in town liked to cruise and try and find parties to bust.

"Yeah, it is. Someday, though."

At last we arrived and I parked my car in the field next to a rusted-out truck and looked for Kyle. I sent her a text and then saw her waving from another row of cars.

Midori and I walked over and joined Kyle and Grace.

"Hey," I said to both of them. I hoped this wasn't going to be painfully awkward.

Kyle just grabbed my hand and then gave me a kiss on the cheek. I was stunned when I pulled back.

"Sorry, couldn't help it."

"They're so cute it's painful," Grace said to Midori.

"Tell me about it."

And that was it.

The four of us headed to the party, Kyle and I holding hands since it was dark and no one would probably see. Grace and Midori started talking about comics (apparently Midori's older sister was going to college to do the art for graphic novels) and completely ignored us.

"Well, that worked out," Kyle said in my ear as we approached the barn. A couple of people had a bonfire going near (but not too near) the barn and were throwing shit on it and yelling as the sparks flared up. There was music coming from the open barn doors.

I sighed and dropped Kyle's hand. It was like a punch in the stomach until she grabbed it back.

"No. I'm not hiding. I'm not stopping myself from touching you because of other people. Seriously, fuck that." I stopped walking and turned to face her.

"Really?"

"Hell, yeah. I was thinking about it all day today and I'm ready. I'm ready for this." She held up our joined hands and I felt tears in the corners of my eyes.

"So this is it? We're doing this at a shitty barn party where everyone will probably be too stoned or drunk to remember on Monday?" She shrugged.

"Guess so."

Midori and Grace had stopped walking ahead of us, just at the entrance to the barn. They both looked down at our hands and then started clapping.

"Oh, shut up," Kyle said.

"I used to think you were a complete bitch, but Kyle has assured me that you aren't, so I'm giving you the benefit of the doubt," Grace said, looking at me.

"Thank you?"

"Uh huh," she said and then started talking to Midori again.

"Let's go, baby," Kyle said, tugging on my hand.

I WASN'T sure what I expected when we walked in. Maybe an explosion. Or for everyone to comically freeze and gasp in unison.

Neither of those things happened.

"We got this," Kyle said, squeezing my hand. A few people glanced over, looked down at our joined hands and then just started talking again. One dude yelled out "Hey, dykes!" but he was standing on a barrel and fell off immediately after.

"This isn't so bad," I said as we found a corner away from the music that had a few rotting benches we could sit on. We had to walk through pockets of pot smoke and I was glad the ceiling of the barn was basically gone so we weren't drowning in it. The beams were strung with lanterns and half-dead twinkle lights, all powered with orange extension cords. The entire thing was probably a fire hazard, but so far, so good.

"We're going to get drinks," Midori said. "Do you guys want anything?" I looked at Kyle.

"Water? Or Coke. Nothing alcoholic," I said and Kyle agreed. Grace and Midori went off for the drinks and it was just the two of us.

"This is so weird," Kyle said, leaning closer to me and then kissing me on the cheek.

"But not weird at the same time," I said, kissing the back of her hand.

"Exactly."

~

A FEW GIRLS from the squad came over and they were stunned for a few seconds, but after we talked to them and said, yes, we were together, they wanted to know everything.

"OMG, can I come to your wedding?" Candace asked.

"Um, we literally just started dating. I think it's a little early for that. Right, babe?" Kyle blushed and there was a chorus of awwws. It was a bit like being an exhibit in a zoo. Finally, their curiosity was satisfied and a bunch of them went to dance.

"I guess we're cute," Kyle said as Midori and Grace came back and handed us our drinks.

"You are cute. It's gross," Grace said, popping the top of her soda. A lot of the cheer girls were dancing with their boyfriends or other guys all in one big heaving clump. I remembered doing that and it had been fun, but I wasn't a fan of having a guy pressing his dick into my ass and then getting a hard-on while we were grinding.

"Whatever," Kyle said.

I expected more attention from the guys, but a lot of them were out at the bonfire, busy with their own girls, or drunk off their asses.

I did hear a few wolf whistles and one guy walked by and asked if we would bang him, but we just ignored him. It honestly wasn't that bad. So far. I kept waiting for the other shoe to drop.

"I shouldn't stay too late. My parents are actually enforcing my curfew now," Kyle said with a rueful smile. "I never had a reason to stay out before you, girlfriend."

"I'm flattered," I said, fluttering my lashes at her.

"Hey, you're not the only gays at this party," Grace said, pointing with her soda can.

Across the room were Tris and her girlfriend, Polly, standing close together and talking with some people. I'd never seen them interacting that much outside of their usual group.

"Should we go say something?" Kyle asked. "What's the protocol here?"

I laughed.

"I have no idea. But maybe we should let them come to us. I'm sure word has gotten out by now." It definitely would by Monday. We'd really done this with a bang, but why the hell not?

Someone turned the music up since more people had moved out to the makeshift dance floor in the middle of the room.

"Do you want to dance with me?" I asked Kyle and her face went white.

"Um, no. I don't think so." She looked away from me. I glanced at Grace and she just gave me a shrug.

"Why not?" I asked, brushing a wisp of hair over her ear.

She heaved a heavy sigh.

"In case you hadn't noticed, I'm not very coordinated. And you are a goddess." I almost laughed. No one had ever called me that before.

"Everyone can dance." She gave me a look as if I'd said something stupid.

"Oh, this is ridiculous, come on." I stood up and pulled her to her feet, against her protests.

"We won't go over there," I said, pointing to the main floor. "We'll dance right here."

I closed my eyes for a second and the song switched to a country song with a fast and driving beat.

"Stellll," Kyle whined. "I don't want to do this." I gave her the quickest of kisses and winked.

"You will."

I turned around and grabbed her hands, placing them on my hips as I found the beat of the music and started moving my hips. Kyle was stiff for a second.

"Just follow me," I said, leaning my head back against her.

She finally started moving with me.

"Fuck," she breathed in my ear. I smiled and melted into her.

Our bodies fit. Perfectly. As if they were made for one another. Curves against curves. Her fingers dug into my hips and I couldn't get over the feel of her against my back and her hips moving with mine.

The only downside was that I couldn't see her face, so I rotated until we were facing one another.

She didn't let go of my hips. I put my hands on her shoulders and then we were dancing face-to-face and I would never, for the rest of my life, forget the way she looked at me.

As if she wanted to devour me and worship me at the same time. I couldn't look away from her green eyes.

I'd never wanted anything the way I wanted her.

The song finally ended and we were both breathing hard. It flipped to another country song that I wasn't as fond of.

"I want you so bad right now," Kyle said, pressing her forehead to mine. My fingers shook a little as I held her face and kissed her lips.

"Me, too."

Our eyes locked and I knew it was only a matter of time. I wanted to take her hand and drag her out and fuck her in the backseat of my car. Hell, I'd settle for a nice patch of grass.

"I can't even think," Kyle said. "I can't even think about anything but you."

The words clogged the back of my throat, desperate to get out. I clamped my mouth shut. I couldn't. Not yet.

Not yet.

"I want to do so many things right now, Ky," I whispered. She made a little sound in the back of her throat that didn't help the situation at all.

"I think I have an idea what you're thinking of."

I smiled.

"Oh, do you?"

"Would you like me to draw you a diagram?" I laughed and then someone cleared their throat. I turned away from Kyle to snarl at whoever had interrupted us, only to find Tris and Polly standing there with amused looks on their faces.

"Can we help you?" I asked, trying to be nice.

"We, ah, just wanted to say hello," Tris said. She and Polly made a cute pair, with Tris rocking a button-up and suspenders, and Polly in a dress that would have made a 50s housewife proud, and bright lipstick. Tonight it was an almost neon pink.

"And you had to do that *now*?" I wondered aloud. Kyle stepped away from me.

"Sorry about her. She's just a little cranky." I gaped at her.

"I know what that's like," Polly said, shooting a look at Tris, who was busy staring at me with her eyes narrowed.

"Don't be grumpy. However cute it is," Polly said to Tris, leaning up on her tiptoes to kiss Tris' cheek. Polly was significantly shorter than Tris, even with her heels on.

"So, looks like you two are . . ." Polly said, trailing off, letting us fill in the blanks.

Kyle rested her chin on my shoulder and slid her arms around me.

"Yup," she said. "Surprised?"

Polly and Tris shared a look.

"A little," Polly admitted. "But you never know, do you? How long have you guys been together?"

"Little while," I said. Tris was still giving me a look like I was just fucking with her.

"We're not faking it. If that's what you're thinking," I said directly to Tris.

"I wasn't thinking anything," she said.

"Yeah, okay. The way you've been looking at us is totally normal, sure." Kyle squeezed my sides to tell me to shut up.

"Just surprised. Didn't expect you to be one of us." That made me want to start chanting "One of us, one of us."

I raised an eyebrow.

"So being gay is like a cult now?" Tris rolled her eyes.

"You know that's not what I meant."

"Okay, then. I'm gay, so is she, and we're super gay together. Got it? Good." I turned around and kissed Kyle full on the mouth. I didn't need to prove anything to them, but I did it anyway.

"Does that clear it up for you?" I asked, turning back around, feeling a little dizzy. Kyle's mouth always did that to me.

"You're really cute together," Polly said, leaning against Tris. "You're like the perfect femme couple." At least she hadn't called us lipstick lesbians.

I leaned back against Kyle again.

"Thank you," I said.

"So, now that we've established that we're all girls who like girls, maybe we could, um, talk like normal people?" Kyle said. "Because it's just been the two of us and it would be really nice to talk to someone else."

That seemed to do the trick.

Tris finally melted and we started talking about our various coming out stories. Guess Tris' family wasn't as accepting as mine and Kyle's and she'd had a real hard time of it.

"I'm sorry," I said, really meaning it. She shrugged it off.

"Not your fault. Just the way things are. That's why I can't wait to get out of this hick town and go to college."

"Where are you headed?"

"Austin," she said, putting her arm over Polly's shoulder. "We're both going to UT." I still hadn't figured out where the hell I wanted to go. Kyle and I had been purposely avoiding college talk. I didn't want to be one of those people who had to factor in their girlfriend for their college decision. Even though I probably would.

"Yup, it's gonna be awesome. We're going to get a little apartment and a dog and it will be sunny all the time," Polly said. She was bright and bubbly and constantly moving. I liked her. The jury was still out on Tris, but she seemed to be warming up. I wasn't really one to talk about being standoffish anyway.

Grace and Midori came over and we introduced them.

Somehow, we all ended up talking for a while and it wasn't a big deal at all.

Kyle squeezed my shoulder.

"Baby, I've got to get home." I turned and gave her a sad smile.

"Okay, I'll go with you to your car." Grace wanted to stay and asked if I could give her a ride.

"See you on Monday!" Polly said, waving at us as we left. I took Kyle's hand as we slowly made our way back to her car. The bonfire had mostly burned itself out, but there were still people throwing shit on it to get it going again.

"That was interesting," Kyle said.

"Just a little bit. What do you think Monday is going to be like?" She shook her head.

"No idea. But if it was anything like this, I think it'll be good. I guess people just don't care. Which is awesome for us." Definitely. I knew it wasn't all going to be good, but so far, my worst fears hadn't come true.

"I loved dancing with you," she said when we got to her car.

"Yeah?" I asked and then had the breath knocked out of me as she pushed me up against the door of the car.

"Yeah," she said before her mouth crashed down on mine and she kissed me like she needed me to breathe.

Her hands fumbled under my shirt and then she was caressing my bare skin and I was honestly going to die or shatter into a million pieces. She didn't get to be the only one doing the touching, so I slid my fingers under the hem of her shirt and brushed the smooth skin of her stomach.

We both trembled and gasped and it was going to kill me.

"I want you so much," she said into my mouth.

"You can have me. You can have everything," I said back.

She laughed. A low, sexy sound.

"Is that so?" Her fingers brushed the edge of my bra and I wished I wasn't wearing one.

"Yes. Fuck, yes."

She pulled back to look into my eyes.

"*Everything?*"

I knew exactly what she was asking, and what my answer would mean for both of us.

"Yes."

Kyle

I didn't really mean to attack her like that, it just kind of happened. There were no protests as I kissed her and shoved my hands up her shirt. I'd been wanting to touch her skin since we'd danced.

Holy shit, the dancing. I hadn't known it was going to be like *that*. I'd pictured tripping over my feet and embarrassing myself, but she'd taken the lead and it turned out that moving my hips with hers didn't require any thinking on my part.

My body just wanted hers. Followed hers. It was natural, to be with her like that. It had made me want to tell her to drive somewhere and park, but then we'd been interrupted. I definitely had to go home now, but I wasn't going to stop thinking about it.

I also wasn't going to stop thinking about telling Stella how I felt about her. *Really* tell her. Because there was only one word for it and I wanted to tell her before we had sex. I wanted her to know that it wasn't just about needing to fuck her.

"Me too," I said. "I want you to have everything. I want it to be you." *I always want it to be you.*

She smiled slowly.

"I will keep that in mind. Later. When I'm in bed." I groaned and she giggled.

"You're just as bad, you know. My wrists have been getting quite a workout since I fell in love with you."

"What?"

She gasped, as if she hadn't meant to say it.

"Oh, shit. I said that out loud, didn't I?" I grabbed onto her shoulders because I felt like I was going to fall over.

"Did you just say that you love me?" My voice squeaked on the word. She swallowed and I could see the panic in her eyes.

"Yes. I did. Because I do. Love you. I don't care if it's too soon, or if we're seniors and heading to different colleges. I don't care. I love you, baby." She stroked my face and I wondered if it was possible for your heart to stop and still live.

"You love me?" There were tears in her eyes.

"Yeah, I do. I tried to fight it, but you're just too damn cute." I laughed a little, still completely overwhelmed.

"Okay. You love me. That's really good, I guess, because I love you too. It would be bad if one of us felt it and the other one didn't. But we're good." She squealed and threw herself on me.

"I thought it was going to freak you out, which is why I hadn't said it before." I leaned into her, smelling her hair.

"I've wanted to say it too. Guess we're both idiots." We laughed together and I reluctantly let her go.

"I really, really have to get home or else my parents are going to kill me. And I don't want them getting mad at me because then they won't let you come over or let me come see you, so." I babbled. Stella gave me one last lingering kiss.

"Okay. I'll see you tomorrow, then." We had plans to hang out all day together, including going to the movies and having lunch. Like a real couple.

"See you tomorrow, baby." I didn't want to let her go.

"Oh, by the way, I love you," she said.

"Oh, hey, me too," I said, getting into my car.

She loved me.

I MADE it home with two minutes to spare.

"Did you have fun with Grace?" Mom asked. She looked up from the paperback she was reading. When I'd texted her to say that I was going out after the game, I told her Grace and I were getting pizza with the rest of my friends. Oops.

"Yeah, we did actually." I didn't want to walk too close to her because I was pretty sure my clothes reeked of pot smoke. The one downside of the night.

"Good, good. Listen, I want to talk with you." Uh oh. I leaned against the wall, but she patted the spot next to her on the couch.

I reluctantly walked over because saying no would only make her more suspicious.

"I know you're going out with Stella now and you know your father and I fully support it, but I don't want you to take that to mean we don't have rules for you. If you were dating a boy, we'd have the same rules." Actually, I'd been wondering when she was going to throw this at me. Stella couldn't get me pregnant, but that wasn't their only concern, I was sure.

"Okay," I said. She stared at me, probably expecting more resistance.

"Okay, so. Your curfew is still in place and when you go out on dates, we want to know where you're going and when you're going to be back. I would also prefer that you seriously consider the consequences of any, ah, activity." Shit, we were having a sex talk. We'd had one before, but now things were different.

"I'm not going to tell you what to do because I know you're smart enough to know what's right for you, but I do want you to be careful. Okay? And I know you're going to be off at college and can do whatever you want, but I'm still having a problem realizing that you're all grown up. When did that happen?" She sighed.

"Thanks. I can do that," I said.

"Good. I can see how much you care about her, and I just want to wrap you up in a bubble so you don't get your heart broken, but I know that I can't do that."

"I really like her, Mom. A lot." She stroked my head.

"I know. I can see it. And I still want to meet her."

I didn't want to share just how much I liked Stella. Not yet.

"I'll ask her about it." I was going to put that off as long as possible.

Mom looked down at her wedding ring. "I fell in love with your father when I was fourteen, so I know that it can happen when you're young and that it can last. Even if I could have dated around and gotten married later, I wouldn't have picked anyone else." I wouldn't pick anyone else but Stella, but it was impossible to know the future.

"Anyway, I just wanted to have that little talk with you. I love you, honey." I leaned in and she gave me a hug.

"I love you, too." She didn't mention anything about pot smoke and I scurried away to change my clothes.

"SO, is this our first real date?" I asked when Stella picked me up the next day. I'd told my mom where we were going and when we were going to be back and she hounded me again about having Stella over for dinner so I guess that was going to happen sooner rather than later. My mom was persistent.

"I don't know. Do you count last night?" Shit. Last night. After I'd gone back to my room I'd undressed and thought about kissing Stella as I got myself off.

Four times.

"I don't know. Let's see how today goes and then we'll decide." I turned on the radio and flipped through the stations.

"But we need to know the anniversary of our first date so we can celebrate." Good point.

"Okay, last night can be our first date and this can be our first date-date." I found the pop station and hummed along to the current song that was playing twenty-four seven.

"What's a date-date?" We argued about that for the rest of the way to the movie theater. I bought the tickets and Stella got the popcorn and sodas.

"I can't believe we're doing this," I said, taking the popcorn from her and handing her a ticket.

"We're dating just like normal people."

"I know, right?" We laughed and headed into the theater.

The movie was one of the latest romantic blockbusters. I hadn't really cared about seeing it, but I figured if we weren't watching the movie, we could potentially make out in the back of the theater.

"Let's sit back there," I said, pointing to the last row of

seats. There were only a few people and they sat way up front, so we were pretty alone back there.

"I know why you want us to sit back here and I completely approve of it," Stella said, sitting down and putting her soda in the cup holder.

"Good. I was hoping you would." I popped a piece of popcorn into my mouth and smiled at her.

"Don't eat it all," she said, shoving her hand into the tub.

"I'll share because I love you." I tilted the tub toward her and she smiled.

"Aw, you're so sweet. You're trying to out-sweet me." We had nearly finished the popcorn by the time the previews started. Stella pulled some wipes out of her purse and we cleaned the fake butter off our fingers.

She leaned over and I put my arm around her.

"I've never done this before. Not even with a boy," she said, leaning closer.

"Me neither," I said watching her eyes glow from the light of the screen.

She kissed me softly and then turned to watch the movie.

I just wanted to watch her, so I did. Half of my attention was on the movie (which was very heterosexual) and half was on her. The way she smiled, the way she laughed, how she concentrated.

"Stop staring at me," she whispered at one point.

"Can't help it," I said. She smirked and then reached her hand over, sliding it slowly up my thigh. I went rigid in my seat and Stella laughed softly next to me.

Shit.

Her fingers leisurely walked their way up my leg and stopped on the top of my thigh. She squeezed gently and then withdrew her hand.

"You are evil," I whispered. "I'm going to get you for that."

"God, I hope so."

"I WONDER if anyone knows we're on a date," Stella said as we were seated at the restaurant. It was just one of those nicer chain places, but I didn't care as long as we were together.

"Probably not. They just think we're friends." I looked around, but no one was paying attention to us.

"I could kiss you and then that would make things clear. Or we could sit on the same side and feed each other." I made a face.

"I love you, but I draw the line at feeding each other. Unless it's like, chocolate strawberries or something." Her eyes lit up.

"Ohhhh, that would be sexy. We should do that for our anniversary or something." I thought the anniversary talk was a little premature, but it was really sweet that she thought that way.

Our server came over and took our drink orders and asked if we were ready to order food.

"I think we'll have the spinach and artichoke dip as an ap, right, baby?" Stella said, winking at me. The server, a guy who probably wasn't much older than us looked from Stella to me and his face went red.

"Sure, babe. That sounds good," I said, grinning at her. The guy stuttered that he was going to put that order in. We waited until he left before we started laughing.

"I think you just gave that guy a heart attack. You're so bad." Stella shrugged.

"If he's scared by lesbians than I have some bad news for him. We're everywhere." I snorted.

"So, what did you think about Tris and Polly? They're really cute, right? I think we could be friends with them," I said and Stella put down her menu.

"Polly is adorable. I feel bad about Tris, though. I can

understand why she was a little suspicious of us at first." It was a reminder that not everyone was as accepting as our friends and families.

"I think we could be friends with them. It would be nice to have gay friends." I agreed.

I told her about my mom's little "talk" she'd had with me last night and she laughed.

"My dad hasn't said anything to me. I guess he figures that since I'm going to be in college he might as well not bother." I wish my mom had felt that way.

"Has she backed off about the practice essays?" she asked me after we ordered our food.

"Not at all. Her new idea is to have me write about being gay. She thinks they'll be more eager to accept me because of 'diversity.'" I put the word "diversity" in air quotes.

"She did not."

"Swear to God. And I might actually do it. I mean, I have a lot of things to say about and it's better than writing something stupid that I don't care about." Our dip came and Stella dove for the first chip.

"That's a good point. Maybe I'll take a leaf out of your book." I snorted.

"I'll let you take a leaf out of my book anytime, baby." Stella threw a chip at me.

"That was a terrible innuendo."

"Made you think about me naked, though, didn't it?" Her face went red.

"Everything makes me think about you naked, Ky."

Chapter Eighteen

STELLA

I finally agreed to go over to Kyle's house for a dinner with her family on Sunday. I figured the sooner I got it over with, the better.

Kyle opened the door and gave me a nervous smile.

"Don't freak out," she whispered as she held the door open.

"Stella, it's so nice to officially meet you," Kyle's mom said. "You can call me Kate and this is my husband Cody." I shook both of their hands and gave Kate the flowers I'd picked up at the grocery store on the way over. I figured it couldn't hurt to suck up a little.

"These are lovely, thank you," Kate said as I followed Kyle into the living room. After Kate put the flowers in some water, we all sat in the living room and I prepared to be grilled.

Kyle took my hand and squeezed it. I stole a glance at her parents, but they didn't seem too upset.

"So, Stella, Kyle says you're a big reader," Kate said.

"Yeah, my father's an English professor so it was kind of inevitable." I laughed a little nervously and then Kate started asking me about my favorite books and that opened up a book discussion and I finally started to relax.

Dinner was roast chicken with mashed potatoes and salad and it went off without a hitch. Kyle kept squeezing my hand under the table to reassure me that I was doing okay.

"What are your college plans?" I'd been hoping I could get out of this dinner without talking about that, since it was a sore spot for me and Kyle.

"I'm not sure yet. My dad doesn't really care where I go as long as I study something I care about." Kate and Cody shared a look. I knew that wasn't their philosophy when it came to Kyle, but I wasn't going to lie.

There was a bit of an awkward silence until Kyle asked for her mom to pass the potatoes and then mentioned that I was a cheerleader, so they started asking me about that.

"Mom?" Kyle said as we cleared up the dishes and took them to the sink. "We're going to hang out in my room, okay?"

"Keep the door open!" she called from the living room.

I gave Kyle a look and she winked.

"ARE we ever gonna talk about college?" she said as we both sat on her bed, me at one end and her at the other. Just in case her mom decided to drop in with a plate of cookies or something.

I looked up at her ceiling.

"How about we not?"

"Baby, why don't you want to talk about it?" Wasn't it obvious?

"Because it makes me think about us being over." She stared at me.

"Why? Because we might go to different schools and then break up?" Obviously.

"It's just . . . it's not realistic." She rolled her eyes.

"That's bullshit and you know it. We're not other people. We're us. And we love each other."

"So?" I said.

"So?! That's the whole point!" Her mom walked by and poked her head in.

"Everything okay in here?"

"Yup, just fine," Kyle said, her voice on edge. I gave her a smile and she left heading back to the living room.

"You wouldn't even consider going to the same school?" she asked, picking at one of her pillows.

"That seems like a recipe for a breakup."

"Okay, so should we just break up now and save ourselves some time?" I groaned.

"That isn't what I meant." She hugged the pillow to her chest.

"Then what *do* you mean?"

"I mean that I don't want to talk or fight about this, which is why I've been avoiding it for so long."

Silence fell over us.

"I'd want to go where you go," she said quietly.

"Yeah?"

She looked up.

"Of course. I figure one college is pretty much like the next and I don't think wanting to go to the same place as the girl I love is a stupid reason to pick one school over another. People pick schools for a lot worse reasons." She did have a point there.

"But what if it doesn't work out?" She stared at me and I was uncomfortable with the intensity in her eyes.

"And what if it does?"

I didn't have an answer to that.

⌒

THINGS WERE a little weird after that conversation, so I decided to head home sooner than I might have. I had a lot on my mind, but I still gave Kyle a kiss goodbye and told her I would text her later in that night.

Dad was home and in the living room with a book, as usual. He looked up and must have seen the look on my face.

"What's wrong? Did the dinner not go well?" I sighed and crashed on the couch, leaning back and closing my eyes. It felt like this day had lasted forever. I was exhausted and it wasn't even eight.

"No, it did. Kyle and I had a little bit of a fight about college. She doesn't see a problem with picking a college based on where I'm going and I think that's a recipe for disaster." He put a bookmark in his book (no dog-earing pages. Blasphemy!) and set it down.

"Why do you think it's a recipe for disaster?" Was he serious?

"Because it's not a good reason to pick a school." He gazed at me.

"Why?"

"Because it's not!" Why couldn't anyone understand this? It was a known fact.

"It seems to me that making a decision based on what matters most to you would be the best way to go. So perhaps making a list of the things that matter to you might be a valuable exercise." I opened my mouth to argue, but then all I could think of was Kyle and I making the list of reasons that girls were better.

"But what if it ends?" I said.

"What if it does? You can always transfer, or, if you're at a big enough school, it might not even be an issue. I'm not telling you to go one way or the other, but what I don't want you to do is make a decision based on what you think you're *supposed* to do instead of what you *want* to do." I gaped at him.

"I don't want you to look back on your life and wish you'd been bolder with your decisions. Just think about it before you decide." Huh. I didn't know what to say. I just sat there for a few minutes and then told him I was going to take a shower.

I started making my list as the hot water poured down my back.

What did I care about? Kyle, obviously. A good English program. I didn't particularly care about the campus size, or if it was in a city or rural. I didn't care about activities, although if they had a cheer program, that would be an upside. I guess I just wasn't that picky. I'd already looked through brochures and online, but no place had really screamed at me. They all pretty much looked the same.

So if they were all the same, how was I going to make a decision?

I braced myself against the shower wall and thought until the hot water ran out. Shivering, I got out and wrapped myself up in a towel. Even though it was still early, I put on a pair of shorts and a tank top and got into bed. I texted Kyle that I loved her and goodnight and she sent me a kissy face.

I scrolled through the pictures of her that I had on my phone. They made me smile and laugh and wish I was with her.

Was I refusing to consider going to the same school just to be stubborn? Was I depriving myself of being happy for no reason?

I thought about it all night.

THE MORNING DIDN'T BRING clarity, but it had distracted me from remembering that it was the Monday after the barn party and everyone was probably going to know that Kyle and

I were together. I texted her to meet me by my car, as we'd planned.

"Hey, I was worried about you last night. Are you okay?" she asked when she got out of her car and hugged me.

"Yeah, just thinking about a lot of stuff. You ready for this?" She kissed my cheek and took my hand swinging it with hers.

"You bet, baby."

~

SO WE GOT A FEW YELLS, a few lewd comments, and a few gay slurs shot at us. Kyle just squeezed my hand and we kept walking together until we had to part to go to our separate homerooms.

Kyle kissed the back of my hand and said she'd see me at lunch and I went off to class.

I got more comments from people in class, but they were such poor attempts at insults that I just let them roll off my back.

Kyle texted me asking how it was going and I sent back that it was nothing I couldn't handle. Actually, those years of psychological torture had really prepared me for dealing with homophobia. Guess I should go back and thank the bullies for toughening me up.

All in all, most people didn't seem to care. Those that did had short attention spans and got distracted or ran out of insults when they saw I wasn't bothered by them.

Kyle and I met right outside the cafeteria with Midori and Grace. The two of them had struck up a friendship independent of us, which was great. No stress about them getting along.

Instead of me sitting with the cheerleaders and Kyle sitting with her friends, we found and empty table and claimed it. Grace and Midori joined us, followed by several of Kyle's friends (some of whom kept giving me wary looks) and surprisingly, Tris and Polly. A few of the cheer girls kept looking over as if they wanted to join, but they stayed where they were. I didn't mind. As long as I had Kyle and Midori, I had who I needed.

"You don't seem like a lesbian," Molly's boyfriend Tommy, said. She admonished him.

"What? She doesn't."

"And what does a lesbian 'seem' like?" Tris asked, narrowing her eyes.

He opened and closed his mouth a few times and then mumbled something.

"That's what I thought," Tris said. "Anybody else have questions?" Everyone looked really uncomfortable.

"Okay, if no one will ask, I will. How does scissoring work?" Grace asked. I burst out laughing and so did everyone else. Even Tris cracked a smile. The tension was broken and the rest of the time was much less hostile.

"You're welcome," Grace said in my ear.

"SO THAT WASN'T SO bad, right?" Kyle said as I met her by our cars in the parking lot. Cheer practice had been cancelled so we were going to hang out together.

"Not really. I have to say, people aren't very creative with their lesbian insults. I got the same ones over and over. They really need better material." She snorted and put her arms around me. We rocked back and forth.

"Oh, I love you, my sexy cheerleader."

"I love you, my cute nerd."

We hadn't talked about the college thing today and I had

the feeling Kyle was purposefully avoiding it. We were going to have to discuss it at some point, but not today.

"You wanna go makeout in my car?" she asked and I jerked back from the hug to find her wiggling her eyebrows.

"Hell, yeah."

Making out solved most problems.

KYLE

I was trying to give her some space on the college thing. I really thought that she was going to come around if I let her think it through. I didn't really want to tell her that I was going to end up at an in-state school, or a private school that gave me the best financial aid package. She didn't have as many restrictions. It would be totally different if she had a dream school she'd always wanted to go to and I would somehow keep her from that. She'd always talked about college in general terms and I knew she didn't have a preference. So why not go together?

We could even be roommates, which would just be awesome. Then we could make out in her bed or my bed, or even push them together. I was trying not to get ahead of myself, but I definitely couldn't stop thinking about it.

Now that we had tackled all the hurdles (so far) to be together, it seemed foolish to put more obstacles in our way that didn't need to be there.

But I was patient. I could wait for her to get there. And while I waited, we could just make out a lot.

I ALSO HADN'T STOPPED THINKING about what we'd said the night of the barn party. About giving each other everything. It kept me up most nights, actually. I thought about all the different ways it could happen. In a hotel room, at one of our houses, in the backseat of one of our cars. I wanted it to be special (in a non-cheesy way), but there wasn't really a way to do that. Unless I lied to my parents, which I really didn't want to do.

So I was out of ideas. I even looked shit up on Tumblr, but that was no help. If only one of us had an apartment.

There were a few times over the next two weeks where we got very, very close. We'd gotten shirts off, but hadn't gone further than that. Either one of us had put the brakes on, or we'd been interrupted for whatever reason.

"What do you think my parents would say if I told them I was sleeping over at Stella's?" I asked Grace when we were hanging out while Stella was at work.

"They would probably say no. But maybe not? If you're really mature about it, who knows?" That was true. She'd told me to be careful, but maybe . . .

The potential of being with Stella for the night was enough for me to get up the courage to ask.

"Mom?" She was in the midst of making dinner and Dad was still at work.

"Yes, honey?"

"What would you say if I asked to sleep over at Stella's?" She froze with a carrot and a peeler in her hand.

She inhaled through her nose and set both the carrot and the peeler down, bracing herself on the counter.

"I'd say . . . I don't know. I know you're both eighteen and technically adults, but I'm not sure I'm ready to condone . . . that . . . either." She finally looked at me.

"I figured. But I wanted to do the mature thing and ask. I would never go behind your back." She gave me a tight smile.

"I'll think about it. Okay? I promise to think about it." That was good enough for me. It wasn't a no.

"Thanks, Mom." I gave her a hug and asked if I could give her a hand.

~

A FEW DAYS later Stella and I were laying side-by-side on her bed just staring at each other. I never knew how good that could be. Just to lay and breathe next to another person.

"I asked my mom if I could sleep over," I said as she walked her fingers up and down my arm.

"You did? Are you nuts?" I shrugged my shoulder.

"I didn't want to sneak around. Because then if we got caught, I wouldn't get to see you anymore. And that's not worth risking. I'd rather have some time than no time. That would kill me." She nodded.

"Agreed. What did she say?"

"The jury is still out. I haven't brought it up again, but I think she might say yes." Stella raised one eyebrow.

"Oh, really? And what if she said yes? Would that mean what I think it would mean?" I grinned.

"Yes, indeed." She threw her leg over mine and moved a little closer.

"So I should get some candles and some fancy sheets and maybe some lingerie?" I almost died at the thought of her in lacy lingerie.

"As long as you don't care about my non-sexy underwear." I had never owned anything made of lace. My undies were utilitarian, not sexy.

"Ky. It's not the underwear I want to see. It's what's *under* the underwear." I giggled.

"I guess you have a point."

"So, you think you're ready?" She pressed her forehead against mine.

"Yeah. Are you?" She bit her bottom lip and said one word against my lips.

"Yes."

~

THREE DAYS LATER, my parents sat me down and told me they would let me sleep over at Stella's.

"As long as you are careful, and you are responsible, and are where you are supposed to be when I call or text. I don't want to find that you two have run off to Vegas or something." I laughed at that, but she was serious.

One of the reasons I even existed was that my mom's parents had forbid her from seeing my dad, so they'd gone around their backs and "been irresponsible." I mean, she didn't put it that way, but it was the implication. Fortunately, Stella couldn't get me pregnant, so that wasn't one of their worries. And since neither of us had been with anyone sexually, we were pretty safe in that department too.

"Sex brings out a lot of emotions. I just want you to be ready for that, but if you tell me that you are, then I believe you," she said. Dad had let her do most of the talking, but had added his two cents here and there. I really wanted to stop talking about sex with my parents, but I sat and listened until they had talked themselves out. Then I scurried to my room to text Stella that all systems were go.

She'd also asked her dad if it was okay, and he had reluctantly agreed. It was a little weird knowing that both sets of our parents knew we were having sex. Or that we were going to. But that was the price we had to pay to be together. And in less than a year, we could do whatever we wanted.

Stella and I were still skirting the college issue, which was becoming more and more of an issue as colleges started sending reps to come and talk to us and convince us to attend their institution above the others.

I honestly didn't care all that much. College was college, I figured and I wasn't heading to an Ivy League, so what did it matter? Just seemed like kids went to fancy colleges so their parents could get a bumper sticker and brag in the Christmas letter.

I was going to wait until she brought it up, or there was a good time for it and I hadn't found that yet. I didn't want us to fight about it. We got along so well and I didn't want to provoke an argument if I didn't have to.

My dad is going away to a conference for the weekend she texted me the day after I'd given her the news about staying over.

You're kidding. That's like, perfect timing.

I know. It's like we planned it.

I couldn't stop the riot of butterflies that started beating their way through my stomach.

Guess I need to do some shopping . . . she texted back. I was going to die. I was going to die before she even got naked. Sex was going to kill me.

Chapter Nineteen

STELLA

My dad definitely knew what was going to happen when he was away, but he just gave me a look and told me to be careful. I told him I would and then waited for him to leave so I could get everything ready. I hoped she would like it. I'd made dinner (buffalo chicken lasagna, avocado and tomato salad, and a double fudge cake for dessert), cleaned my room within an inch of its life, made my bed with new 100 percent cotton sheets, and gotten cute lingerie that I was wearing under my adorable pink dress.

There were also candles and I had a playlist and everything. I'd probably gone overboard, but I didn't give a shit. I wanted this to be perfect.

An hour after my dad left, Kyle knocked on the door.

"Hey," I said, my voice squeaking a little as I looked at her. "Oh, wow."

She'd also put on a dress. A skintight black thing with a hint of gold shimmer. She'd also curled her hair and had mascara and red lipstick on. She was the sexiest bombshell I'd ever seen.

"Holy shit, Ky. Did you do all this for me?" She looked down at her feet. Still in black Chucks. It was so *her*, though.

"Yeah, and I'm freezing my ass off." She didn't have a coat on so I yanked her inside and she set down her backpack that presumably had a change of clothes anything else she might need.

"Well, you look hot as fuck freezing your ass off," I said, taking her hand and twirling her around so I could see the back.

"I wish you could see how your ass looks right now," I said and she turned back around.

"My turn," she said, shoving my shoulder so I'd turn around. I did a little twirl for her, my skirt flaring out.

"You like?"

She stepped close to me.

"I want to eat you alive. And I mean that in every way." I grabbed her face and we started kissing.

"I made you dinner," I said as she started to back me up toward my room.

"Sex first," she said.

"Okay, sure." I completely caved and then I realized that the oven was still on so I reluctantly pulled away so I could go and turn it off.

She stood in the hallway, leaning against the wall and waiting for me.

I stepped toward her, slowly, watching her watch me.

"Give me like five minutes," I said, brushing by her. She groaned, but nodded.

I rushed around my room and lit the candles and got the music going. Lot of Halsey on there. The first was a cover of "I Walk the Line" by Johnny Cash. It was slow and sexy and it made me think of her.

There was a knock at the door and I turned around to find Kyle in the doorway, a smile on her face.

"You didn't have to do all this," she said, waving her hand around the room. I walked toward her until we were only inches apart.

"I know. But I wanted to." I leaned forward and our lips met. She tried to move things faster, but I slowed her down. There was no rush. We had all night.

One step at a time, we walked together toward my bed and sat down. I ran my fingers through her curls, loving how they felt.

"I love you so much," she said in between kisses.

"I love you too," I said and turned so she could unzip the back of my dress. I pulled my hair out of the way and listened to the way her breath hitched as she realized what I wanted her to do.

Her fingers trembled as she gripped the zipper and drew it down slowly. I waited for her to push the straps of the dress off my shoulders, but then I felt her lips on the back of my neck, right where my spine started. She kissed her way down my back, following the line of my zipper. When she was done, she pushed off one strap, kissing the skin she exposed before doing the same to the other shoulder.

I pulled my arms free and stood up, pushing the dress down until it hit the floor.

"You're so beautiful, baby," Kyle said, sounding like she was going to cry.

As for lingerie, when I'd gone shopping I hadn't liked any of the fancy, elaborate contraptions that looked impossible to get in or out of. Instead I'd chosen a dark green silk bra and matching panties with a little lace on the edges. Simple.

Kyle stood and came to kiss me, but I stopped her.

"Now it's my turn."

～

KYLE

I waited as she slowly peeled the dress off me. It got stuck a few times and we laughed.

"It's really tight," I said as an apology.

"I'll cut it off if I have to," she said, finally wrestling the dress over my head. "There."

I'd worn a simple black cotton bra and panties. I knew I didn't have to fancy myself up for her. She looked at me as if I was the sexiest thing she'd ever seen.

"Mmmmm," she said, running her hands up and down my sides, making goosebumps pop up. We backed toward the bed again and lay down next to each other just kissing. I was so afraid that if I slowed down, my anxiety was going to get the best of me.

I had no idea what I was doing. Sure, I could get myself off, but I had no idea what she liked. What she needed. What if I couldn't do it right? What if I scratched her? I'd cut my nails as short as I could get them.

"Ky. Stop thinking." Stella was staring at me. "If you don't want to do this, then we don't have to. Anytime you want to stop, you tell me. Okay?" She pushed my hair away from my face.

"Aren't you scared?" I asked.

"A little. The upside is that neither of us knows what we're doing. And I think I'm going to enjoy finding out what you like." She smiled and I realized I hadn't thought of it *that* way.

"Oh," I said.

"Exactly."

Our mouths met again and I let my hands wander across her body. So much skin to touch. So many places to explore and taste and linger over.

I got her under me and did exactly that until she was quivering under me and saying my name in a way that almost made me come.

She got me back with the same treatment and then we couldn't take it anymore and the lovely lingerie quickly ended up tossed on the floor.

I had no words for how beautiful her body was. None. I just lay there and stared at her. She was perfect.

Me, not so much. I tried to hide my leg, but she caught me.

"You're beautiful, baby. You're perfect." She scooted down and kissed my scars. Loved on every single one. It made me want to cry and then she slithered back up my body and stopped right at nipple level. Locking eyes with me, she very deliberately licked my nipple.

"Fuck, Stella." She laughed and then did it again. I was completely lost as she tortured one nipple and then the other until I was begging her.

"What do you want," she said, kissing down to my navel. "Tell me what you want, baby."

"You. I want you," I said, running my fingers through her hair.

"I know. Where do you want me?" She kissed down a tiny bit further and I was shaking.

"I'm scared." She stopped and rested her chin in my lower stomach.

"What are you scared of? Asking for what you want?" I nodded.

"Well, you'll never get it if you don't ask." She was torturing me.

"Why are you making me do this?" I whined and she laughed at my expense.

"Because I want to hear you say it."

I looked down at her, wondering if she was going to back down. She just lay there like she could wait forever.

"I want you to . . ." Ugh, why couldn't I say it?

"You want me to . . ." she said, waving her hand for me to go on.

I swallowed.

"I want you to go down on me."

She grinned.

"Oh, okay. All you had to do was ask."

I wanted to strangle her, but then she started kissing my lower belly, moving lower and lower until I almost told her to stop. She got close. So close and then stopped. I glared down at her, but she just smiled at me.

"Patience."

She scooted down and started from my knees up, kissing the insides of my legs, traveling further and further toward where I needed her.

My legs quivered as she settled between them and gently pushed my legs further apart.

I almost jacked off the bed as she gently kissed me at the apex of my thighs. She put a hand on my stomach to keep me still and then the real torture began.

As if she had all the time in the world, she kissed me. Licked slowly, up and down, back and forth until I didn't know my name or what day it was or even what planet I was on. I had one hand in her hair and one gripping the blankets of the bed.

She might not have done this before, but she must have done some research because it was good. It was all good. Or at least I thought it was good until she sucked my clit into her mouth and then sneakily slid a finger inside me.

"Stella!" I gasped. "*Please*." She continued to suck on my clit and move her finger in and out of me before adding another finger and then I couldn't take it.

I came so hard I saw stars and I thought my heart exploded. It went on for so long that when it was over, I didn't know if I was ever going to be able to move again.

"Where the *fuck* did you learn how to do that?" I said to the ceiling. I looked down to find her with a very satisfied grin on her face.

"Beginner's luck."

STELLA

I was pretty proud of myself. First time going down on a girl and I made her come. I should get a star or something.

It took Kyle a little while to recover, but once she did, she attacked me and then I was the one begging and pleading.

"You don't have to," I said as she licked her way down my body.

"No way. I want to fuck you with my tongue and watch you come apart." I almost lost it just from that. She still had her glasses on and it was like all my fantasies were coming true in this moment.

Whereas I'd been gentler, she showed me no mercy, but it was exactly what I needed. I barely had to give her any direction as she sucked on my clit, hard, and thrust her fingers inside me, curling them to hit the right spot. It was wild and savage and I wouldn't have had it any other way. I came so fast that I didn't know it was happening until I was already in the middle of it.

"Oh my God, Ky." She kissed my stomach and crawled up to kiss my mouth. I could taste both of us and it turned me on so much that I was ready to go again.

We'd gotten the first rush over with, so we slowed down. Fucked each other at the same time. Tried different positions. Some were failures, but it didn't matter.

It was perfect and it was real.

Finally, exhaustion got the best of us and we both lay together, limbs entwined. She rested her head on my chest and I stroked her back.

"Should we try scissoring?" I said and she giggled.

"Why the hell not? I think we should try everything. I mean, not the weird stuff. You know, I saw a statistic that lesbians have the best sex lives. Better than heterosexual couples." I kissed the top of her head.

"Not surprised. Plus, we can do so many more positions."

Kyle's stomach chose that second to growl and we finally decided to have dinner. I grabbed a robe and tossed Kyle a long t-shirt I wore to bed sometimes.

"I just want to see you in my clothes," I said as she put it over her head.

"Ditto," she said and went to get her backpack. She pulled out a baggy t-shirt and athletic shorts and threw them at me. I put them on and took off the robe.

"Better?"

"Hell, yeah."

WE'D WORKED up quite an appetite and we ate snuggled together on the couch, sharing one plate.

"You said we'd never feed each other," Kyle said.

"We're not feeding each other. We're sharing a plate. That's different," I said. "We each have our own fork. That's the difference." She didn't argue with me. We were both in post-orgasm haze.

"So, I made a decision," I said, stabbing a piece of cucumber.

"About what?" she asked.

"About college." She stared at me.

"And?"

I set my fork down.

"And I'm open to us going to the same school. Because you're the most important thing to me. More than having a cool campus, or anything like that. And there's nothing wrong with that." I'd thought about it until I'd sat with the decision for several days. I didn't get that bad feeling that I was making the wrong choice. All I felt was rightness, but I'd wanted to wait until tonight to tell her.

She took a deep breath.

"Really?"

"Really."

She set the plate down and tackled me.

"I hope your dad doesn't mind if I fuck you on the couch."

I shrugged one shoulder.

"What he doesn't know won't hurt him."

Epilogue

KYLE

"High V! Low V! T! Candlesticks! Low V!"

I was struggling to keep up with Stella's instructions and finally messed up.

"I'm not good at this," I said, putting my arms down. For some reason, I'd thought it was a cute idea for Stella to teach me a little about cheerleading and we were starting at the bottom with motions, which were a lot harder than they seemed.

"Oh, come on, baby, you can do it." I pouted at her and she came over and took my bottom lip between her teeth.

"It's hard," I said when she broke the kiss.

"Well, how about we try something different? Lay on the grass." It was June and we were in her backyard. Stella and I were making the most of the time we had together since we both had full time jobs to help pay for college in the fall.

I lay down and then she told me to bring my knees up.

"Now what?" I asked and then she straddled me, leaning back against my knees.

"I enjoy the view?" she said, giving me a wink.

"You're terrible," I said, reaching up to tickle her. She squealed and rolled off me as I gained the advantage and tickled her until she breathlessly begged me to stop.

"Now who's on top?" I asked and she raised an eyebrow.

"You know what I mean," I said, grinding my hips a little.

"Mmmm," she said, holding onto my sides. "We can't fool around out here. The neighbors." I looked around.

"Eh, who cares?" I leaned down and shoved my tongue in her mouth.

The sunshine poured down on us and I was so glad that we didn't have to spend this summer saying goodbye. We'd both been accepted to the same school in Maine and were headed there in September. She'd chosen English as her major and I was still on the fence. We'd made lists, but I wanted to get to school and then figure out what I wanted. I had time.

We'd decided against rooming with one another, but our dorm rooms were only one building apart, so we'd be spending a lot of time together and maybe down the road we could get an apartment. Stella and I would figure it out. We'd already checked out the LGBTQIA organization so we could meet new people. In just a few months we'd become close with Tris and Polly and the other queer kids at school, but we were all headed in different directions next year. Still, Tris and Polly had given us an open invitation to visit them in Austin anytime and we were definitely going to do that on Spring Break.

I broke the kiss and looked down at my beautiful girl.

"I'm so glad your dad forced you to take AP English," I said.

"Let's *not* talk about my dad while we're making out." I snorted and watched how the light sparkled in her hair.

"Good plan." I pushed my glasses up my nose and she sighed happily.

"I love you, Ky."

"Love you too, baby."

About Chord

Chase Hillier has plans, and nothing will cause her to deviate from them. So far, they're pretty simple: Get through her first year of college with good grades, read a lot of books, and hopefully find a cute boyfriend who could turn into her husband someday. She's got it all mapped out. No one is going to stand in her way. Not even her roommate, Cordelia Scott.

Cordelia Scott has her own plans: Get through her freshman year without too many panic attacks, figure out what the hell she wants to major in, and meet a guy who finally makes her heart flutter.

Fate has other plans for the two when they end up as roommates and neither of them can stop thinking about the other. They're both absolutely sure that they like boys and not girls. But their sparks can't be extinguished and they realize there is a lot more to their connection with each other than either of them thought. How will they navigate a path that neither of them planned on taking?

For all the girls who think they might like girls. This one's for you.

Chapter One

CHASE

"When's your roommate getting here?" my younger sister, Kate, said, flopping on the empty bed on the other side of my dorm room with a squeak. The beds looked like they'd been here since my parents had been in school in, and that was a while ago.

"Not sure. The girl I was supposed to be with dropped out at the last minute, so they assigned me someone new, like, two days ago," I said, pulling my dark hair off the back of my neck. It had grown out a little from when I'd gotten it chopped earlier in the summer and I needed a trim.

"It's not very big," Kate said, glancing around the room.

"It's fine," I said, kicking a box of books across the room so I wouldn't have to bend down and lift it.

Mom and Dad came through the door, both huffing and puffing.

"Don't you have an e-reader, Chase?" Mom said, groaning as she dropped a box of books with a thunk. Dad set my microwave down on the floor and stretched his back.

"Yeah," I said. "Your point?" Mom crossed her arms and

246

narrowed her eyes. Her patience with my sass was running thin today.

"That's supposed to replace the need to carry around a million heavy books. And thus save our backs." I rolled my eyes. My parents were both in their mid-forties. They weren't *that* old.

"How much more?" I asked. We'd thrown everything in the back of Dad's SUV, but it seemed like a lot of stuff in the tiny room. Maybe it was just the boxes of books. Oops. But I couldn't leave any behind. Who knew what Kate would do with them while I was gone? Probably use them to blow her nose just to spite me.

"One more trip, I think. If we *all* help," Dad said, with a pointed look at Kate, who rolled her eyes and let out a sixteen-year-old huffy sigh.

"Good," I said, but my stomach flipped over a few times. When we finished unpacking the car, that meant my parents and Kate were leaving me here. At college. Alone.

Well, except for a complete stranger, which I was now expected to share a very intimate space with. Yeah, sounded like a great idea. I might have been an adult on paper, but in reality, not so much. I still felt like I needed supervision.

I just hoped she wasn't, like, weird. Didn't sleep all day and stay up all night staring at me while I slept kind of weird. Or wanted to be my VERY BEST FRIEND EVER five seconds after meeting me.

There were so many potential awful possibilities.

I should have roomed with someone I knew, but I wasn't smart and by the time I tried that, everyone had already paired up and I was the odd girl out.

And now here I was, waiting to meet the girl who could make my life a living hell. Why did I agree to this again?

∾

THE FOUR OF us got the rest of my stuff up the elevator and down the hall to my room, and I said goodbye with a minimum of tears. After they left, I shut the door and sat on my new bed. The mattress was just one of those thin wafer things and not very comfortable. Good thing I'd brought a memory foam topper for it.

I was just trying to get up the energy to start unpacking when the door banged open.

"Is this it?" A booming voice said. All I saw was a box and a set of heavily-muscled legs before a female voice said "Yeah, this is it" and the walking box entered the room.

The person carrying the box set it down on the other bed and I nearly gaped at him. Standing in front of me was one of the tallest men I'd ever seen. He was also ripped, and had a shock of red hair on his head and a beard on his chin. He wouldn't have been out of place next to some Norse or Roman god.

He beamed at me, flashing white teeth.

"You must be Chase," he said, holding out a hand that could crush two of mine with little effort.

"Uhhhh," I said, and then turned to see who else had walked in.

"Dad, stop it." Standing in the doorway with a duffel bag must be my new roommate.

Cordelia Scott. She was just as striking as her father, but she was definitely on the more petite side. Cute. With red hair a few shades darker than her dad and pale skin that was peppered all over with freckles. I'd never seen someone with so many. I realized I was staring and blinked a few times. My eyes traveled south. She was more well-endowed than I, and I couldn't help but be jealous at the way she filled out her V-neck shirt.

"Sorry about him," Cordelia said, dropping the duffel with

a thunk. "He likes to make an entrance." I still didn't know what to say.

"It's okay," I finally got out.

"It's nice to meet you. Finally. I'm sorry we couldn't have hooked up during orientation, but we're here now." She smiled at me and my stomach did this little flippy thing.

I was *so* nervous about this living-with-a-complete-stranger deal.

"Nice to meet you too," I said, my face turning red. "Do you, um, need any help?"

"No, we've got it," she said, pointing at her dad. "He's a one-man moving crew."

"Okay. Cool," I said, still feeling painfully awkward. She stepped by me and winked before heading out of the room, her giant dad following in her wake.

Whoa.

LESS THAN AN HOUR LATER, Cordelia had all of her stuff in our room and she was giving her dad a hug goodbye. He lifted her off her feet and held her hard. I almost thought I was going to hear cracking ribs.

"You call me, got it? Or else I'm going to come up here and break the door down. And you carry your pepper spray." She rolled her eyes and nodded. He turned to me.

"You look out for each other, okay?" I said I would and then he left, nearly having to walk sideways to make it through the doorway.

"So," Cordelia said, turning to me. "Need some help unpacking?"

"No, I'm okay," I said, clutching two books, one in each hand. Being in this confined space with her was freaking me out.

"Okay, well, let me know." She turned away and started unpacking some of her boxes. I tried not to watch her as I loaded up my bookcase.

"Oh, I love that one," A voice said behind me. I jumped and nearly crashed into her when I whipped around.

"Sorry!" She put her hands up so we didn't collide. Despite being several inches shorter than me, she was just so … vibrant. I guess that was the right word. The hair and the freckles and her energy was too much to be contained by her body. She'd put her hair up on top of her head in a sloppy ponytail and there were wisps around her face.

I was staring again.

"It's okay," I said.

"It's cool that you have so many books. I mostly read on my phone, but it would be fun to swap books back and forth. Looks like we have a lot of the same tastes."

I didn't want to do that, and I was quickly realizing that whichever algorithm had paired us together had made a terrible mistake.

And I'd only lived with her for less than six hours.

CORDELIA

I couldn't tell if she was just shy, or had a hard time with new people, or what. I was trying. Probably trying a little too hard. Dad would probably be telling me to reel it in if he were here. I missed him already.

Chase moved around the room and kept giving me darting glances. Surprise, surprise, she was taller than me (most everyone was) and had the cutest long bob I'd ever seen. She also had widely-spaced brown eyes that made her look like a doll. Chase was definitely not going to have any problem finding a boyfriend, if she didn't have one already. She probably did. I wanted to ask, but she was being so squirrely that I didn't want to spook her on the first day.

So I tried to keep my mouth shut for the most part and unpack my shit and stay on my side of the room.

"I'm going, to, um, go … walk around," Chase said after putting some of her books on the shelves.

She paused in the doorway, as if she wasn't sure she was allowed to or not.

"I could come with you. If you want," I offered. She pressed her lips together and nodded. Nice. Maybe if we got out of the room and away from the stress of moving in she'd open up. I really wanted us to get along, since we were going to be living together. Plus, it would be nice to have a friend.

Chase didn't say anything as we walked down the hall, dodging other people moving in. The floors were filled with hazards and I nearly got bowled over by a guy carrying an enormous TV. I stumbled back against Chase and she caught my upper arms.

"Sorry," I said as she let me go, looking a little stunned.

"It's fine," she said and looked straight ahead.

Okay, then.

"WHAT'S YOUR MAJOR?" I asked. We hadn't exchanged any information like other roommates might have ahead of time, so I didn't really know anything about her, which I was actually kind of excited about.

Dad always called me his little "social butterfly." I guess I was pretty good at talking to people.

Well, under most circumstances. I was kind of striking out with Chase.

"English," she said in a tone that dared me to make fun of her.

"That would make sense with all the books," I said, nodding as we walked down the hill from our dorm. I didn't know where we were going, but I was following her lead.

"What about you?" she said after a second.

"I'm not sure yet. I have a bunch of things I'm interested in, so I want to try a few classes and see first, you know? I mean, I think it's a little stupid to ask people to choose a major and a career before we even know what that involves." I was rambling, but she might as well get used to it because I did it all the time.

"Yeah, I guess you're right," she said. I hoped we were getting somewhere.

"I've thought about English, but then I wasn't sure what I'd do with it," I said, and then realized that was probably insulting.

"I want to work in publishing. Either as a writer or an agent or editor or something. I'll have to get a master's degree, but this is the first step." She said it in a rush and I was thrilled I'd finally started cracking through her outer shell. I had a good feeling about her.

"You have to become a famous author so I can say I knew you when," I said, bumping my shoulder against her arm. I couldn't exactly reach her shoulder with mine because of our height difference. Reel it in, Cordelia.

She gave me a nervous smile and then we were silent again.

"Can I ask you something?" she said after we'd walked a few more steps.

"Sure! We should probably get to know each other since we're sharing a room."

"Have you read *Anne of Green Gables*?" YES. We were going to get along just fine.

I beamed at her.

"Are you asking about my name? It was my dad's idea. When I came out with a full head of red hair like his. He thought 'Anne' was too common, but Cordelia worked since it was the name Anne Shirley always wanted. So there you go." I was so happy she understood the reference. Not a whole lot of people did.

I glanced over at her and saw a real, genuine smile on her face.

"It's a pretty name," she said. "Even without the awesome reference."

"Thanks!"

We made it down to the main part of campus and I asked her where she wanted to go.

"Well, I thought I would check out the bookstore and see how many books I'm going to need, and then maybe figure out where my classes are," she said, pulling out a piece of paper from her back pocket.

Oh, how cute. She was probably going to get all her syllabi on the first day and plan out a schedule too.

"Sure, I'm cool with that. Although, I'm starving. Do you want to get something to eat at the Student Union first?"

"Um, okay," she said, and we walked up the steps toward the Union. I remembered taking my first tour here with Dad. It felt like a million years ago.

Chase held the door for me and I got a little flustered for some reason.

"Thanks," I said, walking through before her.

"Yeah," she said, looking down and blushing a little. Crap, I was busting out of my shirt. I wished there was a subtle way to tuck the girls back in, but there really wasn't. I'd only grabbed this shirt because the rest were packed away.

We didn't really know how to interact with one another, so we just sort of walked around the Union, looking for whatever struck our fancy. I ended up in front of the premade pizzas that were steaming on paper plates.

"Score," I said, grabbing a tray and a plate of plain cheese.

They also had little salads, so I grabbed one of those. Might as well try to be healthy somewhat. Chase grabbed pepperoni and a salad as well. We went through the line, swiping our ID/meal cards.

"Can you believe it? We're really here in college. I keep wanting to pinch myself or something," I said, looking around.

"Yeah, I know what you mean," Chase said. "I'm really afraid I'm gonna get homesick. That's probably stupid, but I don't care." I shook my head and swallowed.

"No, I totally know what you mean! My dad and I are like best friends." Something twinged in my stomach when I mentioned him. Ugh, I missed him already. Hopefully I was going to be able to get through this like millions of other people had.

"That's sweet. Is it just the two of you?" she asked. Finally, we were getting somewhere.

"Yup. Mom bailed and it was just the two of us. I think I was definitely better off. You?"

"Mom and Dad and one younger sister. She's a pain in the ass." I giggled because she rolled her eyes. Cute.

I asked her more about her family and got a little bit more out of her. Maybe it was knowing the origin of my name that helped grease the conversational wheels. Maybe it was something else. But I had the feeling that Chase and I were going to have a big impact on each other's lives.

She was a meticulous eater, rotating her plate as she finished her small slices of pizza. For some reason I found that really adorable.

I had to stop myself from staring at her too much. I was always doing too much. Being too loud. Being too invasive. I had made the deal with myself that I was going to tone my shit down. Starting now. With Chase.

Chapter Two

CHASE

I'd never gotten to know someone that fast before. College seemed to make everything go at warp speed. By our second day together, Cordelia and I had a few inside jokes and had already figured out a chore schedule and when we wanted to go to bed each night. It was like I'd known her for years instead of hours.

"Okay, this one is important," she said as we lounged on our beds/couches. We were tossing a bag of Skittles back and forth. She was eating the purple and green ones and I was eating the yellow and red ones. Neither of us liked the orange ones, so those were in the bottom of the bag and would probably end up in the trash where they belonged.

"Okay," I said. We were currently seeing how much we had in common when it came to food.

"What kind of popcorn is your favorite?" I popped a red Skittle in my mouth and cracked off the coating with my teeth before tossing the bag back to her.

"Movie theater butter. Followed closely by kettle corn." I looked over to find her slowly narrowing her eyes. Uh oh. I wondered if I'd said the wrong thing. Another thing I'd learned about her was that she had strong opinions on a lot of topics. Including popcorn, apparently.

"Is that the wrong answer?" I asked. But the she broke out with a smile that made me want to look away. Something about the way she smiled made me feel weird.

"No, that is the exact right answer. Congratulations. I won't murder you in your sleep." She munched a Skittle and then tossed the bag back at me.

I caught it and sat up.

"So, you're saying if I'd answered, 'with just salt' you would have had grounds for murder?" She nodded, her curls bouncing.

"Of course!" I cracked another Skittle in my teeth.

"You know, you're kind of scary," I said. Her grin got really wide and I had that weird twisty feeling again.

"Thanks for the compliment." I shook my head at her and ate the last Skittle in the bag (with the exception of the offending orange ones).

"Are you scared?" I asked as I tossed the bag in our shared trashcan (which we had already made agreements about who would empty it each week).

"About what?" she asked, pulling her feet up on her bed and sitting cross-legged.

"About *this*," I said, waiving my hand around. "And classes and everything?" So far, I was doing okay with being here and Cordelia was a huge part of that. We were both pretty close with our families, so it was nice to have someone to talk to who felt the same way.

"I mean, not really? I guess I don't really think about it. I try not to worry too much." I wished I was like that. I worried about everything and anything. It was a real problem some-times. I couldn't help it.

"You're much more confident than I am." I got up and

adjusted a few of my books that weren't quite even. I was a stickler for organizing my bookshelves, and it was the first thing I'd done when I unpacked, even before opening any other boxes. Cordelia had tried to help, but she'd quickly realized that I had a system and that system only made sense to me. I was still apologizing about it.

"You're going to be fine. With all that reading, you're going to run circles around everyone else." I felt my cheeks getting hot. I didn't take compliments well. At all. Ever. I was eighteen-years-old and I couldn't take a compliment without blushing.

"Thanks," I finally said.

There was a knock at the door and we both looked at each other.

"Should we answer it?" I asked, and Cordelia shrugged before getting up and peering through the peephole. She had to get up on her tippy toes to do it.

"Oh, it's Laura," she said before she opened the door. Laura was our Resident Assistant, aka, babysitter. We'd met her the night we moved in and she'd had a few meetings and popped in a few times already. Even though she was only a few years older, she seemed to think she was going to be our surrogate parent.

"Hey, I just wanted to let you know that we're having a little get-to-know-you party in the study lounge right now, if you want to come." Cordelia looked at me as if I was the one making the decision. I didn't really want to, to be honest.

"There's free pizza," Laura said in a sing-song voice. Oh. Well, that changed things.

"Sure," I said, and Cordelia nodded.

"Great!" Laura bounced off to ask the rest of our neighbors if they wanted to come.

"You can't turn down free pizza," Cordelia said. I agreed.

~

THERE WERE ONLY a few people in the study lounge when we got there, including one of the girls that lived in our hall. I was pretty sure her name was Stella. Of course, Cordelia went right up to her and grabbed two paper plates from the table Laura had set up.

"You're Stella, right?" she asked, and I took one of the plates.

"Yeah, and you're…. shit, I'm bad with names." Cordelia introduced us and we all piled our plates with pizza before we claimed one of the couches.

Stella was one of those girls who just looked ethereally beautiful all the time. Every strand of her ash-blonde hair was in place and her eyeliner was winged perfection. I had never managed to come even close to that.

Stella pulled out her phone and then looked up at the doorway and grinned.

"Be right back," she said, setting down her pizza plate. I watched as she walked over to a girl with her hair piled in a messy bun on top of her head with black-framed glasses.

"Hey, baby," she said and planted a kiss on the other girl's mouth. Oh. OH. She led the newcomer over to the pizza table and then over to us. They were holding hands and I felt like I was staring. I glanced at Cordelia, but she didn't seem to be affected at all.

It wasn't that it made me uncomfortable, exactly. I just … I hadn't really seen someone be so open before. Welcome to college.

"Hey, this is my girlfriend, Kyle, and this is Chase and Cordelia," Stella said.

"Hey," Kyle said as she and Stella sat down on the other end of the couch.

"Hi," I said, my voice squeaking. Why was I being so weird? Oh, right, because I was me.

"Hey, nice to meet you," Cordelia said. I shoved my pizza

in my mouth so I wouldn't have to talk and Cordelia did her thing, asking Stella and Kyle about themselves.

"We thought about living together, but our parents put the kibosh on that, didn't they, babe?" Kyle said, kissing Stella on the cheek. They were pretty cute, I had to admit. Something about seeing two girls together just made me feel strange, though. Cordelia didn't seem to have the same problem.

"Pretty much. But what they don't know won't hurt them," Stella said. I nibbled on my slice of pizza and wished I could go back to my room without seeming rude.

"What are your majors?" Cordelia asked.

"English," Stella said, pointing to herself.

"Undeclared," Kyle said, doing the same.

"I'm English too," I said, and relaxed a little. It would be nice to know someone in the same program. Or at least have a friendly face in some of my classes tomorrow.

"And I'm Undeclared," Cordelia said, giving Kyle a fist bump.

"What are the chances?" Stella said. She turned to me and started asking about my classes and I found myself able to start talking a little more.

We had two classes together tomorrow, so I was going to see her a lot.

"That is so cool. If you ever want to study together, you can always come down the hall. You're only a few doors away." Guess we'd be spending a lot of time together.

"And we can hang out and try and figure our shit out," Kyle said to Cordelia and they both laughed. We finished our pizza and sat around for a little bit talking. The more time I spent with them, the less I was freaking out, so by the time Cordelia and I headed back to our room, we'd made plans to hang out the next night with Stella and Kyle.

"They were really cool," Cordelia said as I packed up my bag for the next day. I'd already gone around and mapped out all my classes and knew how long it took to get to each one. Cordelia actually had a break at the same time as I did, so we had already made plans to meet in the Union for lunch, so I had that planned out too. I'd called my parents and they'd wished me luck. All that I had to do was get up, eat breakfast, and do it.

I could do this.

"Yeah," I said, as I ran through my last mental checklist.

"You're going to give yourself an ulcer. Calm down, it'll be fine." I turned and narrowed my eyes at her.

"Don't mess with my process. It's worked for me all this time and I'm not going to change it now."

She laughed and flopped down on her bed. Her textbooks were still wrapped in plastic and stacked on the floor in a haphazard pile. It was making my eye twitch every time I looked at it. I didn't know how she could stand it, but from the way she'd organized her stuff, Cordelia wasn't as much of a stickler for "a place for everything and everything in its place" as I was. I guess that was okay. I could just organize her stuff when she was in class. Or sleeping.

"Are you ready?" she asked, as I did a last check. I'd probably do another in the morning. I made sure my alarm was set on my phone and that I had my clothes picked out and sitting on top of my dresser. Good. I was set to go for my first day of college. Now I just had to tell my stomach to stop being upset and my brain to shut down so I could actually get some sleep.

"I think so," I said, giving her a thumbs-up.

"You're going to be fine, Chase. You've got your shit together." I didn't feel like I did. Most of the time I felt like the entire world was spinning out of my control and I was just barely holding on.

"Thanks," I said, lying back on my bed. I turned and looked at my bookshelf. I needed to read to calm my mind.

I was in a young adult mood, so I scanned that shelf. I had

everything from contemporary to fantasy to steampunk to dystopian to speculative fiction. All of it. I tried to read as widely as I could because I wanted to have the whole range of books in my life. Especially if I was going to be a literary agent or editor. I wasn't sure yet. I also kept track of the bestsellers lists and what was currently selling.

I wanted something familiar and comforting, so I grabbed a Cinderella retelling that I'd had for years. I'd read it so many times that I'd had to buy another copy because mine had fallen apart. I loved the spunky Cinderella character because she actually saved the prince in this one. Plus, she didn't take anyone's shit, which was another great part of it.

"What are you reading?" Cordelia asked, as she stretched out. I looked away for some reason as she arched her back and lifted her arms above her head.

I held up the book so she could see the title.

"Wanna read out loud?" Was she serious?

"Really?" She nodded.

"Oh, I mean, I guess?" It seemed kind of strange, but my parents had always read to me as a kid and I'd loved it. Sometimes I read to Kate when both of us couldn't sleep. I guess this was no different.

"Cool," she said, getting up and finding her pajamas and grabbing her toothbrush. "I'll be right back."

While she was gone, I changed into my pajamas and got settled before also going to brush my teeth. Cordelia waved when I showed up in the bathroom and I took the sink next to her. She kept making faces at me in the mirror and I had to stop myself from spraying toothpaste everywhere as I laughed.

Faces washed and teeth brushed, we went back to our room. It was so strange how, after only a few days, we'd gotten a routine down. I was more of a morning person than Cordelia, so I was the designated waker-upper every morning. She looked so grumpy when she woke up, her hair tousled and everywhere. Really cute. I knew I didn't look that cute when I woke up. My eyes were always puffy.

We both got under the covers and I turned all the lights off except for a small lamp to read by, and started the book. I could feel Cordelia watching me out of the corner of her eye, holding onto one of her pillows that she hugged while she slept. It was a little odd at first, but then I melted into the story, and it wasn't.

At one moment I looked over and her eyes were closed and her breathing was deep. She appeared asleep, so I stopped.

"Keep going," she mumbled, but didn't open her eyes.

I did.

~

CORDELIA

I hoped Chase liked reading me to sleep, because I was going to require it for every night that we lived together, and not just because I was a selfish bitch. When she read, she relaxed. At first, her voice wavered, but then it softened and I watched her get lost in the story. It was good for her. Good for both of us. It gave my chaotic mind something to grab onto for a little bit. And it didn't hurt that she had a killer voice. Kind of deep and sexy. Like she knew all kinds of secrets.

Her voice wasn't so deep and sexy when she was yelling at me to wake up the next morning.

"If you don't get up, you're gonna be late," she said, and I could hear the terror in her voice. I cracked an eye open and grabbed my phone.

"Chase, it's seven. I don't have class until nine." What the fuck was even happening? I raked my hand through my hair, and it got stuck. I yanked it out, along with a few hairs. Ugh. Curly hair was a curse sometimes.

"Right, but you have to shower and get your books ready

and eat breakfast …" She trailed off when she saw my face as I looked up at her.

"No," I said, pulling the blankets back over my head.

"Will you at least have breakfast with me?" I groaned under the covers. I wasn't going to get back to sleep at this rate. I peeked out and looked at her. She was practically vibrating with anxiety. I knew she was nervous, but I could see the absolute terror in her eyes.

I was up.

"Okay, did you want to go to the dining commons?" I asked, and she shook her head, her blunt-cut hair swinging and hitting her cheeks. She was already dressed and polished and her bag was sitting by the door. I knew she'd had it packed and had checked it repeatedly for the past few days. She'd mapped out her classes and had even peered in the doors to figure out where she wanted to sit. I'd gone along with her, but hadn't done the same. I wasn't that organized. Plus, thinking the way she did would stress me out. It was much better to ignore things until they became problems. Or went away. It had worked for me for nearly nineteen years. Sort of.

"Breakfast here?" I said, sitting up and stretching my arms over my head. Chase looked away and I realized that I was wearing a white shirt without a bra. Holy headlights. Oops. I crossed my arms and then got up and put a robe on.

"Yeah," she said. We'd also gone grocery shopping, such as it was. You couldn't really cook a whole lot of stuff in a dorm room. Technically we weren't supposed to have a microwave, but Chase, of all people, had brought one and kept it under her bed when we weren't using it.

"Waffles and coffee?" I asked. She nodded, her head jerking up and down. She was really on-edge. I didn't know her that well to know what would be the right thing to say to help her.

This kind of sucked. And it was still too fucking early.

Whatever, I was going to be living with Chase for the fore-seeable future, so I might as well get used to her early-bird tendencies.

I pulled out the tiny coffeepot (also against the rules) and got some water from the fountain by the bathroom. A few other students passed me on their way to class or to the bath-room for their morning showers. I showered at night. Why anyone would shower at the beginning of the day was beyond me.

I tried to stifle a yawn as Kyle shuffled by me, her eyes puffy. She gave me a wave and a nod and I gave her one back.

Another not-morning person.

I got back and Chase was microwaving frozen waffles. Gourmet.

She wouldn't sit still as the coffee brewed and the waffles spun in the microwave.

She set up a little breakfast spot on the floor for us. We'd gotten into that routine, if we were eating in our room, we made a meal out of it by putting a towel on the floor and sitting together. I guess it was like we were at home having a family meal.

I missed Dad so much. I texted him every day and he'd called me more than a few times. But he was trying not to be too needy, which was cute. He was seriously my best friend and I almost wished that he could live next door to us. Almost.

I stirred salted caramel creamer into my coffee, but Chase had hers black. She also only put a little bit of syrup on her waffles. I drowned mine.

"I don't know how you can eat that much sugar," she said, shuddering as I cut my waffles into bite-size bits. I shrugged and shoved a forkful of waffles in my mouth.

Sugar. Sweet, wonderful, sinful sugar. The syrup had butter in it too. Perfection. Chase picked at her food and fiddled with her utensils.

"You doing okay?" I asked.

"Yeah. I guess I'm just nervous."

"That's totally understandable." I mean, if I let myself, I'd be freaking out too. But I would rather focus on the waffles on my plate than entertain the idea that I was facing my first day of college classes that would determine my future.

"I'm just scared that I picked the wrong major. That I'm picking the wrong career, the wrong life," she said in quiet rush. There it was. Now I had something to work with.

"Hey, it's only the first day. You won't know if it's right until you actually go to your classes. And you might even change your mind after you get your degree, or halfway through. It's not a crime to change your mind, Chase." She pushed her waffles around on her plate.

"I know. I just ... I like knowing things. I like knowing my routine and my days and everything. Right now it's all unknown and that scares the shit out of me." She looked up at me with her eyes wide and I thought she was going to cry. I pushed our plates aside and leaned in.

"Can I give you a hug?" She nodded and sniffed. It was still too early, but damn, I was gonna comfort this girl.

I leaned over and put my arms around her and she put hers around me. I nestled my head on her shoulder because it seemed like the right thing to do.

Her hair smelled like mint and rosemary. I was going to have to steal her conditioner.

"It's going to be okay," I said, because what else was there to say? I wasn't so great at the comfort thing, but I could give her a hug and hold her and tell her nice things.

Her head dipped and her cheek rested on my shoulder. My skin tingled, and I tried to ignore it. I nearly jumped when I realized she was running her fingers through my curls.

"Ouch," I said when her hand hit a snag.

"Sorry," she said into my shoulder. Her voice was muffled,

and I couldn't stop the feeling that I didn't want to let go from this hug.

"It's okay," I said back. No one was pulling away and we had passed the acceptable hug period.

But I didn't want to let go. I wanted to hold her and smell her hair and be like this for a long time. I hoped she couldn't feel my heart racing. I didn't know why my heart was racing.

Chase's phone went off and we both lunged back like we'd been shot.

"I have to go," she said. I raised one eyebrow. Her first class didn't start in over an hour.

"I just want to make sure I get a good seat," she said, standing up. I gathered the plates and tossed them in the trash, and put everything else away. Honestly, I kind of wanted to go back to sleep, but that was probably a bad idea. A nap right now would probably screw up the rest of my day.

"Whatever you need to do." She grabbed a tissue and wiped her eyes and blew her nose.

"Do I look okay?" she asked.

"You look great," I said, and I meant it. She looked gorgeous. I was so envious of her legs and her height and her smaller chest. Mine was just too much sometimes. They got in the way of everything. Plus, people stared, and that made everything uncomfortable.

She took a deep breath and gave me a shaky smile.

"Okay. I'm gonna go. Um, good luck to you, too," she said. I wanted to give her another hug, but I thought that might be weird. Since I had literally just hugged her.

"Yeah, good luck! You're going to be fine, I promise."

"Do you?" she asked.

"I do." It was an intense moment, much like our hug. We barely knew each other and yet we'd somehow fallen into a routine and an easy friendship. She smiled and leaned forward to give me a careless hug before she dashed out the door.

Oh.

~

COLLEGE WAS EXACTLY how I thought it would be and nothing like I thought it would be at the same time.

I didn't know if I was allowed to bring snacks or water to class, and then realized that there was a guy in my Intro to Psychology class who was watching one of the Spiderman movies. I couldn't really tell which one. He was too far away and I was actually trying to pay attention as my professor went over the syllabus and outlined what we were going to learn during the semester.

I had three classes back to back my first day, and by the time I got back to my room in the late afternoon, I really wanted a fucking nap. I was regretting not having one earlier.

Chase was back when I unlocked the door.

I was really glad to see her.

"How was your day?" I asked as she put a finger in her book and looked up with a smile that made me feel like I needed to sit down. I dropped my bag and flopped over on my bed. My brain was filled with so many things that I wished I could take some of them out and put them in a folder so they weren't taking up so much space.

"It was okay, I think? A lot of it was a blur. I don't know how I'm going to get everything done that I need to get done. I started making my schedule and had to stop. It was too much." Her laptop was open at her desk and I could see there was a calendar up with different-colored blocks on it. I couldn't read what they said.

"Wait, you're planning out your semester *now*?"

She nodded, as if it was no big deal.

This girl was organized in a way I would never be. She was both terrifying and inspiring.

"I have to. If I don't plan everything out to the minute …" she trailed off and looked back down at her book. "I'm sorry, you probably don't care."

"No, I do care." I probably cared too much. But we were friends and roommates. I was supposed to care. It was a wonder that we had been complete strangers and a computer had put us together and we were getting along so well. Things could have gone so wrong.

"I *need* to have a schedule. If I don't, I can't sleep. I can't do anything. I need structure."

"That makes sense. Is there anything I can do to help? Other than, like, leaving you alone?" We hadn't really gotten into the real college experience, with finals and papers and late-night studying. I didn't know how that was going to work for both of us. We were such different people. What was it going to be like when we got stressed?

I guess we'd figure it out.

"I mean, not yet. I already finished my homework for Wednesday." My eyes nearly fell out of my head. She was hardcore.

"Shit, I hope you influence me. I always leave things until the last minute and then finish under the gun." It was my thing. Somehow, things always seemed to get done, but the stress wasn't super fun.

"Some people like pressure. Maybe you're just one of those people." Chase made my procrastination sound like a positive trait. Huh.

"Guess we'll find out." I sighed, and my stomach rumbled. It was still too early for dinner, but I could definitely have a snack.

Chase went back to her book and I didn't want to talk to her as she was reading because that was really rude, in my opinion. Instead, I grabbed a bag of chips and put my earbuds in. I lay back on my pillow and closed my eyes and did some of my breathing exercises. I was shocked that I hadn't had a panic attack today. Or yet, I guess. So far, so good. But it was going to happen sooner or later. I just hoped it wasn't in public and I had a place to run away to until it passed.

Someone tapped my shoulder and I opened my eyes to find Chase standing over me. I pulled out my earbuds.

"You wanna watch something?"

"Yeah, sure," I said. She turned on the TV and flipped through the channels.

"Oh, oh, oh! Stop!" I said, and she held her hands up, one holding the remote. "What? I love this show."

"What is it?" she asked, sort of squinting at the screen and motioning for me to move over and give her some room. I did, sitting with my back against the wall, clutching one of my pillows.

"Are you telling me you've never seen *Steven Universe*?" How was that possible?

She shook her head.

"Oh my god, I feel so blessed right now. I get to introduce you to the best cartoon ever that will also give you so many emotions, you won't even know what to do with them." She looked skeptical.

"You will thank me, Chase." I knew she would. She would love it. She just had to love it.

"What's it about?"

"Look, I don't want to explain it. I think we should just start from the beginning and you'll see. I want you to go into it knowing nothing. That's the best way." Chase still seemed wary.

"Don't you trust me?" I asked.

"Uh, sure?" I huffed.

"Fine. Don't watch the best show in existence. That's your loss." I tried to take the remote from her to change the channel, but she held it out of my reach.

"That's not fair, you have longer arms," I said, pouting. She stuck her tongue out at me and I went for her belly. She flinched.

"Don't you dare."

"Oh, are you ticklish, Chase?" I asked, wiggling my fingers with menace.

"No," she said, in a completely unconvincing tone.

"Hmmm," I said, tapping my chin. "This could be useful information for later."

Her eyes narrowed and I laughed.

"I'm going to put all your stuff on the highest shelf in the closet." She got up and I grabbed her arm.

"I didn't tickle you! Come on!" She grinned at me and my heart flipped-flopped like a goldfish that fell out of the bowl.

I let go of her arm as if it had burned me and sat back from her.

"Fine, I won't put all of your stuff in the top shelf of the closet. But now you know what could happen if you make me mad ..." Chase said, trailing off.

"So the truth comes out," I said. "You're a menace." A cute, cute menace.

"Only on days that end in y," she said with a smirk.

"I'm doomed," I said, throwing my hands up in the air.

"Only a little doomed." We both laughed and then my phone buzzed with a text from my dad asking how my first day had gone. I replied with an excessive amount of emojis, but he loved them. We could have entire conversations without actually typing words.

"How's your dad?" she asked, as if she'd read my mind.

"I think he's going okay. I mean, he's got friends and he goes out, but we're best friends, you know? I worry about him being alone." He hadn't had a girlfriend in ages, but I was kind of hoping now that he wasn't sticking his nose into my business, he'd get back on the horse, or however that expression went.

"How are your parents?"

She shrugged one shoulder.

"I don't really know. I think they're lying to me to be supportive." I laughed. My dad would never do that, but I wish he did.

"Sorry. I was just thinking how not like that my dad is. Parents are weird sometimes." She nodded.

My stomach growled again.

"Do you wanna go have dinner?" she asked, and I nodded. I turned off the TV, and vowed to tackle Steven with Chase on another day.

As we were leaving our room, we happened to bump into Stella and Kyle.

"Hey, do you want to come with us to dinner? Then we won't feel like losers if there are four of us at a table," Stella said, and I still couldn't get over how perfect her hair was. It didn't seem possible.

"This isn't high school," Kyle said, bringing Stella's hand to her mouth and kissing the back of it.

"Thank god," I said with a laugh. I had been more than happy to leave high school behind.

"Seriously," Kyle said.

There was a tiny awkward moment, but it passed as we all walked down the hall toward the elevator.

"Stairs are evil," Kyle said. I'd noticed that she walked with a limp, but didn't to be an asshole and ask about it. I figured she'd tell me if she felt like it and otherwise, none of my business.

"I'll fight the evil stairs for you, baby," Stella said, kissing her on the cheek as we waited for the elevator.

"Stab them, girlfriend," Kyle said, and I looked away and met eyes with Chase, whose face was a little red. Maybe she was uncomfortable with Kyle and Stella? That didn't really make sense because she and Stella had two classes together, so they'd seen each other today. Huh.

Hadn't read that situation well. I'd have to talk to her about it later, because we couldn't really talk about it with Kyle and Stella standing right there. I hoped Chase wasn't homophobic. That would be a bummer. Still, I had to remind myself constantly that we were still practically strangers.

The four of us walked across the street to the dining commons. I had only been here a few times because I'd felt weird about sitting at the long tables alone and feeling like everyone was staring at me. It felt better being in a group.

We grabbed our trays and moved along the line. I passed by the chicken and went for spaghetti, which was always a pretty sure bet no matter where you ate.

We also nabbed salads at the salad bar and then claimed the end of one of the long tables. Other groups were sitting and chatting and eating. We'd arrived at peak dinner hour.

"I can't believe the first day is over," Kyle said. "I thought I was going to break my neck rushing between classes. Or rushing as much as I can." Stella rubbed her arm and they shared one of those looks that didn't need words. They were so connected as a couple. It almost made me jealous.

I hadn't really dated a whole lot. I'd gone out with boys and they were fine, but I guess I just hadn't found the right one yet. Fortunately, I was diving into an entire pool of dating possibilities. There were literally guys everywhere. You couldn't move because you'd trip over one. Surely on this campus I could find one to hang out with that might be cool enough to date?

"Did you already start the English reading?" Stella asked Chase, and that seemed to relax her. Chase was always most relaxed when she was talking about books, reading books, or standing near books. Maybe we should do a bookstore trip this weekend. I could use some new pleasure reading.

Chase nodded and they started jabbering away. Kyle looked at me.

"So, how is my fellow Undeclared doing?" she asked.

I tipped my hand from left to right.

"I mean, I guess it was fine? I only have two classes tomorrow, so that's good. I don't feel like I really got the full experience, because they just went through the syllabus and assignments and everything. But it's going to be a lot of work and I'm already dreading it." She laughed.

"I know how that is. I knew college was going to be different from high school, but the fact that you won't get a detention if you don't turn your homework in is still so weird to me. Like, if I don't show up for class, they aren't going to call my parents." True. I could sleep through all of my classes and Dad would never know. I mean, he'd know when I failed, but no one was going to call him and rat me out.

I looked around and twirled some more spaghetti onto my fork.

"Are you going to get into any clubs or anything?" I remembered seeing the tables out on the mall on the first weekend we moved in, but I was still too overwhelmed to begin to think about joining anything.

"Um, we're pretty sure we're going to join the campus LGBTQ+ organization, but I'm not sure about anything else yet. I guess there's clubs for literally everything, but I don't want to spend all my time at club meetings, you know? I want to get the whole experience." I nodded because I knew exactly what she meant.

I was still working on adjusting to the fact that I was living with a virtual stranger and eating food that my dad hadn't cooked and going to classes that weren't mandatory. It was all too much to think about adding extras.

I kept looking at Chase as she talked to Stella and I had to remind myself not to stare. It was hard. She was just so pretty. I was totally jealous of her hair and her height and a lot of her wardrobe, which wouldn't fit or look good on me. She was just one of those girls that all the other girls wanted to be. At least I thought sought so.

At one point, Chase looked over at me and smiled just a little bit. I felt the answering smile on my face and it was like everything was going to be okay.

I hoped.

Chapter Three

CHASE

"Are you uncomfortable with Kyle and Stella?" Cordelia asked me when we got back from dinner.

"No, why?" I wasn't really sure what she was talking about. Stella and I had a lot of classes together and I was seriously hoping that we could become friends since we were going to see each other a lot over the next few years. I had hoped I'd be able to find a friend in college that was in my same major and it was looking like that might happen.

"Oh, you just seemed a little weird when they were holding hands in the elevator." I looked at Cordelia. I hadn't been aware of anything. Had I given off something?

"Did I?" I was starting to panic. I didn't want Stella to think I didn't like her because she had a girlfriend.

"Maybe I just saw something that I misinterpreted. I'm sorry. I didn't mean to make you worry." She must have seen the anxiety on my face. I wasn't real good at hiding it. At all.

"Okay ..." I trailed off. "Because I don't care. If she has a girlfriend or whatever. It's fine. I mean, more than fine because they really seem like they're in love." I would be lying if I said I

275

didn't feel something when I looked at Kyle and Stella, but that something wasn't disgust or shame. I thought they were lucky to have found one another. I wanted something like that. With a boy, of course.

"Yeah, they do," she said with what sounded like a wistful sigh. "I hope I can find a boyfriend here. I mean, there's like thousands of dudes on campus."

I nodded.

"Exactly. If you can't find a guy here, where are you gonna find one?" I said.

"We should make a plan to find boyfriends by the end of the year," Cordelia said, holding her hand out. "I'm always more motivated if I'm competing with someone."

Oh. That didn't really seem like something we should be competing at, but what did it matter?

"Sure." I shook her hand and let go quickly. I was trying not to touch her too much.

"Cool. We'll rock our studies and find boyfriends. We've got this." I pretended that I was totally on board with this plan, but the idea of actually putting myself out there to find a boyfriend made my stomach knot up. Ugh. My limited dating experience was going to bite me in the ass. I bet Cordelia had a lot more experience. She was so cute and vivacious, I couldn't imagine that she'd had a hard time in high school with guys. Plus, the red hair didn't hurt either.

"Boyfriends for everyone! Well, everyone who wants one," Cordelia said, punching her fists in the air.

"Yay!" I was trying to match her enthusiasm.

"You're so cute sometimes," she said, and the way she said it made my stomach do a little something. It wasn't an unpleasant feeling. I hoped I wasn't blushing.

"Hey, so since you finished your homework already, do you want to watch *Steven Universe*? I have all the episodes on my laptop so we can start from the beginning. You really have to start at the beginning with this show," she said. Her curls bounced with her excitement. I honestly had no idea why this show was such a big deal, but if she loved it, I was sure I could learn to like it. Her enthusiasm was contagious.

"Uh, sure?" I said, and she made a little squeak of glee.

APPARENTLY, to fully get the entire "experience," we had to turn all the lights off, get under a cozy blanket, and have popcorn. Even though we'd just had dinner. I was trying to think of it as weird salty dessert.

She set up her laptop on her desk, and we had to sit side-by-side on her bed, and since it was so small, we were completely squished against one another. It wasn't a big deal.

I was trying to pretend it wasn't a big deal.

Why was it a big deal?

My right side was touching hers and that was it. Why was my heart racing and my skin prickling? Why was I noticing how warm her skin was? College was really doing a number on my anxiety.

"Are you ready?" Cordelia said as she queued up the first episode. It was a bright cartoon and it didn't seem like my kind of thing, but I was going to give it a shot.

"Yup," I said, reaching into the popcorn bowl. It gave me something to do with my hands.

Cordelia made a little squeaking noise and started to play the show. I really wasn't sure about this. The show started with a cute and catchy opening song. I was going to give it the benefit of the doubt.

"Wait, what's that in his belly button?" I asked. The boy with the black curly hair (who I was pretty sure was Steven) had a red stone in his belly button. Weird.

"Shhhh," Cordelia said, squeezing my arm. "Just watch. All will be revealed in time."

"Okay," I said with a sigh.

SEVERAL HOURS LATER, I was hooked.

"I can't believe I'm crying over this," I said, as Cordelia handed me a tissue.

"Yeah, it kind of sneaks up on you. That's how they get you," Cordelia said, but she was dabbing her own eyes.

"Seriously, what the fuck?" I said, sniffling and blowing my nose.

Cordelia laughed and I realized I was leaning on her. We'd gotten closer as the show played and we were now practically cuddling, but she didn't seem uncomfortable.

"I know. But it's the greatest." I nodded and tossed my tissue in the empty popcorn bowl.

"Wow, it's late," I said, looking at my phone. I should definitely get to bed ASAP. I knew Cordelia liked to stay up late, but then she slept late in the mornings so I didn't see the point.

"Yeah, it is." I turned to look at her and I realized how close her face was to mine. Her freckles were like little paint splatters all over her skin. I probably couldn't count them all.

She blinked at me a few times and I felt my face get hot for some reason.

"I should take a shower," I said, jumping up from the bed and knocking the popcorn bowl on the floor.

"Okay," she said in an odd voice as I bent down to pick up the bowl. My hands shook a little as I tossed the tissues.

"I'll take one too," she said, getting up from the bed. I kept my back to her as I gathered up my towel and shower stuff. I didn't know why, but I couldn't look at her.

We both headed for the large bathroom and didn't speak as

we walked into the stalls that were right next to each other. I tried not to listen or think about the fact that she was taking her clothes off mere feet away from me. Of course, there was a wall, but still. I could see her feet in her pink flip-flops. Mine were black. Everything about Cordelia was bright and fun and I wished I could be more like her. I was just so afraid of so many things. I definitely cared far too much what people thought of me. And I cared a lot about order and schedules and having everything just so. I was hoping her chaos would rub off on me a little. Not too much.

I stripped and turned on the water and heard her humming. I couldn't figure out the tune, but it was sweet. I was normally someone who took real fast showers, but I stayed under the water longer because Cordelia was still humming and had her water going.

So many thoughts ran through my head and I just wanted to hit a switch and shut my brain off for a little while. Too many thoughts. Nearly all of them were about Cordelia. About how her skin had felt against my arm. About how cute she looked when she smiled. About how looking at her face made me feel like I was standing still, instead of running and running and running like I normally did. About how I didn't know how I would have gotten through these first few days of college without her.

So many thoughts. Too many thoughts. I rinsed my hair again, wishing that the thoughts would go with my conditioner down the drain. If only it worked like that.

I left the shower with my towel wrapped securely around me and looked over as Cordelia got out as well. Her skin was bright pink from the hot water and her towel didn't do much to conceal her body. I didn't want to make her uncomfortable so I just gave her a little nod and then shuffled back to our room with her behind me. I should have brought clothes with me and got dressed in the shower.

I turned my back on Cordelia and got my pajamas out. I had mastered the art of getting dressed without getting naked. We still really didn't know each other, and I'd always had trouble with being naked around other people. I wasn't ashamed of my body, but I didn't like to show it to anyone.

As I got my clothes on, I heard Cordelia rustling around in her drawers and I made the mistake of looking up in the mirror that was above my dresser so I could check to see if I needed to pluck my eyebrows. They grew out of control sometimes and I had to keep them constantly groomed or I looked like I had caterpillars above my eyes.

One second I was looking at my own face and the next I was seeing miles of creamy skin covered in freckles. I looked away as quickly as I could, but not before my body jolted with something I didn't understand. It was just her back. She had on shorts, but hadn't put her top on yet. Just a back. Nothing more. Still, I felt my face getting red and my stomach flopped and flipped like a gymnast on a beam.

I coughed and pulled on the rest of my clothes and willed my face to stop being red. A few shaky breaths later, I turned around to find Cordelia combing her fingers through her hair. She made a face when she hit a snag.

"I wish I could brush it, but curls and brushes don't mix." I grabbed a wide-toothed comb from my dresser.

"Would this work?" I held it up and she smiled. My stomach did another swoop.

"Maybe? It's worth a shot." Instead of taking the comb from me, she turned around and put her hair over her shoulder. When it was wet, it fell halfway down her back. My fingers trembled as I sectioned out a few pieces and ran them through the comb, starting with the ends and working my way up.

"I envy your short hair. I wish I could do that with mine, but I would probably end up looking like a frizzy puff." I let out a breathy laugh. I was still having some trouble getting myself relaxed again. What was wrong with me?

Cordelia's hair slid through my fingers.

"You'd still look cute as a frizzy puff," I said and she turned her head to give me a smile. I thought I was going to explode.

"Thanks."

I finished the rest of her hair in silence and she slicked her curl cream through it.

"I'm curious to see the results," she said, getting on her tiptoes to look in my mirror.

I needed to read. I needed to get out of this room. I needed to take a deep breath. I needed to calm the hell down.

Cordelia flopped down on the bed with a sigh.

"We did it. We got through our first day of college. Now we just have a bazillion more to go." I had done the math on how many days I had left of college, but I didn't want to tell her what the exact count was.

"Yeah, we did." Now we just had to get through the next few years of days.

Cordelia looked over at me with a pout as I settled on my bed.

"Will you read to me?" I couldn't say no to her even if I wanted to.

I had no idea if our roommate relationship was normal, but I didn't really care. In this chaotic new environment, Cordelia felt like ... an anchor. When everything was spinning, she helped me stand still.

I definitely wasn't going to share those thoughts with her. Not now, not ever.

"Hey," she said as I picked up the book we'd been reading. I looked up and she was watching me, a serious look on her face.

"Yeah?" I asked, the book almost slipping from my fingers.

"I'm really glad you're my roommate." Her ears and

cheeks got red and I wondered why. She definitely blushed a lot, due to her coloring, so it might be nothing.

"Me, too," I said. She closed her eyes and a smile played on her face.

CORDELIA

Somehow I made it through my first week of college and only got lost three times, fell asleep in class once, was late twice, and had exactly two and a half panic attacks. That was successful for me. Of course, when I told Chase that, she gave me such a horrified look that I laughed until I started crying.

I also made a few friends, including a guy named Atticus in my Intro to US History class, and two girls in my Art History 102 class, Bree and Mariella. I was managing to keep up with homework for the most part, and my dad hadn't shown up at my dorm room to ask me how school was going. I called that a win in my book.

Chase, on the other hand, was already a week ahead in her homework, had written a paper that wasn't due for weeks, and seemed reluctant to venture out too much, except for hanging out with Stella, which usually meant hanging out with Kyle, and I was always up for that. I wished Kyle and I had some classes together, but it hadn't worked out that way. Chase and Stella had two together and I couldn't lie, I was jealous.

On Saturday, Chase told me she was going to the library to study with Stella and asked me if I wanted to come along. Honestly, I wanted to lay in bed and be comfortable as I tried to get my brain to focus on textbook reading, but I wanted to be with her, even if she wasn't paying attention to me. I was fully serious about her work ethic rubbing off on me. It was going to happen. Plus, someone had to be there to stop her before she studied so hard that her eyeballs caught fire. I was happy to be that person.

We gathered up our bags and headed down the hall to pick up Stella, and Kyle was there too. Her bag had wheels on it, and she was using a cane that had blue and purple sparkles swirled on it.

"Ready?" Chase said and they both nodded. She seemed much more comfortable with both of them, and I was glad some random computer had put Stella down the hall. Not only was she completely gorgeous and put-together, but she was whip smart. She could give Chase a run for her money. They quoted books back and forth, far too fast for me to follow. Kyle just stared at Stella as if she hung the moon and it made my heart ache.

I wanted that. I wanted that so much that it kept me up at night. They were just so effortless with each other. They were always touching, always leaning toward each other. As if gravity pulled them together.

I hadn't seen that growing up, since my mom had split and my dad didn't really date much. I think he was worried about bringing someone in my life that wouldn't end up staying. Plus, he spent way too much of his energy on me. I had a lot of guilt about that, but I hadn't known what to say to him to change it. In the end, he was the parent and he could do what he wanted. If that was attending every single dance recital, concert, and award ceremony and not going on dates, that was his choice. Maybe now that he didn't have to do all that, he could find someone to hang out with. I wanted him to be happy. I wanted him to find a woman that could love him because he was pretty fucking awesome.

"Elise was going to come, but Eli surprised her with a date," Stella said. I'd met Elise a few days ago and she was a total doll. Her wardrobe made me drool and her confidence was to be envied. Plus, her purple glasses were adorable. Her figure was thicker than mine, and she rocked every bit of it. I hadn't met her partner Eli, who was non-binary and used they/them pronouns. I'd never met anyone like that before, but I had definitely lived a sheltered life in my small town. I mean, there were probably non-binary people there, too, I just didn't know about them. College was expanding my mind in so many ways.

"They are so cute. Almost as cute as we are," Kyle said, and then puckered her lips for a kiss that Stella gave her.

"You're right. No one is as cute as we are, baby." They both giggled and that ache inside pulsed like a heartbeat. I didn't know what it was, or how to make it go away.

A boy. I needed a boy. Chase and I had made a pact that we were both going to get boyfriends by the end of the year, and as soon as I got my shit together as far as homework, I was going to be on the case. I hadn't really dated much. I'd kissed a few boys here and there (and done a little more than kissing), but it never felt right, and I'd always been a little relieved when they had moved on, or ghosted me. Guess I was just picky. There weren't a lot of options in my town, so I had a much better chance now. I just had to, you know, go out and do it.

IT TOOK a while for us all to find a place we felt comfortable studying at. Kyle finally plopped down on a chair and said she wasn't moving, so we sat at that table.

I pulled out my textbooks first, since they were the worst. I had a few of them as e-books, but I wanted to get the paper ones done. They were definitely the most awful.

I looked up and Chase was already engrossed in one of her books. Biology. She was so smart that she'd gotten into a higher level than I had, so I was stuck in Bio 105. Her mind was amazing. It surprised me every day how it worked. Whereas I could barely think from one minute to the next, she was always five moves ahead and had a map on how to get there. She was just so interesting. And smart. And tall. I had to admit, I loved that she could get things down from the top of my closet for me. I no longer had to jump, or climb on things, or use something else to knock the box of Lucky Charms off the top shelf when I decided to have a snack.

Okay, I was definitely not getting my Algebra done and that was the reason I'd come to the library in the first place. Not to be obsessing over Chase, which was a strange thing to do anyway. I was just trying to avoid doing homework again. Get your shit together, Cordelia Scott.

TWO HOURS LATER, I had made somewhat of a dent in my homework and I was also dying for a snack.

"I'm hungry," Kyle declared, and I was the only one to look up. Stella and Chase had put in earbuds to drown out the ambient noise of the library. I liked it. In fact, I would have preferred for there to be more noise. I thrived in chaos for some reason. I liked to have a lot going on around me. Made it easier to focus. Or maybe it was because I grew up with a dad who was always chopping wood, or building something, or using power tools right next to me, and I had to figure out how to tune him out. Plus, he liked to sing. A lot. Loudly.

"Me, too," I said, giving her a smile. She took her hair down from its bun and then twisted it up again. I fiddled with the ends of my curls. They did look great today, I had to admit. And they weren't going to end up as tangled at the end of the day since Chase had combed them out for me. We'd started that nightly ritual of having her comb out my hair for me and then reading for a while before we fell asleep. It had become a critical part of my day and I didn't know what I would do without it. Her voice and the stories that she picked quieted my brain. When I listened to her, I wasn't thinking a thousand thoughts at once. I wasn't spinning off into five hundred directions. I wasn't worrying or panicking. I was only thinking about the way her beautiful brown eyes bounced along the pages, how she read with such conviction and passion, and how still she was when she read. Often, she was full of nervous energy and always doing one thing or another, but when she read, she was still. I figured it was as good for her to read to me as it was for me to listen to it. Something for both of us.

Kyle poked Stella, who looked up grumpily.

"Babe, I'm starving. Can we take a coffee break and come back?" She pouted, and Stella's grumpy expression melted.

"I can't say no to you," she said with a sigh.

I reached out and tapped Chase, who jumped when she realized we were all looking at her.

"Sorry," she said, pulling out her earbuds. "I was focused." I laughed as she blinked a few times, as if she was emerging from another world.

"Want to go refuel and then come back?" I also needed to get up and stretch my legs. Kyle got up and groaned, stretching her legs. She was pretty open about her disability. She'd been born with one leg shorter than the other and had tons of surgeries, but there was still a difference, so she walked with a limp and needed a cane occasionally.

"You okay?" Stella asked as Kyle flexed and pointed her toe.

"Yeah, just stiff today." She leaned on her cane and took a few steps. "It's fine. I'm fine. Everyone can calm down." She laughed and started walking. I hoped I hadn't been staring too much or treating her differently. I liked her and I didn't want to make her upset.

"Does it hurt?" I asked as we gathered up our things and headed to the coffee shop on the first floor. We were restricted from bringing anything from the shop upstairs, which was a bummer. The first-floor tables and chairs and couches were crowded with students and laptops, all trying to caffeinate and work at the same time. I saw a lot of frantic eyes and it wasn't even close to finals time. I was going to try not to think about that.

"Not really. Just gets stiff sometimes," Kyle said. I didn't want to babble at her, so I just nodded.

"What do you want? My treat," Stella asked the three of us.

"Oh, you don't have to do that," I said, and Chase protested, but she waved us off.

"You'll get me next time. No worries." She beamed and I couldn't believe she was that pretty and that smart and that nice. No wonder Kyle was head over heels for her.

I didn't want to take advantage, so I just ordered an iced vanilla coffee and a small pastry. Chase got the same, but without the flavoring in the coffee. We lurked until we got a table and Kyle sat down.

"To our first week in college," she said, lifting her cup. We all tapped our cups together.

"We liveddddddd," I said dramatically and they all laughed. "I still keep expecting my dad to show up and ask me how it's going."

"My dad is literally a college professor. It's going to be a struggle to write my papers without his approval," Stella said, and I winced. Ouch. That was even worse than my dad.

"Except your dad hasn't threatened to drive up and break into your dorm room if you don't call and check in at least once a day," Kyle said while she made a face.

"Wait, seriously?" I asked.

She nodded.

"Afraid so. I mean, my mom said it in a joking way, but like, that is totally something she would do. She and Dad are like Gold Star helicopter parents." She laughed a little and shook her head and we all started talking about how our respective parents were handling us being away.

It was nice. They were easy to talk to and didn't seem to mind if I got off track and babbled. I also sometimes got kinda loud, but they didn't seem to mind that either. It was usually hard for me to feel super comfortable with new people, but it wasn't that way with them. I didn't think they were talking behind my back about how annoying I was. I'd had that experience before more than once.

The caffeine started having an effect on me, so I suggested we go back to studying so I could use the fuel while I had it.

BY THE TIME dinner rolled around, my brain was fried and I was ready to not think for a while. We all decided to go to the Union and get pizza, and then went back to our dorm.

"Do you want to watch a movie or something?" Stella asked. I looked at Chase and she nodded.

"Yeah, sure," I said. We headed to her room and found Elise there, reading a book and with a notebook next to her and a purple pen in her hand. Her side of the room was a riot of color and rainbows and even a few pictures of unicorns. I loved it.

"Hey, how's it going?" she said, looking up and smiling. Today she had leggings with a star print on them and a black top that had subtle shimmer woven through it. Her lipstick was bright purple.

"Good, how was your date?" Stella asked as we all piled our bags near the door. There wasn't a whole lot of place to sit, but Stella pulled out some fold-up chairs from her closet and set them out.

"Eli is ridiculous. They took me out to this field that I didn't even know existed near campus and we went on a walk only to find they'd set up a picnic. Honestly, it makes me feel like a bad girlfriend." She laughed, but she was beaming.

"Aw, that's so sweet," Kyle said, hooking her cane on Stella's bed and sitting down on her gray and white chevron-patterned comforter. Stella's side of the room was much more subdued, done in shades of gray, white, and pale blue.

"Seriously. I would try and compete with them in the romance department, but I would lose every time." I looked at Chase and she was smiling, but there was something sad in her eyes. I knew the feeling. Hearing about all these happy couples was nice, but it also made jealousy snarl in my stomach. The two of us needed to find boyfriends to do things like that for us ASAP.

Stella asked if it was okay that we watched a movie in the room and Elise said it was fine, and put on a pair of giant headphones and started bopping her head to whatever music she had going and went back to doing her homework.

"What do you want to watch?" she asked us. I had no idea and didn't want to rock the boat, so I said I didn't care and Chase agreed.

"Okay, I'll scan through the movies I've got and if anyone sees something they want, just yell and we'll take a vote." She grabbed the remote and started flipping through. Honestly, I didn't really care. I was just happy to be spending time with people that I liked. Chase was right beside me and her arm kept brushing mine. I jolted a little bit every time she did it. I couldn't figure out why. I swear, the other night when we watched *Steven Universe* I could barely concentrate because she was right there next to me. And that was my favorite show. Looked like I was going to be distracted again.

In the end, Kyle was the decider that we were watching an all-lady remake of an older movie and I was on board with it. Elise softly hummed to herself and Stella started the movie.

"Anyone want popcorn?" she asked, and even though we'd

just had pizza, I figured why not? She pulled out two bags of movie theater butter and I smiled at Chase.

"That's the best kind," she said and the way she smiled at me made my skin feel warm and prickly.

"Exactly," Stella said as she put one of the bags in the microwave and Kyle pulled out two big bowls. Stella had everything. It was impressive. She even had a little hot plate that was definitely not allowed in the dorm.

"I don't even care," she said, pushing it further under the bed. "Sometimes I want to cook and those rules aren't going to stop me."

"You tell 'em," Kyle said, nodding.

The movie started and Stella passed me and Chase our own bowl of popcorn. I situated it on my lap and we both munched from it. Our hands kept colliding in the bowl and I didn't know why it was distracting me from watching. Out of the corner of my eye, I watched Kyle and Stella snuggling. Kyle ran her fingers through Stella's hair and sighed happily. It hurt to look at them.

I looked back at the movie.

Chapter Four

CHASE

It happened again. Sitting next to Cordelia made me feel all kinds of confusing things. Maybe it was just because I was seeing Kyle and Stella on the bed. They weren't doing anything odd, just cuddling and being cute. It was sweet and it was adorable and it made me feel almost ... angry? Was that the emotion that was pacing through my brain? I didn't know. I didn't know what was happening to me lately. And it wasn't just because I was scared about college.

Something else was happening to me, and I didn't know what it was or how to get a handle on it. Whatever it was just kept slipping through my hands and darting just out of my reach.

I didn't really watch the movie. I pretended and laughed when everyone else did, but I spent most of the time silently flipping out. I guess I wasn't doing a good job of hiding it because at one point, Cordelia tapped me on the arm and asked me if I was okay.

"Yeah, just tired," I whispered back. That was a valid excuse in college. She rubbed my arm a little and the strange feelings just started spinning harder. I wanted to go back to our room. I wanted to get away from it all. There wasn't really a way to do that without just bolting and leaving them with questions, so I sat. I stayed in the chair and mechanically ate popcorn and tried to figure out what the hell was going on.

The movie finally finished and Stella yawned. It wasn't super late, but we were all fried from studying earlier.

"Thanks for letting us come over," Cordelia said, handing the popcorn bowl back.

"Seriously, anytime. For any reason. We're always here if you need us," Stella said, and Kyle nodded.

"Me, too!" Elise said, raising her hand. She'd finished her homework and had been reading a non-school book while simultaneously watching the movie. I had no idea how she was doing that, but her level of focus was impressive.

"Thanks, it's really nice to find a few kindred spirits," Cordelia said and looked at me. She knew the Green Gables reference wouldn't be lost on me. I gave her a smile even though it hurt my face.

"Thanks again," I said, and we waved goodnight to the three of them before going back to our room.

"I'm going to shower," I said the second we got back. I must have been giving off a vibe because Cordelia didn't say she was going to take one as well. She just nodded and pulled a book out of her backpack and put some headphones on.

Now I was worried that she was upset with me. I didn't know why she would be, but the idea of her being mad at me made me feel sick inside. I couldn't handle that.

Once again, I took a shower with too many things to ponder. I wished I could crack open my brain and spill some of it out. There was too much.

I changed quickly when I went back to my room, and grabbed my phone.

"I'm going to call my parents," I said, and hoped she

thought that I just didn't want to disturb her by leaving the room to have my conversation. That was the downside of having a roommate who was just a few feet away most of the time. You could never talk about her with her in the room.

She just sort of nodded and kept her eyes on her book. I didn't know her well enough to know if this meant she was mad at me, but I was going to find out when I got back. As soon as I figured out what was going on in my head.

"Hey, Mom," I said and almost cried in relief. I'd talked to both my parents since I'd come to school, but for the first time I thought I might be homesick. I wished I could fold myself into her lap and have her run her fingers through my hair and tell me that any problem I had, she would help me solve. No matter what. I even missed Kate.

"Hey, kiddo! How's school?" I almost broke down, but was able to hold it together as I leaned against the wall.

"It's good," I said, trying to sound as upbeat as I could.

"What's wrong?" Well, guess I didn't do a good job of masking my emotions.

"I don't know," I said, slamming my palm against the wall. Good thing I didn't do it too hard or I might have hurt my hand.

"Talk to me," she said, and I did. I couldn't find shape or weight in anything that was happening, but I tried to give her an idea as best I could.

"Do you think it's just because you're in a new place? You know it takes you a while to settle in with your routine and getting comfortable." That was true, but this felt like so much more than that.

"Is it that you're not used to sharing a room? You and Kate never had to." Maybe that was it. Maybe I was just adjusting to sharing a room with a stranger. That could be it.

"My advice would be to talk to your roommate. Tell her that it takes you a while to adjust. She sounds like a lovely girl and it makes me feel good as a mother that you're making friends." I didn't make friends easily most of the time, so I knew that had been one of her main concerns. And then Cordelia had showed up. Pretty, messy Cordelia.

"I just don't know," I said again. It was the truth. I had never felt this way before and it scared me.

"It's okay. You don't have to have all the answers all the time, love. I know you don't like that, and it makes you feel uncomfortable, but you might just have to live with it a little bit. Give it another week. See how you feel. How are your classes?" I transitioned to telling her about my professors and the other students and I even mentioned my study date with Kyle and Stella. I didn't mention they were a couple, and I didn't know why I did that either. My parents weren't against gay people, I knew that for sure. Mom wouldn't have batted an eyelash or made a comment about them both being girls. And still, I didn't tell her.

"Well, look at you, my social girl! I'm so proud of you, Chase. You know that right?" I felt like I was going to cry again, and asked if I could talk to my dad for a little while. We chatted mostly about how my classes were going and Kate yelled hello and said that she'd stolen one of the sweaters I'd left behind in my closet, and I told her there was a reason I'd left it behind but that it still wasn't hers to take. I finally hung up and felt a little bit of the chaos in my brain slow its mad swirl.

"Hey," I said when I came back into the room. Cordelia looked up and gave me a weak smile before going back to her book.

"How were your parents?" she asked, while she continued reading. Was she trying to ignore me, but she didn't want to seem rude?

"Are you okay?" I asked. I wasn't normally that blunt, but I needed to know.

"Yeah, why? You just seemed like you had a lot on your mind and I didn't want to add to that, so I was giving you space. Was that not what you wanted?" She looked so perplexed that I instantly felt horrible for thinking she was mad at me.

"No, I thought you were mad at me or something. I'm sorry." She sprung to her feet and came over to my bed and sat down next to me.

"No, I'm sorry. I should have asked what you needed. I just … I didn't know what to do." That was fair. I hadn't known what to do either.

"It's okay," I said, and she put her arms around me for a hug. My heart fluttered and I hugged her back. Her hair was in my face and her body was warm up against me.

"Your hair smells really good," she said, her voice soft.

"Thanks. So does yours." It did. I loved her curl crème. My fingers twirled a few of her curls lightly. She held me and we just breathed together.

I knew I needed to pull back, but I didn't want to let go. Cordelia sighed and settled even closer to me. I wasn't letting go.

Her heart pounded against mine and I felt every single place where our bodies met. My skin started to feel hot and tight.

I finally pulled back. Cordelia's cheeks were red and flushed. She looked deep into my eyes. Hers were a shade between green and blue and they shifted based on the lighting. I could watch them for hours. Cordelia was just so … beautiful. Every day she seemed to get prettier. I just loved the way her body curved and how her hair was all over the place and the way her cheeks dimpled just a little when she smiled.

We sat that way, our eyes locked together until she looked away with another blush.

"We should probably go to bed," she said, and she didn't

look at me again as she got under her comforter. I picked up the book that I'd been reading to her from the edge of my desk. My lungs were shaky as I tried to remember how to breathe.

I looked at the words on the page and shoved all that to the side and focused on just reading. Reading the words to Cordelia. Because I didn't have the answers and reading was always where I felt safest. Even if it was reading to the person who was the source of all my questions.

IT WASN'T until a week later that I settled on a potential boyfriend candidate. His name was Titan, which wasn't ideal, but it wasn't his fault that his parents decided to name him that. He went by Ti, so that was okay. He was a sophomore in my bio class and sat a few seats away. We'd been put in a group together for a discussion and he'd been funny and sweet. I couldn't tell if he was flirting with me or being nice, which was part of my issues finding a boyfriend in the first place.

Now every day he said hello to me and had started sitting closer, so I thought that was a good sign. When class ended the next Wednesday, I packed up slowly and watched him out of the corner of my eye.

He was packing up slowly too, and scrolling through his phone. He was cute, I knew. I mean, anyone would think he was cute. He had dark hair and brown eyes and a nice smile. What else was there?

I gathered up my courage in handfuls and smiled at him.

"Are you done for the day?" I asked as we both stood up. He was just a few inches shorter than me.

"Yeah, you?" he asked, adjusting the strap of his bag.

"Yup," I said and then didn't know where else to go from there.

"Do you maybe wanna grab some coffee or something?" he asked, raking some of his hair out of his eyes. It was kind of curly, which was nice.

"Sure," I said, surprising myself. Wow, this was going really well for me. Usually I couldn't talk very well around guys, but I was doing okay so far.

He gave me a smile and I told myself again that he was cute and nice and that was what was important in attraction.

Right?

~

CORDELIA

"How was your day?" I asked when I came back from a late study session that night. I'd caught dinner with Bree and Mariella, so all I wanted to do was crash and maybe watch a movie or something.

"Good," she said, looking up from some homework. Always working, that Chase. Always. She was a professor's dream. I knew already that she was going to beat me in the GPA department and that was fine. She was smart and she worked hard. She deserved every accolade that came her way.

"I had coffee with a guy," she said as I dropped my backpack. I felt like my stomach dropped too. I had to fight to put a smile on my face.

"Ohhhhh, give me details." I sat on my bed and pretended I was excited for her. I was. I guess I was just jealous that she had found someone before I did. To be fair, I hadn't really been trying. Atticus was a friend, plus, he already had a girlfriend and he'd gushed and gushed about how wonderful she was. I had to get my head in the game if I wanted to find someone. Chase was putting me to shame.

Chase told me about Ti and how he'd opened the door for her and paid for her coffee and muffin and had asked her about her major and reading and so forth. He sounded like a great guy. His major was environmental science and he wanted to save the world. That was pretty admirable, I thought.

Everything about him sounded great, but there was something that rubbed me the wrong way. I pushed that aside and gave her my support because she deserved it and I knew how hard it was for her to approach new people and talk to them. Especially a guy.

"You can invite him over to study if you want. I'd like to meet him," I said, but I felt like I was chewing glass shards when I said it.

"I don't know if he even likes me like that. I don't know." She shook her head and closed her books.

"Do you want to do something?" I blurted out. I wanted to stop talking about the guy.

"Sure, what?" I couldn't help but smile. She said yes before she even knew what I had in mind. I liked that. Now I had to come up with something good. I had a car, so we could go off campus if we wanted to. The only problem was our school was in such an isolated area, that there wasn't much to drive to.

I flipped through the potential things we could do on a Wednesday evening that didn't involve alcohol or doing something that would lead to one or both of us to end up in jail. Conundrum. I glanced around the room for inspiration and then saw the wall of books that Chase had.

"Come on," I said, getting up and slipping into my sneakers.

"Where are we going?" she asked, but she didn't hesitate to get her shoes on or grab her coat. It was still fairly warm out during the day, but the fall bite set in when the sun went down and before we knew it the snow would be flying. I wasn't looking forward to slogging to class through the snow. Hopefully they cleaned the sidewalks well.

"You'll see," I said, winging my keys around on my finger. This was going to be good.

~

TEN MINUTES LATER, we were getting out of the car at the closest mall.

"The mall?" Chase said, looking at the building and wrinkling her nose. "I mean, it's fine. I just don't really like shopping that much." I knew that, which was why I told her to trust me.

I steered her through the doors and past the food court, down the right side of the mall.

"There," I said, pointing to the bookstore. The way her eyes lit up made me feel like I was going to burst. Making her happy was just the greatest.

"Oh," she said and then she was the one leading me toward the store.

"I shouldn't be buying books," she said as she plowed through the entrance.

"How about I pick a book for you and you pick one for me?" I liked the idea of making a game out of this.

Chase looked back at me and grinned.

"Okay. You're on." She dashed away from me and I burst out laughing before going for the opposite direction.

I knew where she was going to go, but I wanted to surprise her. I also wanted to get her something that she would unexpectedly love. That was a tall order, but I had faith in my ability to find the perfect book for her.

I went through the bargain books, and skimmed the new non-fiction before drifting over to general fiction. I scanned the shelves, but nothing was jumping out at me, so I looked to see where Chase was and smiled.

"Hey," I said, poking her in the shoulder. She was so engrossed with reading the titles that she jumped.

"Sorry! Didn't mean to scare you," I said, and she shook her head.

"It's fine. I was just in the book zone."

"Find anything good?" She laughed.

"Only about a million things that I want. Nothing for you, yet."

"That's okay, I haven't found anything for you yet either," I said.

"We're bad at this game," she said, and I nodded.

"Okay, if you were to tell me the top ten books that I must read, what would they be?"

Her eyes went wide.

"Only ten?" That made me laugh.

"Yes, just ten." She sighed and blew a breath out.

"I guess I can do that. But this is a lot of pressure." I stroked her arm to comfort her because it seemed like the thing to do. She looked down at my hand on her arm, so I stopped doing it.

"Ten books," she said under her breath as she scanned the shelves. "This one," she said, pointing to a young adult book. I took a picture of the spine with my phone. It was one I had definitely seen on her shelves. She searched and came up with eight more books that I took pictures of. I was going to read every single one of them.

"I'm stuck on the last one, because there are two," she said with a whine in her voice.

"So make it eleven books. Ten was an arbitrary number." I saw her shoulders relax and she picked the last two books.

"And this is just books that are out. There are a bunch that I know I'm going to love that haven't come out yet." My head was spinning. She really was good at this.

"So, tell me what you want in a book." She snapped her attention back to me.

"Oh, I don't know. I think I'm feeling like I want to read something sweet and fun. Not really dark and serious." Chase thought about that. I could see the wheels turning in her head.

She walked away and I followed her. I waited as she muttered under her breath until she pulled a book off one of the young adult shelves.

"This one." It had a cute cover illustration and I flipped to the back to read the cover copy. It was about three best friends in their first year of college trying to figure out what they wanted to do and find love at the same time. Sounded good to me. Plus, one of the girls was fat, so that was nice to see too.

"Cool," I said, looking up at her.

"It's really good. It'll make you feel like you're eating cotton candy and blowing bubbles at the same time." That made me chuckle and I knew exactly what she meant. I hugged the book to my chest. I hoped it was everything that I hoped it would be. Especially for the fat character. She had to get a happy ending. A really good one.

"Now I have to find one for you …" I said, trailing off and looking around. The shelves were so numerous that staring at them made me more anxious. I needed to just … pick something. Not think about it too much.

I looked at Chase and then started wandering around the store. No particular destination. I just walked where my feet led me, which was to a display of new books near the front.

I walked around the table and looked at the covers.

"This one," I said, picking up one that looked good. I didn't even read the back cover. I just handed it to her.

"You're judging this book by its cover," she said, taking it from me. I nodded.

"Yup. If people didn't judge books by their covers, no one would put any effort into cover design. It's a lie that people don't judge covers. And I think we should be allowed to sometimes. Like right now." I tapped her book.

"Come on, let's pay and then get a giant pretzel with tons of salt on it." Chase just shook her head at me.

"You are an interesting person, Cordelia Scott." That felt like the best compliment I'd ever received. I beamed at her.

"Thank you."

Chapter Five

CHASE

To my great surprise, the book that Cordelia picked out for me was actually amazing. No wonder, since it was a bestseller. I started it when we got back and stayed up a bit too late reading and was exhausted the entire next day, but I didn't even mind. It had been a while since I'd been so captivated by a book. And she'd just grabbed one that had a cover she liked. It went against almost everything I believed in when it came to books.

She seemed to be engrossed in hers as well. It was a book I'd read over the summer and had re-read about four times since. It was an interesting choice, but it was one that had comforted me a lot when I'd been nervous about school. Of the three girls, two of them actually end up together, and the third hooks up with a guy she initially hated. It had all sorts of good tropes and fluffiness in it and I figured Cordelia would dig that, and apparently she did.

"I hate you," she croaked at me two days later when I tried to wake her up. I figured it was just her usual morning grumpiness.

"Any particular reason?" I asked as I pulled out the coffee pot.

"I was up so freaking late. I had to finish." She pointed to the book that was at the foot of her bed. I had fallen asleep and she must have stayed up reading with her phone as a light.

"Did you finish?" I asked as she threw some breakfast sandwiches into the microwave. I liked having breakfast in the room with her instead of going to the dining commons. Having those early moments be just the two of us was the best way to start my day. Plus, I didn't have to worry about other people seeing my hair all over the place.

"Yeah, I had to. I had no choice. I can't believe Pearl and Ana ended up together! I didn't see that coming, but it was so sweet and I'm so happy they're happy. Yes, I know they're not real people." She wiped her hands under her eyes and blew her curls out of her face.

"I know. It was unexpected, but then it made total sense. They're perfect for each other," I said. "You might want to have a second cup." She nodded and groaned.

"I don't want to go to classssssss." I didn't know what to tell her. It was way too early in the semester to skip class, even though staying up late reading was a completely valid excuse.

"You're just gonna have to suck it up, buttercup. At least it's Friday." She nodded and poured creamer into her coffee.

"I wish I didn't care about school so I could just ditch. But I'm scared of not going to class. Even though a lot of my classes are huge and the professors don't even know my name. Like, they're not even going to know. Still. I'm scared that they'll assign something that I'll miss and then I will fail and then my dad will give me the disappointed face and shake his head and make noises about how I should have gone to class and not skipped." She took a breath and sipped her coffee. Sometimes when Cordelia got agitated, she rambled without even taking a breath. I'd learned a lot about her in such a short period.

"Think of it this way: you'll get through it today and then wonder why you made such a big deal of it in the first place." She made a face at me and I laughed.

"No, it's fine. I just need some more coffee. And maybe a nap this afternoon." A nap sounded amazing, but I was always too anxious for naps. I usually just ended up laying there and thinking about too many other things until I gave up and just did some more homework.

I bustled around getting ready and eating my breakfast sandwich with one hand.

"Shit," Cordelia said, and I turned around to find her paler than I'd ever seen her, sitting on the floor with her eyes wide. She put one hand on her chest and closed her eyes.

"What's wrong?" She just shook her head and I dove to the floor. She was breathing in and out way too fast.

"What's happening, Cordelia?" I asked, trying not to flip out. Was she having some sort of medical emergency? Did I need to call for an ambulance? What was happening?

"Cordelia?" She gasped another breath and her eyes flew open.

"I'm having," gasp, "a panic," gasp, "attack."

Fuck. I didn't know what to do. I didn't know what to do to help her or make it better and I'd never felt more helpless in my entire life. I reached out and grabbed her hand and started massaging the back of her knuckles.

I felt like I was going to cry because I was scared and I wanted to help her and didn't know how. So I just sat next to her and watched her breathing and held her hand.

After about ten minutes, she started to breathe more normally and her eyes opened. She turned to focus on me and her face went from scary pale to red with a blush.

"I'm sorry," she said, looking down at our entwined hands.

"What are you sorry about?" I asked, still running my thumb across the back of her knuckles. It felt like more than comforting her.

"For that. I'm usually better about hiding them, but that one just snuck up on me. I'm sorry if I scared you." I wanted to pull her into my arms and hold her tight and tell her that she had nothing to apologize for, but I didn't want to overwhelm her.

"Don't ever apologize for something like that, especially not to me. Are you okay? Do you need me to get you anything?" She shook her head and slowly got to her feet.

"No, I'm fine. They only last a few minutes. It's probably the combination of not sleeping, the caffeine and just … thinking too much. Sometimes I know when they're coming and I can head them off, but this one just sort of tackled me. Phew." She had a sheen of sweat on her forehead and even though she said she was fine, I didn't really believe it.

"Maybe you should take today off. Just in case." Cordelia shook her head.

"No, I don't want to. I can't let that crap stop me. Now I'm mad and I'm even more determined to get through today. Fucking panic attacks." She shook her hands out and stretched her neck.

"Seriously, I'm okay. I've had them for years. I have pills I can take that can sometimes stop them if I take them enough in advance. And sometimes they just fucking happen and I have to stop and deal with them. I'm fine, Chase, I swear." She put her hands on my shoulders and now she was the one comforting me.

"I've never seen someone have a panic attack before. Is there anything I can do to make it better?" Cordelia pulled some clothes out of her dresser and I turned around so she could change.

"Not really. Sometimes having something to hold onto

helps ground me. And I have to try hard not to breathe too fast because then I can faint." I almost turned around and gave her a look because fainting? That didn't sound good.

"I've had them for years. It's just a thing I deal with. I've been to therapy and stuff and I have meds. I'm doing all I can do. Just a quirk in my system. They're worse when I'm under stress or in a new environment, like college." That made sense.

"Do you have them a lot?" I took a risk and turned around and she was fully dressed in a pair of cute jeans and a flowy black top with bright flowers on it. She looked amazing, but she always did.

"Um, it depends? Like, I've had them more often since I got here, just because of the high stress and so forth. And then there are times when I can go weeks or months without having one, and then sometimes I get them several times a week. I never really know."

I didn't really know what else to say to that, so I said, "That sucks."

She laughed a little and put on her backpack.

"Yeah, they do. And thank you. For not like, flipping out. It was nice to have something to hold onto." She touched my shoulder and I just leaned forward and gave her a hug. It felt like the thing I needed to do.

I held her close and stroked her hair.

"I was scared. I was really scared." Her fingers dug into my back.

"I know. But you did it anyway, and that's what matters." She pulled back and we stared at each other for a second.

So quickly, before I even knew it was happening, I leaned forward and kissed her on the cheek. It wasn't a conscious decision. It was just a thing I wanted to do, and I did it.

She blinked at me and then smiled.

"I'll see you later?" She had an earlier class than I did on

Friday, but I still was always the first one up and I got a few chores done before I walked down.

"Yeah," I said, and swallowed past a lump in my throat. She slid by me and left the room and I felt like my legs were going to give out on me. I somehow made it over to my bed and collapsed on it.

This had been … some morning.

CORDELIA

So, the panic attack part wasn't great, but after had been pretty great. Having Chase there to hold my hand was honestly the only thing that helped bring me back from that particular spiral. I was completely and totally drained after the attack, and I didn't want to do anything but take a nap, but I had said I was going to class, so that was what I was going to do. Plus, it was Friday. I could sleep in tomorrow.

The rest of the day was even more draining than I thought it would be. I fell asleep three times, which wasn't good. My notes were a complete fucking mess. My brain was like a sieve, all the stuff I tried to put in it leaking out everywhere. Oh, well. It was just one day.

And when I wasn't trying to stay awake and present, the rest of my brain was thinking about how Chase had kissed me. I mean, she had kissed me on the cheek. Like friends did. It wasn't earth shattering.

So why did it feel like it was?

Friends did things like that all the time. I mean, I'd never done anything like that with friends before, but I knew other people did. It was an intense morning. It was a friendship kiss. A kiss of comfort. That had to be it. Chase wasn't … I mean, she didn't …

It wasn't *like that*. I mean, she was looking for a boyfriend. I was reading way too much into it. My brain had a tendency to do that. It spun in five different directions at once and most of them were usually wrong. This was definitely a dead end.

Still, I couldn't shake the feeling I'd had when her lips had pressed against my skin. I'd kissed boys, but it had never felt like that. Whenever I'd kissed a boy, it felt like … I was pressing my mouth parts against his mouth parts. There was real spark or need or want. Just … two mouths smushing against each other.

With Chase it was something else, and I had no idea how to define what that something else was.

That "something else" sat in my stomach and swirled in my skull for the rest of the day, and even when I tried to take a nap before Chase came back to our room, I couldn't sleep even though I was exhausted.

I just couldn't stop thinking about it, so when Chase walked through the door, I felt my face heat. If I had been smarter, I would have pretended I was asleep when I'd heard her key. Of course I didn't, and she walked in to find me all red-faced.

"Hey, are you doing okay? I was worried about you today." She set her bag down and I thought she was going to rush over to me and put her hand on my forehead or something. As if I had a fever instead of a panic attack.

"I'm fine. Just tired. It takes a lot out of me. Some Friday night." She sat on her bed, but the worry was still stamped on her forehead.

"Do you want to take a nap? I can leave if you need me to." Sweet. Chase was so sweet sometimes it was painful. It hit me right in the chest and sometimes it made me want to cry. She was too much sometimes. Too good, too nice to me. Too good of a roommate for me, that was for sure.

"No, you don't have to do that. I'm not going to kick you out of your room, Chase. Do whatever you want to do. Maybe see if Ti wants to do something?" I couldn't believe the words came out of my mouth, but I said them and instantly wanted to take them back. Reel them in and destroy them.

"I don't want to leave you all alone. And I'm still pretty sure he just wants to be friends and isn't interested in me that way." I wanted to roll my eyes. Of course he was interested in her, if he liked girls that way. She was gorgeous and sweet and funny, once you got her to open up. Chase was also smart as fuck. She was the ideal girl in every way.

"It's fine. Go, have fun." I wanted her to have fun, even if it wasn't with me. I could handle my jealousy. I didn't own her. She was just my roommate. Not even my best friend, although, she felt like she had become my best friend in just a few short weeks. Things went fast in college.

"But I'd rather have fun with you," she said, giving me a little smile that made me feel like I was going to burst into a million pieces. She was just so sweet.

"Okay, but my idea of fun involves eating a lot of popcorn and watching a fuckton of *Steven Universe*. I'm all about the self-care tonight." Self-care was something that I was trying to be better at. I couldn't just keep pushing sometimes and I needed to slow down and stand still and just breathe for a moment. It was okay, and I needed it.

"That sounds great," she said and came to sit on my bed next to me. I waited, holding my breath as she brushed some of my curls back.

"I'm glad you're okay."

"I'm okay," I said.

THE DAY HAD STARTED off like complete shit, but ended perfectly. Chase and I sat together and ate too much popcorn and ate marshmallow fluff out of the jar and laughed and cried about Steven and his little alien family.

"I'm so glad you made me watch this," Chase said with a happy sigh. She leaned her cheek on my shoulder and I looked over at her. I was happy she liked it. I would have been pretty sad if she hadn't.

I ran my fingers through her hair and she looked up at me.

Energy buzzed between us and before I could guess or question anything, I leaned over and kissed her on the mouth.

I don't know what made me do it. I just wanted to, so I did. Shock jolted through her, but she didn't pull away. I didn't even know what the fuck I was doing, or what was happening, but I was kissing Chase and after a few seconds of surprise, she was kissing me back.

Chase was kissing me back.

Chase.

Was.

Kissing.

Me.

Back.

Chapter Six

CHASE

I was kissing Cordelia? Like, on the lips? I didn't know why or how it was happening, but it was happening and it was ...

I didn't have words for what kissing Cordelia was. Words hadn't been invented to explain the way her mouth felt against mine. She tasted like salt from the popcorn and something sweet. I trembled, and my breath stuttered in my lungs. I pulled myself closer to her, because nothing had ever felt as good as this. Kissing Cordelia was better than anything else.

I gasped in a breath and felt her tongue dart into my mouth. I felt a moan escape from the back of my throat and I put my hand on the back of her neck to pull her closer. I wanted her tongue in my mouth. I wanted my tongue in her mouth. I wanted her teeth on my bottom lip. I wanted to be completely overwhelmed by her. I was never going to recover from this kiss and I didn't want it to end.

Cordelia made a little whimpering sound and I thought I was going to die. The kiss grew more desperate, more hungry, more and more and more.

I needed more of her. More of *this*.

She was the one to break the moment.

We were both gasping and panting. Her cheeks were full of color and I stared into her eyes. They were more blue today.

Steven Universe was still playing, but I couldn't be bothered to stop it. Noting mattered right now other than this kiss with Cordelia.

I rested my forehead against hers as we both tried to get our breath back. My heart was pounding so hard, I could feel it in every part of my body. I took my hand off the back of her neck and she pulled back a little more.

"I'm not ..." she said, trailing off. "I mean, I don't like girls."

"Me neither," I said, and my voice sounded like it didn't belong to me.

"I ..." she said, trailing off again.

"I know," I said. She sat back and stared at me.

"What just happened, Chase?" she asked.

"I don't know," I said. Things had taken on a hazy quality and my head felt like it was floating above my body.

We both sat across from each other silently for at least ten minutes. Neither of us seemed to be able to find the right words. I knew I didn't have the right ones, but there were a few facts that had to be addressed: One, we had just kissed, and not in a friendship way. Two, we were both heterosexual. Three, there was no going back from that kiss.

"I kissed you," Cordelia finally said, and her hand drifted to her lips, tracing them with her fingers. Her lips were just a little red. I wondered what mine looked like. They were still tingling from the contact with her.

"And you kissed me back." There were definitely two of us in that kiss. I wasn't the only one. If I had been the only one, I definitely would have pulled back.

"I did," she said in a dreamy voice, still touching her lips.

"We kissed." And now we had to deal with what that

meant. In some way, it was almost as if we had been hurtling toward this moment since the beginning. I had kissed her on the cheek this morning.

"I don't know what to do right now," Cordelia said, getting up and starting to pace around the small room. She could only go a few steps in any one direction, so she had to keep pivoting around so she could continue pacing.

"Me neither." My thoughts spun, but my body was still.

"We kissed and it was … well, it was the best fucking kiss of my fucking life and you're my roommate and you're a *girl* and I don't like girls?" The last part sounded like a question.

"I don't like girls either," I said, but she wasn't listening to me.

"I mean, I've thought girls were pretty before and whatever, but doesn't everyone? You're pretty. I mean, that's obvious. You're like, one of the most beautiful people I've ever seen and that's just the truth. It doesn't *mean* anything." She took a breath and put her hands in her hair.

She thought I was beautiful? That made me grin uncontrollably.

"I think you're beautiful," I said, and she stopped pacing and turned to look at me as if she was suddenly remembering I was there.

"You think I'm beautiful?" she said, and her voice cracked.

"Of course. You're amazing, Cordelia." Anyone could see that. She was bright and talented and bubbly and confident and stunning. Being around her made me happier than I had been in a long time.

She came back to the bed and sat down.

"I am?"

"Yes, you are. And I don't know what this means or why it's happening, but I want to kiss you again." I had never wanted something this much. I needed her. I craved her.

"Okay," she said, pushing her hair back. I dove for her and

we ended up horizontal on her bed. Cordelia laughed, and the sound made me feel like I was full of bubbles. I looked down into her face.

"You're really beautiful, Cordelia." She pushed my hair out of my face.

"So are you."

I kissed her again. And again. And again. I explored her mouth with my tongue and teeth and it was everything. She was everything. I propped myself above her and everywhere our bodies touched caught fire. The more I got, the more I wanted. The hand that wasn't used to hold myself above her I used to trace her curves. She had them where I didn't. She was so much rounder and I loved every single inch of her.

Being with Cordelia didn't feel like being with a boy. With boys it was always stressful and anxious and nervous and awful. I just figured that was what it was supposed to be. How you were supposed to feel when you were with someone you liked.

With Cordelia I only felt good. Beyond good. So good I didn't know if I was going to survive it.

The only thing that stopped me was a knock at the door. I bolted off Cordelia as if someone had jolted me with electricity. I looked down at her and we both realized that we weren't the only two people. There was a whole world outside our dorm room. A whole world and a whole lot of questions.

I shakily walked to the door and looked through the peephole. It was Stella.

I opened the door and tried to put a neutral face on. As if I hadn't just been making out with my roommate.

"Hey," I said, pushing my hair back.

"Hey, I was wondering if you wanted to come over and watch a movie or go out or something?" She was all dressed up to go out, but she always looked put-together. I was envious.

"Um," I said, looking back at Cordelia. She just sort of blinked at us.

"Is everything okay?" Stella said.

"Yeah, fine," I said a little too quickly. Cordelia nodded. She didn't seem to be able to form words, which was so unlike her that Stella had to know something was up. I had absolutely no idea how to explain what was happening, and I didn't really want to. At least not until Cordelia and I had talked about what it meant. She was my first priority.

"Okay," Stella said slowly, still looking back and forth between me and Cordelia. "If you want to come over in a few, there will be snacks. Kyle and I went shopping earlier so we have crackers and cheese and soda." I told her we'd be down without even asking Cordelia because I just wanted to get her out of the room so she'd stop staring at us.

She knew. She had to know. There were only so many things that could lead to us both looking and acting like this.

"Sounds good," Stella said, and backed out of the room. I shut it behind her and leaned on it.

"Sorry, I didn't know what to say to her because she definitely knows that something is up." Cordelia sat up and blew a breath out.

"So I guess we have to figure out what the fuck we're doing, huh?" I shrugged.

"Do you really want to do that right now?" I asked. She laughed a little.

"Not really. It's too much to think about right now. Can we go hang out with them and put it on hold? Like, figure it out tomorrow? I'm just not ready to think about all the things I'm already thinking about." I almost started laughing because I knew exactly what she meant. My brain was already firing with so many different thoughts that I wasn't ready to begin pondering over.

"Yeah, sounds good," I said. I ran my fingers through my hair a few times and tried to get my heart to stop pounding so hard.

"So, we're going to go and hang out with Kyle and Stella and we're going to talk about all the other stuff tomorrow," Cordelia said.

"It's a plan," I said.

~

CORDELIA

It was a good plan, but the second we walked into Stella's room (Elise was spending the night with Eli), I felt like I had a spotlight on me. Or that I was in one of those police interrogations and they were just waiting for me to crack.

Somehow, I put on what I hoped was a normal face and tried to fake that my world wasn't crumbling around me. I'd always thought I had known myself really well, and tonight had shaken everything up. My foundation was cracked and shifting and I was barely holding on.

Kyle asked us if things were going well, and I could tell Stella had told her something was up with us, but Chase and I just nodded and said things were going well and that we were fine and everything was good and fine. I didn't know how we did it, but fortunately, we were distracted by a movie and cheese and Kyle and Stella chatting about this and that.

I tried not to sit too close to Chase when we watched the movie. Stella said that Elise didn't mind if we sat on her bed, but sitting on a bed again was probably a bad idea so Chase and I declined.

Halfway through the movie, though, I felt Chase's fingers reaching for mine. I glanced over at her and she mouthed "hi" at me. In spite of trying to sit away from her, I was leaning nearly half off my seat to be as close to her as possible. Oops? While trying not to make much noise, I scooted my chair a little closer to her and then let my fingers twist with hers. It was like when I'd had the panic attack. She ran her thumb across mine. I didn't even know if she knew she was doing it, but it felt good. Holding Chase's hand was right. Like I should have been holding it the whole time. It also made my stomach flutter, and I could feel my cheeks smiling. Things were better with Chase. I quickly glanced over at Kyle and Stella, but they were curled up together, feeding each other popcorn and watching the movie. They weren't paying attention to us. That was fine. I wasn't ready to answer any questions about what Chase and I were doing.

So far, we'd kissed, a lot, and we were holding hands. What did that mean? I had never thought about dating girls. Something like that was never on my radar. I'd had queer friends and had seen queer people my whole live. Several of my classmates had two moms or two dads, or any combination of genders. I had just never seen it for myself.

Now everything had changed. All of my ideas about marriage and who I would marry and how my life would be were shifting and I didn't like that. I didn't like the knowledge that I could be so wrong about myself. How could I have been so sure that I only liked guys and here I was, holding hands with another girl and wishing we were alone so I could kiss the daylights out of her? If I was wrong about this thing, what else was I wrong about?

Ideas and questions burst in my brain like fireworks and I wished I could put my hands on my ears and shut them out. Shut them up.

I wanted to hit the pause button in my mind.

And then Chase squeezed my hand and then leaned her head on my shoulder for a moment and I knew one thing: I liked Chase. I liked her more than I had liked anyone. In fact, I couldn't remember ever having feelings like this before. Crushes on boys had always been lukewarm at best. I'd liked spending time with them, for the most part, but I hadn't wanted to take it further. Even when I thought about kissing them (or doing something further than a little under-the-clothes touching), it wasn't with a rush of desire or excitement. It had always seemed like an obligation. I'd never really been into it, even when I'd told myself I was into the boy.

My brain continued to spin and spin like a bunch of towels in a dryer that wouldn't shut off. I wasn't even paying attention to the movie.

I wanted to talk to someone, but I had no idea who to talk to. The person I wanted to talk to about Chase was Chase. I wasn't sure if I wanted to take this to Dad yet. Not until I was more sure about what I was going to tell him. Was I going to have to come out? Was I going to have to find a label for myself?

I was on the verge of another panic attack, so I squeezed Chase's hand and counted to myself. Starting with one and going up to ten, and then back again until I felt the moment pass. It worked, this time. When I opened my eyes again, the movie was ending and I dropped Chase's hand so Kyle and Stella wouldn't see. They had turned the lights off for the ambience and I was glad it was still dark.

"Thanks for having us over," Chase said, handing back the popcorn. "Next time you'll have to come over to our room and we'll host."

"How about we make it a weekly thing? Either Friday or Saturday night we'll watch a movie or show?" I liked that idea, but right now I wanted to get back to our room so I wouldn't give anything away.

"Yeah, that sounds great," I said, hoping I sounded genuine.

"It's a deal," Kyle said, holding both her thumbs up.

We thanked them again and then walked slowly back to our room.

Chase closed the door and we looked at each other.

"Tomorrow. We'll talk tomorrow," I said, and she nodded.

Getting ready for bed was awkward, because we were both trying not to catch the other changing. I'd pretty much been whatever about it, but now it was different. She had always seemed shy, so I'd given her privacy, but that felt so much more important now for some reason.

I didn't know what to do or how to treat her. This was all new to me. I had lived nineteen years and I hadn't gone through anything like this in a long damn time. It was like being a kid again.

"Can I give you a goodnight hug?" Chase asked when we'd gotten our pajamas on.

"Yeah," I said. I couldn't deny her anything. She hugged me and I wanted to kiss her. Wanted to taste her mouth while it was spicy from toothpaste.

Tomorrow. We would deal with that tomorrow. For tonight, I let her go and got into bed. I wondered if she was still going to read out loud and was about to ask when she picked up the book and got into bed.

I would have been upset if she decided she didn't want to do that anymore. Were things going to completely change now?

Instead of thinking about that, I closed my eyes and listened to Chase as she read. I let myself get lost in her voice and let the story take me far, far away.

Chapter Seven

CHASE

I barely slept. There were just too many things going on. Too much to think about. I listened to Cordelia breathe in her sleep and envied her a bit. I turned on my side and looked toward her bed. She slept on her side with her back facing me.

How had this one girl changed my entire life with one kiss? One kiss that I was having regrets about. If I hadn't kissed her, I might not be up and re-evaluating my entire life up until this moment.

But kissing Cordelia was something that was as inevitable as the sun setting. It was only a matter of when, and last night had been the when.

Today was going to be another story. I didn't even know where to start. I needed to make a list. I needed to read some articles. I needed to sort out my thoughts in an orderly way. I needed boxes for them. Boxes I could sort them into so then I could handle them. Right now it was chaos in my skull and I didn't like that at all.

Part of me wanted to call my parents, but this didn't seem to warrant that kind of emergency phone call. It wasn't like I had a medical emergency. I had just kissed a girl and now I had to figure out what that meant.

There were a few possibilities, and the one that that kept pounding in my brain and in my heart was that I liked Cordelia and I wanted to kiss her again and I wanted to do more than kiss her. I wanted to be like Kyle and Stella. I wanted to be whatever that would mean. Girlfriend, partner, I didn't know. I hadn't gotten that far. I couldn't get that far.

If I didn't know anything else, I knew that I wanted to be with her. And not as friends. Or yes, as friends, but as friends with kissing. And other things. Beyond Cordelia, I didn't have the mental space to figure out what that meant for my sexuality. I had always thought of myself as heterosexual. There had never been any question, for me. I liked boys and I didn't question it.

The night was long and the questions were many. By the time the sun came up, I had few answers.

Cordelia slept much longer than I thought she would and I nearly broke down and woke her up, but I figured that wouldn't be a very nice thing to do, so I let her sleep. When she woke up, everything was going to change and I had no idea how it was going to go.

When she finally moved, rolled over, and opened her eyes, I was so on-edge that I could barely sit still. I'd already been up and had reorganized my bookshelf. Twice. I still wasn't happy with it, but it had given me something to do while I waited for her.

"Hi," she said, blinking at me.

"Hi," I replied.

"Did you sleep at all?" she asked as she stretched and then sat up, her curls a fiery tornado around her head. Seeing her in the morning was my favorite. When she was all soft from sleep and had a little smile on her face, probably from a good dream. I hardly ever remembered my dreams, but Cordelia did. She could tell me about them in extreme detail and I wished I could dive into them at night sometimes when my anxiety was bad.

"Not really," I said, and got up to get the coffee pot out.

"I think I'll have herbal tea today," she said in a small voice. Right, the last time she'd had coffee, she'd had a panic attack. Had that only been yesterday? How had so much happened in such a short time? Lives changed in a matter of seconds, never to be the same.

I put the coffee pot away again and got out some tea. I would join her. I probably didn't need to have caffeine either.

She was quiet as the kettle boiled the water and I put honey in each of our cups.

I didn't know how to start. I didn't know where to start. So we just went about our morning routine in silence. I didn't like it, but I wasn't keen on the alternative.

We sat down on the floor and sipped our tea. I wasn't hungry, and she didn't seem to be either.

"Okay, this silence is too much. I can't deal with it," she finally said, setting her cup down.

"Are you ready to talk about this?" I sure as hell wasn't, but I didn't think I ever would be. This wasn't the kind of conversation you could ever prepare for.

"I mean, not really, but we can't put it off. We can't just go on and pretend that nothing happened, and I don't want to. I can't stop thinking about it."

"Me neither." If I was being totally honest, I wanted to spend the rest of the day kissing her and not talking at all.

"I like you. I don't know what that means, but I do. I like you and I want to kiss you and hold your hand and all of that other stuff. I want to be *with you*, with you," she said. "If you want to be with me?"

I opened my mouth to answer her and then shut it. In spite of spending my entire night thinking and wondering and running through what if scenarios in my head, I still didn't know what to say.

"This is a lot," I said, finally. "I don't know what this means. Because I like you too. I have liked you since we met. I didn't know that's what it was, but then I kissed you and it was so obvious. I didn't plan for this, Cordelia. I didn't come to college expecting to kiss a girl. I didn't expect to go to college and to have these kinds of feelings for my roommate." I twisted my fingers together so hard that my knuckles cracked.

"I didn't plan for it either, but I wouldn't change how it happened. I've never felt this way, Chase. Never. About anyone. You came into my life and now I'm questioning everything. And I'm not so sure that's a bad thing. You're just ... oh my god, Chase, you're just incredible and I feel lucky that I even get to be around you at all." I could feel my cheeks getting red.

She got up and sat right in front of me. Her fingers reached out and stroked my cheek.

"You're the most amazing girl I've ever met." Her voice was quiet and I could barely breathe.

"No, *you're* the most amazing girl I've ever met." My hands stopped clutching each other and I wrapped some of her curls around my fingers.

"So I guess that means you want to be with me?" she asked.

"I don't know what that means, but I'm willing to try." It was such a gamble. It was a potential disaster. What if we tried to be together and then broke up? There were so many questions still to be answered.

"Okay, then. We're doing this. Together. We're ... dating? Is that what we're doing?" That didn't seem like the right word, even though that was what we were essentially doing. Dating a girl.

That was hitting me, and I stood up.

"What are we going to tell people? What are we going to say when they ask? What are we going to tell our parents?" I started pacing around the room until Cordelia put her hands on my shoulders and stopped me.

"I think we should talk to Kyle and Stella. They know what we're going through. Stella told me all about how they got together and told their parents and everything. They were seniors in high school, so it wasn't that long ago. We can trust them." I wasn't sure. I didn't want to share this, but more than that, I didn't want to feel so ... lost.

"I guess," I said.

"You don't sound convincing, Chase." I didn't feel convincing.

"No, it's okay. They have been nice to us and I like them. I'm just scared." She laughed and I gave her a look.

"That makes two of us."

~

CORDELIA

We agreed to wait until Sunday before talking to Stella and Kyle, but then changed our minds when we realized we couldn't sit in our room and be all awkward and weird with each other, so we headed down the hall. I thought about texting Stella first, but I figured she would be doing homework, or we could just come back another time.

Chase made me knock, which I did with a subtly shaking hand.

Elise opened the door. I had never seen her in a less-than-awesome outfit. Today she had a pink peplum top with white polka dots and dark jeans. What made me laugh, though, were the shoes with cat faces on them on her feet.

"Hey, what's up?" she asked.

"Is Stella around?" I asked. Elise shook her head.

"She and Kyle went out a few hours ago on a date, but they should be back soon, she texted me a few minutes ago. Do you want to just come in and wait?" I looked at Chase, who nodded before I said yes.

Chase was pale and she almost looked like she was going to be sick. I didn't know what to do to help her because I was having my own freak-out.

I hadn't really slept either. I'd kept waking up and telling myself if I just pretended I was asleep, that sleep would eventually happen. It didn't until the early morning and I was exhausted. Still, Chase looked like she'd had an even worse time, so I didn't want to say anything.

"Everything okay?" Elise asked. Her hair was in a perfect sock bun that I could never make my mane of a hair do. I was a tiny bit envious.

"Uh, yeah. We just needed to talk to Stella. And Kyle," I said. Chase still looked like she was going to puke. She sat down heavily on Stella's bed.

"Okay," she said. It was completely obvious that something was up, but Elise didn't pry.

"I know you don't know me that well, but I'm a really good listener," she said, hopping on her bed and scrolling through her phone.

"Oh, it's not …" I trailed off. Chase gave me a panicked look and I thought she was going to physically run from the room when Stella and Kyle walked in.

"Oh, hey. I didn't know you were going to be here," Stella said. Kyle came in after her and sat down next to Chase on Kyle's bed.

"Yeah, we, um, needed to talk to you? About something?" Stella looked at me and then looked at Chase and then looked at Kyle.

"And you too, Kyle," I added, looking at her. She raised her eyebrows.

"Just pretend I'm not even here," Elise said, not looking up from her phone. "Or I can take a walk. No big."

I looked at Chase.

"You can stay, Elise," she said. That made Elise smile and she pushed her purple glasses up on her nose.

I sat down on Chase's other side. I definitely needed to be sitting for this whole thing. Stella took the chair from her desk. All eyes were on me, which wasn't new, but it was intimidating right now.

"Do you want me to talk?" I asked Chase. She nodded and pressed her lips together. I had the feeling she was going to be pretty quiet during this whole thing. I had to be our voice. I could do that.

"So, um, Chase and I are, uh, together? I think? We just talked about it this morning and now we're both kind of wondering what comes next. And neither of us has ever liked another girl before. And what do we tell our parents? And what about other people? And do we have to figure ourselves out now? Are we lesbians?" My voice kept getting higher and I had to snap my jaw shut so I didn't pour all of the questions out of my mouth on them.

Chase reached over and squeezed my shoulder. I looked at her and smiled.

"Awwww." Stella was the first one to break the silence. "Don't you remember when we were like that?" She turned to Kyle and they smiled at each other.

"Okay, first of all, I would like to hug both of you, if that's okay," Elise said, getting up. I accepted the hug and so did Chase.

"This is not easy. We've all been there." Stella and Kyle nodded.

"Seriously. Not that long ago," Kyle said. "It's awful." I nodded and Chase started crying. My first reaction was to gather her into my arms and stroke her hair, so I did. Elise produced some tissues and I dabbed at Chase's eyes.

"It's just so much," Chase said. I kissed her forehead and wiped a few more tears.

"It is," Stella said. "It's a lot, but you're not alone. You have all of us here to support you, okay?"

Chase nodded and blew her nose.

"I just never thought this would be me," she said.

"Ditto," I said.

"Same," Kyle and Stella said.

"Yup," Elise agreed. "Because heterosexual and cis is the default. I didn't know I was pansexual and asexual until I was sixteen. It took me months to come to terms with it and tell my parents."

"I know my dad wouldn't care," I said. "He's always loved me no matter what."

"Same with my parents," Chase said. "I know they would support me. But how could I be so wrong about myself?"

"Yeah, we know about that one," Stella said. "Sometimes we don't even know we're lying to ourselves. You can bury something so deep that it takes an entire lifetime to surface." That made sense. I kissed Chase on the forehead again.

"You okay?" I asked. She looked up at me and sniffed.

"I guess. I'm just overwhelmed with it all, Cordelia. I just want to stop thinking about everything."

"Let's go out. Let's go out and do something and not talk about this for a while. Give you a mental break. How about that?" Kyle said, standing up.

"What do you think?" I said to Chase and she nodded.

"I feel bad that you all are taking care of us. Thank you. You didn't have to," Chase said. I put my arm around her and she leaned against me.

"Hey, this is what we do for people we care about. We're

here for you for anything," Stella said. How was it that we had such good people around us? We were so lucky.

"I know what we should do. Come on, we can take my van," Elise said, grabbing her keys. She had about ten different things attached to her keychain. "Do you mind if Eli comes? They should be just getting out of work."

"The more the merrier," I said, and she texted them.

"Another mystery trip," Chase said. "I'm guessing this one won't be to a bookstore, though."

"Hey, does that count as our first date?" I asked as we went toward the elevator.

"I don't think so. It can't be a date if neither of us knew it was a date, can it?"

I laughed.

"I guess not."

We got in Elise's van that she told us was named "Carla." I was pretty sure the van was older than us all, combined, but at least we all fit. Elise drove us down to the dining commons where Eli worked.

"Hey, hot stuff, need a ride?" Elise yelled out the window and honked the horn. Eli loped over with their white chef's jacket folded over their arm.

"Only if you're offering," they said with a wink before coming around and hopping into the passenger seat.

"I'm sorry if I smell like fries. I was on the grill tonight," they said.

"Well, I wasn't hungry until now," Kyle said and we all laughed as Elise headed off campus. Eli took off their hair net and inspected their hair in the mirror.

"You couldn't have given me ten minutes to fix my hair?" they said, pouting at Elise.

"There's a comb and gel in the glovebox, sweetheart. And I have a bottle of water."

Eli leaned over and smacked a kiss on Elise's cheek.

"You, Elise Monroe, are an angel."

She grinned.

"I know."

I looked over at Chase and she was looking at the couple wistfully. I reached over and took her hand, squeezing her fingers gently.

"Hey," I said, and she smiled at me.

"Hey."

Chapter Eight

CHASE

"Bowling?" I said when we all piled out of the van.

"Yup. Good old-fashioned fun. Plus, the shoes are totally cute. And they have really good pizza here," Elise said, slamming the doors of the van shut.

"Come on, let's do this," Kyle said. "I'm going to kick all of your asses."

She and Stella headed toward the doors and I looked at Cordelia.

"Come on, let's go put on some smelly shoes and not think about shit for a while." That sounded like a plan. I thought about taking her hand, but I definitely wasn't ready to be holding her hand in public. Eli put their arm around Elise, and Kyle and Stella were mostly attached to each other, but it didn't feel like we were the odd ones out.

I had a hard time with new people, but I had warmed up to them faster than I expected. Kyle and Stella were cute and hilarious, and Elise was sharp and witty, but so kind and understanding, and Eli made observations that were so smart and funny that we were all cracking up as we got our bowling shoes and picked our lanes.

"Let's do three teams?" Elise suggested, so she combined her name with Eli's to make Eelliise, Kyle and Stella became Style and they put my name together with Cordelia's to make Chord.

"We're not even really together and we already have a ship name," Cordelia said as Elise entered the name into the computer.

She grinned at me and I felt my heart tremble. I really did like her a lot. She was right next to me and I just leaned over and kissed her. She froze, like she had the first time, but she responded a second later and kissed me back, harder than I expected, and I had to pull away so we didn't go too far. She gave me one more little peck.

"You're always kissing me first. Someday I'm going to beat you to it," she said. I laughed and she kissed the tip of my nose. I heard noises and remembered that we were in the middle of a crowded bowling alley.

"Shit," I whispered and took a second to look around.

Kyle and Stella were cuddled next to each other, as were Elise and Eli.

"You two are seriously cute," Stella said. I didn't dare look beyond those four faces at the other people in the bowling alley. It was Sunday night, so it was packed. If I looked around and saw someone disgusted with the fact that I had kissed Cordelia, that would have wrecked me. I didn't even know how I would deal with that. How I will deal with that, if Cordelia and I decide to do this for real.

"Hey," Cordelia said, putting a finger under my chin. "Stop thinking about it." I met her eyes. They were pure green tonight.

"I can't," I said. I felt like I was going to cry.

"Come on, it's our turn." She stood up and reached for my

hand. I took it and she led me over to the lane and handed me a ball.

I looked at her and she smiled.

"Go ahead, C," she said.

"C?" I asked, raising one eyebrow.

She shrugged one shoulder.

"I don't know, I think it's cute." It was cute. She was cute.

"Kiss for luck?" I meant the bowling ball, but she popped up on her toes and planted a kiss on my lips.

"Good luck!" I was stunned for a moment. Cordelia literally put her hands on my shoulders and turned me toward the lane. Right, bowling. Kissing Cordelia made me silly.

I wasn't a great bowler, but I tossed the ball and knocked down a few pins. I handed it to Cordelia to get the spare and she nailed it with perfect form.

"So … you're a professional bowler?" I asked when she did a little jump as the pins went down.

"Um, it's just something me and my dad do together. Every weekend." Her cheeks were red with happiness and I wanted to kiss her again, but I held back.

"We're screwed," Kyle said as she stood up and Stella helped her hoist the ball and then toss it. Between the two of them they got a strike and they were pretty smug about it.

Eli also turned out to be an incredible bowler and my confidence was plummeting.

"Don't worry, you're still cuter and smarter than me," Cordelia said in my ear.

"No one is cuter or smarter than you," I said in her ear and she laughed. I loved her laugh. It was bright and free and wonderful.

As the night wore on, I relaxed. I forgot about the other people around me and focused in on our little group. I had fun and I let myself go. I hadn't done that in ages. It was hard for me to let go. I had to feel completely comfortable with the people I was with to relax.

I let myself cuddle close to Cordelia and steal a kiss here and there. I didn't want to not kiss her, so the solution was to kiss her. She kissed me a few times too, probably to make up for me initiating so many of them.

It was … easy. Being with Cordelia that way was easy. The hard part had been putting up barriers between us. Constantly convincing myself that my feelings for her weren't romantic. Constantly telling myself I couldn't feel that way about her because she was a girl and I didn't like girls that way.

I still hadn't gotten my head around if I liked girls, period, or of it was just Cordelia. Right now, I was going to let myself enjoy bowling with Cordelia and kissing her, and I was going to worry about that tomorrow. If I could let myself do that.

"I HATE YOU ALL," Stella said. She was grumpy about coming in third in bowling. Cordelia and I came in second, with Eli wiping the floor with us all.

"I can't help it that I have natural talent," they said, smirking.

"You're going to be insufferable now, aren't you?" Elise said, but she was grinning.

"Possibly," they said and gave Elise a peck on the cheek.

"You're pretty much always insufferable," Elise said.

"But you love me anyway," Eli said.

Elise sighed. "I do."

We all stuffed ourselves with pizza, except Eli, who got wings because they had Celiac disease.

"Are you having fun?" Cordelia whispered in my ear. She knew I had a hard time in social situations, but I was having a really good time.

"Yeah, I am. I'm really glad I'm here with you," I said, and she kissed my cheek.

"I'm happy that you let me kiss you. I like kissing you." Her eyes sparkled and I wondered if she was remembering when we'd kissed yesterday on her bed. I got tingly just thinking about it. My blood raced and I had the urge to pull her to her feet and press her up against the wall and attack her mouth. I was grateful no one could read my mind because those kinds of thoughts were unusual for me. I had never thought about doing that with anyone before. With Cordelia, everything was different.

I wanted to do so many things with her. I thought about what it would be like to touch her body. To touch her all over. To kiss her all over. To do everything with her.

"You're blushing," Cordelia said, running a finger down one of my cheeks. I jumped.

"Am I? Guess I'm just hot."

"Yeah, you are really hot," she said with a grin. I was too busy trying to tamp down the lust that had surged in my blood. Was that what being turned on felt like? This was a new experience. I would have rather not had it at a bowling alley, but it definitely wasn't unpleasant.

"Shush," I said belatedly to Cordelia's comment about me being hot.

"Never," she said, getting up and throwing our plates away. She said she was heading to the bathroom, and Kyle said she needed to go as well.

I found Stella looking at me.

"What?" I asked.

"Nothing. You just remind me of myself a little. Things with Kyle were complicated at first, too." I hadn't heard the whole story of how they'd met yet.

"Yeah?" I asked.

She nodded.

"Yup. Totally complicated. We didn't know what to do. And it all seemed insurmountable. But then we talked and we talked to our families and our friends and it turned out fine. I mean, there are moments, but if I have any regrets, they're only that I didn't get more years with her." Wow. That was powerful.

"Same with us," Elise said, looking at Eli, who agreed.

"For what it's worth, you two are very clearly into each other. You can't stop smiling," Eli said. I put my hand to my face. They were right.

"I don't know what I'm doing. My dating experience is almost nonexistent. I was always too scared." I shook my head at myself. I was still scared, but I was scared of different things. And more than being scared, I wanted to be around Cordelia. More than anything.

"That doesn't matter. What matters is right now. And how you feel and how she feels. The rest will come later. Or never. You don't have to put a label on yourself if you don't feel comfortable with it. You can just … be. Some people feel better with a label. Others don't. Find out what works for you," Elise said.

"If you want, you can come to the meeting of the campus queer organization. No pressure. But you'd be around other people who are questioning." Questioning. That was definitely me. I was made of questions and uncertainty.

"I'll think about it," I said. That seemed to be a good enough answer for now. Kyle and Cordelia came back and there was a rush in my heart when she sat back down next to me. I was giddy around her.

"Stop talking about me," she said, pushing her hair over her shoulder.

"Never," I said.

∿

CORDELIA

Bowling was a blast and it had helped taken my mind off things. Chase had a good time too, and I could feel her relaxing next to me as the night wore on. She talked more than I expected her to and I could tell she and Elise had really bonded. She was so cute when she got a strike. The shock on her face made me burst out laughing. I didn't know what I would do if she wasn't in my life. How different my college experience would be if she hadn't been paired as my room-mate. I wasn't sure if I believed in fate, but somehow, this girl's name had ended up being paired with mine and I would always be grateful for that. No matter what happened. I would always be grateful that I met Chase Hillier.

Kissing her was off the charts. It made my brain just STOP whenever she did it. As the night wore on, the kisses became more frequent, and I was relieved Chase felt so safe with Stella, Kyle, Elise, and Eli. I wished she could be this free all the time. Not many people got to see her like this, and it was a shame because they were missing out on what an incredible person she was.

We decided to head back to the dorms after we ate, since the bowling alley was getting more of a night crowd and they had fired up the karaoke machine.

"Hell to the no," Stella said, and we all agreed.

"I'd only do it if everyone was doing it," Elise said. "Or if one of you dared me. I'll pretty much do anything. I have no shame." I saw Chase's look of terror.

"C, I would never make you do something like that. Ever." No one who cared about her at all would.

She leaned on me as we walked back to the van.

"Thank you for being you," she said.

"Thank *you* for being you."

~

337

WE WERE both exhausted from the turmoil of the past few days, so we said goodnight to the others and went back to our room.

"I wasn't expecting you to be the most aggressive in the PDA department, that's for sure. You're always surprising me," I said, putting my hands on her shoulders.

"I guess I just wasn't thinking about it. I wanted to kiss you, so I did. I'm not usually like that. I can stop if you want."

"Don't you dare," I said, pushing up on my toes to kiss her. I wanted Chase to kiss me as many times as she wanted to. Kissing Chase was better than ice cream. Better than swimming in the ocean. Better than a roller coaster. Better than anything else I'd experienced. Kissing Chase was going to ruin me for kissing anyone else, and right now, I wasn't worried about that. I wasn't going to worry about tomorrow and the next day and the next because right here, in this moment, everything was awesome. The prettiest girl in the whole world wanted to kiss me and that was more than enough.

"What are we doing, Cordelia?" she whispered.

"I don't know. But if this is wrong, I don't want to be right." She laughed a little.

"Should we go to bed?" There was an added layer of question.

"In separate beds, right?" I asked. She nodded.

"Kissing is one thing, but …" she trailed off.

"Yeah." I mean, I would be lying if I said I hadn't had thoughts about being with Chase that way. Being naked with her. Sliding my body against hers. Kissing her everywhere. The idea of being with her like that made me more turned on than I had ever been in my entire life. It made me ache.

I didn't want to freak her out with that kind of desire being so strong, so quick. Apparently, I had unlocked the door to my inner Lust Room and it was all spilling out.

"You're blushing," she said, stroking my cheeks.

"Just thinking," I said.

"About?" She raised one eyebrow.

"Things?" Chase laughed.

"You wanna tell me about those things?"

"Not really?" I mean, at some point, yes. I hoped we would get to that point.

"I bet I could guess. You wear your emotions on your face, Cordelia." I couldn't get over how sexy her voice was when she said my name.

Sexy. My roommate was beyond sexy and she had been this whole time. I was just lying to myself about it. Telling myself that the feelings I had for her were friendship feelings.

"You can't prove anything," I said in a sing-song voice.

"Yeah? Is that a challenge?"

Ohhhhh. A delicious shiver went down my spine. This was new. This was new and exciting and overwhelming.

I felt myself biting my bottom lip between my teeth.

"Maybe," I whispered. I watched so many things flit through her brown eyes.

"I don't know if either of us is ready for that yet, Cordelia," she said, stepping back. I knew she was right, but part of me howled in rage.

I had no idea what I had gotten myself into with Chase. She had already changed my life and I had the feeling we were just getting started.

MONDAY MORNING WAS AWFUL. I didn't sleep well on Sunday night, mostly because I kept having very graphic dreams involving kissing Chase and they wouldn't let up and give me a rest. I felt like I needed to sleep the entire day, but I couldn't. I had to get up and there was Chase, reminding me about all those dreams. Hiding my constant blush was my main goal when I was around her. I even went to class way early so I wouldn't have to answer questions about why my entire face looked like a tomato. Sometimes being so pale was the worst.

"Are you okay?" Mariella asked when I sat down in art history. Bree swiveled in her chair and raised her eyebrows.

"Yeah, why?" I said. I was totally flustered even though I had gotten to the building so early. I'd thought that since I was so early, I could go and get one of the really good blueberry scones from the little coffee shop next to the art building, and it had taken way longer than I thought it would, so I'd barely been able to make it in a few minutes before class. Add on top of that all the thoughts I was still having about Chase and this weekend and I was a hot fucking mess. I wished it wasn't so obvious to everyone else.

"You just look a little ..." Mariella said, trailing off and looking at Bree.

"Flustered," Bree supplied.

"Yeah, I just got up late. Couldn't sleep." Even though I'd been in public with Chase last night and if they were at the bowling alley they would have seen us, I wasn't ready to tell everyone that I was dating a girl. Chase and I hadn't talked terms yet. Could I call her my girlfriend? Would she call me her girlfriend? Would we go on dates? What about our parents? I hadn't talked to Dad in a few days and I knew this was something I couldn't not tell him. I could try to leave it out of our conversations, but he was going to know that I was omitting something and want to know what it was. And then he probably wouldn't cave until I told him every single detail. I wanted to do this on my terms. I had to prepare for it and I hadn't done that. I needed to talk parameters with Chase.

"Ugh, I know how you feel. I know we're just a few weeks into the semester, but I'm already stressed about finals and losing sleep worrying about studying for them. How ridiculous is that?" Bree said, rolling her eyes.

"You stress too much," Mariella said. "Calm down. Finals aren't here yet. Breathe." Bree took an exaggerated deep breath and I was relieved the heat was off me. A few seconds later, our professor started the class and I was able to let my brain do something else other than think about Chase. Or at least try to.

∼

"AM I YOUR GIRLFRIEND?" was the first thing I said to Chase when she got back from class. I'd been sitting and wondering and worrying and had worked myself all up, so I had no filter when she finally walked in.

"Uh, hi?" she said, setting her bag down.

"Sorry, I sort of shot that question at you. But I've been thinking about it all day and I really need to know." She opened and closed her mouth a few times.

"I ..." she sat down with a thump. "Yeah. You are."

"Haven't you thought about that?" I asked.

"Yeah, I have, but I guess I didn't think about it actually happening. Like having you as my girlfriend. Having a girlfriend, period." It was a lot and I was probably pushing too far. I mean, we had just kissed a few days ago. We'd just realized we liked each other a few days ago. In other ways, this felt like it had been building since the moment we met. It was all confusing as fuck.

"You're my girlfriend," she said and then started laughing. "That's so weird to say out loud, but it feels like that's how it was supposed to be?" I got up from my bed and sat on hers. I had missed her today. I missed her whenever we weren't together. I always had something that I wanted to tell her. Always wanted to see her reaction to something.

"I know. It feels so easy and so hard at the same time." I

reached out and took her hand. She fit her fingers in the spaces between mine. So easy.

"Yeah, it does. But I want this. With you. If things don't work out—"

I interrupted her.

"We don't have to worry about that now. We'll figure things out. We're just starting. I don't want to be constantly wondering if we're going to break up." I couldn't handle that. I had to think about the positives, or all the potential negative voices were going to get into my head and sabotage me. I knew myself enough to know that it could happen. My brain was a complete asshole sometimes. Especially about things I wanted. And I wanted to be with Chase in the worst way.

She opened her mouth, maybe to argue with me, but then she closed it and squeezed my hand.

"Okay. We can talk about that later." I didn't want to talk about it later. I didn't want to talk about it at all, but I knew she would. Chase liked to sit with something and imagine every single possible outcome. Like plotting a point on a map and then figuring out all the possible paths to that point. Her brain worked so differently than mine.

"Okay," I said, bringing her hand to my lips and kissing it. "Can we kiss now?"

She laughed and the negative thoughts retreated from my mind for a little while.

Chase leaned forward and pressed her lips to mine. I almost sighed in relief because I hadn't kissed her goodbye this morning and I regretted it the entire day. I had never had a girlfriend, so I wasn't sure if I should or not, plus I'd been all wrapped up in my sexy dreams and I'd basically run away before thinking about it.

"I'm sorry I didn't kiss you this morning," I said, breaking the kiss.

"It's okay. I didn't expect you to. Should I have expected

you to?" She was so cute and so perplexed that I had to kiss her again.

"I don't know, C. This is all new to me, too."

Chase sighed.

"I don't like not knowing what I'm doing, Cordelia. But if I don't know what I'm doing, I'd rather not know with you than with anyone else." I thought my heart was going to explode. That was the most wonderful thing she had ever said to me. Other than when she said she wanted to be with me.

I kissed her forehead.

"Just tell me where you want to go and I'll go there with you," I said.

She squeezed my hand and kissed me again.

Chapter Nine

CHASE

In less than a week, I had gone from a girl who was looking for a boyfriend to a girl who had a girlfriend. Beyond that, I had no idea.

The next time I saw Ti in class, I smiled at him and tried to look at him objectively. Yes, he was cute. Yes, he was nice. But other than that? He was just a guy. There were thousands of guys on campus. Thousands that I had walked by and not looked twice at. I put him next to Cordelia in my mind and he just disappeared. Next to her, he was no one. Even thinking about her made a wave of happiness and excitement crash over me.

I couldn't even imagine being on a real date with Ti, let alone kissing him. I didn't want to. I didn't want to kiss him. I wanted to kiss Cordelia.

Did that make me a lesbian? Would I have to change my wardrobe and watch new shows and hang out with only other lesbians? Some part of me knew those questions were ridiculous, but another part of me was really wondering. Would my entire life have to change now?

I didn't know the answer to that and that question was the one that hovered in the back of my mind. That snuck up on me when I least expected it. That tried to yell at me when I was with Cordelia. Kissing her was the only thing that made it shut up. I decided I needed to kiss her more.

I turned away from Ti and didn't think about him for the rest of class. I honestly forgot he was even there until he tapped on my shoulder as I was gathering my things.

"Hey, you busy?" I didn't know how to answer him. "I was just wondering if you wanted to get coffee again." Oh, crap.

"Yeah, I actually have to get back. I have plans," I somehow said. It wasn't a lie. I did have plans with Cordelia. Plans that hopefully involved her lips and my lips. I had to bite back a smile when I thought about that.

"Oh, okay. Maybe another time?" He was cute and nice, but that wasn't enough. Not for me. He would be right for someone else.

"I'm actually seeing someone," I said. I knew I was taking a risk, but I wanted to cut things off so he didn't get the impression that I was busy today, but I was still interested in him.

"No, sure, that's fine. We can have coffee anyway, can't we? Unless that's not okay with your boyfriend." He chuckled a little and I had a moment of panic. Was I supposed to correct him?

I stuttered that we could have coffee as friends and then rushed away as quickly as I could.

When I got back to my room, Cordelia was there with Elise.

"Hey," I said, going over and giving her a kiss.

"Hey," she said, smiling up into my face. I could stare at her for weeks and never get tired. Her eyes were halfway between blue and green today. Like tropical water.

"You're just so cute. I'm so happy I get to witness this," Elise said with a sigh.

"So, Ti asked me out for coffee again and I said I was seeing someone. Then he said something about still being friends, as long as that was okay with 'my boyfriend' and I didn't say anything." Why did I feel like I was confessing something awful? "Should I have corrected him?" I asked.

"You don't owe him anything," Cordelia said. Part of me had worried a little that she would be upset. Like I was hiding her. Or I was ashamed of being with her.

"I know. But I didn't want you to think that I was hiding us." Cordelia shook her head and then kissed me.

"I don't think that. You don't have to tell every single person that you have a girlfriend. No one is entitled to that from you. Not him, not anyone. It's fine, Chase." I hoped it was.

"I didn't want to tell you this originally, but coming out isn't a one-time thing. I happens over and over. It happens to me every time I talk about Eli with someone new. It happens every time someone asks if I'm single. It happens hundreds of times. I've skirted around it, I've lied, I've changed the subject, I've done everything. Sometimes you don't want to and that's okay. It's shitty that you have to keep doing it, but that's the way things are right now. I hope it will change," Elise said.

"Oh," I said, sitting on the bed. "I didn't think about that."

"You don't have to, until you do," Elise said.

"Hey, we don't have to do anything right now," Cordelia said with her hand on my face. I knew she could see me spiraling.

"I know," I said. "I'm fine. Really. It surprised me, that's all." My stomach growled.

"Do you want to go have some dinner?" Cordelia asked. I nodded.

"You want to come?" I asked Elise.

"Sure, Eli is working so I can poke my head in and hassle them. Kyle and Stella have a date tonight, so they're out." I should take Cordelia on a date. A real one. Maybe with a fancy restaurant or something. She deserved to be taken on dates. Plus, we both needed to learn how to date another girl. Not that I had had much practice dating boys either. I mean, I'd hung out with guys in group settings and gone to the movies and so forth, but usually I ended up not calling them back, or ignoring them until they stopped contacting me. I always chalked it up to my anxiety, but lately I was wondering if I liked boys *at all*. Since I had never really found one that I had wanted to date. Looking back, all of those dates I'd been on had been awful. I mean, I had fun with the guys but when it came to kissing or other romantic stuff with them, I hadn't wanted it. Couldn't make myself do it.

As a result, I had only kissed two guys in my life, and both were awful. I wished I could wipe the memory of those kisses and fill the spaces with Cordelia. She was my authentic first kiss. Everything else I had done before her had been a lie.

I thought about that as we walked to dinner. I didn't hold Cordelia's hand, but I thought about it.

The three of us loaded up our trays and sat down, talking about this and that.

"I can't believe I haven't been home in weeks," Cordelia said. "I haven't been away from my dad for this long since maybe I was in camp years ago. But I feel okay about it? I'm not really homesick. I guess I've been a little distracted." She looked at me and smiled.

"Yeah, me too. I've missed a few things here and there. Sometimes I wish I could have my dad's lasagna, but then I remember Kate would fight me for the best piece and she would usually win," I said with a laugh. Oh, Kate. She was probably reveling in the fact that she got the choice lasagna piece.

"My parents are all the way in Vermont and I'm okay with having the distance. They're supportive, but they don't really understand my life, and they don't understand Eli. They get misgendered when we visit and I just don't want to put them through that. So I'm fine being here. There's not a whole lot to miss back home, except for my grandmother's empanadas. Those I miss." That got us talking about what food we missed and we started swapping recipes.

"I wish we had a kitchen we could cook in. Stella's hot plate is okay for some things, but others, not so much. I wish I had an oven," Elise said, and we all agreed.

At one point I felt a hand on my thigh. Thankfully, it was Cordelia's. I snuck a hand under the table and put my free hand on hers and squeezed it. I glanced over at her and she gave me a little half smile.

I couldn't believe she was with me. That she liked me even a little bit. Things had happened so fast, but it didn't feel too fast. Yet.

She squeezed my fingers back and went to take her hand away, but I stopped her. I liked holding her hand under the table. Sure, we were both over eighteen and holding hands wasn't seen as a big deal by a lot of people, but this was the first time I'd held hands with someone I wanted to, and I was going to enjoy and treasure it. I didn't care what anyone had to say about that.

WE ENDED up doing homework for the rest of the night. I'd gotten behind on my personal schedule, but not actually behind since I had already been ahead. Basically, I was on track, but that wasn't good enough for me. I didn't like to even be close to behind.

"You're being very distracting over there," Cordelia said, and I looked up from my notebook.

"Huh?" I said. I'd been deep in taking notes with the

Norton Anthology (which could be used as a serious weapon if needed) next to me.

"You're being distracting," she repeated.

"Am I?" I raised one eyebrow.

"Mmmm, very." She bit her bottom lip and her cheeks were bright with color.

"Well, I'm so sorry about that," I said in a way that told her I wasn't sorry at all. I tucked some of my hair behind my ear.

She sighed.

"I might have to just get up and come over there and distract you back." I narrowed my eyes.

"Don't you dare, Cordelia Elizabeth Scott," I said, pointing my pen at her.

"Ohhhh, the middle name. I shouldn't have told you that," she said, taking her hair down from its messy bun. Her curls exploded everywhere and I wanted to get my fingers all tangled up in them. Get all tangled up in her.

"That was your mistake and my gain," I said, setting the pen down. I was ready for a break and I was ready for her.

She shook her head slowly. Her curls bounced around.

"Too bad," I said, getting up and walking slowly over to her. Cordelia's bed was mere feet away from me at all times. It was so strange to be doing this relationship thing with her so close.

I put my hands on the edge of her bed and leaned toward her.

"You distracted me, so now you're going to pay the consequences," I said. I had never, ever been like this, but something about being with Cordelia brought out a side of me that I didn't know I had. She brought out a lot of sides of me that I had never known. I liked myself when I was with her.

"Oh, no, that sounds terrible," she said in a monotone voice.

"You are in so much trouble," I said, pushing her books aside. She was smiling at me.

"Am I?"

"Mmmm, yes," I said, crawling onto the bed. This was the first time we'd done anything like this and I was freaking out a little, but also so turned on that I could barely think.

"What are you going to do about it?" she said, and her cheeks got redder and her breathing was labored.

"What do you want me to do?" I asked. Our mouths were inches from each other.

"I want you to kiss me," she said in a low voice.

"Then I guess that's what I'm going to have to do," I said, pressing forward just a little bit so our mouths could meet. Kissing Cordelia was my favorite way to spend time. Even better than reading, and that was something I never thought I would say.

Cordelia made a little whimpering sound and I pushed a little harder, running my tongue along her lips. Her mouth opened and I dove in. She worked her tongue against mine, surging forward and pulling back, giving and taking. We worked perfectly together. I didn't have to fumble or wonder what I was supposed to be doing. It was easy with her.

I used my teeth to nip just a little at her bottom lip and that always made her gasp a little. She pulled back and caught her breath.

"I don't know where you learned to kiss, but holy shit, Chase," she said, her voice trembling. I was shaking a little. Who knew a kiss could be like that? I had always thought people were making it into something way more than it was. Now I knew that they hadn't gone far enough, but those people hadn't gotten to kiss Cordelia.

"I guess you just bring it out of me," I said, brushing her cheek with my fingers.

"Sometimes it scares me when we kiss," she said in a whisper.

"Why?" I asked, sitting back.

"Oh, not like that. Just … how good it feels and how much I want you. That's what scares me." This was new.

"How much do you want me?" I asked. I wasn't sure if I wanted to know the answer. I knew I wanted her. The want seemed to grow each and every day and I was probably going to combust any moment now. Somehow I was going to have to find an outlet, because it was downright ridiculous.

"More than I know what to do with," she said. "It keeps me up at night. It wakes me up in the morning." Oh. I didn't know she was going to really tell me. We hadn't talked about that kind of thing yet. We hadn't done anything other than kissing. I think both of us were reluctant to do anything more than that. Not because we didn't want to though.

"I know how you feel," I said. "Sometimes I'm doing something and right in the middle of it, I think of you and then I have all these ideas." I looked up to see her reaction.

"What kind of ideas?"

"Naked ones." I hoped that didn't shock her too much.

Her eyebrows shot up.

"Are we having that conversation now?" I wasn't sure what she meant.

"I mean, I feel like we should sit down and figure out what we're both ready for. Since this is new for both of us." I didn't want her to do anything she wasn't ready for and I didn't want to let myself get carried away either and have regrets. As much as I wanted to keep kissing her and see where it went, I knew that would be a mistake.

"Yeah, we should," she said with a sigh. I burst out laughing when she pouted.

"I wanted to keep making out."

"I mean, we can make out and talk later. I'm not opposed to that plan." Her eyes lit up.

"Good. Making out now, talking later." She shoved the rest of her books off her bed and nearly tackled me to the floor.

CORDELIA

We'd been dancing around that conversation for long enough, and I knew kissing was only going to put it off for a little while, but kissing helped my brain shut the fuck up and it was awesome. I was going to require a certain amount of kissing to get through every day. It was just essential.

We kissed so long that we ended up horizontal on my bed, my hair ended up completely knotted and tangled, and somehow my hands started to make their way under Chase's shirt.

I wasn't sure which one of us put that brakes on, but somehow we sat up and got our shit together.

"Okay, we need to talk," Chase said. "I'm going to go sit on my bed so we're not tempted." Her lips were a little red and her normally straight hair was all over the place. Her shirt was wrinkled and messy and I honestly just wanted to throw her on the floor and do some more kissing and other stuff.

Alas, she was right, and we needed to talk. Without kissing. Probably without touching because that would also be distracting.

"Talking," I said as soon as we'd calmed down a little.

"Yes," she said, and then shook her head as if she was trying to clear it.

"So, we're dating. You're my girlfriend and I'm your girl-friend," she said.

"Yes, we've established that."

"Okay. Good. So do you want to tell people that we're together? Do you want to tell your dad?" she asked.

"I mean, I do. Mostly because if I try to hide it from him, he's going to get it out of me anyway, and also because I want to tell him. I'm so happy with you, Chase. I want to share that with him so he can be happy for me."

She beamed and I almost fell over.

"Good. I feel the same way. The only issue is what are we going to tell them about how this happened? I mean, I'm not ready to really commit to any kind of label until I've figured myself out." I agreed.

"Cool, me neither. I'm thinking about going to Kyle and Stella's club, at least to talk to some other people and maybe that will help me figure things out? Or maybe there are books or something that can help." She nodded.

"I want to go too, if that's okay with you." Of course it was.

"So, with that said, um, what else?" she asked, and I could feel my face getting red.

"You mean sex?" She groaned and hid her face with a pillow.

"You didn't have to be so blunt with it," she said, her voice muffled.

"I mean, that's what we've been beating around the bush about for a few days so I figured I'd just come out and say it. Lay it all out there. I mean, not literally." She groaned into the pillow.

"Why are you like this?" she said, and then put the pillow down.

I shrugged.

"You're the one dating me."

"Oh, right, that," she said. We both laughed.

"How do two girls even have sex?" she asked. "I mean, I've

seen porn before. I've heard jokes, but I honestly don't even know." That was more blunt than I was expecting her to be.

"I mean … I've never …" she trailed off and looked at me desperately.

"You've never had sex with anyone," I said for her.

"Yeah. I didn't really want to tell you that, but I can't keep going without you knowing that. I just … I never even got close. Like, one or two guys tried to cop a feel, but I flipped out and bailed as soon as I could. The idea of having sex with a guy made me want to throw up. At the time, I figured I just wasn't ready, or it wasn't the right guy. Now, of course, I'm thinking that it was something more. So there you go. My entire history."

She held her hands out and then dropped them.

"Guess that means it's my turn? Okay, I've had like, full sex, whatever that is, with a guy once. And oral a few times. Does oral count as sex?" She nodded.

"Okay, then I guess I've had sex about five times? It was never really great. I just assumed all sex sucked and people were liars. I was never into it, but I tried to be. It was never, like, bad. I was never into it. But I'm into you." I couldn't tell what her reaction was. She seemed to be thinking.

"I'm sorry you felt like you had to do that." I shrugged one shoulder.

"It's fine. Who knows if I hadn't met you if I would have gone out and done it again? Honestly, the idea that I don't have to have sex with a guy is such a fucking relief." That made her smile.

"Oh my god, I know, right?" Huh, I hadn't been able to quantify that feeling yet, but hearing Chase say it made complete sense.

We laughed and the tension was broken.

"I guess we can figure it out as we go along?" I said.

"I'm not sure how ready I am for … stuff," she said, and I could tell she was reluctant to tell me that.

"It's okay, Chase. I don't want either of us to do anything we're not ready for. And there's no rush. We literally live together. We have all kinds of time." I got up and went to sit next to her. I kissed the side of her head.

"Okay?"

She nodded.

"I really like you, Cordelia," she said. That made my heart feel like it had grown several sizes.

"I really like you, Chase."

She kissed my cheek and then rested her head on my shoulder.

"I'm glad we had this conversation," she said.

"I know. I knew we needed to, but it's hard to talk about this stuff sometimes." She nodded against my shoulder.

OUR TALK DIDN'T LEAD me to have less sex dreams, but at least I knew that Chase and I were on the same page. Or, at least, we were open to talking about what pages we were on.

When it came to sex, I had always been sort of meh on the whole thing, but that had been when I was going to be having sex with guys. Now, when I thought about sex with Chase? Phew. It made sweat trickle down my back and my skin buzz and my body ache. Was that what sexual attraction was supposed to feel like?

I had tried masturbating before and never really liked it, but now that I knew Chase pushed my buttons, I figured I could maybe try it again. When she wasn't in the room, of course. I didn't have a vibrator or anything. I had always been too scared to buy one, in case my dad was doing laundry and found it and then we'd have to have an awkward as hell conversation. Having him give me a talk before I'd gotten my period had been bad enough. We were so close, but there were just some things I didn't want to discuss with him.

Plus, it wasn't like I had anyone else I could really talk to about it. I'd had friends in high school, and we'd talked about this and that, but you could never say "hey, how do you all masturbate?" There was the internet, but I'd gotten overwhelmed with all that and had shut down.

I guess I could just try it.

On Monday afternoon, I had a short window when Chase was at class and I was in the room by myself. The fact that she was so predictable and wouldn't skip class unless she was at death's door was in my favor.

I set my bag down, turned my phone off and pulled the blinds. I also turned off all the lights. Honestly, I didn't know what I was doing, but I might as well figure out now. Should I be naked for this? I figured I probably should, so I took all my clothes off and got under the covers. Then I decided that I couldn't see what I was doing if I did that, so I lay on top. Totally naked.

Okay, I could do this. I wasn't afraid of my own body. I guess I was just worried that it wasn't going to work and I was going to be frustrated again. Still, I wanted to try.

I closed my eyes, since that seemed to be the natural thing to do. I figured the best way to do this was to go slow, so I started with my fingers touching my chest. Caressing carefully along my collarbones and shoulders and arms. Goosebumps popped up on my skin. So far so good.

From there, I moved to my breasts. I cupped and stroked them, and then worked on my nipples. They went from flat to standing straight up and hard. My breathing changed and I could feel myself getting hot. Okay, I was doing it. This was nice. It felt good, so I kept going. Moving down to my belly, touching it all, and then I moved my legs apart to start with my inner thighs. Part of me was impatient to get going, while another part told me to slow down and not rush. I had time. I had time to get to the other parts. The tension and the ache were building, and I knew I was coming up to something. Something good.

Tentatively, I touched where my thighs joined. Not on my clit, I wasn't ready for that yet, but above it. I pressed a little with my fingers, trying to learn what kind of pressure felt the best. I moved my hand in a circular motion like I'd seen some girls do in porn, but way slower than they did. I cringed when I remembered seeing videos of girls slapping their clits and moaning in pleasure. No, thank you.

My breathing got faster, almost desperate. I continued circling my hand and moved it lower. I flinched when I hit my clit. It was a good flinch. I touched it again and it made the ache worse. My hand went lower, fingering my opening. I started with a pinky, and pushed it in slowly, trying to relax. Putting in a tampon was one thing, a finger was something else. Sure, I'd had a penis in there before, but this was different. I moved my finger in and out, and then replaced it with my middle finger, adding my ring finger when I felt comfortable with the other one.

A moan escaped my mouth as I thrust my fingers in and out. Was this what I'd been missing? Shifting my hand a little, I moved it upward so when I pulled my fingers out, the heel of my hand hit my clit.

Ohhhhhhhh. Yeah, that was so good.

I hadn't been thinking about anything in particular, but now, an image of Chase looking over her shoulder at me flooded my mind. I moaned again and thought about how beautiful she was and how I felt when we kissed and suddenly, it was like a train of sensation had slammed into me and my legs were convulsing and wave after wave of painful pleasure nearly drowned me. I gasped and made noises I'd never heard myself make and pulsed with the most powerful sensations I'd ever felt.

After it ended, I felt like I was glowing from the inside out and I could feel a smile on my face.

That was fucking AWESOME. It took until my freshman year of college, but I'd finally had an orgasm. I lay on my bed for a while, sitting with the feeling. I didn't think I was the first or the last person who hadn't had an orgasm, but it definitely was a little weird sometimes when other people talked about it like everyone had had one, and that was a given.

I stroked my clit and it was hypersensitive and the touch hurt a little. I should probably get up and get dressed, but I was dopey and sleepy and all I wanted to do was take a nap. Unfortunately, I happened to glance over at the clock on the microwave and HOLY HELL, Chase was due back very soon. I needed to get my shit together and put some clothes on. The idea of her finding me naked wasn't horrible, but I wasn't sure if she was ready for all that yet, so I was going to wait for her to make a move on that.

Moving a half-speed, I got up and put my clothes on. My skin was so sensitive that feeling the fabric slide against it made goosebumps pop up. I checked myself in the mirror. My hair was all over the place, as usual, and my cheeks were bright. I pulled my hair back in a curly bun and tried to slow my still-racing heart.

By the time Chase walked in, I had made up my bed and was sitting on it with a book, pretending to read.

"Hey," she said, coming in and walking right over to give me a kiss. We'd decided that hello and goodbye kisses were mandatory.

"Hey," I said, my voice a little too high.

"Did you have a good day?" she sat on my bed and set her bag on the floor. I set my book aside. Not that I'd been reading it anyway.

"Yeah, you?" I wanted to keep her distracted so she didn't figure out what I had been doing not ten minutes before. Not that I was embarrassed. I guess I didn't know how to talk about that with her. Yet. We shared a room and I thought I knew her really well, but I'd never really heard or seen her doing anything like that, so I wasn't sure if she did.

"Yeah, it was good. Stella said the funniest thing in class, we were dying. I'm starving, though, do you want to go to dinner?" That second, there was a knock at the door.

Chase opened it and Stella, Kyle and Elise were on the other side.

"Dinner?" Stella said.

"Yeah, we were just talking about that." I didn't exactly want to be in a group of people, but what else was I going to do? I couldn't say no and give a vague reason.

"Sounds great," I said, getting up and shoving all my masturbatory thoughts to the back of my mind for a while.

∽

DINNER WAS a good distraction and there was no talk of masturbation. Thankfully.

"You're quiet tonight," Chase said when we got back to our room. I had a pile of homework, including a paper for art history and a chapter to read for my US history class, including notes and highlighting. It was going to take a long time, since the print was microscopic in my book and it was a lot of information at once.

"Am I?" I said as I gathered my supplies, including my favorite highlighters. I didn't know why, but using them somehow made me remember the reading better.

"Yeah, is something wrong?" Her voice was casual, but I could tell she was worried I was having second thoughts.

"No, not really. I was just thinking about all this homework

I have to do. Not all of us are a month ahead like *some* people."
I meant her.

"I told you if you wanted, I could sit down with your syllabi and make a schedule." I laughed.

"Oh, C, I know you would. But that's not how my brain works. I wish it did. That would make my life easier. No, it's fine. I'll get it done. I always do." Somehow, even though I got things done at the last minute, I always got them done. I'd never missed one yet. I guess it worked for me, in a weird way.

"Is that it?" she asked, pulling at one of my curls and the letting it spring back on itself.

"Uh, yeah," I said. I couldn't meet her eyes. I'd never lied to her before.

"Cordelia?" Her voice cracked, and that pretty much destroyed me.

"I masturbated this afternoon and had my first orgasm ever and I didn't want to talk about it because I didn't know if it would make you uncomfortable or feel weird so I didn't tell you except now I'm telling you." The words came out in one long rush. Shit. I didn't mean to say it that way. Guess that ship had sailed.

"Oh," Chase said, her face getting a little red.

"Yeah."

"I mean, I'm happy for you?" She laughed, and I felt my face get red. "Sorry, that came out wrong. I'm happy that you had your first orgasm. And, um, yeah, I masturbate. Mostly in the shower, because then you're less likely to get caught. It's kind of weird to do it when your roommate, who you are also attracted to, is laying a few feet away."

"Yeah, that was why I did it when you were gone," I said. "So, um, do you do it a lot?" I had gone from embarrassed one minute, to being ragingly turned on at the thought of Chase masturbating. I wondered if she'd ever thought about me when she did it.

"I mean, I don't know, what's a lot?"

"Twice a day?" I suggested. Now that I knew how to do it, I was probably going to be spending a lot more time doing it.

"I definitely don't do it that much. Would it be bad if I did?" I shook my head.

"I mean, it's pretty fucking great. If I could spend at least two hours a day doing that, I'd probably be a happy girl." We both chuckled.

"I wondered why you looked so dazed," she said, yanking a little on one of my curls.

"Hey!" I said and smirked at me. Her face was so close and I wanted to kiss her so much. I was also horny as fuck with the current topic of conversation.

"I bet you look beautiful when you do it," I said, and she stopped smirking.

"You can't say things like that to me," she said, and I noticed that her breathing sped up.

"Why not?" The air had gotten thick and hard to breathe. My blood pounded in my ears.

"Because it makes me think about so many things I want to do with, and to, you." Fuck.

"Are you ever going to tell me about those things?" I asked. Her mouth quirked up on the side in a seductive smile.

"I'd much rather show you."

I nearly fell off the bed.

And then I leaned forward and kissed her. What else was I going to do?

She kissed me back. Hard. We had been leading up to this, and I was still fired up from my earlier orgasm. I was horny and she was here and we wanted each other.

Her hands went into my hair and she pulled the elastic out, letting my curls loose.

"Are you okay?" she asked with a gasp.

"Yeah," I said, going right back to her mouth. Her fingers

pulled at my hair a little and I let my hands wander down her arms to the hem of her shirt. I'd been here before, but now I wasn't going to stop myself.

My hands dove under her shirt and found her stomach. She trembled at my touch and I stroked her mouth with my tongue. There was so much going on that my brain couldn't even think of anything other than how she tasted and how she felt. I pressed closer and she ended up on her back, with me over her. I straddled her hips with mine and looked down at her.

I took her hands and put them on my hips. Her eyes went wide, but I nodded to show her that it was okay. I wanted her to touch me.

She squeezed my hips a little and I groaned. Ever so slowly, she slid her hands up and touched my stomach under my shirt. I had a lot going on in that department, and I'd been a little hesitant about her touching me there, but she stroked me and didn't seem to want to stop.

"I want you so much, Cordelia," she said in a hushed voice. "You're so beautiful. I can't believe I get to do this." There was wonder in her voice and reverence. As if I was the most beautiful thing she'd ever seen. It almost made me want to cry. No one had ever looked at me quite like that.

"You're gorgeous, Chase. Every single part of you."

"What are your favorite parts?" she asked.

"All of them?" I said, and she laughed under me, shaking a little.

"All of your parts are my favorite," she said, digging her finger into my sides.

"Do you want to see some of my parts?" I asked. She nodded and I put my arms up so she could take my shirt off.

She propped herself up on her elbows and helped me get my shirt over my head.

"Wow," she said. "Your body is amazing."

Her hands ran up and down my arms and I shivered at her touch.

"Are you cold?" she asked.

"No." I wasn't. I was hot. I was burning from the inside out.

"You're so hot, Cordelia, holy shit." I smiled down at her. Fortunately, I had worn my favorite bra. It was hard to find one for a larger chest that was pretty, and this had been a serious investment. It was black with lacy cups and it made me feel sexy and mysterious.

"Can I take your shirt off?" I asked. She nodded and we both moved so I could get hers off. She had a very simple Chase-like bra on, but it had the tiniest little pink bow where the cups met in the front.

Her skin was more brown than mine and I was a little envious. I bet she didn't burn after five minutes in the sun like I did. I had to practically bathe in sunscreen in the summer. I was also a huge fan of big hats and lots of gauzy cover-ups.

"Your body is incredible," I said. This was the first time I was really seeing her in just a bra. Somehow we'd been really modest with each other. Guess I knew why now. I dragged one finger from her throat all the way down to the top of her jeans.

Her stomach quivered.

"There's so much to touch and I don't know where to start," I said.

She puckered her lips and I burst out laughing. Kissing seemed like a good place to start, so I leaned down and joined my lips with hers.

While we kissed, I let my hands wander all over her shoulders and the front of her bra, and down to her belly button. I discovered that certain parts of her side were ticklish, so I tried to avoid them for the time being, but I tucked that information away for future reference.

I didn't know if she meant to do it, but her hips started

rhythmically pressing against mine and I thought I was going to black out from the pressure in that particular place. Fireworks of sensation exploded in my brain and I had to stop and take a breath for a second.

"Okay?" Chase asked.

"Yeah," I gasped.

"Can I have a turn now?" she asked. She'd been running her hands up and down my sides while I'd been exploring and I could tell she was getting impatient.

"Yup," I said, and shifted so she could get up and we could switch positions. She laid me on my back and looked down at me.

"I can't believe I get to touch you," she said.

"You can. You can touch me," I said, and she let her fingers meander across me. It was maddening. I arched and strained against her fingers, but she kept up just the lightest pressure. A tease. A prelude.

"Why are you doing this to me?" I said, and it came out as a moan.

Chase chuckled.

"Because I can," she said in a deeply seductive voice.

Yes, she could. I was a complete quivering mess in her hands and she could do what she wanted with me and I would let her.

I'd been on top, but she was definitely the one who was steering this ship.

Her hands traced the cups of my bra.

"This is really pretty, but I'm guessing what's underneath is even prettier," she said. For someone who wasn't usually confident in social situations, Chase was completely taking charge and it was the most erotic thing that had ever happened to me. Somehow, it didn't surprise me at all.

"Would you like to find out?" I said. Chase nodded, and I sat up so she could get the back closure undone. After a few fumbles, she got the hooks undone and I moved the straps off my harms. I was taking my bra off with Chase and I was a tiny bit terrified.

"Wow," she said again, cupping my breasts with her hands. They spilled over her fingers. I was more than a handful.

She scraped her thumbs over my nipples, and I jerked in response.

"Oh, do you like that?" I nodded, and she did it again. She was going to drive me wild, just from touching my nipples.

And then she dipped her head and licked one of my nipples with her tongue and I was actually going to die. I was going to die and Chase would be the cause.

"Oh, fuck," I said, arching up into her mouth. She fluttered her tongue somehow and I felt my eyes roll back in my head. Incoherent sounds came from my mouth and I could barely breathe

There was a phone ringing. Somewhere. There was the sound of a phone ringing and Chase had removed her tongue from my body and was fumbling for her shrieking phone.

"Hello?" she said, answering it, totally breathless. I gaped up at her, my brain still hazy.

"Oh, hey, Mom," she said, getting off me as her face turned redder than I had ever seen it.

"Not much. Hey, I'm right in the middle of something, can I call you back?" I had to muffle a laugh. She was right in the middle of something, that was for sure.

"Okay, later ... Love you too ... bye." She hung up and looked down at me.

"Oh my goddddd." Chase burst out laughing and set her phone down on her desk. "Of course my mom would call right now. Of course she would." She sat back down on the bed and I started laughing too.

"We got clit blocked by your mom." Her eyes went wide for a second and she laughed so hard she started crying.

"You're the funniest person I've ever met," she said as she wiped her eyes.

I still had my tits out, and I wasn't sure if the moment had passed.

"Come back here," I said, reaching for her.

"Mmmm, yes, back to business," she said, putting her hands back on my breasts.

"Yes, pleaseeeeeee," I moaned.

Chapter Ten

CHASE

She was so ridiculously hot and I was losing my mind. I couldn't even believe that I'd gotten to see her without a shirt. Miles of creamy skin dotted with freckles, and so much to touch and stroke and tease. Being with Cordelia brought out a ferocious side of me that I didn't know, but I wanted to get to know—she was confident, she knew what she wanted, and she wasn't scared. I liked who I was with Cordelia. I liked her a lot.

I played with her nipples some more, and listened to every sound and thought about going further, but I pulled back and put the brakes on by kissing her.

"Can I touch you now?" she said. I nodded and she took my bra off. My chest wasn't even close to as ample as hers, but she looked at me as if I was something she very much wanted to devour. And she did.

Cordelia touched me and kissed me with all the fiery enthusiasm that I knew she had, and then some.

I squirmed on the bed and gripped the covers and made sounds that I'd never heard myself make. I was wild and uninhibited and she was plucking each and every string. Her lips found the undersides of my breasts and the spot above my belly button and my sensitive sides and licked right above the button on my jeans.

I gasped and she chuckled. Her breath rippled against my skin. I was coming apart.

"Mmm, what do you say about stopping it there for tonight?" she said, and I looked up at her. It took a second for me to realize what her words meant. I wasn't firing on all cylinders at the moment.

"Oh, yeah. Sure." She was probably right. I didn't want to get in over my head. "Can I hold you for a little while?"

She nodded and I opened my arms so she could lie on me.

"Your boobs are so much bigger than mine," I said, pouting.

"Your boobs are awesome. They're perfect and perky and you don't have to wear a bra all the time. I'd love to do that," she said.

"I'd love to actually fill out a bra."

"Hey," she said, "You're perfect." She gripped my chin. "Understand?"

I nodded.

"You're pretty stubborn," I said.

"Of course I am. It's the red hair." Cordelia yawned and snuggled into my chest. I let my fingers wander through her hair. There was so much of it, and it was fun to play with.

"I love your red hair," I murmured.

"I'm glad you do." I looked down and her eyes were closed. I kept stroking her hair until her chest rose and fell more slowly and I realized she was asleep. I pressed a kiss to the top of her head and closed my eyes too.

∾

THE NEXT THING I KNEW, I was waking up with a cloud of red hair in my mouth and it was the middle of the night.

"Shit," I said, realizing Cordelia and I had fallen asleep on her bed all wrapped up together.

"Huh?" she said, as I moved some of her hair out of my face. "What time is it?" She sat up and stretched her arms. All the lights were on and she still wasn't wearing a shirt. I was momentarily distracted by her breasts and forgot what she'd asked me.

"What?" I said.

"I asked you what time it was." She followed my eyes down to her chest and then laughed.

"You're never going to let me put these away, are you?"

"I mean …" I trailed off and she gave me a playful shove in the shoulder.

"My eyes are up here," she said, pointing to her gorgeous eyes.

"Yes, and they're beautiful." She blushed just a little bit.

"Stop it."

"Never." We stared at each other for a moment, and then both realized that we should probably go to bed. And put some shirts on so we didn't get distracted.

"What would you say if we shared a bed?" I asked, as she pulled on a baggy T-shirt and took off her jeans.

"I'd say that would be really nice. These beds aren't really that big, so I'd get to be pressed up against you all night, and I can't think of anything better," she said. "But which bed?"

"Yours. Your comforter is softer." It didn't matter so much, since both beds were the same, but I liked the idea of sleeping in her bed, surrounded by her blankets and her scent.

"And your pillows are nicer." I grabbed them off my bed and put them on hers.

I put a T-shirt on and she turned her back as I changed out of my jeans and put some shorts on to sleep in.

"Come snuggle," Cordelia said, getting into bed and holding her arms out. I pretended to run and dive into the bed. She squealed and I crawled into her arms. She pulled the covers over us. I lay my head on her chest. It was the actual perfect pillow.

"This is awesome. We should have started doing this from the beginning," she said, kissing my forehead.

"That might have been a little awkward at the beginning," I said with a laugh. "Hi, I'm your new roommate, let's snuggle."

"I mean, I knew I wanted to kiss you. I had no idea why I was so attracted to you and couldn't stop staring at you. Right away I had these feelings and didn't know what to do with them," she said. "I hope I didn't come on too strong. I was kind of reeling it in at the beginning. You were so shy and I was worried about scaring you."

"I was scared of you, but I thought it was just because of you being a new person and being in a new place and being around all these new people. Now I know what it was, but at the time I thought I was scared of you for different reasons."

I could tell she was looking up at me in the dark.

"Are you still scared of me?" she whispered.

"Yes, but for completely different reasons."

"Which are?"

I took a breath.

"I'm scared about how much I want you. I'm scared about how much I miss you when you're gone. I'm scared about how fast this has happened. I'm scared about what will happen if things don't work out. I'm scared about people finding out. I'm scared about telling my parents. I'm scared about a lot of things, Cordelia." She might as well know. We had to be honest with each other.

She squeezed my hand and kissed my cheek. We both had class in a few hours, but this was the kind of conversation that you needed to have in the dark. It was easier to talk to her like this. When we were both drowsy and uninhibited by the light of day.

"I'm scared, too," she said in a low voice. "I'm scared about how I feel about you. I'm scared about devoting all my time to you and fucking up in school and then dropping out. I'm scared about what my dad might say. I know he loves me no matter what. But I'm his only child and I just don't know. I'm scared about redefining myself. Because I've never felt this way about a guy, so what does that mean? Does that mean I like girls, or is it just you? And how do I figure that out? How does anyone figure this out?" I didn't have an answer for that.

"We could go to Kyle and Stella's club with them. They said there were other people like us there. So maybe it would be good?" She nodded and then yawned so hard her jaw cracked.

"Yeah, I think so. We don't have to figure it out tonight. There's time." She nodded and made a cute little sleepy sound.

"We should probably get to sleep. Tomorrow is going to be rough," I said.

"Uh huh." She was already halfway there. Strange, because she didn't usually fall asleep that fast.

"Goodnight, Cordelia," I said, kissing her forehead. She mumbled a goodnight and I finally let my eyes close.

It had been an interesting night.

CORDELIA WAS beyond grumpy the next morning. It was pretty cute though. I did feel partially responsible, but I didn't regret how we had spent our night. As she moved around the room (stumbled around the room), all I could think of was how she'd looked last night, laying out on her bed, naked from the waist up. Her body was unbelievable. It was perfect. I couldn't wait to touch her again. I couldn't wait to get her clothes off again.

I'd never been so wrapped up in another person. I wasn't running through my lists and schedules constantly. I had something to look forward to every single day. I had someone who smiled when she saw me. Someone who was so glad to see me. Being with her was the best part of my day.

"You're staring at me," she said, and I realized I had been. Oops?

"Sorry," I said. She grinned.

"Don't be. You can stare at me all you want." She wiggled her hips and I laughed, but then realized how sexily she was moving and that shut me up.

"If you want either of us to get to class, you're gonna have to stop doing that immediately." She raised one eyebrow.

"Oh, really? Maybe I don't want to go to class today. Maybe I want to spend all day in bed with you." Images of what that could lead to flashed through my head.

"Cordelia," I said in a warning voice.

She smirked at me and then sighed.

"Okay, fine. I'll let you go to class. Only because I know that you'll be mad at me later if I let you miss class." That was true. I might want to skip now, but I would regret it later.

"Thank you," I said, and she smacked a kiss on my cheek.

"See you later, C," she said, flouncing off. I sat on my bed and just breathed in the silence of my room. It felt so empty without her in it. I looked at her bed, where the covers were in disarray and my pillows were on her bed. Since my pillows were white with blue stripes, and her covers were bright fuchsia, they clashed. Kind of like me and Cordelia, on the surface. We didn't look like we went together at all.

I shook my head and started getting ready for class.

∽

MY MOM CALLED me that afternoon and I had completely forgotten about her previous call when I'd been messing around with Cordelia. We hadn't really talked in a few days and a lot had happened.

"Hey, you sounded distracted last night and you didn't call me back. What's happening, Chase?" I could hear the worry in her voice. It wouldn't have been a big deal, normally, but I was me and she knew me. I was a victim of my own past actions.

"I'm sorry I didn't call you back. I was hanging out with my roommate and then I fell asleep early." I mean, neither of those things was a lie. I'd simply left out the fact that we both hadn't been wearing shirts at the time.

"How are things with Cordelia? Are you two getting along?" I was lucky Cordelia was still at class because I didn't think I could have this conversation with my mother while she was in the room. No way. I wouldn't have been able to keep a straight face. Then Mom definitely would have known that something was up. As it was, I didn't know if I could talk my way out of this conversation without her getting suspicious.

"They're good. We get along great," I said, and my voice sounded fake even to my eyes.

"Is she there, can you not really talk to me right now?" I sighed.

"No, that's not it." I heard a sharp intake of breath.

"Are you not getting along? What's going on with you, Chase? I feel like we haven't heard from you in ages." It had been a week, tops, but that was out of character for me.

"I know, I'm sorry. I've just been busy with everything." That distracted her for a little while and I was able to take a breather and talk about less-fraught topics.

Of course, we circled back around to my social life. I mentioned Kyle and Stella.

"They sound so nice, are they best friends?" It was a perfectly innocent question.

"No, they're a couple," I said, and braced for the impact.

"Oh, how sweet. They sound like really nice girls. I'm glad you're making friends, Chase. I didn't want to worry too much about you, but I did anyway." Phew. That was good. I knew both of my parents had progressive politics and had often been vocal about their support of the queer community, but it was a whole different situation when it was your daughter who was the queer one. If I was. I still didn't know yet. I knew I wasn't heterosexual, but other than that, it was all a giant mystery. I wasn't ready to take that to my parents until I had something I could tell them besides "hey, I'm dating a girl and I really like her, but I have no idea if this makes me gay or not." I was worried they might pressure me to find a label and slap it on, but I wasn't ready. Fortunately, Cordelia wasn't ready either and she told me that all the time.

"You sound busy and happy. I can put my mom worry away for now," she said, and I laughed.

"Yes, you can put your worry away for now. Or maybe use it on Kate since you don't need to focus on me." Since I was the first born, I got more attention than she did, which she was still bitter about. I had told her time and again that she could have had that attention anytime she wanted it.

We finished our chat and I breathed a huge sigh of relief just as Cordelia got back from her class.

"Hey, how was your day?" I set my phone down and gave her a kiss.

"Good. I just talked to my mom. Somehow I was able to talk my way around everything, so I don't think she suspects." Cordelia flopped on her bed. I'd made it up after she left. Cordelia never made her bed.

"I'm still trying to figure out what to tell my dad." She rubbed her eyes. "Why is this shit all so complicated? Why can't I just be with you without any of the other bullshit? If you were a guy, none of this would be stressing us out." She pouted and I went over to sit next to her.

"Sorry, not a guy," I said.

"Thank god. Although, you'd probably be the hottest guy." I laughed about that.

"We should go on a date," I said. "Like a real one, with just us."

She turned her head to the side a little.

"Really? You think we're ready for that?"

"You were literally licking my nipples twelve hours ago." Her face flamed up and I felt a bolt of lust go through me. And how good she'd been at it.

"Mmm, fair point. But can the date involve nipple licking? Because I think I'm getting really good at it." I snorted.

"I think we can arrange that when we get back. I don't think a restaurant would be okay with public nipple licking."

"Well, that's just rude," she said.

"You're so cute," I couldn't stop myself from kissing her.

CORDELIA

Chase seemed to want to take the lead in planning our date, and she was the planner in this relationship, so I went ahead and told her to go for it. I figured if I was the one planning, she'd just be anxious about what we'd be doing and might not have a good time, so I let her take the lead.

My first date with a girl. It was surreal. I never thought I would be here, but I couldn't imagine not being with Chase, now that I was. Ever since that first day, I'd known there was something special about her, something I had to be around.

I happened to run into Stella one afternoon when I was coming out of the bathroom. My last class had been cancelled, so I'd come back to my room and was trying to use the time constructively with doing homework, but I'd spent most of the time daydreaming about my upcoming date with Chase.

"Hey, how's it going?" she said. "Are you busy right now? Do you want to hang out in my room? Everyone else is gone and I'm bored." I didn't even bother with the homework excuse. I could do it later.

"Sure," I said, and we walked down the hall to her room. "Hey, I actually wanted to ask you something."

"Go for it," she said as we both sat on her bed.

"So, Chase and I are going on our first date, which is bizarre, but I'm wondering … how do I date a girl? Like, who pays? I know that's a weird thing to ask, but I feel like if she was a guy, there would be all these established rules and I have no idea what the rules are for girls dating girls." She smiled and put her hair over her shoulder.

"You're reminding me of my first date with Kyle. Neither of us really knew if it would qualify as a date. She was still really new, but I'd known I was a lesbian for a while. Still, it was a lot of guesswork. And I think we figured along the way that we could make our own rules. That a lot of the rules for heterosexual couples were rooted in old ways that, sometimes, were completely misogynistic and outdated. So, really, you can do what you want. What feels right. That's one of the best parts of being queer. You make your own rules."

Wow. I hadn't thought of it that way. Right now, it was like we were both walking forward without a map. The way Stella put it, we were in the process of drawing our own. Forging a new path that was whatever we wanted it to be, instead of being completely lost.

"I like that, thank you."

"You're welcome. Anytime you need advice, don't hesitate to ask. We're here for both of you. This can be hard to navigate, and we didn't really have anyone so we fumbled along for a while." She was right. We did have a lot of people to ask and who were supporting us. Even though our parents and families weren't there, we had made up a new family somehow. A family we didn't even know we needed until now.

"I really appreciate it. All this is still so surreal." Stella nodded and gave me a knowing smile.

"I remember exactly what that was like. I was so scared to tell even my closest cheer friends and my brother." I raised my eyebrow.

"You were a cheerleader." She nodded and pulled up some pictures on her phone.

"Yup. Loved it. I thought about cheering here, but it's such a huge time commitment and I didn't want to take time away from being with Kyle. Cheer is important, but she's more important." Hearing her talk about Kyle almost made me want to cry. They were just so in love and that love shined out of both of them. It was a ferocious light that everyone could see. Only a tiny part of me was jealous.

Not that I loved Chase. Oh, hell, I wasn't close to that yet. I couldn't be close to that yet.

"When did you know?" She looked down and smiled.

"I don't know exactly when it started. What moment, what clicked in my brain. I actually didn't mean to say it out loud the first time I said it." She laughed at the memory. "It just came out and by the time it was said, I couldn't un-say it. And I'm lucky that she loved me too." Her story was making my heart ache in the worst way. I wanted that.

"You look really happy together," I said.

"We are. I mean, everything isn't perfect, we still have our moments, but I love her. Sometimes it's that simple." Huh. I liked that. I was glad I'd run into her. I had needed to have this talk with someone.

"Seriously, thank you, Stella." She brushed me off and asked if I wanted a snack. I did and we talked about other things until Elise got back and I realized that Chase would also be back any moment.

"Go get your girl," Elise said, pushing me a little out the door.

My girl? Was Chase my girl? If she was my girl, did that mean that I was hers?

We still had so much to figure out, but Stella had helped a little.

I was only in the room for a few minutes when Chase got back. I almost tackled her before she had even got through the door.

"Oh, hey," she said as I launched myself at her. I attacked her lips and her hands immediately went for my hair. She loved touching my hair and I loved it when she pulled on it just a little. Maybe I was kinky and I didn't even know it?

I licked and kissed her mouth, reveling in her taste. I loved that she was taller than me. Loved the way her lips were curved. Loved the way her tongue played with mine. Loved the way her eyes got dark and she got a little bossy. Everything about her was designed to drive me wild, make me want her more.

I gasped and had to catch my breath. I always chose kissing over breathing with her.

"What was that?" she asked as we both held onto each other and trembled.

"I missed you?" I said, and it sounded like a question.

"I was only gone a few hours." I laughed a little hysterically.

"I was talking with Stella and the way she was talking about Kyle, I don't know, it just made me realize how much I like you. Because I do, Chase. I know this is new and scary, but I want to do this with you. I want to do all of this with you." So far, we'd been girlfriends behind closed doors, but I thought I was finally ready to be out and open about being together.

Even if people would ask a ton of questions. I could handle them, as long as she was by my side.

"I'm glad you talked to Stella then, Carrots." I smiled at the nickname. It was the same one that Anne Shirley's love interest, Gilbert Blythe, had called her. First as a taunt and later as an endearment. It was perfect.

"You can call me Carrots anytime," I said. My knees were still wobbly from the kiss. I stumbled a little and she caught me.

"Are you ready to go to dinner?" Dinner? I blinked at her. I was still to flustered by the kiss and the nickname and the warmth flooding my chest by being near her.

"Yeah," I said at last. "Let's go to dinner, C." Chase put her bag down and pushed the door open. I reached my hand out and took hers. She looked at me with surprise.

"Are we doing this now?" I had wanted to take her hand so many times and I was finally ready.

"I can't let you have all the control. I *did* kiss you first." Her eyes got dark.

"Mmm, but wouldn't you like it if I had all the control?" she said in my ear as we walked down the hallway.

I shivered with desire and willed my face not to get red. She chuckled under her breath and knocked on Stella and Elise's door. My brain had almost completely shut down and it was all I could do to walk down the hallway to the elevator with them and then to the dining commons next door.

"Earth to Cordelia," Elise said, waving her hand in front of my face. I blinked and realized that I was holding up the line for food. I grabbed a tray and got a plate of pasta with meatballs, a side of garlic bread, and a small salad. For some reason the meatballs here were out of this world. I didn't know what they put in them, but I always went back for seconds.

Chase was behind me and got the same thing. I could feel her presence, could feel her breathing near me. Just getting myself and my tray to the table without incident was a miracle.

I sat down next to Chase and she gave me a look, raising one eyebrow slowly. She was still thinking about what she'd said earlier, and I was still thinking about it too.

What was it about her? I'd never really considered what role I'd play when it came to sex. With a guy, I guess I had assumed that I would be the submissive one. I mean, that was what you saw everywhere. The guy was the aggressor and the woman submitted. Now, though, I was thinking about what it meant that Chase and I were both girls. It was like Stella had said, we could make our own rules.

Chase was so shy and so reluctant in most situations, but when things got heated between us, she turned into someone who knew what they wanted and knew how to get it from me. And I became someone who wanted to give it to her. I liked it, a whole fuck of a lot. In fact, I couldn't stop thinking about it.

"You're staring, Carrots," Chase said in my ear. I felt my face flame up. Her hand stroked my thigh under the table and I was ready to slide to the floor in a puddle.

"Why are you doing this to me?" I whispered back, whining a little.

"Mmm, because you like it?" I did. I liked it a hell of a lot. I made a little frustrated sound in the back of my throat and she laughed softly.

I looked up and realized we were with other people and being wildly inappropriate. But everyone else was chatting and eating and didn't seem to be paying attention to us. Either they were doing it on purpose, or it was just a coincidence. I didn't really want to know which.

Time to put my focus on my food. I looked down at my spaghetti and meatballs and picked up my fork. Eating. It was time for eating. Not time for thinking about Chase pushing me up against a wall and pulling my hair and kissing me hard. I took a breath.

People were talking around me and I was trying to pay

attention, but I couldn't. I needed to get out of here as soon as I could so I didn't have to pretend that I wasn't a million miles away and thinking about doing naughty things with Chase.

Dinner lasted forever and I tried to clean my plate, but I couldn't. Not even the incredible meatballs were going to occupy my mind. I didn't remember anything anyone said to me and couldn't tell you what was said or what I said.

It wasn't a complete disaster, but as Chase held my hand on the way back to the dorm, she leaned down and said, "You're awfully distracted tonight, Cordelia."

"I can't help it, you keep saying things," I hissed back at her. She squeezed my hand.

"I thought you were enjoying it."

"Yeah, I enjoy it too much, that's the problem. I can't think about anything else right now." I couldn't look at her, but her hand tightened on mine.

"Do you think we need to do something about it?" Her voice was casual, but I knew what she meant.

I took a breath.

"Yes," I said.

Chapter Eleven

CHASE

Honestly, I didn't know what I said affected her so much. I knew it turned me on more than I'd ever been before. I didn't even know what I was doing, but whatever I did, Cordelia responded to.

We somehow got back to our room without saying or doing anything in front of everyone, but the second I had the door shut, I was pushing her up against it and diving for her mouth.

"I want you so much right now," I said, and she moaned and clutched onto me. My skin hummed with need and I couldn't get enough of her. I plunged my fingers into her hair, yanking it just a little and making her gasp.

"Do you like that?" I asked, and pulled a little.

"Yes," she said, her voice thick with desire.

"Interesting," I said, before going back to her mouth. I couldn't get her shirt off fast enough, and she was having similar difficulties. We were both so desperate to get the other one's shirt off that we weren't getting anywhere.

"Whoa, hold on," I said, laughing a little. "One shirt at a time."

I pulled hers over her head.

"Hey, why is my shirt the first one to come off?" she said, her voice muffled as I got it over her head.

"Because I said so." Her eyes went a little wide.

"Okay, but can I take yours off now?" I nodded, and she unbuttoned my shirt. She got huffy when she found a tank top under it.

"Why are you wearing two shirts?"

"Because if I didn't, my bra would show through?" She made grumbling noises as I got the tank top over my head and we were both down to our bras.

Today hers was cotton and pink and she was almost falling out of it.

"I didn't know I was going to be showing you this one, or else I would have put on another one this morning." My eyes nearly fell out of my head.

"Don't apologize, you look amazing," I said, cupping her breasts in my hands. Or, at least, trying to.

"You're so sweet and pretty," she said, touching me. I gathered her hands in mine and slowly put them above her head.

"Is this okay?" She pulled her bottom lip between her teeth and nodded. Her cheeks flushed with heat.

I wanted to give her my complete and total attention. The attention that every single inch of her deserved. I stopped holding her hands, but she kept them above her head. Good girl.

A fire had been lit within me and it was burning me alive. I had so many thoughts firing in my head and I wanted to do everything at once, but I needed to make a list in my head. I needed steps. First step, kissing her neck. I hadn't done it enough, and it was an area I wanted to explore.

I dragged my mouth from hers and down her jaw to the underside of her face. I tasted and licked and gave her little soft kisses and tested my teeth. I wanted to know what she wanted, so I tried a little bit of everything and waited for her reaction. I was learning Cordelia, and I needed to know every single thing.

She liked it when I kissed hard, liked it when I scraped my teeth against her skin, liked the little feather-light kisses I placed on her skin. Hard and soft.

Her hands didn't stay on the door, they moved into my hair. I didn't mind. In the back of my mind, I knew I could tell her to put her hands up and she would do it. She would do what I wanted and that drove me even more wild.

I raked my hands across her skin and decided that the bra was nice, but it needed to go. I wanted nothing between us.

"Bra off," I said between kisses and she reached behind and undid the clasp, letting it fall to the floor. I fell to my knees and buried my face in her stomach. She bent down and kissed the top of my head.

I looked up and she pushed my hair out of my eyes.

"You're so fucking beautiful right now," she said.

She was beyond beautiful, and I was going to show her.

I stood up and tugged her toward the bed. I needed her on her back. Hovering over her, I looked down at her spread out on the bed. Her body was lush and perfect. I had seen her like this before, but each time was incredible.

This time, I let my mouth follow my hands, tasting every inch, kissing every part of her, licking her until she squirmed and begged beneath me.

"I want ..." she gasped.

"What, Cordelia? What do you want?" Her eyes opened and she looked up at me, her eyes full of want.

"I want to touch you." I wasn't even close to being done with her yet, but I figured it was only fair.

She tugged at my bra as if to make her point.

Her impatience was so adorable. I stripped off my bra and her eyes went wide. I didn't know what she saw when she looked at me, but judging from her face, she liked what she saw.

"Your boobs are so great," she said, cupping them.

"If you say so."

"I do," she said, sitting up to kiss me.

Now it was my turn to be on my back and let her have what she wanted.

Cordelia didn't waste any time and went right for my nipples. She experimented with biting them softly with her teeth and that was mind-blowing. My body arched off the bed and pushed my nipple further into her mouth. She smiled up at me as she flicked my nipple with her tongue and moved to give the other the same treatment. She sucked, hard, and I wondered if she was going to leave a mark. I almost wanted her to. So I could look at it later and remember that her mouth had been there. I wanted her to mark me.

She didn't stop, and kept going until she reached the waistband of my jeans. Cordelia locked eyes with me as she popped the button of my jeans, and gripped the zipper.

She was asking permission. I nodded and she pulled the zipper down. The sound was louder than the pounding of my heart.

We hadn't traversed this territory yet, and I didn't think either of us knew what we were doing, but Cordelia didn't hesitate as she pulled my jeans a little lower, exposing my white panties. I didn't have fancy underwear because I didn't think anyone was going to see it. I might have to remedy that.

"So sweet," she said, stroking the edge of my panties. They had just a tiny bit of pink lace on the top. I thought I knew what would happen next. I mean, I sort of knew what people did in this situation. But Cordelia had had sex before and I hadn't. Did this count as sex? What did count as sex?

"C. Are you okay?" I blinked down at her.

"Huh?" I had so much going on in my brain and in my body and couldn't form it into something coherent.

"Do you want me to stop? I felt you drifting away from me there."

I took a deep breath.

"I'm not sure if I'm ready. For that, anyway." I cringed and hoped she wasn't mad.

She kissed my stomach and zipped my pants up.

"That's fine. I wouldn't want you to do something you weren't ready for." She was too good for me. Too wonderful. Too awesome.

"What did I do to deserve you?" I said, touching her face as she rested her cheek on my stomach.

"You need to flip that question around. I'm pretty sure I'm the luckiest one." I wanted to argue with her, but I decided not to.

"Would you like to go down on me?" she asked after a few minutes of silence.

The second she said it, my blood ignited and I was ready to fucking go. It wasn't that I hadn't wanted her to go down on me, but my anxiety had been louder than my desire and I didn't want to get into it and then bail. I definitely hadn't wanted to do it and then have any sort of regret. That would be horrible. I would not have any regrets with Cordelia.

"Mmmm, yes," I said, grinning at her. She popped up and shoved me so she could lie down.

"Good because I have been dying to see what you can do with that tongue, Chase Hillier." I made a little growling sound and she squealed.

"Are you sure you're ready for this?" I asked.

"I don't think I'll ever be ready for you, Chase, but that's not going to stop me." I'd take it. I dragged my hands down her front, stopping briefly to tweak her nipples and make her jump before I got to the button on her pants.

"Just take them off before I die from anticipation," she said, and I laughed. I popped the button of her jeans and started to tug them down her legs. I left her underwear on. For now.

There was a little struggle to get them off over her feet (they were obscenely tight), but with a little wrangling, I got them off and tossed them on the floor.

Her legs were thick and curved perfectly. So much freckled skin spread out before me. Cordelia's panties were black with red cherries printed on them. Strangely appropriate for the current situation.

"Your body is just so fucking great," I said, running my hands up her calves. She parted her legs just a little bit for me and blushed and those two things together were making me want her even more.

"I don't even know what to do," I admitted. I kept stroking her legs, going a little higher each time.

"Do whatever you want, Chase. I'm all yours." The fact that she trusted me so much was intense. I knew if I sat here and worried about where to start, I would end up not doing anything and be paralyzed with indecision and we'd never get anywhere.

I wanted to touch her, so I reached out and brushed my hand along the front of her panties. She made a whimpering sound. I stroked her again, and pressed a little harder. Her hips reached for me. I stroked downward, right through her center and her legs twitched and spread wider for me. What a good girl.

I hooked my finger under the top edge of her panties and started to pull at them. She lifted her hips to help me. I could barely breath as I revealed her and worked the panties off her legs to join her pants on the floor.

I had Cordelia Scott completely naked and I had never seen anything sexier. My hand shook as I touched her at the juncture of her legs. Before I could think about it, I brought my head down and kissed her. She made incoherent sounds and I thought she was asking me for more, but her words were garbled. Still, I could tell she liked what I was doing. I brushed her with my fingers, letting them play with her clit, with her inner and outer lips, tickling and teasing. Her legs were shaking.

Finally, I made out one word that she said, "please."

"Please, what?" I asked, looking up as I let my index finger hover at her entrance.

"Please, Chase," she said, pushing herself into my hand.

"Tell me what you want," I said again. I wanted to hear dirty words from her pretty mouth. I wanted to hear her ask me for what she wanted. And then I would give it to her.

"Please fuck me with your tongue and your fingers, oh god," she said in a rush. I didn't expect her to ask so easily, so now it was up to me to comply.

"My pleasure," I said. "All you have to do is ask."

I teased her entrance with my fingers and then moved them so I could touch her with my tongue. I had no idea what she would taste like, and the second her taste hit my tongue, I wanted to devour her. Savor her. I licked her up and down, and found her clit, flicking it experimentally. Oh, she liked that. She liked that a lot. I continued until she was a complete mess, moaning and begging me. My hands continued to stroke her opening and I tentatively inserted one finger. She gasped at the intrusion, so I stopped. I could feel her internally tugging at me, as if she was begging with her body and her words.

"More please," she gasped out and I pushed my finger further.

"Fuck!" she said, her back coming off the bed. I flicked her clit with my tongue as I pushed my finger all the way inside. She threw her head back and panted and I loved every second of it. I retracted my finger and then dove into her again, and then again, and then again. I kept up my assault of her clit with my tongue. When it felt like she was ready, I added another finger, curling it forward to where I hoped her g spot was. Sure, I didn't have experience doing this to someone else, but I had the same set of equipment and had been getting myself off for years. I figured I would try what worked for me and go from there.

My fingers kept up a steady rhythm and I matched it with my tongue. Her hips thrust toward my mouth and I worried a little about her knocking my teeth out with her pelvis, but honestly, I wouldn't care all that much. As long as I got her off, that was what mattered.

"Fuck, Chase, fuckkkkkkkk," she drew the word out and I wanted to ask if she was close, but my mouth was busy and it seemed like a foregone conclusion as her inner walls pulled at my fingers and her hips shook with tremors. I kept it up with my mouth and my hand to draw her climax out.

The sounds she made ... I would never forget those sounds as I made her come. I made a decision right then to devote a portion of my time to getting her to make those noises as often as possible.

Her body quieted and I smiled up at her from between her thighs. I was the actual happiest girl in the entire world.

"Holy fucking fuck shit fuck," she said. Her cheeks were beautifully flushed. She smiled down at me and stroked some of my hair out of my face. The strands had gotten in the way and now they smelled like her.

"Was that okay?" I asked, but I pretty much knew the answer.

"Fucking fuck, I thought I was actually going to die from too much pleasure. That was just ... holy shit, Chase. I mean, I know I literally had my first orgasm like a few days ago, but holy fuck." She giggled a little and pushed her hair back. It was all over the place and I wanted to bury my face in it.

"Well, that was my first time going down on anyone, so I didn't really know what I was doing, but I guess it worked?" She growled and grabbed my face, pulling me up so she could kiss my mouth.

"Yeah, little bit," she said, and then devoured my mouth. My face was wet from her, but she didn't seem to mind at all. She kissed me long and hard and everything below the waist ached with want and need. It would have to wait for another time. I didn't want to be reckless and say "sure, go for it," if I wasn't ready, and I didn't think I was. I wouldn't let the lusty thoughts override my sensible thoughts.

"Fuck," she said again and wrapped her legs around me. It did not escape my attention that she was completely and totally naked as she grinded against me and kissed me.

I grabbed onto her because she was like a tornado of red hair and need and desire. I reached a hand between us and started fiddling with her clit, which made her thrust herself against my hand and I got her off again that way in only a few moments. This time I watched her face as she came, as she fell apart and came back together.

"You are pretty much the best thing that's happened to me, ever," she said. I knew what she meant. I rubbed my head against her hair.

"I wish we could just stay in this room sometimes. Just the two of us having a world of our own. Nothing to face outside," I said. That would be heaven.

"I know. But I feel like we'd get hungry eventually. And we do have supportive friends." That was true. We did have supportive friends. And we would probably have supportive families, when we decided to tell them. Right now it was just easier and safer to be like this. Just the two of us.

"We could order food online. And our friends could come and visit us here," I said. She giggled.

"But we'd get pretty stinky after a little while, I think." Oh, she had a point there. We didn't have a bathroom attached to our room. We'd have to leave to pee and take showers.

"Damn, that plan is out the window."

CORDELIA

It was perfect. Everything with her was always so much better than I thought it would be. I imagined what it would be like to have Chase in bed, but the reality? Far exceeded that in every way. For someone who had never gone down on someone else, holy fuck. She must have been blessed by an angel or something, because she pushed every single button I had. The other times when guys had gone down on me, I'd been so uncomfortable that I hadn't even gotten close to enjoying it and pretty much just told him to stop. With Chase I could let go. I didn't have to hold myself back. I was free.

I left to take a shower after we messed around, and when I came back, she was in bed reading. Walking in and seeing her sitting there, tugging on the ends of her hair and with that little concentration wrinkle between her eyebrows took my breath away. She was just so beautiful.

"Hey," I said, closing the door. She finished her page and looked up at me with a smile.

"That was really great, by the way. In case I didn't make that clear." I kissed her and she grinned back at me. She was pretty pleased with herself, that was for sure.

She stuck her tongue out at me and wiggled it.

"Okay, you need to stop that immediately unless you want me to tackle you." She put her book down.

"Is that a challenge?"

"Definitely."

We didn't end up going to sleep for a long time.

MY DAD CALLED me the next afternoon when I was in between classes. I was hanging out with Mariella when my phone rang, so I excused myself from the table we'd been sitting at in the Union and went outside.

"Hey, Dad," I said.

"Hey, Sprite!" he said. My dad didn't talk at a normal volume. I bet anyone standing near me heard him calling me by the nickname. He was lucky I didn't embarrass easily. I had more than one story of him saying something that should have been said in a whisper at an extremely high volume so that everyone in the grocery store knew I needed regular size tampons and not supers.

"How's the college life?" he asked.

"It's good. Busy. Stressful, but what else is new?"

"You behaving yourself? No frat parties?"

"Uh, nope. Haven't done any of those yet."

"Good, you stay away from those boys up there, Sprite. They're only after one thing." I rolled my eyes. Sometimes my dad had outdated views about people. I knew he meant well, but it was frustrating.

"I'm not interested in boys, Dad," I said, and then realized what I had said. Shit.

"No one caught your fancy? That's fine, you don't need any of that in your life. Keep your focus on studying." I bit my tongue and had to stop myself from saying "I'm not interested in boys, but there is a girl," but I didn't. I chickened out.

"That's what I'm trying to do," I said. Telling him about Chase wasn't the kind of thing I could do with a bunch of people standing around me. And definitely not before I had mentally prepared myself and thought out what I might say.

He asked me a few more questions and I asked him how work was going. My dad was an archivist and historian, and I think it broke his heart a little bit when I hadn't been interested in getting a degree in history, even art history. I figured I was taking a class, and maybe I'd change my mind. I honestly had no idea what I wanted to do or how to commit to something like that. How could I pick a fucking career to do for the rest of my life when I couldn't even decide which Pop Tart flavor I liked better? It was beyond ridiculous. I knew Chase had all her shit planned out and mapped and everything and sometimes it made me feel like a failure. I tried to tell myself that we were different people and had different brains and that was okay, but it still got to me.

I hung up with my dad and went back to Mariella.

"Sorry, my dad calls and checks up on me. I'm an only child, so he's a little protective." Plus, my mom wasn't around, so it had been just the two of us for my whole life. I was his world, and I wished I could help him feel less anxious about me being at school.

"Yeah, I know what you mean. My mom is really protective too. And then there's my aunts and my grandmothers too. I can't even sneeze on social media without them texting or calling and asking me about it." I laughed. At least my dad wasn't that bad. He hated social media. Thought it was a waste of time. I hadn't been able to explain to him that social media could connect you with people all over the world and he could make friends with people anywhere. He was never going to get it.

Mariella was a sophomore and lived off campus with three roommates in a tiny ass apartment, but I still thought that was cool. Having an apartment seemed so grown up.

"Sometimes I miss the dorms, honestly. I have class and I have to drive to campus and then there's work and by the time I get home from that, I'm exhausted and all I want to do is sleep and I still have to make food and everything." The idea of all that responsibility made me feel panicky. I had a car, but my dad had helped me pay for it and I worked all summer to have money for this school year. I was hoping I didn't have to get a job, since Dad said he would send me money so I could focus on school and not have to work, at least for this year.

"That sucks," I said because there didn't seem to be much else to say.

She sighed.

"Yeah, it does. But it's what I have to do, you know?" I nodded. Yeah, I did. My anxiety made it hard for me to do things like making phone calls and going to appointments, and most of the time I had to suck it up and just do those things because they had to be done. Even if I had a panic attack on the way to an appointment.

She looked at her phone and realized she had to get to work, so I said bye to her and then walked back to the dorm. I couldn't wait to see Chase, but what else was new? I couldn't wait to see her every day. We were finally going on our first date this weekend, and I knew she had been planning it all out. No matter what we did, it was going to be awesome. It was going to be both our first dates with another girl, so I knew she was probably going to go all out. Like she did everything else. Meticulous and sweet.

I wished I could wipe away all those other dates I'd been on and declare that this would be my first one. Still, if I hadn't gone on all those dates with guys, I might not have figured out that I didn't want to go on another date with one. Ever.

Figuring out my sexuality had been put on the back burner for now. I wanted to enjoy my time with Chase without the anxiety of that ruining things. I hadn't talked to her about it recently, but I knew it was something she worried about too. Why couldn't things just be easy and uncomplicated?

I walked through the door and there she was, my girl. I rushed to kiss her and she was right there to meet me. She caught me as I did a flying leap into her arms.

"Well, hello," she said as I tried to kiss her.

"Hello," I said into her mouth through a kiss.

We ended up falling over onto her bed. It had become our couch, since we were using my bed to sleep in. It was cramped and we ended up all curled around each other and my hair was in her mouth each morning, but I wouldn't want to wake up any other way.

She rolled us so we were both on our sides.

"My dad called today. I didn't tell him anything," I said. I didn't mean to blurt that out, but it had been bothering me the entire walk back.

"Did you want to?" she asked, stroking my curls.

"I mean, yes. I share nearly everything with him. But I'm just not sure how to go about it? How do I tell him something so life changing happened? How do I casually drop that into a conversation?"

"Yeah, I know. I've thought about so many different ways of doing it. Just dropping it like a bomb, or doing it in a more subtle way. Honestly, I don't think there is an easy way to do this. Which is what makes it so difficult." I nodded and pressed my forehead to hers.

"We are gonna figure this out."

We'd have to.

Chapter Twelve

Chase

The night before our date, I barely slept. I just kept running everything through my mind, making sure I hadn't left anything out. I wanted everything to be perfect. Statistically, I knew something was going to go wrong, but I wanted to prevent anything big from going wrong. I couldn't let our first date flop. I wouldn't let that happen.

I knew that if I told anyone how nervous I was, they would say I was making a big deal out of nothing. That Cordelia would be content to literally drive to the middle of nowhere, get out of the car and stare at each other for three hours and then go home. I knew that was true, but I also knew that she deserved everything. She deserved fireworks and helicopters and dates like they had on those cheesy reality shows. I wanted her to have the best.

As she slept, I held onto her and hoped that things would be fine. That we would be fine. If this whole relationship blew up in our faces, there was going to be hell to pay. What if we broke up and couldn't bear to live with each other anymore? We'd have to switch room assignments and I had no idea how to do that since it was still the beginning of the year. I had the feeling it was complicated, to prevent people from playing musical roommates. I liked our room. I liked our hall. I liked where we were. Changing that would be awful. Not to mention the thought of losing Cordelia completely made me want to scream and cry and break things all at once. I would do anything possible to prevent that from happening, if I could.

Finally, morning came and it was go time. I had barely gotten any sleep and I was going to be exhausted for the entire day, but who the hell cared? I was going on a date with the greatest girl in the entire world.

When she finally opened her eyes, I noted that they were extra blue.

"Hi," she said in a sleep-thickened voice.

"Hi, Carrots," I said. She always smiled when I called her that. "You ready for our date?"

She yawned and stretched her shoulders until they popped.

"Mmmm, after a little bit of coffee," she said.

"Would you be okay with getting breakfast on the road?" She raised one rust-colored eyebrow.

"Is our date starting now?" I nodded and she bounced out of bed quicker than I'd ever seen her before.

"Yeah, it is. So we both need to get dressed." I pulled my sleep shirt over my head. I hadn't worn a bra to bed. Her eyes got wide.

"How about I have *you* for breakfast?" I put out a hand to stop her.

"No time for that, we have things to do." She pouted until I leaned down and kissed her. She threw her arms around my neck and tried to pull me back into bed, and it took everything in me to resist her. We had a schedule to keep.

"Later," I said into her mouth as I unlatched her arms from my neck.

"This date better involve kissing at some point," she said,

standing up and then stripping her own shirt off. Now I was the one who was second-guessing the schedule. Her breasts were so perfect and so full and so touchable.

Without even realizing it, I'd reached for her, but she waggled her finger at me.

"Now, now. We don't have time for that." She went to her dresser and pulled out a bra. I growled in frustration. She laughed as she put on her bra and then presented her back for me to do the hooks. For a second, I thought of pushing the bra off and onto the floor, but then an alarm on my phone went off, reminding me that we needed to get going.

I reluctantly did the hooks and brushed the tops of her shoulders, settling her straps into place. She shivered a little and looked over her shoulder at me.

"You look so sexy right now," I whispered and then kissed her. The alarm buzzed again. Dammit.

"Time's up," she said as the alarm continued to blare.

SOMEHOW, we made it out to the parking lot and I steered her toward Elise's van. I'd asked her if I could borrow it for the day and she'd handed me the keys, but not before she let me take it for a spin around campus to make sure I could handle it.

Cordelia raised her eyebrows at the van, but I opened the door for her and held my hand out so she could climb in. It was a little bit of a hop for her, but she made it and I closed the door behind her.

I jingled the keys as I got into the driver's seat. Elise and I were almost the same height so I didn't have to move the seat.

"You ready?" I asked.

"As long as we're not driving off a cliff," she said.

"Uh, no. No cliff driving."

"I mean, to be honest, I probably would drive off a cliff

with you, C." My heart fluttered in my chest. More than fluttered. It had wings that thrashed inside my ribcage.

I started up the van and then remembered that I had made a playlist for this. Since the van was so old, there were a bunch of cords that I had to plug my phone into to get it play through the speakers. There wasn't even a tape player. I was pretty sure the van was older than both of us.

Just as I was leaving the parking lot, the first song played and Cordelia smiled.

"Of course you made a playlist. You never do anything halfway."

"Never," I said.

Cordelia hummed along with the song. Making the playlist had been so easy, I had pretty much done it before we even had gotten together. I had a list of songs that made me think of Cordelia and I'd added them as I went. I didn't even know I'd been making it until after everything had happened. Since then, I'd added more and more songs until I had a list of over a hundred. It was probably excessive, but I didn't even care. Like Cordelia said, I didn't do anything halfway.

"There better be food on this date," Cordelia said, and I gave her a look.

"Do you really think I would neglect something as important as food, Carrots?"

"I'm sorry. I'm just really hungry," she said, whining a little.

"Well, you're in luck, because we're almost there."

"Where is that?" she asked, looking around. I hopped on the highway right off campus and listened as the GPS in my phone interrupted the song to tell me where to go.

"I would have thought you'd memorized the directions," Cordelia said.

"Nope. Not even I'm that good."

I looked over at her and smiled. Her hair was down and messy from sleeping on it. I'd told her to wear something casual, so she'd put on her favorite pair of jeans and a loose top with flowers on it, along with a leather jacket. I loved the mix of hard and soft. It was perfect for her.

What she didn't know was that I had a second outfit for both of us in the back of the van, hiding under a blanket.

I was going to make this a day she wouldn't forget.

OUR FIRST STOP was a diner that was made out of a converted railway car.

"Oh thank god," she said as I pulled into the parking lot and the GPS announced that we had arrived.

"So. This place is special because it's the oldest diner in Maine. It used to be open twenty-four hours a day to serve the railway workers." There were only two dozen seats in the entire place, and there was already a line out the door. We probably should have gotten here before they opened, but I knew that wasn't going to happen, so I'd had to compromise and we would probably have to wait. I had planned for that as well.

"Score. Let's get in line before someone else does." She jumped out of the van and ran to the door to get in line as I came behind her. There were a stack of menus on a bench outside, so she picked one up and we put our heads together to read it.

"Oh my god, I don't even know what to get. Everything looks incredible. Can I just order everything?"

"If you want to," I said.

"You're so good to me," she said, kissing me on the cheek.

"You deserve it." She snuggled into me and it was about twenty minutes until there were two seats next to each other at the one and only counter. The place was tiny and cramped, but everyone was in a good mood and the food smelled incredible.

Rosemary Clooney crooned from hidden speakers and one of the cooks whistled along.

"This is so cool," Cordelia said, looking around. "Thanks for bringing us here." I had the feeling she would love it here, which is why I'd picked it.

A waiter with more tattooed than non-tattooed skin came to take our order once we'd stared at the menu and made the difficult decision of what to get. I ordered the Silver Dollar Pancake Plate and she got The Deluxe Sandwich that had bacon, egg, cheese, and jalapeno on an English muffin.

She hummed along to the music as we waited for our food.

"Even if this is the only part of our date, it's already perfect. Just so you know," she said, grinning at me.

"Being with you is perfect." She leaned forward and kissed me. It was only the second time we'd been out together in public, but no one yelled or made any comments. I let out a breath.

"You're so sweet, I can't even deal sometimes," she said. I blushed and looked up as our waiter brought us both coffee and water.

Our food came a few minutes later on plates so hot, we didn't dare touch them for a few minutes.

"Cheers to our first date," I said, raising my coffee cup. She clinked it with hers and we dug in.

There wasn't much talking as we both stuffed our faces and switched plates so we could try everything. I finished her sandwich, which was probably a bad idea, but it was so good I didn't care.

When our plates had been cleared, they were whisked away and the slightly damp check deposited between us. I snatched it before she could even reach for it.

"I planned this, I pay," I said, waving it in front of her.

"Fine, fine. But on our next date, I'm paying."

"Deal," I said.

"Kiss on it?" We smooched and I put enough cash on the table for our meal plus a generous tip. We'd timed things right because the line was nearly thirty people deep when we walked out.

"Look," Cordelia said in my ear, nudging me. There were two girls in line holding hands. They were probably a few years older than us. I tried not to stare as we walked by them to the van.

"I hope you don't have anything that involves running in the near future planned," she said, rubbing her stomach.

"Nope," I said. I plugged the next location into the GPS, hiding my phone so she couldn't see it.

"What *is* planned next?" she said, trying to see. I pulled my phone away and started the music.

"That's for me to know and you to not know until we get there," I said, being careful to maneuver the van out of the parking lot without taking out any other cars. I was doing pretty well for someone who had literally never driven a car larger than a sedan before. I conveniently left that out when I asked Elise to borrow it.

She huffed in the passenger seat, but she was smiling.

CORDELIA

I knew she had planned this down to the minute. Probably to the second. There had also been spreadsheets involved that she wouldn't tell me about.

She was having so much fun with this all and it was so fucking cute, I could barely stand it. The diner was just the first part of the date and it had already exceeded my expectations. Not that I'd had any expectations. All kinds of potential scenarios had gone through my head while I was trying to get to sleep last night. Some of them were a little absurd. Like her taking us to the airport and getting on a plane to go to another country for lunch. After all, we were college students. Plane tickets weren't in the budget.

Part of me wanted to tell her to pull the van over in a secluded spot so we could make out in the back for a while. If we took the seats out, we could very easily put a blow-up mattress in the back and do all kinds of things.

The only thing stopping me was the fact that Chase would hate going off the schedule that she'd so carefully planned. Oh, and the fact that we'd borrowed the van from Elise and I wouldn't be able to look her in the face if we had sex in the back of the van.

It took us a while to get to our second stop. I hadn't been in this part of Maine before. I was from the coast, so I stuck mostly there. We were heading up north.

"We're not going to Canada, are we? I didn't bring my passport." I was only half-joking. I wouldn't put it past her to drive to another country. I'd never been to Canada and Quebec was supposed to be amazing.

"Uh, no. We'll be staying in the country for this one. Although, that would have been a good idea. Fuck, I should have done that." She slammed the steering wheel with her hand.

"C, calm down. Whatever you have planned is going to be incredible. I know it." I rubbed her shoulder. I needed to not say things like that.

"Are you sure?" she said. Oh, she was so cute.

"Pull over," I said. We were still on the highway, but we were getting into a more rural area.

"What?" she said, looking at me as if I had asked her to set the car on fire.

"Pull. Over." She did and put on her warning lights.

I leaned over and grabbed her face in both hands.

"This date is perfect. You are perfect. This day is perfect." I kissed her before she could protest. I kissed her until she melted in my arms and I crawled into her lap and nothing would have dislodged me.

"You're perfect," I said, rubbing my nose with hers.

"I'm not, but that's a really nice thing to say," she said. I tucked her hair behind her ears. The steering wheel was digging into my back and the shifter was digging into my leg and my head was hitting the roof, but I didn't really care that much.

"Every time you doubt yourself, I'll be here to remind you." She kissed me again and squeezed my ass. I squeaked and jumped a little, hitting my head on the roof.

"Ow," I said.

"Sorry!" I figured I couldn't stay in her lap for much longer without doing myself serious injury, so I reluctantly scrambled back to my seat.

"A concussion definitely isn't in the plan for today, I'm guessing," I said while rubbing my head.

"Definitely not. No injuries allowed," she said, looking over her shoulder to turn back onto the highway.

We had to stop for gas a little while later.

"I promised to fill up the tank for Elise," Chase said. It wasn't cheap and I winced at the price on the pump, but she paid it with her card. This date was getting expensive. I hoped she wasn't going to go into debt just to make this special for me. I didn't need a fancy dinner or fireworks. I just needed her.

"Where the hell are we going?" I asked a little while later.

"You'll see," she said.

I sat back in my seat and listened to the music.

"WE'RE HERE," she said as we pulled onto the campus of one of the sister schools to our college.

"Uhhhh, are we transferring?" I was completely at a loss. What could we possibly see here?

"Nope. Come on." She got out and ran around the side of the van to open my door for me. Chase held her hand out to me and I didn't hesitate to take it. If she was leading me into an open flame, I'd go with her. I'd go anywhere with her.

Chase tugged me toward one of the buildings.

"The Northern Maine Museum of Science," I read. I mean, neither of us was that wild about science, but I figured maybe they had something cool here that I just didn't know about. I'd grown up on the coast with a ton of lighthouses and colonial settlements and forts. This was completely new.

She pulled me through the door and down a hall, passing a ton of exhibits, but I didn't say anything. Chase was a woman on a mission.

"Here we are," she said, motioning to a giant yellow arch that went from the floor through to the ceiling.

"What is this?" I asked.

"The sun. You are looking at the start of the Maine Solar System Model. The sun is here, and the other planets are in other places. It spans 95 miles. We're going to see it all. Including Pluto, even though it's not a planet anymore. RIP, Pluto." Her face was completely lit up and I couldn't stop looking at her.

"I thought I could show you the universe, or at least a little part of it."

Fuck. I felt like I was going to cry.

"This is amazing, Chase. Holy shit." I hugged her.

"I hoped you were going to like it."

"I love it, seriously." I held her and I felt as if I was going to explode with happiness.

"Thank you," I said, pulling back to look at her face. She was brighter than the sun. There were other people coming into the building and looking at the arch, taking pictures, and chatting, but they might as well have been in another galaxy. Right now, there was just me and her. A girl who was my entire world.

I fucking loved her. I fucking loved her and I didn't know when it had happened, just like Stella had said. Maybe it had been on that first day. Maybe it had been when we first kissed. Maybe it was when I first showed myself to her. It didn't matter, really.

The revelation settled into my bones and I didn't know what to do with it. Did I tell her? I couldn't tell her. It was too soon. I was always the more impulsive of the two of us. Granted, I had kissed her first, but everything else had been all her. Kissing was one thing, saying those three words was something else entirely.

Plus, we hadn't even finished our first date, my dad knew nothing about what was going on with Chase, and I hadn't begun to untangle the mess that was my sexuality.

It wasn't the right time. Even though I knew it, now not the time to tell her. I held the words in my mouth, swallowed them down.

"Let's take a picture," she said, and we posed by the yellow arch, with me tucked under her arm. I made her take one where we made silly faces, as well as a serious one.

We walked slowly back to the car and I pushed her against the door and kissed her senseless for a little while.

"Does that mess up your schedule?" I asked.

"Yes, but I'll allow it."

"You didn't factor in any kissing breaks? Shame on you, Chase Hillier. I'm going to punish you for that."

Her eyes were bright.

"How are you going to do that?" she asked. In response, I stuck my tongue in her mouth. That seemed like the best way to answer.

We had a few minutes of breathless making out until

Chase's phone went off. She'd set alarms so we didn't stay too long at one place.

"Time to go see Mercury."

WE MADE it through Jupiter before we had to stop and have lunch. Chase had that planned out too. That one was massive, and had just been repainted. We were lucky they had put it back up or else we would have been missing a planet.

The restaurant was a nice bistro where we gorged ourselves on brie with mango chutney with crackers, and I had the best grilled cheese Panini in my entire life. She paid again and I let her without much of a fight.

Then it was on to the other planets, finishing in Houlton with Pluto, which was itty bitty. You could barely see it in the pictures we took, but it didn't matter.

Then it was on to an old-fashioned candy shop where we bought too many jelly beans and sour worms and gummy bears and tons of other things. We probably went a little over-board, but we had enough candy for the rest of the school year.

"This is study food," Chase said with a serious face. "We need the candy for studying." I decided to just go with it as I filled a bag with salt-water taffy.

We were driving back to campus, I figured based on the GPS directions, and I decided it was time for me to change things up.

"Pull over here," I said, pointing at an exit. "I have to pee." That seemed like a reasonable excuse.

Chase drove until we found a gas station and she pulled in.

"Okay, so I lied about needing to pee."

"Why?"

"Because I really want to make out with you in the back of this van?" She gaped at me for a second.

"You could have just said that." She nearly peeled out of the gas station, which was saying something since she was driving a van. Chase drove for a few more minutes until she found a more secluded place to pull the van over. She turned the key and faced me.

"Okay. Let's make out."

I laughed and dove into the backseat. She followed me more carefully.

"Get over here," I said, pulling at her. I was laying across the bench seats. It was fortuitous that she'd borrowed the van. My small car wouldn't be as good for this situation.

"Thank you for this day, Chase. It's been totally amazing. No one else would have done something like this for me." The words that I wanted to say, the words that I had swallowed earlier threatened to jump out of my mouth and make themselves sentient. I couldn't tell her.

"You deserve all of the best dates, Cordelia. You deserve everything. I know I'm not what you were expecting, but I'm so happy you picked me." I didn't feel like I had. I feel like some other force had picked us for each other.

"So do you. I know I'm a mess and I'm all over the place and I'm a lot to take, but I'm so happy you picked me back." I had to stop talking or else I was going to say them. Those words were desperate to get out. They didn't want to be silenced. So I kissed her. I pressed my mouth to hers and then bit her bottom lip. I knew that would distract both of us.

She moved her hands from my hair to my waist, and started rubbing the front of my jeans. I hadn't gotten her pants off yet in any of our encounters, but I figured now was as good a time as any to see what she might be comfortable with. I mirrored her movements, putting my hand against the front of her jeans, pressing just a little bit as she kissed me.

A little gasp escaped her mouth and I wondered if she was going to tell me to stop. But after a second, she moved her hips against my hand. Oh, fuck. If that wasn't the hottest thing ever.

I rubbed her harder, wishing there wasn't anything between us. I was adventurous, but I wasn't get-naked-in-our-friend's-van-on-the-side-of-the-road adventurous. Not yet, anyway.

Her hand kept up a steady rhythm that made my eyes roll back in my head. I was barely able to keep up with what I was doing with my hand. My wrist started to cramp from the angle I was at, so I moved my hand, but put it on her ass, urging her to move so that we were lined up together.

We both moaned as we pressed our hips together. In spite of the layers of material between us, having the most needy part of her grinding against the same parts of me was enough to make my head explode.

"More," I said and she arched into me harder. I rose up to meet her and we set a pace that was both hard and soft at the same time. I dug my hands into her ass and urged her on.

The friction was killing me and I could barely breathe and I couldn't stop.

"Fuck!" I said, and it wasn't because I was about to come. My calf had seized up. I nearly kicked her in the stomach with my effort to massage away the cramp.

"What?" she said, her eyes unfocused, her breathing frantic.

"Cramp in my leg, ow," I said. What a way to kill the mood. "I'm sorry."

"Where does it hurt?" Chase asked, ignoring my apology. I pointed and she started massaging the lump that my calf had become. After a little while, I felt the muscle loosen and go back to normal. I let out a sigh of relief.

"You okay now?" she asked, and I nodded.

She gazed down at me for a moment and I wondered what she saw when she looked at me.

"Thank you," I said. "Sorry I kinda killed the mood." I was still horny as fuck, but I didn't know if Chase wanted to put on the brakes before we got more carried away.

"You didn't. I was thinking that we should probably hit the pause button. At least for now." I raised my eyebrows.

"For now?" She grinned at me.

"Yes. For now." What did that mean? She gracefully extricated herself from me and got back in the driver's seat.

"You ready for dinner?" she asked. "We have a reservation."

It took me a second to move. My limbs weren't exactly obeying me. Somehow, I made it back to the passenger seat without any injuries. Well, except for the fact that I was still so turned on that my labia were literally aching with need. I squeezed my legs together and willed the feeling to pass. It was distracting.

Chase put the music on and we drove back toward campus. This had been a day, and I didn't want it to end. I had this fear that once this date was over, a spell was going to break. The clock would hit midnight and I'd go back to being a single pumpkin who didn't have a girlfriend.

"This day has been incredible," I said. "Honestly. Best date ever. And I'm not just saying that, because I have been on other dates. Have I told you about the one where the guy ate so much popcorn that he ended up having to go and throw up halfway through the movie? And then tried to kiss me after?" I shuddered at the memory. I'd had quite a few bad dates, but not any good ones. Until now.

"Yuck. That sounds disgusting. I never really did the one-on-one thing with a guy, but I can tell you about the first time I kissed a guy." I hadn't heard this story, and I weirdly wanted to know. I guess I was a little smug over the fact that the guy she had first kissed wasn't the one who got to kiss her now. That was me.

"It was this party my parents had made me go to because everyone in my grade had been invited. The only problem was that my best friend from school was at her grandfather's funeral, so she couldn't go. I was basically on my own, and it was a nightmare. We were in this girl's basement and her parents were pretending to supervise, but not actually doing it?" I laughed because I remembered going to those kinds of parties. I'd always had to lie and tell my dad that we were being VERY VERY supervised. Sometimes I got away with it, sometimes I didn't.

"So anyway, everyone was sort of hanging out and there was this one kid, Griffin, and I guess he'd been flirting with me, but I was too oblivious to know that was what was happening. We got talking about movies and that was fine. It was nice because most of the people there ignored me. I think some of the girls were trying to see if they could sneak upstairs and maybe get a hold of some alcohol. I hadn't been in on that, and I hadn't wanted to be. So I was talking with Griffin instead." That sounded about right. I had never really been part of those kinds of shenanigans at parties. I'd been the one to suggest a few adventures, but I'd never participated. My dad would have murdered me.

"And we were sitting on one of the couches and he just sort of ... went for it? He dove at me lips-first. He smashed his mouth onto my mouth and I was so shocked that I didn't even know what to do. And then his tongue was doing something and I finally was able to push away. He got all red and embarrassed and basically ran away. I called my mom and begged her to let me go home. I didn't tell her about the kiss, but she found out about it because everyone at school talked. For a hot second, a few of the other girls thought I was cool, but then they moved on to something else. It was kind of a disaster.

Griffin moved away later in the year. I have no idea what happened to him. Might be interesting to look him up online." I officially wanted to punch this guy. Yes, he was young, but no, that was not a thing that was okay to do.

"He'd better not ever see me, because I would give him a piece of my mind. That's awful, Chase." She shrugged one shoulder.

"I mean, I think it sounds worse than it really was? Honestly, it wasn't super traumatic in the moment. It was only later when the complete and utter embarrassment set in." I shuddered.

We talked more about our past dating experience. I glossed over the times when I'd had sex, but she wanted to know. I still didn't give her everything because it didn't feel right, and I didn't think she needed to know absolutely everything. Those times hadn't mattered. My time with her was the important thing. If I could, I would wipe out all those times and fill them with her.

At one point, I reached over and took her hand. She squeezed me back and the radio played the next song. It was one I hadn't heard before and as I listened to the lyrics, I knew it was a love song. I smiled as the song played and felt my heart squeeze a little.

This was honestly one of the best days I'd had in my entire life and it was ending soon.

"I don't want this date to end," I said.

"I know," she murmured and brought my hand to her lips.

Chapter Thirteen

CHASE

The day had gone exactly to plan. Except for the part when we made out and got busy in the backseat, but that had been completely and totally worth it. I stopped at a gas station near the restaurant and brought out the fancy clothes I'd packed.

"You are such a sneak," Cordelia said when I handed her a bag with her outfit (including shoes) in it.

"I try," I said, and she scampered off to the grungy bathroom to change. When she came out, I almost fainted. I'd gone through her closet when she was at class and had picked a sparkly black dress I'd found in the back. I wanted to make sure that she didn't notice that it was missing.

The dress was form-fitting and clung to every single curve of her figure.

"Holy shit," I breathed. Her legs were on display and her breasts were pushed up and on display. "I almost don't want to take you anywhere so no one else can see you because holy shit, Cordelia." She did a slow spin for me, the glitter in the dress catching the sad lights above the gas pumps.

"You picked my sexy dress," she said when she got back around. She'd done something with her curls and they were a little more defined.

"Did I? Oh, no, I didn't mean to do that," I said, pretending I was upset.

"Do you have a sexy outfit too?" she asked. I pulled out another bag and she squealed.

"Hurry up, I want to see," she said, smacking my butt as I hurried to change.

I didn't have a lot of fancy clothes and I wasn't much of a dress person, so I'd found my favorite nice pair of black pants and paired them with a button-up shirt and a blazer. I felt more at home wearing that than I would if I'd put on a dress. I'd also brought a small silver bow tie that I'd bought on a whim, but had never worn because I didn't really know how to wear it. I had learned how to tie one online and had practiced, but had never had the courage to wear this ensemble. Once I had the outfit on and the bowtie all set, I added some silver dangly earrings and a pair of black boots. I hardly ever wore makeup, but tonight I made an exception and put on some silver eyeliner and mascara.

I wasn't sure what Cordelia's reaction would be, so I hesitated before leaving the bathroom.

"Holy fucking shit fuck," she said. She shook her head slowly. I hoped that was good.

"Is this okay?" I asked when she didn't say anything for a while.

"I honestly don't even know what I've done to deserve this moment, but I must have done something good because fuck, Chase. You look fucking incredible." Okay, that had to be good.

"I didn't have a dress," I said, looking down at my pants and fiddling with the sleeves of my jacket.

"You look ... I just don't even have words. And like,

words are my thing. I usually talk enough for two people, but I have no words." She puckered her lips and I gave her a kiss.

"You look hot as fuck. There. How's that?"

"You look hot enough to fuck," I said. I was still fired up from earlier in the backseat. Honestly, it had been hard to drive after that.

"Mmmm, maybe we can skip dinner and you can just eat me," she said.

"Fuck, Cordelia, you can't say things like that," I said in her ear and then softly bit down on her earlobe. She whimpered and I pushed her up against the van.

"You can't say things and then not expect me to do them. It's like a dare." I licked the side of her neck and moved her hair out of the way. She arched into me.

"I'm hungry and horny and I don't know which one is stronger right now," she said in a strangled voice. As if to make her point, her stomach growled.

I made a sound of frustration and pushed away from her a little, but not before I put a little kiss on her neck.

"Let's feed you first. Food before fucking." I normally wasn't so free with my language, but it happened around her. And especially when I was turned on.

"Food before fucking. We should get that painted on a distressed wooden sign and put it above our doorway." I spanked her ass and handed her into the van.

THE RESTAURANT WAS upscale and I'd been a little apprehensive about it, but I wanted her to have the best and this was the nicest place that I could afford close to school. The lights were low, there were candles and fine china, and a huge wine list.

I knew neither of us was going to get away with ordering wine without getting carded, so I didn't even bother to try.

I ordered a Coke and she got a large Shirley Temple with extra cherries.

"You look so good, Chase," she said. "I can't stop saying it. You just do. You should dress like this more often." I fiddled with my bowtie, hoping it was straight.

"I really wasn't sure. I've never worn this before. I bought it when my mom took me clothes shopping and I told her it would be good for job interviews." That had been a total lie. I'd been wanting a suit or something like it for a long time, but was too scared to ask. Funny thing was, my mom bought it for me without even batting an eyelash or making any comments. She told me constantly that she wanted me to be happy, no matter what that looked like. Still, I didn't want to disappoint her. Not even a little bit.

"Are you worried about your parents?" she asked after our drinks arrived.

"I mean, no, but how will I know until I tell them? There's no litmus test for this." She sighed and reached for my hand across the table.

"I know."

Soft music played in the background and she glowed in the light of the candles. I had an idea and I wasn't going to second-guess it.

"Will you dance with me?" I asked. I stood up and held out my hand. A few people around us glanced over, but quickly went back to their own dinners and conversation.

"Yeah," she said, taking my hand and standing up. The piano music wasn't really appropriate, but it didn't matter. She put her hand on my shoulder and I put my hand on her waist and our other hands clasped together.

I started to sway and she matched me.

"I've never danced like this with a girl before," she said, laughing softly.

"Me, neither. But we'll figure it out." We had so far. We hadn't figured everything out, but that would come with time, I hoped. Right now was all that mattered. The most beautiful girl in the world was in my arms and she was looking at me as if I was everything.

We danced for a while, and then we had to stop when our food came. The waitress didn't comment at all on us dancing, and no one else seemed to have noticed. I still had the fear that a homophobe was going to pop out of nowhere and throw tomatoes or scream bible verses at us. I didn't know if that fear would ever go away.

Cordelia got a burger that had fiddleheads on it with a pear and spinach salad. I'd gotten the house salad and the duck. I had never had duck, so I figured now was the time to try it.

"I feel like I'm not fancy enough for this food," Cordelia whispered.

"I know what you mean," I whispered back. We both put our napkins on our laps and Cordelia tried to decide if she wanted to eat her burger with her hands or a knife and fork. She tried the latter, but then gave up.

"Screw it," she said, picking the burger up with both hands and biting into it. Her eyes rolled back in her head and she moaned.

"This is so fucking good," she said, and an older woman at a table near us threw her a dirty look. I stifled a laugh as I tried to eat my salad as carefully as possible. I didn't want to get anything on my clothes, especially my white shirt.

My duck was unbelievable. I wasn't sure what to expect and I was totally surprised. The reputation of this place was well deserved. We finished our food and then split the chocolate torte.

I paid the check and then we went back out to the van.

"I have had some of the best food in my life today. You went above and beyond, Chase. This date has ruined me for all other dates."

"Good," I said, and she laughed.

BY THE TIME we got back to our room, we were both exhausted.

"Wait," I said, blocking the door from her. "I have to give Elise back her keys and do something. Can you maybe chill with Stella for a few minutes?" This was the only thing I hadn't really been able to do ahead of time. I'd thought about giving my keys to Stella or Elise to have them set up before we got back, but I didn't trust anyone else to make it the way I wanted. I had a hard time delegating.

"Yeah, sure," she said, hiding a yawn behind one of her hands. She still had the sparkly black dress on and I could barely keep my hands off her. She took the keys and walked down the hall. I watched her move and nearly fell over. She looked almost as good as she did when she had nothing on.

She gave me a little wave as she knocked on Stella and Elise's door and was admitted. I heard their exclamations about how good she looked and then the door shut.

I hurried to unlock the door and get everything done. I picked up the room that we'd sort of left as is this morning. Next was making the bed up, and then I pulled the battery-powered candles out and placed them around the room. I didn't want to take a risk and set off the smoke alarms. That would definitely be a mood killer.

I had thought about putting on a sexy outfit, but honestly, I didn't feel very sexy in the kinds of clothes that were supposed to be sexy. I liked what I had on, and I thought Cordelia liked it too. Letting her undress me was part of the fun. At least I hoped it would be.

When I was finally satisfied and had stopped fiddling with the locations of the candles, I texted Cordelia to come back. Just before she knocked on the door, I realized I'd forgotten the music and plugged my phone into my speakers. I'd made a playlist for tonight, too.

"Come in," I said, hoping I sounded more confident than I felt. My voice trembled, but I took a breath to steady myself.

Cordelia peaked into the room.

"Oh, wow," she said, closing the door and leaning on it.

"Do you like it?" I asked. It wasn't as if I'd done anything major, but I hoped this was still good.

"You're the most romantic person I've ever met and I cannot believe I get to be with you." She crossed the distance between us and grabbed my face to kiss me. I kissed her back, but pulled away because there were things I needed to say.

"I'm ready. Tonight. I think. I want to try." I had been thinking about it for days and going over and over it. I wanted to be with her.

"Are you sure?" she asked. I was tired of overthinking everything. I was tired of planning. Tired of stressing out. Tired of everything going on in my head. I just wanted all my anxiety to shut the fuck up for a little while.

"Yeah," I said, and then pulled my jacket off and tossed it to the floor. I hoped that made a statement.

"Then how about you help me get this dress off?" She turned around and I started unzipping the top of the dress, my fingers trembling a little. I'd seen her naked before, but tonight was different. I exposed her shoulders and her black lace bra that was my favorite.

She helped me by taking her arms out of the sleeves, and then I pushed the dress over her hips and stomach and to the floor. Her panties were also black lace and matched the bra. I stroked her spine and she shivered. I pushed her hair over her shoulder and kissed her shoulder. She arched back into me, pushing her ass into the front of my pants. I groaned and grabbed her hips, pushing back.

Cordelia made a little moaning sound and I did it again.

"I just want you so much all the time and sometimes it's so much I can't even breathe," she said. I knew what she meant.

I bit her shoulder lightly, and then followed it with a kiss. Was it bad that I liked leaving marks on her pretty skin? I hoped not. My hands caressed her hips and her ass, and she continued to rub against me. I continued my path across her shoulders and then turned her around.

"Do you want to see how much I want you?" I asked. Her eyes got wide, but she nodded.

"Yes." Good.

I reached for her mouth and kissed her so hard that our teeth clicked together. I dove in with my tongue and she kissed me back with as much force. I backed her up until her legs hit the bed and then pressed her down until she was on her back.

"It's not fair," she whined. "I want to see you." I took her hands and put them over her head.

"Later. Right now it's my turn." I squeezed her wrists. "Okay?" She nodded and I pressed her wrists into the bed.

"Leave them there." My voice was commanding and I knew that she would do what I asked her. My blood sparked and fizzled in my veins.

I took my time, tasting every bit of her. Touching every inch of skin, pushing her bra straps aside and then helping her remove it altogether. Her panties followed, and she kept her hands above her head.

"Good girl," I whispered, just before I settled myself between her thighs. I was still learning what she liked, but I had a pretty good idea of what could send her through the roof. This time, though, I was going to make her work for it. I wanted to tease her. To torment her. To hear her beg.

I licked her slowly and fluttered my fingers at her entrance. She bucked her hips up to bring my mouth closer, but I put my hand on her belly.

"Stay still," I said. She made a sound of frustration. "Impatient girl." My tongue went back to work, and I brought her to the brink, only to back off. She practically screamed in frustration, but didn't move her hands. I was impressed.

"Chase, *please*," she whimpered after I brought her just close enough again.

"What do you want, baby?" I said, leaning my cheek on the inside of her thigh. Her legs were shaking so badly that she couldn't stay still anymore.

"I want you to make me come," she said, not even messing around.

"You want me to make you come?" I curled my finger inside her, hitting the exact right spot. She jacked her hips up and nearly took my teeth out.

"Please." The word was a mere gasp.

"If that's what you want." She made a garbled sound and I laughed a little as I finally put her all the way over the edge. Cordelia came like she did everything else, hard and soft at the same time. I brought her through it and rested my head on her stomach as the last shudders ripped through her.

"Fucking fuck," she said, and looked down at me.

"You can put your arms down now," I said, and she grunted as she brought her arms down from above her head.

"That was hot, Chase," she said, running her fingers through my hair. "We can do that again."

"You like it when I take charge?" I asked. I knew she did, but I wanted her to do it because she liked it, and not just to make me happy.

"Yeah, it's fucking hot. I liked it. I like everything you do.

It's like you know what turns me on without me even having to say it. Kind of freaks me out sometimes."

"If there's anything I do that you don't like, you can tell me. It's not going to hurt my feelings. I just want to get you off in the best way possible. That's my main goal in life." She laughed and put a finger under my chin.

"Now get up here so I can get you off." Mmmm, I liked that. When she got a little bossy. I crawled up the length of her body and kissed her. She inhaled me and now it was her turn to undress me. We had a few mishaps when she tried to get everything off at once, so I had to help her a little to make sure I didn't get strangled with my bowtie.

Cordelia got my pants off and lay me down on my back. I had been this naked with her before, but we'd never gotten my panties off. I always sort of froze up and backed out. No more.

She kissed her way down my body, paying special attention to my nipples as she kissed and licked them into stiff peaks that ached and throbbed. I let myself go as she made her way down to the edge of my panties.

"Can I take these off?" she asked, looking up at me. Her ass was up in the air and her hair was all over my thighs. I raked it back from her face and held it with my hands.

"Yes," I said, and she hooked her fingers in them and I lifted my hips so she could get them off.

"You're so fucking beautiful," she said, and I knew she meant it. I still had to hit pause on the urge to cover my chest or my lower half. I didn't hate my body, but being naked with someone else was new and scary for me.

"Can I kiss you, here?" she asked, pointing. Instead of answering her, I widened my legs and nudged her head down with my hands. She gave me one last look before she gave me a sweet little kiss. Even that was a shock to my system.

"Now who won't stay still?" she said and kissed me again. I tried to keep my hips from moving, but it was difficult. And then she stuck that tricky little tongue out and licked my clit and I was sure she was going to be the death of me. Was that what I had been missing?

Instead of going back to my clit, she kissed up the insides of my thighs, getting just close enough, but not touching it again. I knew exactly what she was doing because I had been doing it not that long before. The ends of her hair added to the sensations and my brain was on sensory overload.

Cordelia took her time. She tormented me until I was actually pissed.

"I swear, Cordelia if you don't—" and that was when she flicked my clit with her tongue and I lost the ability to make words. I lost the ability to do anything but feel and exist in a body that was made solely of nerve endings. With only her tongue, she fucked me. She circled my clit and pressed at my entrance and then used it to plunge inside me.

I was completely lost, and she hadn't even used her hands.

～

CORDELIA

Okay, so I didn't exactly know what I was doing. I'd only ever given blowjobs before. But I'd had her go down on me so I knew the basics. Probably more so than someone who wasn't working with the same equipment, so at least I had that.

I was nervous, but I didn't want her to know, since this was the first time she was trusting me like this. I could not fuck this up. I wouldn't let that happen.

I decided to take my time, to give her space to back out if she decided it was too much. I'd wanted to taste her for ages, so I started with my tongue and that drove her so wild that I wasn't even sure if I needed to do anything else. Besides, I was having a great time. She tasted amazing and I loved the feel of her against my tongue. She was so soft here, and I was getting off on the sounds she was making. This was one of the best moments of my entire life.

She trembled and quaked around me and gasped out "I'm close." I wanted to pump my fists in victory. Hell yeah. I sucked harder and licked faster and fucked her deeper with my tongue and then her fingers dug into my scalp and her legs bucked and she was making a lot of noise. It seemed to go on forever and I could barely breathe, but what did that matter? I was getting my girl off.

When her body stilled at last, I risked a look up at her. My hair was all over my face, my mouth was full of the taste of her, and my tongue had had a good workout.

"Well, fuck," she said, and then started laughing a little. "You are very good with your mouth." I snorted and grinned up at her.

"I'm glad my efforts met with your satisfaction." I needed to wipe my face and wash my hair, but that didn't matter right now. I slid upward so I was tucked into her chest.

"Thank you for being so patient with me," she said, kissing my forehead.

"Of course. You were worth the wait." We lay together in silence for a while, the candles flickering artificially.

"This really has been the best day ever. I don't know how I'm going to go back to class and regular life on Monday," I said.

"We don't have to go back to completely regular life. We can go on more dates. Maybe not all-day ones, especially not around finals time, but we can still do dates. And I'll plan them, if you want."

I looked up at her.

"You would really love that, wouldn't you? Planning all our dates?"

"I mean, do you want me to lie and say no?" I burst out laughing. Fuck, I loved her so much. Today had just cemented it. She stared down at me and the words were dancing around on the back of my tongue, begging to come out.

"No, you can plan most of our dates. I want to plan *some* things."

She sighed as if it was a huge imposition.

"I guess." I poked her in the stomach in her ticklish spot.

"No fair, no fair!" She wiggled and tried to get away, but I wouldn't let her.

"Hey," I said after she calmed down.

"What?"

"Hey, this has been the best date ever, do you want to take a shower with me?" I figured post-coital showering would be a cute and sexy end of the night. Then we could cuddle up together and fall asleep. Perfection.

"Only if we can come back and have tea in our towels while I brush your hair." Oh, yeah. Perfect.

I SOMEHOW WAS able to keep the biggest secret of my life, that I was in love with my roommate, from said roommate. But somehow, I did. I kept the secret when we cuddled and watched *Steven Universe*. I kept it when we woke up in the morning on top of each other. I kept it when she made me come harder than I knew was possible. I kept it when we held hands as we walked to dinner. I kept inside even as it beat with my heart. I didn't know what to do. I wanted to talk to someone, but I didn't know who. Everyone at school was out because I didn't think they'd be able to keep that secret from Chase. I really wanted to talk to my dad, but that would mean explaining about Chase. And I couldn't do that yet.

Almost an entire week went by and October break was coming up. Both of us were going home and I knew that if I was going to tell my dad anything, I was going to do it in person, and that seemed as good a time as any. So I just had to hold out until then and after I'd talk to Chase. Simple enough.

Except for the fact that I was horrible at keeping secrets and it was damn hard to lie to someone when you lived with them. Sometimes I would just hum with the need to tell her and sometimes I would almost say it without even thinking and then I had to stumble and reel the words back in, like a thrashing fish on the end of a line.

Chase asked me multiple times if I was okay, if there was something that was bothering me, but I just told her it was nothing and I was just thinking about going home and talking to my dad about everything.

"I don't know if I'm going to tell my parents yet. I can't decide. I feel completely out of my depth for this." We both did, so at last we decided to attend a meeting of the group that Stella, Kyle, Elise, and Eli belonged to. They were having a pizza party in their office at the Student Union, so it seemed like a less-intense environment.

"You'll be fine," Stella and the rest assured us. "If anyone says anything, just grab us and we'll handle it." I had a death-grip on Chase's hand and her skin was pale and white. I was just hoping I could get through this without a panic attack.

Chase and I had also made an exit strategy, just in case we needed to bail and not tell anyone we were bailing if it turned out to be not for us.

I stopped Chase just outside the door. The temperature had dropped, and our breath looked like smoke in the air.

"We've got this," I said, kissing her briefly.

"We've got this," she repeated, pressing her forehead briefly against mine.

I took a shaky breath and we walked into the lobby area where everyone else was waiting for us.

"They won't bite, I promise," Stella said.

"I mean, unless you want anyone to," Kyle added and that broke the ice a little.

The room was in a row of offices in the basement of the Union, and all of them were dark and quiet, except for a room at the end of the hall, where music was blaring. I resisted the urge to turn and run in the opposite direction. Instead, I squeezed Chase's hand harder and we approached the door.

Everyone else went in first and then we came behind them.

"Hi everyone, I just wanted to introduce Chase and Cordelia. They're new and if anyone is mean to them, you'll have me to deal with, okay? Okay," Stella said, giving a death glare to everyone.

Kyle let out a dreamy sigh.

"She's so hot when she's protective," she said, smiling at Stella. "Did you know that she was called the Ice Queen in high school?" I shook my head. I hadn't known anything about that.

"Yeah, it was hard to break through that to really get to know her, but she thawed. Every now and then she puts on that armor again and I remember what I used to think about her before I really knew her."

I looked up at Chase. I knew exactly what I thought when I first met her. That she was cute as hell and painfully shy and I was afraid to scare her.

"You okay?" I asked her. She was busy looking around the room. There were probably about twenty-five people total, and a few tables set up with boxes of pizza, sodas, some veggie trays, and a few containers of cookies. There was also a stack of blank nametags and pens and pronoun pins.

"Yeah," she said in a low voice. I was about to tell her that we could leave when she smiled down at me.

"I'm okay. Promise."

At first, no one really approached us, so we inched closer to the pizza and each got a slice. There was a small area set aside where a few mismatched couches and tables and chairs were set up, so we sat down with Elise, Eli, and Kyle. Stella was flitting around the room, saying hello and talking with everyone.

"She's like the cruise director. Or the dictator. It varies," Kyle said, grinning at Stella.

"I heard that," Stella said, walking by, with a few people trailing behind her.

"Hey, Chase, Cordelia, this is Andrea, Noah, and Alyx." The three people waved in turn. They already had their nametags with their pronouns under them.

"Hi," I said. Chase just nodded. I figured I was going to have to carry all the conversational weight. Chase shoved her piece of pizza in her mouth.

"Nice to meet you," I said, and then there was a brief but painfully awkward pause.

Andrea sat down next to me on the couch with a plate full of veggies. She had gorgeous dark skin and long dreads pulled into a bun, and gave me a warm smile. Her nametag said her pronouns were she/her.

"Stella is always bringing in new people, she's a great recruiter," she said, and snapped a carrot in half with her teeth.

"Yeah, we're not really sure what we're doing yet. Um, we're together, but we both thought we were completely heterosexual up until now. So I guess we're ..." I trailed off and shrugged.

"Questioning. Totally valid! I was there last year, believe me. I'm still working on my labels, but lesbian feels good for me right now. You don't even need to figure out a label ever." I started to relax and talk to her. Noah came down and sat next to Chase and Alyx sat next to Noah. Alyx's pronouns were xie/xer, which I had never seen before. There was a whole lot more to this than I guess I ever thought. It was a lot of information to take in at once.

Chase started talking quietly with Noah and I was relieved she was talking with someone. I finished my pizza and told Andrea the story of how Chase and I had gotten together. She declared it painfully romantic.

"I'm going to tell my dad when I get home, but I really don't know how he's going to take it," I said. "I know he loves me, but he keeps asking me about a potential boyfriend and I can't get the words out." Andrea nodded.

"Yeah, I know how you feel. I thought my parents were going to lose their shit when I told them I thought I liked girls, but they were completely supportive. My sister has been on a crusade to find me 'a nice girl.'" She put air quotes around "a nice girl" and rolled her eyes.

"Wow, I hope my dad doesn't do that, especially since I already found a nice girl." The best girl.

"Yeah, you did." I finally felt comfortable enough to leave Chase on her own and did a circuit around the room. I met a trans woman with pink hair named Jac, a few other couples of various genders, and the president of the group, who was a senior named Chris who had two boyfriends. Everyone was incredibly warm and welcoming and didn't pester me to know what my deal was. I got another slice of pizza and went back to Chase.

"Hey," I said, bumping her shoulder.

"Hey, Carrots," she said with a grin that lit up her whole face. I almost tripped over the couch. Her smile destroyed me.

"Carrots?" Noah said, lifting an eyebrow.

"Nickname," Chase said before turning back to me. "You doing okay?" I was going to ask her the same thing.

"Yeah, I met a lot of great people. Everyone here is so nice."

"This the place that I feel the safest," Noah said. "I know I pass pretty well, but you still never know." I didn't know what he meant about passing. I didn't know if it would be rude to ask. He must have seen my confused look.

"I'm trans. I've been on T for a year and a half, but I haven't had top surgery yet." That was a lot of words that I didn't know. I was going to have to do some research before I came here again, if Chase and I decided. I think even if she didn't want to, I would. I liked it here. I felt like I could breathe. And it was easy to talk to everyone. Like we had met before, or known each other for years. I'd only really felt that way with a few people, including Chase.

"Uh, yeah, if you want to know anything about it, I'm fine with questions. I know some people aren't, but it doesn't bother me," Noah said. I had questions, but I wasn't comfortable asking him. I figured I should probably do the basics on my own and then maybe ask him after.

"I'm not really sure what letter I am," I said, looking up at a huge rainbow poster with all the letters of the queer acronym. There were more than I knew about. Not just L, G, B, and T.

"That's fine. You can just hop under the Questioning Umbrella and live there forever." That was what everyone had said, but I still didn't really believe it.

"I want to find my label," Chase said. "I don't like it when things don't fit into lists and boxes and definitions." Typical Chase.

"We have some books, if you'd like to borrow them. Or there's a few pamphlets and lists of web sites. The information is there, if you want it." Noah was being super helpful too. I didn't know why everyone was being so kind to us, but it was unexpected and almost embarrassing.

"Thanks, I might look some stuff up," Chase said.

"Get the books. You know you want the books," I said, nudging her shoulder. She blushed a little.

"Chase is going work in publishing," I said to Noah. I knew I was bragging, but I didn't even care.

"Cool. Maybe you can help some queer authors get their work out there. Or you can write your own. We need more of it in the world. And not just the stories where we all die."

"Who's dying?" Stella said, coming over. Kyle had been chatting with Andrea and a few other people about a new movie they were really excited about.

"No one," Noah said, grinning. "Chase is going into publishing and I was saying that she can help get good queer stories out in the world. No more of this Bury Your Gays bullshit."

"Hell yeah," Stella said.

I added "Bury Your Gays" to the list of things I needed to look up. I should have written all of this down. Maybe Chase would help me remember later.

My brain was starting to fire in too many different directions and I was getting overwhelmed with too many new people and too much new information. I nudged Chase and tried to convey to her that I wanted to leave soon.

She gave me a soft smile.

"We should get going. I have an early class tomorrow and I still have a paper to work on." I knew she didn't have a paper and it made me feel warm and sloshy inside that she lied for me.

"Seriously, it was so nice to meet you," I said to Noah.

"Sure, and if you see me around campus, say hello. I also work in the library if you need anything there. Take a look at the books here before you go." I said that I would, and we said goodbye to everyone else. We were leaving early, but it was okay. I had reached my limit.

Just before heading out, we checked out the bookshelf. Chase pulled a few titles off the shelves and signed them out. I wanted to look online first.

We slipped out as Chris was telling a story about being at Pride with his two boyfriends that had everyone roaring with laughter.

"Wow," Chase said, taking my hand. I let go of it and instead tucked myself under her arm. I needed some support. "That was way different than I thought it would be."

"How so?" I asked as she pushed the door of the Union open.

"I don't know. I didn't really know what to expect, but that was so nice. Welcoming. I didn't feel like we were outsiders, or that they didn't know why we were there. I didn't have to make excuses, or feel like anyone was judging me. I guess I just never thought it would be like that." She kissed the side of my head.

"I'm glad you got some books." She had them under her other arm.

"Yeah, I think starting is the biggest part. Just starting to think about what I want my life to look like. It seems so easy, but it's not. I had this path all set out in my mind. I have one year plans and five year plans and ten year plans. All of those plans included finding a boyfriend. I'd never even considered any other possibility." She stopped walking and pulled me into an alcove between two buildings.

"And then there was you. You, Cordelia Scott, who burst into my life like a fireball and turned all those plans to smoke." I was freezing, but it didn't matter. The girl I loved was saying amazing things about me and if I turned into a human popsicle, I was going to stand here and listen to her talk.

"And do you have new plans?" I asked. She smiled slowly.

"The thing is, when I'm with you, the plans don't matter so much." Well, if that wasn't the nicest fucking thing anyone had ever said to me.

"I didn't mean to fuck up your plans, Chase. You fucked up mine, too, such as they were. I guess we're not competing to find boyfriends now." She laughed and pressed a warm kiss to my mouth.

"No boyfriends for me. Just you. Only you. Always you." Holy shit, was she ...

I pulled back from the kiss and gave her a look.

"What is it?" she said.

Fuck. I must have misread the situation.

"Nothing, I just ... nothing." I shook my head.

"No, what is it?" How the fuck was I going to get myself out of this situation?

"I guess I just thought ... I thought you were going to say that you loved me. But I was wrong. So, um, yeah." I finished and clamped my mouth shut so I didn't ramble on. Chase didn't need to know that I loved her yet. It was still too much too soon.

"Oh," she said, and then she inhaled deeply. "You weren't wrong."

"What?" I blinked at her.

"You weren't wrong. I do. Love you, I mean. I just ... I thought it was too early to tell you. I thought it was too early to feel this way." I would have laughed if I wasn't so knocked off my feet by what she was saying.

"You love me?" My voice squeaked and she beamed at me.

"I do. I love you, Carrots. Even if I don't know why or how it happened. I'm going with it." I was going to die. Like, actual death was happening to me.

"I love you, Chase. I was waiting to tell you until I had gone home and talked to my dad, but it's been killing me this week. That's why I was being so weird. Oh my god, I can't believe this is happening." She pulled me closer. My entire body was shaking and I couldn't seem to stop it. And it wasn't just because I was cold as fuck.

"I guess I have to tell my parents now. Tell them I'm in love with the most beautiful, funniest, wildest girl in the entire world. And that she loves me too."

"I do. I do love you. So much that it hurts." I kissed her desperately, as if I was afraid to lose her. In a way, I was, but in this moment, I had her. I had her right here.

"This is absurd," I said. "How the hell did this happen?"

Chase shrugged.

"Does it matter?"

No. It didn't.

Chapter Fourteen

CHASE

It had been a big night for both of us. I realized Cordelia was freezing her ass off when her chin started trembling as we kissed, so I hustled her back to our room, shoved her in front of the heater, and put a fuzzy blanket on her shoulders.

"You love me," she said through chattering teeth.

"Yeah, I do." I had been feeling inklings of it for a while, but it was the date that really sealed it. When I let down all of my walls with her and was completely naked, physically and mentally, I knew. I didn't plan on when I would tell her, I decided when the time felt right. Tonight was right. I honestly didn't expect anything back from her, so hearing her say it back was a complete shock that I was still recovering from.

I stood with her by the heater and rubbed her shoulders, trying to get her warm again.

"Do you want to take a shower?" She nodded and I pushed her in the direction of the bathroom, grabbing our shower stuff and towels. The stalls weren't exactly big enough for two people, but we made it work. I wasn't going to complain about being pressed up against her warm, wet skin. There were worse things in the world, by far.

The water was on when I smushed myself into the shower stall. Cordelia was still trembling, but I hoped she would warm up soon.

"Why didn't you tell me you were cold?" I asked.

"Because you were declaring your love to me. I didn't care if I was cold. I could have been on fire and I would have stood there." She reached and turned up the water, sighing as it pounded down on her head, making her hair a dark brownish color.

"Okay, that's fair," I said, and she laughed.

It took a while before she let me under the stream of water, and by that time, I was the cold one.

"Come here," she said, opening up her arms. Showering with each other was probably supposed to be sexy, but there really wasn't room for a whole lot of movement. Someone would get a full spray of water in the face, or smash their arm on the tile, or slip and slide into the wall. It was a futile activity. And we had tried.

"I love you," she whispered in my ear.

"I love you," I said, nuzzling into her hair. Being with her was still so easy. I kept waiting for the other shoe to drop. I was betting it was going to happen when we told our parents, and when everyone else found out. Things between us had been basically smooth so far. There were bound to be bumps in the road ahead.

But I wasn't as scared as I had been when this first started. Maybe it was knowing that she was completely, totally in this with me. And meeting everyone at the group tonight. That had also helped. There were people out there like us, people who didn't know they were gay or trans or ace or whatever when they were five and grew up with that knowledge. There were people who spent their entire lives not knowing, shoving that part of themselves so deep down, that it took an entire lifetime to unearth. We were lucky, in a way. That we had found each other. Because who knows how long I would have tried to find a boyfriend and maybe found one and gotten into a relationship.

The thought of a relationship like that with a guy now made me shudder. I had been so lucky to find Cordelia.

We stood under the hot water for longer than we needed to. She let me wash her hair, and she reached up to wash mine as I ducked so she could scrub my head with her fingers and then turn my shampoo-soaked hair into a mohawk.

"You'd look good like this," she said, tilting her head to the side.

"You think?" I had never thought about it.

"You'd look good with your hair any way. Or bald. You just look good always," she said with a sigh. "It's so unfair."

"What are you talking about?" She was literally the most gorgeous creature on this planet.

She rolled her eyes.

"Come on, Chase." Oh, this was not going to fly.

I held her face in my hands.

"Every time I look at you, I can barely believe that you're real. You're the most incredible human and I would not change a single freckle. You are made of stardust and magic, Cordelia." She opened her mouth and then shut it.

"And that's all there is to it," I said, and that settled it.

"You sure know how to say things that make me speechless," she finally said as I rinsed my hair out.

"I don't mean to. I only speak the truth."

THE NEXT WEEK was the best week I'd had since I started college. I woke up to a (sometimes naked) Cordelia and I went back to her every evening. We barely left each other's side and I thought that we should maybe get out of our room more often, but snuggling with her always seemed like the best option on the table. Plus, we were going to be apart for a week, and I didn't know what I was going to do without her. That sounded dramatic, but it was true. She was an integral part of my life now. She was part of my new family. As were Stella, Kyle, Elise, and Eli. And maybe some of the people from the group, especially Noah. He and I had clicked and there was something about him that I really liked. He was so open and so willing to share himself with others. I didn't know how to be like that, but I wanted to learn.

Stella and I talked a lot in between classes about what we wanted to do with our careers and made a tentative plan to work together on it.

"My dad wants me to teach, but I don't think I want to. Or, at least, not in a classroom setting. I'm not sure it's for me. Honestly, thinking about working in publishing, with books, is really where I want to be, I think. Maybe an editor. I think I'm a hardass enough for that." I laughed because Stella would be a brutal editor. She would pull no punches and be amazing at it.

"Maybe I'll be an agent. I don't think I'm ruthless enough to be an editor. I just don't know." I didn't know, which was part of the problem. And how did we find out?

"I can do some research and we can look together. Help each other out. And then when we're both successful, we can say that we knew each other when we were just starting out." I liked that. I didn't know if it would happen, but it was nice to think about navigating those unknown waters with someone else. I wasn't in the dark alone.

I told Cordelia about my plan and she loved it.

"You're going to be this big-time agent and get tons of book deals and make a buttload of money and I'm going to be there, cheering you on. Doing whatever I end up doing. I seriously still have no idea." I knew she didn't know, and that was okay. She would be a success at whatever she did. Cordelia was all in, when she made up her mind.

"Do you think we'll still be together?" I asked.

"Don't you?" She gave me a look as if the answer was obvious. I guess I was more pragmatic than she was.

"The statistics are against us," I said. She snorted.

"Those statistics were made with non-queer people, probably. And fuck statistics." Well. She did have a point there.

"Okay, fine. Fuck the stats." She tackled me on the bed and that was the last time we talked about statistics.

MY PARENTS WERE PICKING me up since I didn't have a car. I had arranged it with them ahead of time, so when Cordelia offered me a ride (even though we lived hours apart), I had to decline. It would have been awesome, riding back to my hometown with her, but I couldn't tell my parents the reason I wanted to ride with someone else. They were all excited about coming and seeing my dorm room and taking me out to lunch and having me show them around campus. They were also dragging Kate so I could get her excited about college. Her grades weren't that great, and she had been talking like she didn't see college as an option, and they were freaking out a little. I was sure she was going to be fine. She'd figure her shit out, they just needed to let her do that and stop hitting the panic button.

"I don't want to sleep without you," she said into my hair the night before break.

"I know. It's going to be strange sleeping in a bed by myself." I'd completely adjusted to sharing a twin bed with her. Sure, I didn't get much room to stretch out, but she was always there and I always had someone to hold onto. It was a trade-off.

"I might like it for a little while, but I don't want to be without you for more than a night. We're completely hopeless." We were. Totally and hopelessly in love.

"Are you sure you don't want me here when your parents come?" They were going to be here tomorrow afternoon, and Cordelia had planned on leaving in the morning.

"Yeah. I think it'll just be too hard to, you know, not be the way we are right now. I can't keep my hands off you. And I don't want you to have to deal with any questions from them, and I don't want to put you on the spot. So I think this is better." She didn't say it, but I knew she was relieved about that. She still hadn't met my parents, and that was a pretty awkward way to meet the parents of your girlfriend for the first time when they didn't know their own daughter liked girls in the first place.

"It'll be fine," I said, kissing the tip of her nose.

"I hope so. I'm actually excited about seeing my dad. We'll get to do all the goofy things we used to do."

"Like what?"

"Like having pancake making competitions, and marathoning movies with a theme and going for dips in the ocean in the off season. We were pretty much best friends. I don't really know how to navigate things with us now. It's going to be strange. I feel like I haven't seen him in forever. I do miss him." I rubbed her shoulder and she turned over on her stomach so I could rub her back.

"It's okay to miss him. I'm not trying to take his place. I couldn't. He's still your dad." She nodded and closed her eyes.

"I know. But it's still hard to figure out what we are to each other now that I'm an adult and not his little girl anymore. I know he still wishes I was." I wished I had a solution for her. Some wise words.

"It'll be okay, Carrots." That was the best I could do. She smiled softly.

"I hope so."

I DIDN'T WANT to get out of bed the next morning, so Cordelia and I kissed for what felt like hours and used our hands to get each other off before we realized that she needed to get on the road.

"I don't want to go," she practically wailed. "Why is this so hard?"

Someone looking from the outside would probably think we were being too dramatic, but they didn't know. I had spent nearly every single day with her for over a month and she had been my anchor. She had been my safety. My home in this new place.

"I know, baby, I know." I held her close and breathed in the scent of her hair. I wanted to burn that smell into my brain so I could call it up when she wasn't with me.

"We'll call and videochat and text. It's only for a week," I said, and she nodded against my shoulder. I felt like I was going to cry. Instead, I swallowed any tears and helped her carry everything to her car. We hugged and she kissed me hard.

"I'll see you later," she said.

"I'll see you later," I repeated. It wasn't goodbye. Just see you later. "I love you, Carrots."

"I love you, C." She squeezed my hand and then got in the driver's seat.

"Drive safe," I said, but the window was up. She waved sadly and then she was off, and I tried to dull the feeling that my heart was going with her.

~

MY PARENTS WERE ON TIME, as usual. They were never late and almost always early. I had put my pillows back on my side of the room and tried to hide anything that would give them clues about my relationship with Cordelia. It wasn't like we had framed pictures of us kissing, but you never knew.

She texted me once when she stopped to get gas with a lot of kissy faces and a list of things she wanted to do with me when we were together again. I messaged her back that it was unfair that I had to face my parents when I was horny as hell and she said it was fair because she had to see her dad the same way.

I was laughing at that when they knocked on my door.

"Hey, college girl!" my mom said, rushing in and sweeping up into her arms.

"Hi, Mom," I said, my voice muffled into her shoulder. I had missed her. I'd missed my whole family, and so much had changed that I wanted to share with them.

"Hey, kid," Dad said, hugging me tight. Kate was next, and she looked like she was already over it. To be fair, she had been trapped in the car with them for nearly two hours. It wouldn't surprise me if she'd gotten more than one lecture while she was a captive audience.

"Hey, Kate," I said, giving her a tentative hug. She huffed, but she hugged me back.

"Hey," she said, and her bitter attitude dropped just a little.

"Wow, it looks great," Mom said, turning around. "I was expecting it to be full of dirty laundry and Pop Tart wrappers." I raised an eyebrow.

"Do you know me at all?" My room at home had always been spotless. I needed order in my brain and in my space. Always had.

"Oh, well, you know. It's college. Where's Cordelia?" I flinched at the mention of her name and my chest ached.

"She already left this morning. She lives further away and she had to drive." It was an effort to smile while talking about her.

"She seemed like a really nice girl, are you still getting along?"

"Yeah," I said, my voice sounding choked. *More than you know, Mom.*

"I'm hungry," Kate said, and I wanted to hug her for the distraction.

"How about we go and have lunch?" I said. Anything to get out of this room that smelled like Cordelia and reminded me of Cordelia.

Everyone was on board with that plan and I locked the door and gave myself a second to breathe before we walked down to the Union. Mom was chattering away, telling Kate all about how she could come here someday and Kate was being surly and trying to ignore her. I shuffled along behind them and Dad fell into step with me. My mom and I were closer, but Dad and I had more similar personalities.

"You doing okay? Really?" I nodded immediately.

"Yeah, I am. I'm doing good in all my classes and I have friends and I haven't woken up naked in the hallway yet. I'd say that's successful."

He laughed.

"You're right. I don't know if it's the fact that you've been away, but you seem different." Of course my perceptive dad would say that.

"Do I?" I tried to be casual about it, but I was also panicking at the same time. Breathe, Chase.

"You seem ... I don't know. Maybe less anxious? More settled? Calmer?" Well, that was good. My parents had seen me at my worst and had held my hand through some of the worst anxiety spirals. I didn't get panic attacks, but I did act out in other ways when my anxiety spiked. Some of those ways had been destructive when I was younger and I'd been in therapy to help.

"I'm not trying to insult you, Chase. College looks good on you, that's all." I bumped him with my shoulder.

"Thanks, I think." He smiled down at me and gave me another hug as we walked.

"I'm going to have to save Kate from your mother," he said with a sigh.

"What's going on with her?" I asked. I was glad to turn the attention on someone else, even if it was throwing my sister under the bus.

"Not sure, but we're doing the best we can. If you could talk to her, maybe? That would be a big help. I think she misses you, although she would rather die than admit it." Sounded like we needed to have a chat later. I could be her big sister again. Even if she didn't want me to be.

We made it down to the Union without Kate running away or screaming, so that was a success. I showed them around, and helped my mom pick out what to have while Kate slunk off to get tacos at the little taco counter and Dad went right for the pizza.

We all got our food and I offered to pay for them all with my meal card, since I didn't use it that much. Too much eating breakfast in bed with Cordelia.

The Union was quiet and the rest of the campus was still. Everyone had pretty much bailed for the break, and it was strange to see it so empty.

I talked more about my classes and then Stella came up when I told them that we were going to check out publishing careers together.

"That's so great you've found a good friend," Mom said, cutting her meatloaf into precise pieces.

"Yeah, she's great. Her girlfriend, Kyle is cool too. We hang out with them a lot." I figured I could drop a few statements like that and see what the reaction would be.

Mom grinned and Kate picked at her tacos. Something was seriously up with her and I was going to get to the bottom of it. A little pang of guilt went through me for being away at school and not there for her, but what was I supposed to do? She was sixteen and she could always come to me if she needed to talk. She knew that. Kate was just so damn stubborn. I had no idea what that was like.

After lunch I took them on a tour, showing my parents and Kate where my classes were. Kate sulked along and I tried to pull her aside, but she brushed me off. I'd have to deal with her later at home.

We went back to my dorm room and they helped me pack up some clothes and my pillows. Of course I had those at home, but I wanted the ones that smelled like Cordelia. I'd also snuck a few of her shirts in my bag to bring with me when my parents weren't looking.

I texted Cordelia to let her know that I was heading for home and she didn't answer, but I figured she was driving and would get back to me later. Still, it sucked to be away from her and it had only been a few hours. How was I going to make it a whole week?

"I MADE sure to get all your favorite things," Mom said the second we walked into the house. "And if there's anything else you want, I can go out and get it." I wanted to tell her that she was being a smother, but I knew she had just missed me and this was her way of showing it. I could deal with her shoving pieces of cake at me.

Kate disappeared to her room and I took my stuff upstairs.

My room was across the hall from hers and she slammed her door. If that wasn't a statement, I didn't know what was. I finally got a message back from Cordelia. Phew. She had made it home and was making her way through a pineapple upside down cake, her favorite. Apparently her dad and my mom were two of a kind.

I shoved my phone in my pocket and knocked on Kate's door.

"What?" she snapped.

"Can I come in?" I asked. I heard her huff.

"Sure, whatever." I poked my head in and she was on her bed, messing with her phone.

"Are you okay?" I figured trying to be blunt first might work.

"Yeah, why?" She finally looked up at me.

"Because you have been a pain in the ass for the past few hours and you were fine when I left. What's going on?" She lifted her eyes to the ceiling and sighed.

"I'm fine. Seriously."

I took a few tentative steps and then sat down on the edge of her bed.

"Okay, okay," I said, putting my hands up in surrender.

"What about you? There's something you're not telling Mom and Dad. I have no idea what it is, but you're not very good about hiding it. Just so you know." She smirked at me and I felt like I'd been slapped. I stood up.

"You have no idea what the fuck you're talking about, Kate. And I came in here to try and be your big sister and give you someone to talk to, but I guess you'd rather be an asshole alone. Fine." I stormed out and went back to my room. I didn't hear if she muttered anything after me, but I bet she did. Fine, she was on her own. I wasn't going to let her treat me like that. So much for a happy homecoming.

❧

CORDELIA

Dad would not stop staring at me and it was starting to freak me out.

"Why are you doing that?" I asked. His eyes were narrowed, as if he was trying to figure something out.

"Did you get your hair cut?" he asked. I shook my head.

"Nope."

"Color it?" Another head shake.

"No, Dad. What are you doing? It's annoying." I slumped further over on my side of the couch. Away from his judgey gaze.

"There's something. I can't put my finger on it. Maybe you look older. Or it's something else." He took up most of the couch with his frame and it creaked every time he moved. He was hard on furniture.

"You're being weird, cut it out." I threw a few pieces of popcorn at him. We were knee-deep in a Keanu Reeves movie marathon. I knew he'd been waiting for me to do this, so I didn't tell him I'd rather watch something else. I was going to humor him. At least for now.

In the back of my mind were the words I had to tell him. The conversation we had to have before I went back to school. I was leaning on having it sooner rather than later, even if it would make things uncomfortable. I could always get in my car and leave if I had to. Not that I thought it would come to that, but I had the contingency plan in case.

"I'm not the one who went off to college and now won't really talk about what she's been doing." I looked away from the movie and him.

"What are you talking about?" I had been yapping about college plenty since I'd been home.

447

"You're telling me all kinds of things, Sprite, but you're not telling me other things." Well, shit.

"What do you want me to tell you?"

He shrugged his massive shoulders.

"I don't know. I feel like you're keeping something from me. And I'd like to know what it is, but I'd also like to know why you feel you *need* to hide something from me." I took a breath. Guess it was happening now.

"I'll tell you what's been happening, Dad. But you have to let me get it out and not interrupt me." He nodded and paused the movie.

"Of course."

Another breath.

"So. Chase, my roommate? We're, uh, we're seeing each other. It totally took us both by surprise, and I don't know what it means, honestly. But I love her and she loves me and we're together." My dad wasn't the silent type, but he didn't say anything for a long time while I trembled so hard that I thought I was going to fall right off the couch.

"Dad?" I finally said. It had been a lot of information to drop on him at once, but I needed him to say something or else I was going to have a panic attack.

"Yeah, I'm just processing this information and trying to find the best and most supportive thing to say." That sounded good.

"Anything right now would be good," I said. "It doesn't have to be perfect."

He reached for my hands and held them.

"I love you, Cordelia. You are the light of my life. My Sprite. I love you unconditionally. Always. There is nothing you could tell me that would change that. Not who you love. Not anything, Cordelia. Nothing would change the fact that you are my daughter and I love you." Those words turned on the faucet and I couldn't stop crying. He pulled me into his chest and I curled up like I had when I was a little girl.

"I love you, Dad," I said through my tears.

"I love you, too. This has been quite a year for you, hasn't it?" I nodded and wiped my face on his shirt. I knew he didn't care.

"Yeah, little bit."

"You want to tell me about it?" I did.

At last, the tightness in my chest loosened and I could fully breathe. I told him about how I'd felt when Chase walked in, I told him about my confusion and feelings, I told him how I kissed her first I told him about our date. I did NOT tell him about everything, because, well, some things were private. I also didn't think Chase would really like my dad knowing about our sex life. So I skipped that part.

"I don't know what this means. Obviously, if I'm in love with a girl, I'm not completely heterosexual. But other than that ... I don't know. Do I still like guys? Was I only liking them because I was taught to? Do I like other girls, or just Chase? What about people of other genders? It's all so confusing and overwhelming and I can't even begin to untangle it all. It makes me so tired. I started looking stuff up online, and it almost gave me a panic attack, so I stopped. I don't know what to do." That started me crying again. It was a rush of relief to have this talk with him.

"Hey, hey, it's okay, Sprite. You don't have to put yourself through that if you don't want to. Maybe just take some time and be with Chase and see where it goes. I don't have a lot of experience with this kind of thing, but I don't think you need to force something that makes you feel that anxious. Just enjoy what you're doing. I knew there was something different, and it's that you're happy. If Chase is making you happy, then I'm ecstatic." He had a point. Trying to figure all this out had been making me stressed out. Was it really worth it?

No, not right now. It wasn't. I would support Chase in whatever decision she made, but right now, I wanted to focus on loving her, and trying not to be so distracted by how hot she was that I flunked out of college. Plus, I had to figure out what I wanted my major to be. That was going to take priority over my sexuality. At least for now.

I sat with that decision for a few moments. It felt right. It was what I needed.

"Thank you, Dad," I said, hugging him again.

"You're welcome, Sprite. I'm here for you. No matter what."

"Even if I murdered someone?"

"I'll get a shovel."

"You know, it would be better to dissolve the body in acid. Less evidence." He raised his bushy eyebrows.

"I don't even want to know how you know that."

I HAD BEEN TRYING to text Chase as much as I could, but I wanted to hear her voice when I told her what had happened with my dad, so I asked if we could call or even videochat.

She said that was fine, so I told Dad I was going to my room and that I was talking to Chase.

"Keep it G rated," he said. I almost tripped over my own feet.

"What?"

"I'm just saying. You never know who might be watching or listening." I blinked at him.

"Okay, sure, Dad," I said and ran away as fast as I could, shuddering the whole way. I didn't need my dad giving me that kind of advice.

"Hey!" I said when Chase picked up the call. Just seeing her face made me want to squeal with glee.

"Hey, Carrots," she said, and I felt my face flame up. Every time. She got me with that nickname every time.

"How's it going?" she asked.

"Well, I told Dad. And he was totally supportive. I think he ships us." He had basically said as much.

"Oh, wow, okay. You went ahead and told him." I hoped she didn't feel pressure to also tell her parents.

"I mean, he wouldn't leave me alone, saying that I looked different and I kind of caved. As I do." I shrugged and lay back on my bed.

"No, it's fine. I'm glad you did and I'm glad it went well. I love you."

I beamed at her. The only way this could be more perfect is if she was here with me.

"I love you. How's everything going there?" She sighed. Oh. I guess things weren't all rosy at the Hillier house.

"My mom is kind of up my butt because she missed me and my dad knows something is up and my sister is being a brat and won't talk to me about it. Oh, and she knows that something is up, too. Because I guess I'm not very good at keeping secrets from my family." She sighed and raked her hand through her hair.

"I'm sorry. I wish I could be there to do something. I have no idea what I could do, but I still wish I was there." She gave me a weary smile.

"It's okay. I think it's going to be fine. Just … not what I was expecting. I was hoping for more time. Since I don't have a car and I'm trapped here if my parents turn out to be secret homophobes."

"If your parents are like that, I will get in my fucking car and come and rescue you. I wouldn't even need a cape. I don't even care where you are, I will come get you, Chase." I wished neither of us had to deal with that kind of uncertainty, but that was the way the world worked in our lifetimes.

"I know. And I *know* they're going to be fine. But still, a little voice in the back of my mind is questioning everything."

"I would like to punch that voice in the face." That made her laugh. Finally. She relaxed a little after that and I told her about my travel adventures and some of the plans my dad had for this week. He had to work during the day, so I was going to take a lot of baths and hog the couch while he was gone. I also, unfortunately, had homework that needed to get done as well. Chase, of course, had already done hers because she was an over-overachiever.

"What do you think is up with your sister?" That seemed like a less-fraught topic than if she was going to tell her family about us.

"I honestly have no idea. She's always been the kind of person who won't tell anyone when something is wrong and just sort of holds it all in and snaps at anyone who tries to help. It makes loving her hard sometimes. She's a pain in the ass, but I would honestly do anything to help her." I didn't have any siblings, but I knew that fierce feeling, and I admired it a lot in Chase.

"I'm trying not to feel guilty for being away at college and not talking to her often enough," she said.

"C, you can't help someone who doesn't want you to help them. You can try, but if she doesn't want it, she doesn't want it. I wish I could give you a hug."

"Thanks. I know you're right." I heard a pounding sound in the background. "Hold on a sec." She set the phone down and I had a view of her ceiling as she talked to someone and then came back.

"Sorry, that was my mom asking me what I wanted for dinner. I don't know why she asked, because she literally had all the lasagna ingredients out on the counter and she knows it's my favorite." Oh, lasagna. That would be so good. I didn't want to make it, but I wanted to eat it. Maybe I could go out and get a frozen one and throw it in the oven.

"If you need to go, that's fine. I just wanted to let you know what happened with Dad." I was lying. I didn't want her to go, but I understood that I had to share her with other people.

"If I don't go down, she's going to pester me until I do, so I probably should. But before I do…" she lowered the phone and then pulled up her shirt.

"Chase Hillier! You naughty girl." She giggled as she flashed me her bra.

"Just something to remind you of what's going to happen when we're together again." Fuck, now I was turned on. I figured it was only fair that I showed her, so I pulled my shirt up.

"Fuck, you're so hot. Okay, I love you. We'll talk soon." She made kissy faces and I said I loved her and we hung up.

I rubbed my chest where my heart beat. God, I missed my girl.

Chapter Fifteen

CHASE

Things that night were fine. Or as fine as they could be. Mom was still hovering, Kate was still surly, I was still upset with her, and Dad was just sort of sitting back and watching how everything was going to go.

Cordelia had told her dad and it had gone well. I was so happy for her, but now even more nervous about my parents. That little voice that told me they were going to disown me kept getting louder and I wanted to drown it out, but I didn't know how. Not even my mom's delicious lasagna could do that.

"You're awfully quiet, Kate," Mom said, finally taking her focus off me.

"Yeah," she said.

"Why is that?" Mom asked and I looked at Dad. This was not going to go well.

"I dunno," she said. Right now she was the picture of the grumpy teenager, slumped at the table.

"Kate, you're being ridiculous," Mom said. I wanted to tell Mom to lay off, that she wasn't helping, but I kept my mouth shut. I wasn't going to make waves now.

"Linda, leave her alone," Dad said.

"May I be excused?" Kate said. Mom looked like she wanted to say no, but after a wordless discussion with Dad over the table, she agreed. Kate went upstairs without clearing her place.

"What is wrong with that girl?" Mom said, looking after her. She almost looked like she wanted to cry.

"I don't know, but nitpicking at her isn't going to help. Let her alone. Let her come to us," Dad said. I felt like I didn't want to be here anymore if they were going to be talking about Kate. I wasn't done eating, but I did want to get out of there, so I excused myself as well.

I figured I could give it another shot with Kate, even if I was hurt by what she had said earlier. I knocked on her door and she let me in. I figured that could be a good sign.

"Look, I know you don't want to talk to me. And I know you think I'm hiding something and I am. So I'm going to tell you. And then maybe you'll trust me enough to tell me what's going on with you." It was a risk, but I figured I could start with one family member and work up from there. Plus, Kate wouldn't mind keeping a secret from both of our parents. If we got along better, I would have told her sooner.

"So what, we're trading secrets now, is that how this works?"

"Look, you can be as snotty as you want, but this is a big deal for me, okay? Can you just be my sister for five minutes?" That seemed to shut her up. She tossed her long dark hair over her shoulder. It was easy to tell we were sisters. We shared the same hair color and brown eyes, but her face was rounder than mine and she wasn't as tall. Still, we were the spitting image of one another. Our mother's genes were strong.

"Fine," she said, folding her arms. I figured that was as good as I was going to get.

"I'm dating Cordelia. My roommate. We're together. She's my girlfriend." Kate's mouth dropped open.

"Are you fucking serious?"

"Yes." And she started laughing. Literally laughing.

"What the fuck, Kate?" I had no idea what to do with that reaction. Did she think this was funny? It wasn't funny at all.

"I'm sorry," she said through giggles as she wiped her eyes. She had laughed so hard she was crying. She took a deep breath.

"I'm sorry. I'm not laughing because it's funny. I'm laughing because I think I'm bisexual. There's a girl I really like and she's been flirting with me and I don't know what to do about it and I don't know how to tell Mom and Dad and here you are telling me you have a girlfriend and if this isn't irony, I don't know what is." I nearly slid off the bed.

"You're bisexual?" She nodded.

"Yeah. I think. I've been feeling that way for years, but I haven't had a crush like this on a girl yet. Just boys. Honestly, I could probably date anyone, who knows. But right now I'm head over heels for this girl and I figured Mom and Dad were going to find out and I didn't know how to tell them." This was a shocking development.

"Huh," I said.

"Exactly."

"So we're both not heterosexual."

"Guess so."

We sat and stared at each other for a few seconds.

"So what do we do now?" she asked.

"I guess we tell them. Together. If you're ready for that. I had planned on telling them this week sometime, but Cordelia already told her dad and I feel guilty for not doing the same. I'm not hiding, but I also don't know what they're going to say." Kate rolled her eyes.

"Are you kidding? You're the golden child. You could tell

them you murdered someone and they would throw you a party to celebrate." That was an exaggeration, but I got her point.

"I can tell them without you, if you want. But I think if we do it together it will be better."

Kate snorted.

"You sure about that?"

I stood up.

"Only one way to find out."

"Guess so."

We both walked downstairs to find Mom and Dad in the kitchen loading the dishwasher and talking about Kate.

"You want me to go first?" I said. Somehow, having Kate next to me was making me feel like I could do this. All my uncertainty was gone. This was happening.

"Sure," she said, standing behind me.

"Mom, Dad?" I said, and they looked up, realizing we were both standing there. They shared a look.

"Can we talk to you?" I indicated myself and Kate.

My parents blinked a few times and then nodded.

"Do we need to sit down for this?" Dad asked.

"I mean, I don't think so, but we could," I said, so we went to the dining room.

"So," I said, taking a breath, "there's something I wanted to tell you. I know both of you noticed that I seem different. Well, the reason is that I'm dating someone." My mother made a squealing noise.

"I knew it. Who is it? Is he cute?" Dad hushed her.

"He isn't. Because he's a she. I'm dating my roommate, Cordelia." Thick silence descended on the room.

"So, does this mean you're …" Dad trailed off.

"I don't really know. I'm still working on that one. But I think it's safe to say that I'm not heterosexual." I looked at Kate.

"I'm bi," she blurted out. Mom's eyes got the size of dinner plates.

"Hold on, hold on, one daughter at a time," Dad said. "How long have you been dating this girl, Chase?"

"Uh, for a few weeks? I wanted to tell you in person. So that's why we waited. She told her dad today too. We didn't plan on it, obviously. It just happened. And I know it's complicated because we live together, but I'm happy. She makes me so happy." Now I was going to cry.

Dad got up from the table and wrapped his arms around me.

"Thank you for telling us. It's going to take me a little while to wrap my mind around the fact that you are dating your roommate, but I'll get there. I love you, Chase. Always have. Always will." I hugged him back and looked at Mom.

"Why didn't you say something sooner?" She got up and attacked me with a hug. "You've been letting me yammer on about boyfriends. I had no idea, Chase, I didn't."

"It's okay, Mom. I didn't know either. It's a shock to all of us." I laughed a little and Mom kissed my forehead.

"Oh, Chase. I love you so much. And I'm sure Cordelia is a very nice girl. Are we going to get to meet her anytime soon?" I gaped at her.

"I don't know."

"Don't pressure her, Linda. Give her some breathing room."

"Uh, hi?" Kate said and then they hugged her too.

"So you're bisexual?" Mom said, and Kate nodded.

"I think so."

"Okay, then." And that was that. That was what Kate had needed. They had given me what I had needed. They sat back down and I told the story of how I had gotten together with Chase (leaving out the more salacious aspects) and Kate talked about the girl she had a crush on. We laughed and it was comfortable. They were fine, as I knew they would be. The doubt was gone. We stayed up talking for hours, like we hadn't done in years. It was good and I was happy I could text Cordelia and tell her that everything was fine. And that now my mom was pressuring me to bring her over so she could meet her. I was going to put that off as long as I could. If my mom would let me.

THE REST of the week flew by, surprisingly. I hung out a lot with Kate, who also had a few days off from school. While my parents were at work we hung out and talked about queer things and laughed about all the signs we had missed when we were growing up. I hadn't felt close to her like that in a long time.

I also talked a ton with Cordelia, who's dad had gone out and gotten a rainbow flag to hang on the front of their house and had joined PFLAG (Parents, Families and Friends of Lesbians and Gays), an organization for the parents of queer kids.

"He's really gotten into this whole thing. It's kind of freaking me out, if it wasn't so sweet." I didn't want to tell my mom about PFLAG because she would inevitably want to join it too.

Everything had worked out, as it rarely did in life. I didn't know how I'd gotten so lucky to have an amazing girl and an amazing family behind me. I also talked with Kyle, Stella, Elise, and Eli during the break and they were all thrilled for us. It was a big step to tell our parents.

I'd also read several of the books I'd borrowed from the queer organization and I still hadn't landed on a label. I was thinking I was probably a lesbian, but then there were so many different genders and I just didn't know. Cordelia and I talked a lot about working on our labels and definitions together, and she had decided to shelve it for the time being. The idea of not knowing did not work for me, so I was still going to try and figure it out. But it wasn't essential for my survival. Right now, I was enjoying being with her, and enjoying having a supportive family. The label stuff could wait until I got back to school. I might just go with "queer" since it encompassed so many things and was an umbrella term. At least for now. I just wanted something that felt right for me, and I hadn't found it yet.

~

CORDELIA

The rest of the week with my dad was a blast. He dove headfirst into the fact that he had a daughter that was dating another girl and I thought he was almost too enthusiastic about the whole thing, but I couldn't fault him for it. He loved me and he didn't do anything halfway. We had that in common.

Missing Chase sucked, but I was thrilled that her family was on board with everything. Apparently her sister was also bi, as she'd recently found out, so they had bonded over that. It was so sweet and it made me want to be a big sister-type to Kate as well and we chatted a few times. She wanted to come up and visit Chase and stay with us for a weekend sometime. We just had to convince their parents it was a good idea.

In between pining for Chase and hanging out with my dad, I got my work done, even though I hated every second of it. I really needed to pick a major at some point. My classes weren't great, but they were all required, no matter what my major was, so I had to do them anyway. Art history was not my jam, and I told my dad that. He seemed to accept it, at least for now. Weird that he had a harder time with that than the dating girls thing.

I arrived back at school on Sunday afternoon before classes started back up on Monday. I was ready to go the second the sun came up on Sunday, but Dad forced me to have pancakes with him and watch too many baking shows. Guilt stabbed me as I packed up to leave again.

"You're not lonely?" I said as he grabbed me up in a bear hug.

"No, I'm not. I have work and I go out. I do have friends, you know. Other than you." He was an adult, but I still worried.

"You should get a girlfriend. Or a boyfriend?" He chuckled at that.

"I think I'm just interested in women, but I can't seem to find the right one. It's not what I need right now." I hugged him back and figured that was all I could do. I couldn't force him to date someone, and I knew he was still so hurt after my mom left. She'd really broken his heart.

"I love you," I said, jumping up to kiss his bearded cheek.

"I love you, Sprite. Drive safe."

I waved goodbye to him and got in my car. It was time to drive and see my girl.

IT TOOK FOREVER for her to get back. I kept looking out the window and checking my phone and nibbling on my nails. At last, there was the sound of her key in the door and I yanked it open before she could get it unlocked.

"I fucking missed you," I said, hurling myself into her arms and kissing her hard. She dropped everything she was holding and grabbed me so we didn't both topple over.

"I missed you," she said in between kisses and then set me down. I couldn't stop looking at her, but a throat cleared and I looked away from her beautiful face.

We weren't alone.

"Oh," I said, my face going redder than it had ever been before.

"Cordelia, this is my mom, my dad, and my sister, Kate." They were all here. They were all here and they had seen me tackling her. Welp. This was awkward.

"Uh, it's nice to meet you?" It sounded like a question.

Her dad looked like he was trying not to laugh and her mom was beaming. Kate had a smirk on her face. She and Chase looked so much alike, but Chase took more after her father in height and body shape. Her coloring was all her mother.

"It's nice to meet you," her dad said, sticking out his hand. I was pulled into a hug by her mother and Kate gave me a hug as well.

"Do you want to come in?" I asked. I didn't want to prolong this horrible encounter, but I also didn't want to be rude.

"No, that's fine. We just came up to say goodbye to Chase," her mom said. They hugged and then they left. Kate gave me a little wave.

"Have funnnn," she said with a knowing look. I wanted to die.

"Did that just happen?" I said, finally looking at Chase.

"Yeah, it did." She burst out laughing and dragged me into the room.

Epilogue

CHASE

"So are you *sure?*" she asked me for what felt like the millionth time.

"Yes, I'm sure that I want to live with you next year. It would be impossible to live without you at this point," I said. It was next to the last week of classes and Cordelia and I were signing up for next year, including where we wanted to live and who we wanted to live with.

"Okay, I'm typing your name in," she said in a sing-song voice. Our parents had cautioned us on living together next year, but we'd made it one entire year without killing each other or breaking up, so I figured we could do another one. I loved living with her. Even when she made a mess or didn't wash her dishes. Even when I found her hair everywhere. Even though we had to share a bed that didn't really accommodate two people. It was all worth it.

"I'm typing you in," I said and submitted the request form. It came back immediately confirmed that we were set up to be roommates for the coming school year.

"Yay!" Cordelia said when she saw the confirmation. She dove into my lap and kissed me.

"You're not sick of me yet?" she said.

"Nope. You're not sick of me?" She shook her head.

"Not even a little bit. But I'm thinking maybe we might want to bunk our beds and put a futon on the other side. Or see if we can get rid of the beds and just have a futon." She had a good point.

"We can look for a used one. I bet someone is selling one."

"I can't believe we have to be without each other for a whole summer." Most people probably looked forward to summer, but I wasn't this year. All I wanted was to be with Chase the whole year, but we were going to be apart. Since we were both going to be working as much as possible, our face-to-face time was going to be limited. Still, other couples had done long distance before and at least we would be in the same state.

"We'll get through it," I said. My phone buzzed with a text. "Hey, Kyle is wondering where we are." We were having another bowling night and Elise was out front waiting for us.

"Are you sure we can't just stay in?" she said, reaching her hand under my shirt. "We only have a few more days to get in as much sex as possible."

I snorted, but her clever hand was making me think about things other than bowling.

"You're being distracting and our friends are waiting for us. Maybe if you're a good girl at bowling, you'll get a reward later." She made a little whining sound.

"You're so unfair."

"Mmmm, you love it," I said, taking her hand.

"You're right, I do. I love each and every thing about you." She put her arms around my neck.

"I love each and every thing about you, Carrots." She wrinkled her nose at me.

"Even though I messed up all your plans?"

"Yup. Now I have new plans and they all involve you." I stared down into her eyes. They were like the ocean again today.

"That's so weird, all my plans involve you."

"What a coincidence." I smiled down at her and smacked her butt.

"Come on, our friends are waiting."

THANK you so much for reading Style and Chord! Please take a few moments to leave a review, even if it's just a few words and a star rating. Reviews help other readers find books they might love, and they're so appreciated by authors!

Afterword

Sign up for my newsletter for access to free books, short stories, sales, other bonus material, sales, and new releases!

About the Author

Chelsea M. Cameron is a New York Times/USA Today/Internationally Best Selling author from Maine who now lives and works in Boston. She's a red velvet cake enthusiast, obsessive tea drinker, former cheerleader, and world's worst video gamer. When not writing, she enjoys watching infomercials, eating brunch in bed, tweeting, and playing fetch with her cat, Sassenach. She has a degree in journalism from the University of Maine, Orono that she promptly abandoned to write about the people in her own head. More often than not, these people turn out to be just as weird as she is.

Connect with her on Twitter, Facebook, Instagram, Bookbub, Goodreads, and her Website.
If you liked this book, please take a few moments to **leave a review**. Authors really appreciate this and it helps new readers find books they might enjoy. Thank you!

Also by Chelsea M. Cameron

The Noctalis Chronicles

Fall and Rise Series

My Favorite Mistake Series

The Surrender Saga

Rules of Love Series

UnWritten

Behind Your Back Series

OTP Series

Brooks (The Benson Brothers)

The Violet Hill Series

Unveiled Attraction

Anyone but You

Didn't Stay in Vegas

Wicked Sweet

Christmas Inn Maine

Bring Her On

The Girl Next Door

Who We Could Be

Castleton Hearts

Mainely Books Club

Style is a work of fiction. Names, characters, places and incidents are either the product of the author's imagination or are use fictitiously. Any resemblance to actual persons, living or dead, events, business establishments or locales is entirely coincidental.

No part of this book may be reproduced, scanned or distributed in any printed or electronic form without permission. All rights reserved.
Copyright © 2016 Chelsea M. Cameron
Editing by Laura Helseth
Cover by Chelsea M. Cameron

Chord is a work of fiction. Names, characters, places and incidents are either the product of the author's imagination or are use fictitiously. Any resemblance to actual persons, living or dead, events, business establishments or locales is entirely coincidental.

No part of this book may be reproduced, scanned or distributed in any printed or electronic form without permission. All rights reserved.

Copyright © 2018 Chelsea M. Cameron

Editing by Laura Helseth

Cover by Chelsea M. Cameron

Ingram Content Group UK Ltd.
Milton Keynes UK
UKHW020743070623
423023UK00015B/830

9 798215 445440